Praise For Ava Miles

Nora Roberts Land
"Ava's story is witty and charming."
—Barbara Freethy #1 *NYT* bestselling author

Selected by *USA Today* as one of the Best Books of the
year alongside Nora Roberts' *Dark Witch* and
Julia Quinn's *Sum of all Kisses*.

"If you like Nora Roberts type books, this is a must-read."
—Readers' Favorite

Country Heaven
"If ever there was a contemporary romance that rated a 10
on a scale of 1 to 5 for me, this one is it!"
—The Romance Reviews

"*Country Heaven* made me laugh and cry...I could not
stop flipping the pages. I can't wait to read the next book
in this series." —Fresh Fiction

Country Heaven Cookbook
"Delicious, simple recipes... Comfort food, at its best."
—Fire Up The Oven Blog

The Bridge to a Better Life
Selected by *USA Today* as one of the Best Books of the
Summer.

"Miles offers a story of grief, healing and rediscovered
love." —USA Today

"I've read Susan Mallery and Debbie Macomber...but
never have I been so moved by the books Ava Miles
writes." —Booktalk with Eileen Reviews

The Gate to Everything
"The constant love...bring a sensual, dynamic tension to
this appealing story." —Publisher's Weekly

More Praise For Ava

The Chocolate Garden
"On par with Nicholas Sparks' love stories."
—Jennifer's Corner Blog

"A must-read...a bit of fairy magic...a shelf full of happiness." —Fab Fantasy Fiction

The Promise of Rainbows
"This is a story about grace, faith and the power of both..."
—The Book Nympho

French Roast
"Ms. Miles draws from her experience as an apprentice chef...and it shows...I loved {the} authenticity of the food references, and the recipes...looked divine." —BlogCritics

The Holiday Serenade
"This story is all romance, steam, and humor with a touch of the holiday spirit..." —The Book Nympho

The Town Square
"Ms. Miles' words melted into each page until the world receded around me..." —Tome Tender

The Park of Sunset Dreams
"Ava has done it again. I love the whole community of Dare Valley..." —Travel Through The Pages Blog

The Goddess Guides Series
"Miles' series is an **exquisite exploration** of internal discomfort and courage, allowing you to reclaim your divine soul and fully express your womanhood."
—Dr. Shawne Duperon, Project Forgive Founder, Nobel Peace Prize Nominee

"The Goddess Guides are a **world changer**. Well done, Ava." —International Bestseller Kate Perry aka Kathia Zolfaghari, Artist & Activist

Also by Ava Miles

Fiction

The Merriams Series

Wild Irish Rose

Love Among Lavender

Valley of Stars

Sunflower Alley

The Love Letter Series

Letters Across An Open Sea

Along Waters of Sunshine and Shadow

The Dare Valley Series

Nora Roberts Land

French Roast

The Grand Opening

The Holiday Serenade

The Town Square

The Park of Sunset Dreams

The Perfect Ingredient

The Bridge to a Better Life

The Calendar of New Beginnings

Home Sweet Love

The Moonlight Serenade

The Sky of Endless Blue

Daring Brides

The Dare River Series
Country Heaven
Country Heaven Song Book
Country Heaven Cookbook
The Chocolate Garden
The Chocolate Garden:
A Magical Tale (Children's Book)
Fireflies and Magnolias
The Promise of Rainbows
The Fountain of Infinite Wishes
The Patchwork Quilt of Happiness

**Dare Valley Meets Paris Billionaire
Mini-Series**
The Billionaire's Gamble
The Billionaire's Courtship
The Billionaire's Secret
The Billionaire's Return

Non-Fiction

The Happiness Corner: Reflections So Far

Home Baked Happiness

The Goddess Guides to Being a Woman

Goddesses Decide

Goddesses Deserve The G's

Goddesses Love Cock

Goddesses Cry and Say Motherfucker

Goddesses Don't Do Drama

Goddesses Are Sexy

Goddesses Eat

Goddesses Are Happy

Goddesses Face Fear

Sunflower Alley

THE MERRIAMS

AVA MILES

ISBN-13: 978-1-949092-13-4
www.avamiles.com
Ava Miles

To all the people in the world like my heroine, Louisa, who inspire me with their real-life examples of commitment, kindness, empathy, and love.
May more rise.

And to my divine entourage, who brings people and stories to me that remind me that the world really is a wonderful place and can be transformed at any moment with love.

Acknowledgements

Writing this book changed my life and expanded my ability to love.

But it didn't start with the first words on the page...

It started on a cold and cloudy afternoon in a Manhattan hotel when I met a billionaire. Of course, I didn't know he was a billionaire when he approached our table and commented how rare and wonderful it was to see people laughing and being happy in the Big Apple. Inviting him to join us changed me and sparked this book. Over the course of the afternoon, we shared our life stories about what had led us to choose happiness, and here's where it intersects with Connor's story. As he walked to a soup kitchen where he was volunteering, a homeless man mistook this billionaire for homeless too and told him everything was going to be all right and that things would get better. This billionaire said it was like the homeless man had seen inside him. In his heart, despite seemingly having everything, he was homeless. It prompted him to change his life and start choosing happiness and doing more good things in the world. After our encounter, I just knew I needed to write that into one of my heroes, and who better than Connor?

I also want to thank Martha White for sharing her friend's story that inspired part of Boxer's back story. You see, this woman was afraid of the homeless man sitting across the street from her house, but he was pleasant to her when she'd walk her dog, so she started to say hello back to him. Amazingly, it was this man who saved her dog when her house caught on fire.

There are two other people I have only read about that I'd also like to thank for inspiring me. Former Chicago police officer, Lisa Negro. She started serving the homeless coffee and sandwiches out of a little red wagon and has since founded an acclaimed service organization that includes Inspiration Kitchens. Her empathy and vision is beautiful, and I for one, am happy to know she and others like her are in our world. Also, Keanon Lowe, a former Oregon Ducks football player and now a high school football coach in Portland, Oregon. He disarmed a student that brought a gun inside and then hugged him when the boy broke down and said no one cared about him. That act reminded me yet again how we can bring empathy and love into a violent situation and transform it into a moment of grace and example.

*Matchmaking is a lot like investigative journalism.
Both require relentless pursuit—
especially when the object of inquiry is
a man like Connor Merriam.*

The five journalistic questions reign supreme.

The who: My nephew by my beloved wife, Clara

*The what: The newly fired CEO of
Merriam Enterprises has disappeared.*

The when: A week ago

*The where: Location unknown
but speculating Chicago*

*The why: Best friend and cousin died in Merriam
Enterprises accident with other employees; Connor
blames himself and has gone wild with grief.*

*Clara and I have had a lot of challenges matchmaking this next generation, but leading Connor to love
will be our biggest challenge yet.*

Good thing I believe in one truth:

*When a person is in dire straits and the stakes are
high, their soulmate tends to show up.*

*With Connor, she is going to have to be one hell of a
woman.*

*Arthur Hale, Pulitzer Prize-Winning Journalist
and Matchmaker Jedi*

CHAPTER 1

HE'D FAILED HIS BEST FRIEND AGAIN.

The freezing Chicago weather wasn't numbing Connor fast enough after his brief encounter with his cousin's widow. Neither was the bottle of Irish whiskey he'd bought at a dilapidated corner store adjacent to the run-down South Side park where he was currently sitting, defeat covering him like the falling snow. He'd ended up at the liquor store after taking a hard run to Corey's gravesite in Oak Woods. Seeing his cousin's shiny new tombstone again had somehow made everything worse. Not that his confrontation with Olivia, Corey's widow, hadn't been crushing enough.

I don't want you to see my sons right now.

Hearing that had made him feel worse than being fired by his family a week ago.

"Max and Joseph are my godsons, for Christ's sake." He was talking to himself like a crazy person, but who the hell cared? No one was out in the snowstorm but him. He took a pull of the whiskey.

How had it come to this? He'd gone to visit Olivia and the kids, only to discover their South Side neighborhood had fallen into alarming disrepair. He'd come across a couple of needles and enough unsavory characters to give him nightmares. Olivia had turned him down flat when he'd offered to buy her a house in a safer neighborhood like Lincoln Park. Sure, the home she lived in had belonged to his grandparents. But what were happy memories compared with safety? On Corey's wedding day, Connor had promised to take care of his family should anything happen to him. He intended to carry through on that promise.

But what had Olivia done? Turned him down flat. She'd insisted they wouldn't give up on their neighborhood.

"She's the crazy one," he muttered to himself, lifting the bottle to his lips and welcoming the harsh burn in his mouth.

Who was she kidding? The neighborhood had deteriorated so much he didn't recognize it, and he'd gone to the University of Chicago in the adjacent neighborhood, Hyde Park. Even back then, everyone had known not to venture too far from the campus, but this part of South Side had never looked so dangerous. He couldn't fathom why Corey hadn't noticed. Of course, his cousin had spent most of his time on a Merriam offshore oil rig for the company Connor no longer ran.

I don't want my boys following you around like my husband did. Look where that got him.

Everyone kept telling him he wasn't at fault for the deaths at the oil rig. Hell, hadn't he tried to convince himself of that? Not Olivia. Truth be told, he'd welcomed the lash. Hadn't he been president of Merriam Enterprises at the time? Couldn't he have reinforced the steel on the rig? He should have done something...

All he'd done lately was fail, and people kept getting hurt. Olivia hadn't pulled any punches.

I don't trust you or your judgment right now, Connor. I won't have my boys getting hurt by being around you.

He wanted to crush the whiskey bottle in his hands.

Someone in the family must have told her what had happened with Michaela. His sister had nearly died in

Kenya, on an assignment he'd sent her on. His poor handling of the situation had only worsened matters. One of many bad calls he'd made since Corey's death. Truth was, he'd deserved to be fired for conduct unbecoming, which was why he'd driven his family to do it.

Getting fired had felt like rock bottom at the time, but he'd fallen even deeper into a pit of hopelessness. He'd thought making good on his promise to Corey would help fill the emptiness inside him. But how could he take care of Corey's family when Olivia wouldn't let him? When she wouldn't even let him see those wonderful boys who looked so much like his best friend? What if something happened to them while walking these gritty streets?

No. He wouldn't allow that to happen. He was Connor Merriam, a freaking billionaire, someone *Forbes* had called "a visionary leader of our time."

He'd find a way to fulfill his promise to Corey.

If he didn't, he had nothing left.

"Hey, buddy!" he heard someone call out.

Snow wetting his face, he took a long pull on the bottle. He used to think people just drank out of paper sacks to disguise the alcohol, but he realized now they had another purpose—the paper gave a person something to grip in freezing conditions. The bottle would be wet and slippery otherwise in his numb hands.

"Man, it's snowing like crazy out here," he heard again. "You got somewhere to go?"

A big black man in a puffy black jacket with shoulders the size of a forklift bent over in front of Connor, a dark stocking hat on his enormous head.

"Get the fuck away from me."

"Not looking to hurt you." The man stood back and held up his giant gloved hands. "Just a concerned citizen. It's six degrees out with snow coming down hard. You're wearing next to nothing and drinking in a park. I'm not about to let you freeze to death."

Freeze to death? He was boiling on the inside with anger and guilt. "Still a free country last I looked. Buzz off."

"Hard case, huh?" The big guy cracked his neck. "Fine then. I'll be back in a jiffy."

Connor didn't bother to follow the man's progress. Taking another pull on the bottle, he stared out across the park. The snow was quickly covering the cracked sidewalks—ankle busters, Grandpa Noah used to call them—and God knows what other trash on the ground.

His grandparents would be appalled. Back when Grandma Anna and Grandpa Noah were young, their church had helped pull the community together. Grandma Anna had taught at the Catholic school, working with the legendary pastor, Father Shaughnessy, and the church had helped feed, school, and clothe the local kids. But according to Connor's Weatherby cousins, the new pastor hadn't filled his shoes, nor had the one who came after him. Diminished attendance and church scandals had helped seal the church's decline.

Like religion ever helped a damn thing, anyway. Connor wasn't a religious man and sure as hell wasn't going to worship a God who didn't take care of his flock. Corey had been a churchgoer when he wasn't on a rig in the ocean, and where had that gotten him?

"Boxer here tells me you're a tough guy," a feminine voice said, a vein of steel in it.

He turned his head in its direction to see a woman standing in the amber light. A blast of heat punched through his numbness as he looked at her. She was standing beside his bench, five foot nothing, in a red parka with a soggy navy stocking hat covering her long black hair. Maybe the cold was getting to him, but she looked like Rihanna's doppelganger with her caramel skin, arched brows, and full lips.

She had his attention.

Her accent was pure South Side and those wide-set,

captivating eyes were locked on him with a directness he rarely saw. Most people hesitated to challenge him, whether in the business world or his own family. It was why he'd earned the nickname of the Big Bad Wolf. Her high cheekbones bespoke beauty while the pointy chin signaled strength. The big black man he'd met earlier stood behind her protectively. Were they a couple? And what the hell were they doing out here in a snowstorm, least of all talking to him?

"What's it to you?" Connor shot back.

She sat down on the snow-covered bench next to him and folded her hands in her lap, her entire demeanor calm while her eyes—golden, he could see now—roved over his face. "You think it's 'tough' to get frostbite or die from exposure? I can promise you it hurts like hell."

He laughed, happy to play devil's advocate. "It won't hurt if you die."

"You looking to die?" she asked in that same serious tone.

Since he didn't have a flip response, he blew out a breath, the cold freezing it in front of his face.

"Things that bad, huh?" she asked, placing her gloved hand on his thinly clothed arm.

Her touch shocked him. He was a stranger sitting in a run-down park drinking from a bottle. Why did she care what became of him? "You some do-gooder who's got nothing better to do on Friday night?"

Something dropped onto his legs. "It's just a blanket," the woman said. "I'm Louisa, by the way, and this is my friend, Boxer. Do you have someplace we can take you?"

He thought of the motel room he was staying in only a few blocks away. A snowy street was cleaner and more inviting than that shithole, but it was serving its purpose. The owner took cash and didn't require a credit card for amenities—because there were none. It didn't make for a comfortable stay, but his tech-savvy brother, Flynn, couldn't track him there. Other places would have accepted cash too, but this one had another advantage: no one would ever think to look for him there. He was too ashamed to see his family.

"I'm fine." He pushed the soft blanket back to her and took another long pull from the whiskey. "Got my friend Jameson here. Don't need anything else."

She worried her rosebud of a mouth. "Jameson, huh? I have two glasses back where I work. Why don't you come back with me, and we'll have a drink?"

He was sure he smirked. "You looking for a little slumming on Friday night? Like the bums in a park, do you?"

"You'll want to watch your tone, man," Boxer said.

Louisa shook her head at her friend. "He's only testing me. How about this, tough guy? If I can guess why you're sitting in this park drinking in a snowstorm, you'll come with Boxer and me to where it's warm."

She was negotiating with him? Connor Merriam loved a good negotiation, and he hadn't done it since being fired. It had been a disarming transition for a man accustomed to twenty-hour workdays. Each day loomed long and empty, and even though it had only been a week, his mind was already itching for a challenge. "You have to guess at least five things about me out of seven. If you don't, you walk away." Then he had a thought. "And you won't call the police on me." He didn't want to go back in just yet—despite the weather—and he certainly didn't need the hassle.

"So you're smarter than you look." She nodded. "You're on. How about this? You just lost your job and don't have a line on anything new."

His cold lips forced a half-smile. Was he that obvious? "Score one for Ms. Goody Two-Shoes."

"Second, you can't go home," she added.

The kick to his guts was sure and swift. "No, I can't." After the board meeting, he'd driven home to pack a few things and grab some cash, and then headed straight for

Chicago, storing his car in an underground garage down-town. He'd promised himself he wasn't going home until he did something right. He felt pretty far off the mark just now.

"Three, you don't have any family you can go to."

His throat thickened with grief, hearing that hard truth out loud. He had six younger siblings that he couldn't look in the eye right now, and his parents... He'd let them all down. They'd pushed at him to get help, telling him the grief had skewed his thinking. But who could possibly help him? Nothing could bring Corey back. Nor could some therapist undo the decisions he'd made that had led to Michaela almost dying.

"Four, you're staying at Ferguson's Motel," Louisa said, her hand still on his arm.

Surprise stole his breath for a moment. "How did you—?"

"Cash only and not far from this park or the liquor store that sells Jameson," she said. "There's another liquor store to the south, but it doesn't sell Jameson."

"You that big of a Jameson fan?" he asked.

"I drink it when I watch Notre Dame play," she said. "Now, that's four I've gotten right so far."

He handed her the bottle. "Since you like it so much."

She laughed but pushed it back at him, and he noticed a small hole in her right glove. "The Irish aren't playing right now. I'm superstitious."

He shook his head. "An Irish fan and a superstitious one at that. God help me."

"So you don't like the Fighting Irish?" she asked. "I won't hold that against you. Boxer doesn't either, but I still love him."

He glanced at the man still standing behind her. Snow covered his shoulders, but he hadn't moved from his pro-tective stance. "He only your friend?"

"Yes, and it looks like you need one. Last one," Louisa

said, "and then you're coming with me and Boxer. You don't like yourself much right now."

He hated himself, in fact, but it didn't take a genius to see that. "Too easy. You'll have to do better than that."

She raised those arched eyebrows. "You're incredibly smart but self-destructive and stubborn to boot. And you're not an alcoholic despite your intentions this evening."

He lifted the bottle to his cold lips before answering, "Not yet, I'm not."

"You're not even drunk," she said, standing up. "Now, I've more than fulfilled our contract. You going to fulfill yours?"

Contract? "You talk like we made a business deal. Lady, sure you're pretty and all, but I don't know what you're selling, and I've had enough of it. I'm going to sit here and drink as long as I damn well want, and if my fingers fall off, that's my problem."

She put her hands on her waist. "Do you have health insurance?"

"I'm not sure." Shock rolled through him. Billionaire Connor Merriam might not have health insurance. Sure, logically speaking, he knew he could get COBRA, but it felt like everything he'd taken for granted was crumbling beneath him like rocks in an avalanche.

"Listen to me. You don't want frostbite. Trust me, it's horrible."

She sounded like she knew, which was weird. Everything about her suggested she was well taken care of.

"If you don't come with me, then I'll be forced to stay out here with you until you see reason."

Boxer gave a gusty sigh. "Man, please just come with us. Don't make Louisa hang out here in the cold with you."

Connor stood up and studied her. She stared right back, lifting her chin in stubborn emphasis. That look told him she wasn't about to back down.

"You could freeze yourself," he said. "Why would you

do that? I won't be responsible for that." He couldn't take one more person getting hurt because of him. Not even this stranger.

"So you'll come with us," she pressed, reminding him of a baby pit bull.

He didn't want company. Maybe he should just head back to the motel. This woman seemed determined to stay with him.

"All right, last guess about you, and if I get it right, you leave with us. No excuses or complaints."

"Lady, you are some—"

"Someone you loved very much died because of you, and you're out here because you blame yourself."

His sharp intake of breath was audible in the silent expanse of the snowy park. "How could you—"

"I know the look." She grabbed his forearm in a solid grip. "You're coming now, right? Because if not, I'll have to make Boxer get me more blankets and some coffee. I'm not leaving you alone out here."

"I can go back to Ferguson's—"

"Too late. I won. You don't want to welch on a bet, do you?"

God, she was relentless. "Lady—"

"The name's Louisa, and I'd very much like to know your name if you don't mind. You don't have to tell me your last name or anything. I understand privacy issues."

Privacy issues? Who in the hell was this woman? His mind shifted back to St. Patrick's and the way the neighborhood used to be.

"You aren't a nun from a local convent, are you?" She didn't look like a nun, but he knew there were plenty of them in Chicago, and they helped people on the street.

She started laughing. In fact, she bent over and guffawed. "That's a good one."

Boxer joined in, his baritone laughter a harmonious counterpart to her higher-pitched one. "You've been called a lot of things, Louisa, but never a nun. Sister Louisa. I might have to tell the staff."

"Don't you dare," she told him, swatting his massive chest. Turning back to Connor, she said, "Come on... What's your name?"

"Connor," he found himself saying. The man and woman started walking, and to his surprise, he fell in with them.

She slipped behind him and wrapped the worn blanket around his shoulders, a simple piece of kindness that cracked through his numbness for a moment. How long had it been since someone had done something like that for him?

"Sorry the blanket's so wet and cold." She sluiced some snow off with her hand. "You held out for a while, and it's snowing pretty hard. We'll find you something warm when we get back to Sunflower Alley."

He stopped short. "Sunflower Alley? You a florist?"

Her laughter trickled over him again. "Another good one. No, Connor. I'm the director, working with Boxer here. It's a homeless shelter."

He fell back a few steps on the sidewalk, staggered by her words. "*You think I'm homeless?*"

She stared him straight in the eye. "You don't have a job, a home, or a family to go to. You're staying at Ferguson's, which probably means you don't have much money. And you're sitting in the park in a threadbare University of Chicago T-shirt, drinking out of a paper bag during a snowstorm. Trust me, you check most of the boxes."

He checked the boxes? He looked down at himself. His favorite college T-shirt was worn and faded, and he had a rough blanket around his shoulders and a brown-bagged bottle in his hand. He *did* look homeless. How had it come to this? He was a man who'd graced the covers of *Time* and *Fortune*. Done anything he wanted. Had anything he wanted.

If she could think he was some homeless bum in the

park, the man he'd been was truly gone. Shame coated him, and something hot and angry clawed at his throat.

Rock bottom gave out again, and he fell farther.

This was the worst moment of his life.

She put her hands on his shoulders. "Connor, right now you feel like you have nothing to live for. I'm going to help you see that's not the truth. If you let me… Trust me, I've been there."

She had? It went along with what she'd said about frost-bite, but she didn't fit any image he'd ever had of homeless-ness. "But you couldn't…"

"I'll tell you my story if you come with me."

Standing in the amber lamp light with snow falling around her, she looked like an angel. Grandma Anna had always told them the right people showed up when times were the darkest. He didn't want to keep spiraling down.

He simply had to find a way to set things right. He'd promised Corey, and he had a duty to his own family as well, as the oldest sibling, even if he didn't have a clue how to regain their trust.

Louisa held out her hand to him.

He took it.

CHAPTER 2

THANK GOD HE'D FINALLY AGREED TO COME WITH THEM.
Louisa had been fighting off the shivers as the temperature kept dropping with the snow still falling hard. Connor's entire head and shoulders had been covered in a thin layer, and his dark beard looked like a frozen mask on his face. He'd been freezing right before her eyes, and her heart rate had kicked up the longer he'd fought her.

Her dad would call him a tough cookie. Of course, she and Boxer faced hard cases all the time. People off their meds didn't always understand she was trying to help them. Homeless ex-cons often thought the two of them might be undercover police. And women afraid of going to a shelter due to long-term abuse were difficult to persuade.

Connor fit none of those categories, and yet his lack of trust in anyone or anything was evident.

She knew how hard it was to live with guilt over causing someone's death. She didn't know this man's story yet, but she knew what that particular pain "looked like" on a person. He might have done something to consciously hurt someone—like getting into a fight that went wrong— or it might have been negligence on his part. There were a million ways it could have happened. Whatever the case, she hoped they could help him see his way through it so his life didn't continue to spiral out of control.

Like her mother's had.

Her mom had died outside on a night like tonight. They'd seen each other only once that winter, a few months after her dad had finally been granted full custody. Her mom had tracked her down at school, wanting to wish her a Merry Christmas and give her another damn doll. Louisa had been angry back then, but she'd still asked her mom to go somewhere warm with her. Her mother had refused, and it was the last time she'd ever seen her alive.

Louisa now never took no for an answer from someone at the end of their rope. If someone refused to leave the park on a snowy night, she'd sit beside them in the snow or walk with them until they agreed to come with her for a cup of soup or warmer clothes. Her tenacity was one of the keys to Sunflower Alley's success. Everyone needed to know there was at least one person who wouldn't give up on them, who cared—her father had first taught her that— and this man was no exception.

She studied Connor in the soft lamplight. He was tall— six three to her eye—well built, and handsome despite the haggard grooves around his eyes and mouth, clear signs of fatigue and grief. He wasn't malnourished and had straight, healthy teeth, so she'd guess whatever had befallen him had been recent. If he kept drinking like he'd intended to in the park, his aura of health would diminish quickly. She'd seen it time and time again.

He turned his head, tugging up the blanket when it slipped off his broad shoulders. She helped him, and he gazed at her warily. No, he wasn't used to kindness. In fact, he was downright suspicious of it.

Which was probably why he'd assumed someone like her, who wanted to help, had to be a nun. She couldn't help but smile at that. A nun? Well, she didn't have much of a social life, but still.

"What are you smiling at?"

She almost said, *you*, but he'd bristle. Instead, she said, "The nun comment. Man, that was funny."

"A nun who looks like Rihanna," he murmured. "Funny or tragic?"

His mouth tipped up, and she heard Boxer snort out a laugh as they padded across the snow-slicked sidewalk. The Chicago streets were mostly quiet for a change as the storm raged its forecasted ten to twelve inches. They'd dig out tomorrow, but right now, the smart ones were at home and off the roads.

But not this one.

"Only a couple more blocks to go," she told him.

"You like living in this dump?" he asked.

So he didn't live here normally. Something to remember. "This part of South Side isn't pretty, but I do what I can to make it a good neighborhood."

"Let's be honest here. This section is a shithole, and it's not safe for average families."

She was tempted to argue that the streets were lined with so-called average families. Sure, they didn't all have white-picket-fence lifestyles, but how many people actually did? Debating the matter wouldn't get her anywhere with him, however. This man was angry at the world and itching for a fight, and even though she'd known him all of fifteen minutes, she could tell he was stubborn.

And yet he seemed smart. He'd *negotiated* with her, for heaven's sake, while drinking from a bottle. Not normal.

"So where are you from originally, Connor?" she asked.

"All you need to know is that I've spent time in this part of South Side," he responded in that firm, crisp, eff-off tone. "It's gotten worse."

Here she was thinking some of it had gotten better, but he was right. One block would improve, another would worsen. Most years it was like playing whack-a-mole. "We do what we can."

"Pardon me, but you're not doing enough."

The accusation burned, and she heard Boxer growl. "You think you can do better?" she asked.

"Maybe," was all she got in response.

That *maybe* held the promise of gasoline on a bonfire. She wondered what he had in mind. Some wanted to dispense good old-fashioned justice themselves to the corner drug dealers and gang members. She'd only seen that breed more hate and violence. The police did their best, but some of the community didn't trust them. She tried to stay out of that fray. She didn't dispense justice. She dispensed hope and a second chance at life.

"Lot of abandoned buildings on this street," Connor commented as they turned the corner.

"High rents. Increased crime."

"Bad investments," he finished for her.

Boxer glanced over at her, and she smiled. So this one knew about investments. More evidence of his smarts. "Exactly."

Her dream was to make something out of those bad investments. She hoped to buy a large, abandoned school building a few blocks from Sunflower Alley and turn it into a job training center. She had about a hundred thousand dollars left to raise, and then hopefully Sunflower Alley could give people a full-service program that provided both a fish and a fishing pole.

"Here we are," she announced, extending her hand to her pride and joy, a two-story office building she'd bought on the cheap after the owner had declared bankruptcy. Sure, the radiators were ancient and they had window air-conditioning units, but it was a safe place for their clients to stay while they turned their lives around.

"How did you come up with the name Sunflower Alley?" Connor asked.

"My dad grew sunflowers for me when I was a kid. He did it to show me that something could be beautiful

and tough. I wanted to share that message with others."
She waited for him to make a cutting remark. Others
had.

"He sounds like a good dad," Connor said instead,
shocking her.

Boxer unlocked the door and opened it for them.
"Coach Evans is the best."

"The sunflowers are also inviting to women and children," she added.

His brow winked up. "Children?"

"You'd be surprised how many homeless children
there are in the greater Chicago area."

"How many?" he pressed, despite Boxer holding
open the door. He had to be hungry for that warmth, but
he didn't take a step forward.

"About twenty thousand," she replied. At one time,
she'd been one of them.

His mouth formed an impressive scowl. "That's the
size of a small town."

"Yes, it is, which is why places like ours matter so
much. So... Welcome to Sunflower Alley, Connor. Unfortunately, you'll have to leave your bottle outside."

"You let people leave their bottles out front like
they're umbrellas?" he spat back.

She took the bottle he extended. "Some people are
reluctant to part with their friend Jameson or Jack Dan-
iel's. We try and get them inside without riling them up
too much. It's not a perfect solution. There are lots of
gray areas for us to handle when working with people."

"Gray is an understatement," he shot back, anger in
his tone.

She fumbled with her keys for a moment, her fingers
numb with cold, but managed to open the short cabinet anchored to the wall beside the door. Once his bottle
was secured inside, she locked it up.

"What?" she asked, feeling his scrutiny. "You didn't

think we were just going to leave it on the ground for anyone to pick up, did you?"

He made some sound, something between a laugh and a snort. One thing was for sure. He didn't care much for what people thought of him.

"Louisa, why don't you check in with the staff while I take care of Connor?" Boxer said as they walked inside. "Connor, normally we'd have someone sitting at our reception desk, but it's after curfew and we're closed."

"A reception for the homeless? Now I've heard everything."

She locked the door again. "We have an intake process. There are practical matters to address, like the person's situation and needs. Are they single, or do they have children? Do they meet the guidelines we have for safety at the shelter?"

"What happens if someone comes to the door after curfew because of the storm?" he asked, gazing around like he was sizing up the place.

"If anyone needed shelter tonight, they'd have to buzz for the night caretaker. Boxer, I'll take care of our guest. After all, I owe him my story."

"I'm not a guest," Connor said in a hard tone. "You were right about where I'm staying. I'm not homeless."

No, he wasn't homeless yet if he had a room at Ferguson's, but he could be on the cusp of it. He was a danger to himself just now, and she wouldn't have been able to sleep if she'd left him in the snow.

"Regardless, you'll feel a lot better once you have some hot coffee and warm clothes," she said, waving Boxer off. "Come on, Connor."

Boxer narrowed his eyes. "Find me if you need anything."

"Don't I always?" she shot back with a wink, making him throw his hands up as he left them.

"Who writes the Hallmark cards?" Connor asked.

She turned to see him studying the big chalkboard she'd hung in the bright entryway. Each morning she wrote what she called her daily love note. "I do. People don't hear good things often enough if you ask me, especially the people we serve. Do you have something against kindness and inspiration?"

"'*If you're reading this, something wonderful is about to happen.*' I'm sorry, but do the people staying here really buy that?"

This time she gave him back her best smirk. "Depends on the person, but I want them to know we care from the moment they walk in."

He made another sound in his throat, and she nudged him with her elbow gently.

"In your case, Connor, something wonderful *has* happened. You're here and not freezing to death outside. Sounds like a win to me. Now, let's get you some clothes. You're—"

"Lady, I'm not wearing someone else's clothes," he ground out.

"It's Louisa, and you're freezing."

"I'm not that bad," he said, his tone fierce. "I tend to run hot."

Sure, he did. She'd humor him and circle back, a fine art she'd perfected with the tough guys. "Do you want to take a shower while I dry your clothes in a dryer then?" She eyed his bare legs, red from the cold. "They should dry quickly."

"Is the shower clean?"

"Yes, it's cleaned daily like the showers at your local gym," she said, imagining he worked out. "Are you going to question *everything*? Because if you are, let me at least take my coat off and get warm myself."

"Your cheeks are red, and your stocking hat is so soggy it's falling off your head. Also, you need new gloves." He pulled the hat off, surprising her. "God, you really do look like Rihanna."

She laughed. "You're not the first to say so. I'm mixed, but my dad's people are originally from the Caribbean. Some of our guests think I've missed my calling as a singer. It crushes them when they find out I can't carry a tune or dance." She did a horrible hip-hop step, one that usually guaranteed a smile or laugh.

He did neither. His eyes had crested over her face, and she noticed one of his eyes was green and the other blue. It wasn't completely obvious at first, but when you looked a little closer...

My goodness, he was handsome in a rough kind of way, dripping snowmelt with that dark beard.

Be professional. She switched her regard to checking for any yellow tinge around his pupils, indicating any medical issues. There were none.

"You freaked out by my eyes?" he asked. "They call it *heterochromia iridis*, but that's just a big word for having weird eyes. Yours are beautiful. Gold with green and brown around the iris. Quite unusual as well, and very compelling."

He stated it more as a fact than a compliment.

"I think yours are rather cool actually," she said. "Then again, I don't like the same-same. Come on."

She led him down the hall to the men's locker room. When she got there, she knocked on the door. No one answered, which she'd expected given the hour, but it always paid to check.

"It's after curfew here, so you'll have the place to yourself. Showers are on two-minute timers out of concern for our water bill. Hope you understand. Let me grab you a towel." She walked to a cabinet and dug her keys out to grab him one.

"Do you have to lock everything up?" he asked.

"Unfortunately, yes. Some people would never think to take a towel, but others who have nothing..."

"And no ethics," he finished, pulling his blanket off and folding it neatly.

"You call it ethics," she said. "To some people, it's survival. I try not to judge."

He took the towel from her, and those strange, entrancing eyes held her gaze as he placed the wet blanket in her hand. "How's that working for you?"

Challenging him seemed the best response, which was fortunate, because it was the only one she could manage. "You're here, aren't you?"

"Indeed, I am, Louisa." He opened the door to the locker room and left her standing there.

It was the first time he'd used her name, and it seemed significant. Maybe she'd be able to get through to him, help him out of the cycle that could end in him being homeless and worse. She dropped the wet blanket in the laundry hamper and took off her coat, heading back to her office.

"Hey! You want my clothes?"

She stopped in her tracks and turned around. He was holding out his shorts and T-shirt, his body hidden mostly by the door. But she could see the firm muscles in his arm and part of his chest.

In the harsh fluorescent light, she admitted the truth. She was attracted to him.

It had never happened with anyone they'd come across on the streets or in the park. The realization caught her off guard, even more so because it wasn't just his looks that spoke to her. He wasn't like anyone she'd ever met.

He waved his hand at her, his long muscled arm beckoning her closer. She felt her insides warm, thinking about him on the other side of that door. Her feet wouldn't move.

Shake it off. He was totally and completely off-limits. She didn't fraternize with the people they served. She was here to help—that was a sacred trust—and given her brief acquaintance with him, he was deeply troubled. He needed kindness and only kindness.

"Why are you standing there like a lump of clay?" he asked, and then he was opening the door and striding toward her in a towel.

Her breath stopped in her chest, an instinctive reaction that was completely unwanted. She purposely looked away. He had to pick up her hands and plop the wet, soggy clothes into them.

"You were taking too long," he said, "and this way you can see that I don't have the body of some homeless guy."

Hadn't she just been trying to ignore that? "I've seen some homeless ex-cons and drug dealers with bodies like that." That sounded more fair-minded, didn't it?

His mouth twitched. "More august comparisons. First homeless and now a criminal. Man, what a night."

She couldn't help but notice as his towel slipped lower, showcasing a fantastic V. Maybe she should call Boxer in, after all.

"The locker room isn't too bad, by the way." Then he was heading back to it.

She laid a hand on her chest. Her heart was racing. *Stop this.*

She put his clothes in the dryer in the laundry room, then headed to her office to shed her coat and check her voicemail. The most recent message was from the director of another downtown shelter who had an overload situation and was hoping Sunflower Alley could take in an extra family. Louisa called their Uber contact—his tab was picked up by a benefactor—and asked if he would brave the streets to pick the family up. It was only ten minutes without traffic, and he'd done it in the snow before. After talking to the driver, she called the shelter back to confirm pickup. When she clicked off, she heard someone clear their throat.

Connor was standing in a towel in her office doorway as if he owned the place. "I didn't want to interrupt you, but I need my clothes."

She flew out of her chair, tamping down the tightness

in her belly at seeing all that hard muscled flesh again. "I'm so sorry. I had an urgent matter. Come on, let's see if your clothes are dry. Do you need another blanket? Are you *sure* you don't want warmer clothes?"

"I'll be fine," he said, matching her stride as she hurried down the hallway to the laundry room. "I had a chance to read your job postings on the community bulletin board. You're looking for someone to create a business plan for a new job training center?"

Her insides started humming for an entirely different reason at the interest in his voice as she pulled his clothes out of the dryer and handed them to him. "They're mostly dry. As for the job, I don't have the time to get to it, and I thought someone might see the posting... We have volunteers and visitors, you know. Anyway, I don't have the building now, but I hope to acquire it within the next six months." She had some serious fundraising events planned to get her to her goal.

"I might be able to help with that." He frowned. "Were you really arranging for a family to come here in the snow? I didn't mean to overhear while I was waiting."

"Yes, another shelter didn't have beds for them, so they've been calling around. Luckily, we have a couple open tonight."

"What would have happened if no one found beds for them?" He shrugged on the long-sleeved T-shirt right in front of her. No body shame or modesty here.

She wasn't sure what he was going to do about the shorts, so she spun around. His laughter erupted immediately. "I wasn't going to pull the rest of my clothes on until I went back to the locker room, but it's good to know even women try to be a gentleman."

Snorting herself, she spun back around to face him. His wet hair looked like he'd run his hands through it, and it somehow made him more appealing.

"We aren't supposed to take clients home with us, but

in weather like this, if all the shelters are full, some of us will meet the family and decide whether to make an exception. On a wintry night like this one, many, many years ago, someone offered my mom and me a break, something that might have saved our lives. That experience and many others taught me not to draw hard and fast lines."

His mouth dropped open. "*You were homeless*?"

"Yes. You asked about my story. My mom came home from the Gulf War with PTSD and an injured shoulder from when her team's Humvee hit an IED. She was the only survivor, which she never got over. She started using oxy for the pain, and later the escape, and developed an addiction. There's more to it, but yes, after my parents divorced, my mom and I went from the streets to shelters to temporary housing and then back again."

He swallowed thickly. "That must have been terrible for you. No wonder you help the homeless."

Her laugh was ironic this time. People always assumed that. "For a while, I wanted nothing to do with them. Something happened that changed everything, but that's a story for another night."

He regarded her for a long moment. "You promised me your story earlier, and I want it now. How did you stop being homeless?"

He wanted it now? Demanding was too tame a word for him. "My dad. He lost custody when they divorced. It's horrible, but addicts lie, and she made up damaging stories about him. Being the mother, white, and a veteran, the judge believed her." For years, she'd carried around rage at her mother for lying about her father. Thank God, she'd finally put that to rest. Forgiving her mom had been hard but necessary for her to move forward with her life.

His mouth was twisted, as if in disgust. "How did your father regain custody after she maligned his reputation? That's not an easy thing to overcome."

Did she discern something more personal in his query?

If he did feel responsible for someone dying like she'd guessed, perhaps he was facing some questions about his own character. "My dad appealed the ruling and continued his work as a teacher and coach and community leader, hoping the truth would speak for itself in the end. Of course, my mom's addiction and our homelessness helped his case, although the court system took way too long to overrule the decision and give me back to him." Her dad had confessed his agony and guilt over his inability to make it happen sooner.

"Good for him for fighting and not giving up," he said, nodding. "What happened to your mom?"

The wrenching of her heart wasn't as painful as it used to be, but it was still there despite all her counseling. "She froze to death on a night like this when I was fourteen."

"Jesus, I'm sorry." He studied her. "No wonder you don't back down at the park. Who could live with that?"

It sounded as if the words had been ripped from his chest. Yeah, he had deep hurts, ones she could understand, ones she hoped she could help. "For a while, I couldn't. I got counseling and tried to move on."

His face shuttered. "How long did that take?"

"A few years with some forward movement and some bumps along the road, but I got there. I was lucky. I had my dad, and the woman he married—my stepmom—was terrific. Her heart gave out a couple years ago, it was so big. My half-brother is also really great."

"So you ran from the homeless after that. Understandable. What changed?"

Rapid-fire questions. Did he realize how intense he was? "I was working my first job out of college in advertising, feeling far away from it all, and wouldn't you know it, a homeless man took to sitting on a bench in the park directly across from my apartment building. I used to walk past him every day with my dog. I tried ignoring him at first, but he always said hello to me. I felt guilty after a while and started to say it back. We did that for three months, and then I got laid off and went on a vacation to reassess things. My apartment building caught fire while I was gone."

"Jesus, you've had it rough."

"Maybe, but I was lucky too. I had a friend dog sitting, but she wasn't there during the fire, thank God. Anyway, the homeless man saw the blaze and broke into my apartment to save my dog since he heard him barking. He ended up helping a few other people escape the blaze as well."

"That's a pretty incredible story. Some would call it full circle."

Wise as well. His intriguing factor kept going up. "It gets better. That man is Boxer."

His rapid blink was the first indication he was disarmed. "What happened next?"

"I was so moved he'd saved my dog, I asked if there was anything I could do to help him. He told me his story, one I don't mind sharing since most of it is up on our website. The factory he'd worked at for years moved its production overseas and laid everyone off, and his wife left him. When he couldn't find a new job, he fell into a deep depression. He just didn't care anymore until the day of the fire. Helping save those people and my dog gave him a renewed sense of purpose. The same thing happened to me in some ways. I had this big life moment. Felt like I'd lost my job in advertising because it didn't speak to my soul. As you said, full circle."

"A big life moment, huh? That's pretty deep." Except his body language closed up like a clam.

"Life *is* deep," she said, "especially when it comes to taking our hurts and turning them into something good. After the fire, I knew without any doubt that I was supposed to help the homeless, people like Boxer and my mom. I especially wanted to help families. So I did my homework and saved some money and talked Boxer into working with me. We started out small, but we've been steadily growing our organization to help more people. You might not believe it, but homelessness is actually down in Chicago for another consecutive year."

"And yet this neighborhood looks worse than I remember it." Once again, his tone suggested an anger she didn't understand.

"When was the last time you were here?" she asked.

His eyes shuttered a moment before he met her gaze straight on. "You promised me *your* story. I didn't promise you mine."

She knew a wall when she saw it. "You're right. Why don't you finish dressing? I'll get us some coffee."

"In a minute. Regarding the job posting... I'll give you an outline of what I have in mind for a business plan tomorrow. If you like it, I can draw up a full one for you."

To her surprise, she didn't question his qualifications or ability. Somehow she knew this man absolutely knew what he was talking about. No, what she wanted to know was why.

"Why would you do that, Connor?" she pressed, studying him.

He inhaled deeply and looked down at his bare feet before meeting her eyes. "You were willing to take a homeless family into your own home tonight if need be. You put your own safety and comfort on the line to help a stranger in a snowstorm—even though I'm not homeless. If you want to create a job training program, that's more than simply helping the homeless. That's rebuilding a community."

Succinctly put. Like he was used to summarizing points. Damn but she wanted to know his story.

"Besides, you were right. I don't have any prospects right now. I'm used to keeping busy." He paused. "And you were willing to sit beside me in a snowstorm tonight until I saw reason. Very few people challenge me, and it's exactly what I needed tonight."

Somehow it was a compliment, and her throat grew

thick with emotion. "How did you know I wasn't bluffing about sitting with you?"

His easy smile stole her breath, the beauty and charm of it so unexpected and captivating. "Louisa, I *always* know when someone's bluffing."

She believed him. "I'd be happy to see the outline if you're serious."

"I never say something I don't mean."

"Neither do I."

"Then we seem to understand each other," he said, the smile fading from his mouth. Maybe he wasn't used to anyone understanding him either. Something told her that was the case.

"I believe we do. Now, it's cold and the snow is likely heavy by now on the road and sidewalk. I have a bed for you, if you'd like to stay here tonight."

His mouth twisted harshly. "I told you, Louisa. I'm not homeless, and I sure as hell don't plan on ever being a client of yours."

"Why is that?" she asked, equally direct.

"Because I think you're beautiful and tenacious, and if I end up asking you out, I don't want you to have any ethical concerns about accepting."

His words were a punch to the gut, but she didn't want him to know how they'd affected her, how *he* affected her. "Ask me out? Now who's getting ahead of themselves? An hour ago you were freezing to death, drinking in a park. You might not be a client, but you're still troubled."

He leaned in, the scent of donated Irish Spring soap catching her nose. "An hour ago, I was feeling sorry for myself after a bad meeting. The liquor was part of the pity party. But I'm over that."

Her brow winged up. Who had he met and what had transpired to drive him to such dire straits? "Are you?"

"Mostly." He grimaced. "I'm trying. Tonight seems

to have given me that renewed purpose thing you mentioned earlier as well as the answer to a problem I was facing."

"And what is that?"

"I'm going to help you turn this neighborhood around."

CHAPTER 3

ARTHUR HALE WAS TOO OLD FOR STAKEOUTS.

And yet, here he was, sitting on a snowy bench the morning after one of Chicago's notorious snowstorms, freezing his ass off next to his beloved wife in a place he hoped to avoid for a few years longer—a graveyard.

Clara sat next to him, a Chicago tourist brochure in her hand, reading about all the famous people buried in Oak Woods Cemetery. Graveyard tourism. He wondered what the cemetery's residents would think of that. Would boss Big Jim Colosimo still want the attention? Would Olympian Jesse Owens want the cheers? A big bummer, as far as Arthur was concerned. "Put that brochure down and keep your eyes peeled."

She gave him a look before putting the brochure in the pocket of her fur coat. Not a hard-core environmentalist, his wife, but he loved her to pieces just the same.

"Hargreaves prepared a flask for you if you'd like to add a touch of mother's milk to your coffee," she said, scanning the graveyard like he'd asked. "Your cheeks are red, dear, and you're a bit grouchy."

"They don't like this lake-effect wind any better than my backside likes this Icelandic bench, and whiskey is the water of life, Clara. Guinness is mother's milk. Jeez, you should have that one down after our trip to Ireland."

She rapped his arm with her gloved hand. "Why didn't you let Hargreaves stake this place out with me instead of canvassing the area? You could be reading a newspaper in the warm confines of our hotel room."

He snorted. "Like I would let your butler—who has no head for investigation, by the way—outdo me. My God, woman, what kind of a man would I be if I let my wife and her butler do *my job*?"

"We all want to find Connor, dear," she said, her pink-painted mouth worrying. "Thank goodness he finally went to Olivia's last night, or we wouldn't even have confirmation he's in Chicago."

He didn't bring up the fact that they'd only missed Connor last night because Clara had talked him into staying inside due to the snowstorm. Arthur wouldn't put it past Connor to have planned the meeting with Olivia during harsh weather to avoid detection. He'd certainly made a point of not being found. No credit cards used. No devices or cars registered to him. Nothing. To Arthur's knowledge, even the boy's tech-savvy brother, Flynn, hadn't found one bleep of him.

"I know he was the runner I saw the other day, but he didn't slow down." And his eyes weren't twenty-twenty anymore, even though they were pretty sharp for a man in his eighties.

"We should have chased him down," Clara said, hitting her hand into her palm. "Hargreaves had the limo all ready."

Why she'd insisted on renting a limo in one of the nation's worst cities for traffic, he couldn't fathom. But he'd learned not to make a fuss if he didn't object strongly to one of her whims. Unless it was to poke at her a bit. Like he was about to do. "This Irish fisherman sweater you knitted me is starting to itch."

Her beautiful baby blues rolled his way before she pulled her brochure out again in outright challenge. "That wool is the softest I've found yet. Arthur, I swear. If you're going to keep complaining, I'm joining Hargreaves. He packed us a nice picnic, and my stomach is rumbling."

"A picnic? Clara, for heaven's sake, this is a stakeout. Not a garden party."

"You have your way of enduring the waiting, and Hargreaves and I have ours." To punctuate this, she pulled out a curvy pocket flask from her purse and took a drink. Her eyes closed, and she made a sound of delight.

"You made that sound this morning for an entirely different reason," he said with a chuckle. "What are you drinking?"

"Marital bliss and martinis go together like yellow and purple in a rainbow."

"Your analogies need work. Are you seriously drinking a martini?"

"It's lunchtime, Arthur, and you know I feel European on the inside."

He just shrugged. The martinis made her happy. Besides, Clara could drink like a fish. He'd never seen any amount of alcohol affect her. Her family called it an alcohol supergene.

"A man fitting Mr. Merriam's description is running this way on the east side of the graveyard," Hargreaves' voice sounded on the walkie-talkie Arthur had insisted on buying. Of course, his wife had suggested simply texting any sightings. Hell, no, not on his watch. This was a proper stakeout—minus the fur coat, tourist brochure, and martinis.

Arthur picked up his binoculars. Sure enough, a man wearing nothing but shorts and a long-sleeved University of Chicago T-shirt was running at a healthy clip toward the grave of none other than Corey Weatherby. But he was sporting a short beard.

Good camouflage, Arthur suspected. Or maybe the boy wasn't taking care of himself out of grief. They'd soon find out.

All that mattered was they'd found him. Connor needed his family right now more than ever—despite his insistence on pushing everyone away—and Arthur knew he and Clara were about to have a hell of a fight on their hands. Still, he whispered almost reverently, "At last. We've got you, son."

Clara picked up the walkie-talkie. "Hargreaves, head to the limo. If Connor flees, you'll have to chase him down."

Arthur cut her a look. "Did you watch an old Steve McQueen movie after I fell asleep last night? We're not going to chase him down, Clara. We're going to reason with him." Or play hardball, if need be.

Clara stood, grabbing the binoculars out of his hand. "He's heading to Corey's grave as you predicted. Bravo, Arthur. Let's get moving. The attendants might have shoveled a path through the graveyard, but it's slippery. You'll need to go slow."

"You're as old as I am, woman," he said, rising and extending his arm to her like the gentleman he was. "We'll both go slow and hope to hell Connor doesn't bolt."

"You can count on Hargreaves if that happens, dear."

He harrumphed as they started down the path. Connor was standing in the freezing cold in front of Corey's grave, hands folded in front of him. Had he gone mad? The temperature was in the low twenties and he was ridiculously underdressed.

"He looks different with the beard. Darker somehow." Clara gripped his arm. "Arthur, what happens if he won't let us help him? His family will be devastated."

We'll all be devastated.

Which was why he didn't intend to take no for an answer.

"We won't stop pressing him until he does listen. Are we not two stubborn old people?"

She gave him a watery smile. "Stubborn I am, indeed, but not old."

"No, you're in the prime of your life." Arthur kissed her cheek. "Now buck up. We're about to lock horns with the Big Bad Wolf." As a family nickname, it was telling. None of the Merriam kids were tougher than Connor—Arthur didn't know if it was being the oldest of seven, knowing he was expected to take over a multi-billion-dollar conglomerate that had made him that way—and he prayed to God none of the others ever would be.

They stopped a few feet behind Connor, and he must have sensed them because he turned slightly and nodded like he might to other mourners. Then he turned around the whole way, facing them with the wariness a bull might feel toward a matador. "This can't be a coincidence."

"It is not," Clara said, lifting her regal chin. "We've missed you, my boy. Everyone has been worried about you."

His face fell. "Is Michaela—"

"She's completely recovered from her fever, don't worry," Clara said, reaching for his hand.

He lowered his head, his profile a still life of agony. "Thank God. I was..."

Carefully, he took Clara's hand and set it away from him. Arthur felt a pinch in his heart seeing the conscious withdrawal.

"Now that we've established the state of her health, why else are you here?"

Clara looked over at him. "Arthur had a mind to see if his old investigative journalist skills might assist him in finding you."

"Which explains why you're here, freezing in a graveyard after a Chicago snowstorm." Connor tucked his gloveless hands around himself. "I knew seeing Olivia was a risk."

"It only confirmed my suspicions," Arthur said, taking hold of Clara more firmly. "We've been canvassing this graveyard and Olivia's house for a week now. Missed you last night due to the storm and the other day when you didn't stop running. Happy you finally slowed down."

His mouth twitched as if amused. "I apologize for causing you any inconvenience, but like I said, I didn't want to be found. I certainly didn't want to see anyone in the family after what transpired, but after last night, I'm surprised to discover I'm not unhappy to see you. In fact, I feel like we have a mutually beneficial deal to make."

This was what Arthur loved about life—even after eighty years, it still had the ability to surprise him. The last time he and Clara had seen Connor, they'd taken him to task for some exceptionally bad judgment regarding his sister and her work with a local village in Kenya. Connor didn't seem to be angry with them, but it was hard to see beyond his rock-solid poker face.

Clara met Arthur's eyes before standing taller in her snow boots. "I'm eager to hear your proposed deal."

Oh, these Merriams. Sometimes Arthur wanted to knock them on the backs of their heads for complicating things with deals and negotiations, but business was in their blood like journalism was in his. He could make allowances. Plus, the boy wasn't running. That was something. His old bones weren't great at chasing anymore. "Outline what you have in mind."

Connor looked off for a moment. "I assume Hargreaves is driving the limo coming this way."

"Of course," Clara said. "When I say we've all been worried, I'm not exaggerating."

"No more talk of worry or the past," Connor said in the hard tone he was famous for. "This is a short-term business deal. You don't share my whereabouts with my family in exchange for working with me, which will allow you to keep tabs on me. Something you clearly want."

Arthur ran his tongue over his teeth. Could he keep something like this from the boy's family? They were all beside themselves with worry. "This had better be good because I can't fathom not telling them."

"I can disappear again," Connor said, snapping his fingers. "No one would find me. Not even Flynn."

"And yet we found you," Clara said. What was she trying to do? The boy already had his back up, and hell, if he ran, they wouldn't be able to catch him.

"You only found me because I was overly sentimental coming here," Connor said, his mouth twisting. "It won't happen again. I can and will disappear for good and no one would ever find me."

A spasm rolled through Arthur's gut at the thought. Connor would do it. He wouldn't think twice. "Let's not get ahead of ourselves. Tell us what you have in mind."

Clara folded her arms. "I'll need to hear the terms before agreeing."

Connor rolled his eyes as Hargreaves came into sight, walking up the path from where he'd parked the limo on one of the roads running through the graveyard. "Are your butler duties never done, Hargreaves?"

The man was carrying what looked like a full-length winter coat, and for once, Arthur could have kissed him.

"Your coat, sir," Hargreaves said, unfolding it and holding it out for Connor.

"In my size, of course." Connor sighed, shaking his head. "Fine, I'll wear the damn coat, but I run hot. When I went to school here, I rarely wore a light jacket in the winter."

"You get that fire from your Grandpa Emmits," Clara said. "He was the same way."

"Genes," Connor said, chuckling. "Can't escape them. I guess I should be glad Hargreaves didn't bring me a blanket. Everyone seems to want to cover me up lately."

"Please, sir," Hargreaves said with a slight scoff. "A blanket? I have standards to adhere to."

Clara shot Arthur a puzzled look, but even though he was equally curious, he suspected it wasn't the time to press the boy.

"Are you hungry, sir?" Hargreaves asked. "I have some lunch items in the car."

"I'm fine, Hargreaves," Connor said. "Is everyone worried I'm not taking care of myself?"

"Yes," Clara responded.

Arthur nudged her. "On with the conditions."

Connor buttoned the coat with precision. "I find I'm in the mood to improve the neighborhood Olivia and her boys live in. If you've been staking it out, you'll have noticed it needs it."

"It seems to have fallen on some hard times," Arthur agreed. "Some blocks are better than others." He'd been worried about having Clara in the car with him, but she'd insisted on coming along. Of course, he'd chosen an old Buick. There was no way they were going to stake out in a limo. Leave that for Hargreaves' daytime canvassing.

"I want to buy up as much of the neighborhood as I can. Help it find an urban spring," Connor said. "Uncle, I imagine you are well informed on successful urban renewal models. I have some thoughts already. Stayed up all night researching and preparing some ideas."

Arthur rocked back on his feet, feeling the healthy bite of excitement. This was the kind of challenge he'd missed after retiring. "I am, and I can research more on ones used successfully in comparable cities."

Connor nodded, finishing with his buttons. "Music to my ears. Aunt, I assume you chartered a plane to come here."

"I did," she responded cautiously. "In need of a flight?"

"Yes, to Switzerland, and perhaps Luxembourg," he said, scratching his beard as if he wasn't friendly yet with its presence. "I need to move some money. Set up a few new corporations in names that won't track back to me."

"Ones your family can't trace," Clara said.

"And other inquiring people," Arthur added. "One person buying up that much property in South Side might raise some eyebrows."

"It's legal, but yes, I don't want anyone to raise objections," Connor said. "I'll have to buy up enough property to convince some of the bigger box stores to come in and put up their shingle to turn things around, and I need this done quickly and without complication."

The boy was talking about gentrification. Strong feelings defined the topic, but Connor had never been one to shy from opposition. His nephew seemed resolute.

"Why the sudden interest in improving South Side?" Clara asked.

Arthur looked to Corey's grave.

"Because Olivia won't leave the neighborhood," Connor said, his jaw tightening. "I promised Corey I'd look after her and the boys, and it's not safe. Right now, this seems the only way."

A smart and canny workaround, Arthur thought, but it was a great weight for one person to take on. "It's a big investment with a lot of hurdles and uncertainties," he said carefully.

Connor held his arms out, and Arthur saw a sparkle of that old Merriam magic—the certain something that had helped lift his mentor, the great Emmits Merriam, Clara's grandfather, to greatness. "If a billionaire can't take risks, what the hell is the money for? Besides, it's not like I ever had the time to enjoy it. Working at Merriam... Never mind. That's over, and I don't ever want to speak of it."

Arthur's heart grew tight in his chest. The pressure and demands of running a company like Merriam Enterprises were enormous and never-ending. For years, Connor had devoted his every breath to the family business, but Corey's death had deeply wounded him, and the ill-advised decisions he'd made in the thick of grief had led to this—a family divide so deep Arthur wasn't sure it could be bridged.

But he and Clara were going to damn well try.

"What else?" Clara asked crisply.

"I'd also like you to donate a significant sum to a South Side homeless shelter—money I will give you. Without boring you with the long version, the director approved the outline I created for the job training program they're going to be implementing."

"I see," Clara said in an even tone, but Arthur caught her sidelong glance.

Connor Merriam was helping a homeless shelter? He didn't know if it was lunacy or the perfect thing to get the boy's head on straight.

Connor wiped his face as the wind gusted up a sheen of snow, almost as if flicking away a fly. "I told her I'd need a week to flesh out a full business plan, and I should be able to make that deadline even with my travel schedule... should we come to terms. There's another caveat. I don't want the director of the shelter to know we know each other."

Well, well. The plot doth thicken.

"If this shelter is deserving, I'll give *my* money to it," Clara said haughtily.

"Never argue with her when it comes to her name or reputation, son," Arthur said, smiling suddenly amidst the tension. "A job training program could help you turn the neighborhood around. Clara will make the donation, and I'll tell them I'm doing an article on the homeless in America. Which I'll publish when it's perfect enough." Hell, he could win another Pulitzer.

Clara nudged him. "It's on an important topic so I won't quibble about you being retired."

"This shelter works especially with homeless families and children, but they seem to have a knack for screening people who want to pull themselves up by their bootstraps,"

Connor said. "People like me have a very negative view of the homeless. The bums. The crazy people who talk to themselves on the streets. The vets who get violent when you don't give them money. San Francisco was full of negative examples."

Arthur saw things differently, but he didn't correct the stereotypes. Not when Connor was admitting to them. "What changed your mind?"

"Let's say the director of the shelter helped me see this problem in a new light. She's compelling. She's also seriously trying to make life better for people in need. I intend to help her."

Arthur's matchmaker radar sounded. Compelling, huh? This woman had to be that and more to have inspired Connor to undertake such a task.

He glanced at Clara, who raised her brows. Yes, she was thinking the same thing.

"You'll meet her when you visit Sunflower Alley. I'd like that to happen when I get back from my trip. Be nice to have the money come in right around the time the business plan's ready. She'll see it as a miracle. She's into those things."

Oddly, there was no derision in his tone. If Arthur had to characterize it, he'd say it was amused respect. "I imagine you'd need to believe in miracles to work with the homeless."

"She sounds like an incredible woman," Clara said. "Sunflower Alley. Is that the shelter's name?"

Another smile from the Big Bad Wolf. "Yes."

She clapped her gloves together. "I love it."

"You would, Aunt. No offense." He held up his hands for good measure, which was the only reason Arthur didn't give him a set down.

"So you've taken it on yourself to single-handedly turn around South Side," Arthur said, feeling the need to add a dose of reality to the conversation. "Do you know anything about Chicago politics? They have a long history of doing things their own way. South Side especially."

Connor just grinned at him, the kind of grin that had more of that Merriam magic to it. "They haven't dealt with me before. Besides, this is a win-win situation for everyone."

Was it? He suspected not everyone would see it that way. But if finding a new purpose in life helped Connor manage his grief, Arthur was all for it. "Clara and I will need to discuss the secretive nature of your plan before we can agree. If you'll excuse us... Hargreaves, please join us."

He led his wife a few yards away, shielding her from the wind. Hargreaves joined them and stood next to his mistress—the term Clara insisted Arthur use even though it seemed ludicrous to call his wife someone's mistress. Weird butler language.

"The boy seems set on this plan with or without our assistance," Arthur said, "and I'm inclined to help. He might think he's over his grief and guilt, but I think we know better. I'd like to be around if and when it kicks back up. Clara? What say you?"

"I agree with you," she said, shaking her head a little, "but I hate the idea of keeping this from his family—*our* family. Even if I felt they could forgive me for it, I hate knowing they'll be worrying. Hargreaves? I value your insights. They've been helpful to me for decades."

Arthur almost said, *why do you think I invited him to join us*? But he kept his mouth shut. This was serious business, and Connor was tapping his snowy tennis shoes on the snow-packed ground impatiently.

The butler's ever-calm demeanor didn't falter. "I believe Mr. Merriam is serious about disappearing. I imagine his family would prefer for us to assist him in a healthy enterprise without their initial knowledge than for him to flee to parts unknown doing God knows what."

That phrase—*God knows what*—chilled Arthur to his

bones. "A man like Connor needs purpose and work," he added. "He's used to it. He'll wither away otherwise. And this might help him feel like he's fulfilling his promise to Corey."

Clara drew back her shoulders, and that slight gesture was all the proof Arthur needed to know she'd reached her decision. "We're going to back him and pray we can convince him to let us tell the rest of the family. I'm willing to risk their ire, but I'm hoping for their understanding."

A family disagreement had kept Clara and her brother at odds for decades, but they'd finally made up. Something she was hesitant to risk, especially since she and Arthur had been involved in the family rift between Connor and the others.

"They are inclined to trust you, Madam, and you too, sir," Hargreaves said. "After all, you have helped the other Merriam children quite admirably. This seems an exceptional situation, yet you are still helping a Merriam."

"Thank you, Hargreaves," Clara said with a regal nod. "Then I guess it's settled. We'll help Connor with this new project, including this woman who's managed to impress him so, and keep an eye on his overall well-being."

And yet, Arthur couldn't help but worry. In the four months since Corey's death, Connor had taken to making unilateral decisions in his drive to keep the people he loved safe. It had resulted in increasingly erratic behavior that had ultimately cost him his job as CEO of Merriam Enterprises. Was this new project another manifestation of his ongoing obsession with keeping the people he loved safe?

Arthur feared it might be, but he didn't see any other choice than to help him and hope they didn't fail. Perhaps they could do some real good in the process.

CHAPTER 4

A MAN SHE'D MET IN A SNOWSTORM WAS GOING TO HELP her launch her dream training program.

Even more miraculous, she'd mistaken him for a homeless person. A week later, Louisa still couldn't believe it. After Connor had left in the Uber that had brought the homeless family to her door, she'd concluded one hundred percent: he wasn't homeless or on his way toward it. No, he was unlike anyone she'd ever met.

He'd dropped off his outline the next morning like he'd promised, an outline so detailed, concise, and freaking brilliant, she'd almost thrown her arms around him when she said, "Yes, I want to see your full business plan." He'd nodded, given her a make-your-knees-weak smile, and promised to deliver it to her in a week's time. With that, he'd left.

Of course, she'd immediately raced the outline over to Boxer's office. His eyes had opened a little wider with each page. "Yeah, this is super impressive," he'd conceded, "but we still don't know nothing about him, and he doesn't seem interested in filling us in."

Maybe so, but how could they pass up this kind of help? She trusted her gut, and it was telling her to work with Connor. Louisa had been on pins and needles all week, waiting for today. And not only because Connor was delivering the business plan.

He'd been flirting with her via text all week, and she'd caved in a few times and flirted back. His first text had completely shocked her.

Louisa, it's Connor—the guy you saved the other night. If I didn't mention it, thanks for that. Low moment for me. You make a beautiful knight in shining armor. I'm sending you a gift as a thank you.

When his surprise arrived, she got a little gooey on the inside. The fleece-lined gloves, a scarf, and a slouchy stocking hat were all in lipstick red, one of her favorite colors.

The price tags had been cut away, but she could tell they were good quality. Where had he gotten the money? But she made herself set aside that concern because he wasn't one of her clients.

The card was simple yet touching, and she'd tucked it inside her purse for safekeeping. Usually she was the one who wrote the love notes around here. She couldn't remember the last time someone had handwritten a message to her, much less one like this.

Louisa,
This set is waterproof since you seem to enjoy spending time out in snowstorms. I don't like the idea of you being cold, but I like the idea of you continuing to help people like you helped me.
Connor

Okay, she'd admit it: he was charming and had a serious way with words. No cute little emojis for this man. Sitting at her desk, anticipating their meeting, she pulled up their message chain and reread it for the tenth time, like some pathetic schoolgirl.

Working on your plan, and it's like you're in my head, Louisa. I can almost hear you telling me what you want and what you don't want. Of course, I push back a little because there are some things you don't know you want yet.

Connor, you're terrible. Send me your draft as is, and I'll tell you if you're on the right track.

Louisa, you are as impatient as you are tenacious, both qualities I admire. I'm savoring the anticipation of seeing you again and sharing my ideas with you. Both are going to be really, really good.

All right, that text made her want to combust. She knew she wasn't reading too much into his words—he'd been thinking about sex. Hadn't he said he might ask her out? The gift seemed a slam dunk on that score. She still wasn't sure what she was going to do about that, but maybe today's meeting would help her decide. She eyed the last series of texts from him.

Can't wait to see you tomorrow. Your plan is fresh off the presses. I'm wondering if I'll still hear you talking to me once I deliver it to you. Not sure I want it to stop. That isn't meant to sound crazy. Despite appearances at our first meeting, I am quite sane. Obviously eager for a real conversation with you.

You should probably delete that last text. I just read it again, and I do sound a little crazy. About you.

Okay, I'm going to stop texting you right now.

It didn't sound crazy to her, but it suggested the man approached everything with the same brand of intensity, something that intrigued her. Each day, she'd found herself checking her phone multiple times for texts. Usually, she'd found one. Connor might not have told her much about himself, but he wasn't the type to play games.

She checked the time. He was supposed to be at her office in five minutes, and she fought the urge to rush to the bathroom and check her appearance.

Someone rapped on her doorframe, and she looked over to see Boxer standing there in navy sweats. "You still going gaga over those texts from Connor? Girl, I'm worried about you. You need to get out more if a few texts are enough to turn your head."

He'd caught her re-reading Connor's texts yesterday, twice, and had grabbed her phone and started reading them out loud. Thankfully, he hadn't made it all the way back to the part about the gift, so he hadn't teased her about it. Hadn't given her any of his brooding looks either.

"Don't you have someone else to harass?"

He shrugged his massive shoulders. "It's obvious you want to meet with this guy on your own so I'm heading to the gym. But in all seriousness, are you one hundred percent sure you want to open this can of worms?"

"We both size people up quickly," Louisa said, setting her phone aside. "Have to, right? What's your take?"

"Well, he's not dangerous, he obviously likes you, and he sure as hell is smart." Boxer tapped the side of his head. "One night of work, and he came up with an entire outline full of ideas we'd never considered. Hell, he even identified various classes of homeless folk and made individualized suggestions for industry placement. Yada, yada, yada. I get it."

"We can't pass this up."

He sighed. "I know this looks like one of your miracles."

"*Our* miracles," she reminded him. "Who saved my dog in a fire and turned his life around?"

"I miss that dog."

She'd cried when he had passed away. So had Boxer.

"Who would have imagined you and me could look back on that day in a positive light now?" he asked.

She grabbed a paper and pen and wrote, "'Your worst day may one day end up becoming your best day.' How's that for a love note?"

Chuckling, he said, "You really are a greeting card wrapped up in one cute little package. All I ask is you use your heart, which is the biggest I know, *and* your head. Perhaps tell your girl parts to cool it."

She'd ignore that last comment. "If his business plan isn't good, I'll reevaluate," she told him. "But I don't think that's going to happen."

He waved at her. "I don't either, but I still want to look it over when I get back. Speaking of... Connor is gracing our hallway. Hey, man. You got past our reception desk?"

She heard a robust laugh in response.

"I'm running out for a while, but I'm looking forward to reading this plan of yours once Louisa gets through with it."

Connor extended his hand to Boxer, who shook it. "Here. I made you a copy."

Their gazes met and held—they looked like two giant pillars of testosterone sizing each other up. She couldn't stand it, so she hummed "wa-wa-waaaah" from *The Good, The Bad, and the Ugly*. "Take your Clint Eastwood impressions outside."

Boxer dropped the challenge first. "Eastwood? Please, I'm taking my *Denzel* impression to the gym. See you later, Connor, and thanks for the copy. I'll read it after I lift weights. Be good with my girl here."

"Boxer!" Louisa called out, throwing a pen at him, which he deftly caught.

Connor didn't move so much as an inch, only locked eyes with her. "Hello, Louisa."

The way he said it almost made her gulp. She could almost hear him saying, *Both are going to be really, really good.* "Hi, yourself."

Connor's mouth twitched. "Boxer, don't worry. Your girl is safe with me."

As Boxer left with an indelicate sound, Louisa pointed to the chair in front of her desk and nodded to the gray slacks and black sweater he was wearing. Again, she wondered where he'd gotten the money. But goodness, he was handsome with that strong bearded jaw and those arresting eyes trained on her. "Still no coat?"

His mouth turned up as he took a seat and set the business plan between them. "I told you I run warm, but yes, I have a coat now. If I need it, I'll wear it. Okay, Ms. Evans?"

He was teasing her for being bossy, she knew, and yet her name sounded downright sexy on his lips. "Speaking of being warm, thanks again for the present. I'm pleased to see *you* have something beyond running clothes to keep you warm."

"Are we going to talk about my wardrobe? Maybe you'll also be glad to know I've rented a furnished apartment on a month-to-month basis?"

"I'm relieved to hear you're out of Ferguson's." Bad things went down there.

"What else can I tell you?" he continued. "What I ate this morning? Who I met with after my run? I would have texted you the play-by-play if I'd known you were that interested."

Actually she was, but it wouldn't be wise to push his limits this soon. "I'll introduce you to our in-house chef later, and if you're hungry, we can find you something."

"I'm not one of your projects, Louisa. I'd hoped we could move past your misperceptions about me."

And yet she couldn't get the picture out of her mind of him sitting in the snow in the park drinking out of the bottle like he had nothing to live for. *Be careful, Louisa. This one could break your heart.* "Fine, I'll stop. Now give me that file. I'm dying here."

His smile was as slow and sexy as the way he slid it across her desk. "I meant what I said. This is going to rock your world."

She wanted to purr in response but acted all casual as she picked it up. "I sure hope so. This is a pretty heavy business plan for only a week." So thick, her mouth was salivating as she held it up as if weighing it.

"I'm thorough, and when I agree to do something, I do it well," was all he said.

"On that we agree. I can't wait to dig into it. You must have worked on it all week."

His mouth tipped up. "No, I had something else to see to, but I had plenty of time to research, craft, and refine my thoughts for the business plan. After reading about all of your programs and plans, my main takeaway is that you're thinking too small."

She leaned forward and drummed her fingers on the plan. "No one has *ever* told me that. This shelter was supposed to be impossible, and yet—"

"You did it," he said, "and now you want a bonafide job training center. But what does a successful one look like, the kind that trains people *and* helps them find good paying jobs?"

Oh, she wanted to bounce in her chair in excitement. "Talk to me."

"Fine, you have some interesting people you're helping. Some have records. A history of mental illness. Disabilities too, right? It won't be easy to get those types stable, well-paying jobs."

"I know that. The food industry has been good for hiring a few of the people who have records, so long as we vouch for them. I can't guarantee people with mental illness will continue to take their meds."

"Exactly! I'm glad you're thinking about these issues already. As I understand from your website, your inhouse chef and your brother train some of your people for food service. Impressive, but still too small. Three people a year."

Placing her elbows on the desk, she said, "Trust me, to those three people, it's not too small."

He nodded quickly, drawing her attention to the crisp line of his jaw beneath his facial hair. His presence was more potent today, and it moved her to see the change in him. "Point taken. However, we'll have to diversify. Most people in food service can't make enough money to live in a safe, no-cracks-in-the-sidewalk kind of neighborhood."

"You've done your homework," she said, picking the plan up with the reverence someone might show a special holiday present. "I knew you were going to hit a home run. Your initial business outline was way too detailed and thoughtful. Are you finally going to tell me your last name and who you really are? Obviously you're in some kind of major transition. You aren't homeless."

"I'm glad you've finally accepted that," he said, crossing his arms. "I'm not ready to tell you anything else about me. Is that going to be a problem?"

She began to leaf through the first few pages. "No, we're good. But I might need a minute. Dying of curiosity here." She scanned the table of contents. "Holy—"

"You can read that later," he told her, pulling it out of her hands and standing up, waving it in the air—inasmuch as a person *could* wave such a massive document. "You promised me a tour. Tonight, maybe you'll let me take you out for pizza. I know a great place."

She stopped trying to grab it out of his hand as the enormity of the situation settled on her. This was her dream. "Connor, your business plan is everything I could have hoped for. And that creates a problem for our...back and forths. I'm not comfortable dating an employee."

He made a deep sound in his throat, almost like amusement. "There's no problem here. Louisa, I'm *volunteering* my services. Any assistance I provide is strictly pro bono. Like a consultant."

She was sure her mouth was gaping open. "But you don't have a job."

"That doesn't mean I don't have money, Louisa."

She thought of the gloves and his wardrobe today. His assertion only drove home how little she knew about him, and her gut instincts wavered in the face of it. "I don't even know your last name. Don't take this wrong, but some drug dealers are less mysterious than you."

"Know some drug dealers, do you?"

It was time he stopped seeing her as some goody two-shoes. "When you work on the streets you come across them. I also know gang leaders, community and religious leaders, and some politicians thrown in for dessert. Actually, almost all of them put together are less mysterious than you."

His compelling eyes studied her, and then he said, "Louisa, I know you're tough. You went a couple rounds with me and won. No one does that. It's one of the reasons I haven't been able to stop thinking about you all week. Like I told you in my texts, which you answered by the way."

His strong, masculine body suddenly seemed too big for her office. The room had never felt so small before. "What's the other reason?"

He leaned forward, his strong hands resting on his knees, almost as if he had to grip them to keep from reaching for her. Their gazes locked. "You're one of the most beautiful women I've ever met, and I haven't been able to keep you out of my head. You must have guessed that from my texts. What you might not know is how unusual that is for me."

Goosebumps raised over her arms, and she was glad

she was wearing a sweater so he couldn't see how much he affected her. Maybe it was time to negotiate again. "Not good enough. I want more information about you."

He gripped his knees and then settled back in his chair as if he had all the time in the world. "I've had a week to think about you and other factors, and I've decided. Now it's your turn to decide if we're going to have something personal in addition to our business interactions."

"You want me to decide right now? You're pushy."

He chuckled. "So are you. I figure that's one of the reasons why we're both intrigued and attracted to each other. Other than broken people, how many people actually challenge *you*?"

A fair point. He was one of the most compelling men she'd ever met, whether half-freezing in the park or sitting like a caged lion in her office. "Fine, you want me to decide. You may not have promised me your personal story, but I did give you mine. Give me something to work with here. You told me you feel responsible for someone dying. What happened?"

He looked off, his jaw ticking, and she sat there quietly, wondering if he was going to answer her or walk out. Then he turned back and looked her straight in the eye, his intense stare arresting her breath. "I was the business manager for a project when a natural disaster occurred. He wasn't the only one who died. People tell me it wasn't my fault, but inside I feel differently. He was my best friend. I should have protected him better. All of them better."

Those words sounded like they were clawing their way out from a broken place inside of him. Her own heart hurt hearing them. "They're right, you know," she said softly. "It's not your fault. I learned that with my mom, but it took a long time."

A breath escaped him, and she knew he didn't believe her. She'd seen it a million times—survivor's guilt carried a heavy toll. It could take years for a person to move on.

"I don't make excuses," he said, holding up his hand. "I made some...careless decisions in response to what happened. That's ultimately why I got fired, and why I'm here in Chicago. Right now, that's all I can tell you. I can't give you personal or professional references or refer you to my LinkedIn page. But what I can tell you is that I encounter people all the time—I've dated them, recruited them, trained them, negotiated with them, led them— and you're the first person who's both captivated my primal side and impressed the hell out of me. That's why I haven't been able to stop thinking about you. I wouldn't text a business associate like that, and I certainly wouldn't buy them personal gifts."

Her belly tightened at the way *primal* rolled off his tongue, and despite the fact that she'd won numerous community awards, the praise of this somewhat anonymous man meant something. "I don't quite know what to say, Connor."

He rolled his eyes. "Sure you do. You're too self-aware not to. Would it be less complicated if we didn't go out? Certainly, but I still find myself asking. I want to sweep you out of this office right now and have you all to myself."

Her breath stopped in her chest. No one had ever been this direct with her. And the way he'd said it, holding eye contact the whole time... "Keep going."

His brief laugh had her smiling. "I can't offer you forever if that's what you're looking for. I'm not sure anyone would want that with me anyway. I'm too aggressive, and I work too hard, and I have what some see as a million faults."

His self-loathing made her want to cross the short distance between them and give him a hug. "A million? I doubt that, Connor."

He rubbed his beard. "We'll see what you think when you've had time to tally them. For now, that's all I can tell you. Louisa, I would like to spend time with you outside the shelter while I'm here. If you don't want to, just say so. I'll still want to help you turn this neighborhood around. You'll never hear or feel anything else from me except professional courtesy. No more texting. Gifts. Nothing. I give you my word."

And she already knew she could trust his word. "I appreciate that. And your directness. In fact, it's refreshing. Most of the men I've dated like playing games. Either that, or they run the other way when they realize I'm married to my job."

He gestured to her. "I don't play games unless I have to. As for you being married to your job, I get that. I personally don't see anything wrong with it. Why is settling down, getting married and having kids, and working a regular forty-hour week the gold standard of happiness?"

"Amen," she said.

"Glad you agree. Personally, I want to do big things with my life, not live in Pleasantville. Not that there's anything wrong with that. Don't get me wrong. I know a few people who are quite happy with that kind of life. It's just not for me."

Had she ever had this much in common with a man in terms of personal philosophy? No. Her skin was tingling, she realized. She was totally going to go out with him. She thought back to her talk with Boxer. She could no more pass up what Connor was offering personally than she could reject the incredible proposal he'd brought her. "If I catch a whiff of anything in your background I don't like, we're done. Personally and professionally."

His smile started slow, like the fuse on a stick of dynamite, and then the fire connected, and she felt the full force of his emotion—pride, achievement, and primal desire.

She couldn't wait to kiss that smile, because she was honest enough with herself to admit she wanted that. And possibly a lot more.

"I knew it wouldn't take long for you to decide," he said, his eyes locked on hers. "You're a spur-of-the-moment kind of person."

"I kinda am."

He stood, walked to the doorway, and leaned against it in an ever-so-sexy way. "Now, show me around. I'd like to especially focus on the kitchen, since you're already training people for food service careers, and your special reading program for children. You'll see I'm suggesting you spin off the childcare program, expand it, and establish it as an official daycare and after-school care program open to the public, not just the homeless, with a fee per child about thirty percent under the Chicago average for daycare. Not for your homeless clients, obviously. I did some research, and I couldn't believe how much the typical program costs."

"It's incredible, isn't it? Then again, that's your child."

He nodded. "Exactly. Your literacy program is innovative and well recognized. I imagine there are other areas you could emphasize in an expansion, like math and science. I noticed the director of your current daycare program for the homeless has won numerous teaching awards."

"Greta," she said, her heart picking up speed at the thought. "Yes, she's fantastic."

"Your father is also a respected educator and coach. I imagine he could make some suggestions for sports and exercise programs and also has good contacts in the teaching community."

She'd never considered leveraging her father's knowledge that way, but it made sense. No, more than that, she knew he'd welcome a chance to be more involved. "He'd love that."

"Your focus on literacy is just the tip of the iceberg," he said, a slow smile on his face. "You can tell me what you think about the rest of my ideas in the business plan when I pick you up tonight."

She laughed and stood up as well. She couldn't wait to show him what they'd done so far on limited resources. He needed to see that what Sunflower Alley did went beyond business—people's lives were involved. "I love those ideas, but you *are* bossy. Luckily so am I."

"We'll have to see if I like you bossing me around..." he said in a heated tone as she came around her desk. "I figure we're a good match. You don't pander to me."

"I don't pander to anyone," she said, meeting his hot gaze. "In fact, I'm only giving you a tour now because it's convenient for me. And to further ground your ideas in reality. Got it?"

He extended his hand toward the hallway almost in deference. "Yes, Ms. Evans. Lead on."

She passed by him, and with only a few inches between them, his body heat made her want to shiver. He *did* run warm, or maybe he'd been affected by their conversation too. "Eight o'clock is when things calm down around here. I can go out with you then. Now, time for the tour."

He smiled again as he took a step closer, inches away from her body now. His nostrils flared as if he'd inhaled her scent, and her belly gripped again in desire.

"I have a feeling both of us are going to remember how this moment changed things," he murmured.

"Me too," she replied in all honesty. Searching his face, she found herself learning his features: the intense gaze of his beautiful two-color eyes, the dark brows, and the downright sexy square jaw. But something else struck her. Although he'd kept so much of himself from her, his eyes hid nothing—when she looked in them, she could see the weight he carried as well as the desire he had for her.

She wanted to touch his face, to trace the line of his cheek, but this wasn't the time or place. Still, her heart told her he was right about the importance of this moment. Because in it she'd made a promise to herself: he might be helping her turn the neighborhood around and start her training program, but she was determined to help him too. Whatever had happened to cause the deaths of his friend and those other people wasn't his fault, and she was going to help him heal.

She only hoped he'd let her.

CHAPTER 5

THE MOST AMAZING WOMAN HE'D EVER MET HAD AGREED TO go out with him.

Somehow Louisa's response felt like the greatest victory in what was a string of defeats. This moment was another turning point, he sensed, much like the night he'd met her. He put his hand briefly on the small of her back as she walked down the hall, not only because he simply had to touch her, but also to tell her how much her response meant to him.

He was going to treat her well for as long as they were together.

Some of his other siblings, especially his sister Caitlyn, believed in love at first sight. Connor had always scoffed at the idea. However, after a week of nonstop fixation on Louisa, he had to acknowledge the power of instant attraction and understanding. That was a more apt description of their connection. He was glad she was so grounded. Neither of them could get hurt that way.

As she took him through the front, she explained that clients were restricted from wandering around the shelter for safety and practical reasons. He dropped his hand at the doorway to the kitchen, and she turned to him and put her hand on his chest.

"The people you're about to meet mean the world to me. They're family. They also feed about eighty people three times a day."

Did she think he'd disrespect them? "You can trust me, Louisa. I respect hard work and service." If his parents hadn't raised them that way, he'd have come to it himself, traveling to the various Merriam job sites, meeting everyone from factory workers in Oklahoma to oil drillers in...

Corey's engineering crew in Indonesia came to mind, and he had to box that thought back down again.

"Great. Just saying." Something flashed through her eyes—relief, maybe, and pride—and then she was moving into the kitchen quickly. "Hey everybody! I have someone I want you to meet."

The punch in her voice was the kind he'd heard in motivational business speakers, the kind that got an audience up on their feet, clapping and cheering after a long day of meetings and workshops. She was pure brilliance in action, and he couldn't wait to have all that brilliance turned on him when they were alone.

He walked into the large industrial kitchen, surprised to see it opened into the empty dining room. There were two sliding aluminum panels he imagined could be closed. He wondered if they served guests through it cafeteria-style or if people were served at their tables. Apparently a potato dish and salad were on the menu today. Peeled potatoes were mounded on one table while another held large trays covered in salad greens.

He made sure to make eye contact with the four people Louisa was greeting with hugs and arm pats. The faces were ones he recognized from the website.

"This is Connor," she said, gesturing to him, "and he's going to help me create the best formal training program ever. He's blown in from the land of Oz to deliver yellow bricks for all the roads we want to build with this community and the people we serve. I know you'll make him feel welcome."

"Good thing I left my monkeys at home," he said, following her lead. "Great to meet everyone."

The giant black man at the stove came forward, cleaning his hands on his white apron before extending one for Connor to shake. "Us too, man. Boxer said Louisa had someone giving her a business proposal today. I'm Carter, the head chef around here. It's good to have another helper around. We have lots of people who'd like jobs."

Louisa put her arm around the man's waist as he returned to his workstation. "Carter was one of the first people who embraced my early vision of a training program."

Connor nodded. "I read your story on the website. Very impressive." The man had gone from being homeless to working in the kitchen of Louisa's half-brother, the award-winning chef at Soledad. He'd managed to get the money and references to attend culinary school. Instead of getting a job at a top restaurant, though, he'd come back to the shelter. Somehow Connor knew it was because of Louisa. "Man, I thought Boxer was big. Just how tall are you, Carter? Even at six three, you tower over me."

"Six eight," the man said with a laugh. "I figure it's a good thing. Keeps what hair I have left safe with all the time I put in on that temperamental stove."

Since Carter was mostly bald, Connor couldn't help but chuckle. "I'm terrible in the kitchen, but I hadn't thought about setting myself on fire before."

Louisa grinned and smacked one of the others on the back. "Spicy here has a young Eminem fanboy thing going on with that pretty dyed blond hair of his, but he's magic with salad and desserts. He was on the streets young like I was, but he made it out."

"Because someone stopped me on the street one day and asked if I was feeling okay," Spicy said. "I had the flu. Louisa brought me here, put me to bed, and brought me soup. She kinda won me over."

"She has that way about her, doesn't she?" Connor said, shaking his hand. "Good to meet you."

"And this is Jewel," Louisa said, bringing over a large black woman in her fifties. "She's just like her name."

"She's always said that," Jewel said, hugging Louisa tightly before extending her hand to him. "I've been around here as long as Carter. The good Lord blessed me when I met Louisa on the streets during a snowstorm."

He glanced over at Louisa and they shared a long look. "The weather wouldn't stop her. I know that much."

"Nothing does, and thank God," Jewel said, turning to the remaining woman yet to be introduced. "Come on, girl. He looks tough but he won't bite."

Her comment about him made him wonder. Had he changed so much that she didn't see the wolf others used to see so clearly?

"Connor, this here is Maria," Jewel continued. "She'll make you the finest tamales and beans ever. Here at Sunflower Alley, we don't just feed people's bodies. We do our best to feed their souls too."

"We do at that," Louisa said, beaming, "although I can't cook. Hence why I needed help."

"I still think Jewel's cornbread is better than my tamales," Maria said with a shy smile, crossing her arms at her waist. "It's good to meet you, Connor."

He didn't step forward to extend his hand to her. She might not trust him or like to be touched, he imagined, but there was a vein of courage behind that shy smile. "Maria, it's an honor to meet you."

"An honor?" a dry, male voice asked. "Maria, have you been sharing your tamales with someone other than me?"

Connor turned to see Louisa launch herself into the

arms of a young man who shared her smile. He recognized him as her half-brother, Damien Evans—chef of Soledad and, from what Connor had read online, one of Chicago's most eligible bachelors.

"What are you doing here?" Louisa asked. "It's almost lunch."

He waved a hand. "I have minions to handle prep. Lunch doesn't get going until twelve thirty anyway. Right, Carter?"

"Hey, man," the giant man said, coming over and giving Damien a bear hug that lifted him up off the ground. "You gearing up for the shelter's next cooking competition, because I'm going to destroy you."

"In your dreams," Damien said, hugging and kissing Jewel and Maria on the cheeks before fist-bumping Spicy. "You'll be crying for days after I beat you this time."

"Connor, you probably saw this on the website," Louisa said, "but the shelter brings in local chefs to compete against Carter every month. We invite the community to join us and our clients. It's a grand time."

He had seen it and thought it a brilliant way to fundraise and engage the community. "I'm looking forward to the next one."

"It's pure hell for Damien since I kick his ass whenever he's the visiting chef." Carter laughed, a deep sound that reverberated throughout the room like a church bell.

"Laugh all you want," Damien said with a wink at Maria. "You're going to be unseated."

Louisa came over to stand beside Connor as the chefs continued their bantering. "Damien! Come meet Connor."

Her brother crossed the short distance to join them. Connor could tell the siblings were close from their easy way with each other, and there was no mistaking the protectiveness in Damien's gaze. "I hear Soledad is the place to eat," he said. "Good to meet you, Damien. I'm Connor."

"*Connor...*" Damien said, a clear call-out for his last name.

Louisa punched him in the arm. "You know we don't require people to give their last names. Connor prefers to keep his to himself, and we're going to respect his wishes."

The look she gave Damien was pure older sibling, one he'd given to his younger siblings a million times.

His heart clutched a moment, thinking about them. He had to lock down a rush of emotion. It was weird not to know what they were doing, if they were okay. Was he ever going to see them again? How did he start to make up for what he'd done?

Louisa's hand on his arm brought him back. "Connor handed me the most thorough business proposal I've ever seen this morning. The table of contents would blow your mind."

"I'd love to see it," Damien said. "We're always looking for good examples to model in the food industry. In a couple years, I want to open another restaurant. I'll need more staff. Hint, hint."

"If you're a good boy, I'll show you the proposal. Later." Louisa cut Connor another look. Yeah, she knew Damien had shown up to check on him. Boxer's work? Connor would lay that bet. "You can get a start by helping Spicy with all of those potatoes. We're going to get moving."

"See you all later," Connor said, lifting his hand.

Damien inclined his chin. "Come by Soledad anytime. Dinner will be on me."

Connor simply nodded and waited for Louisa to precede him out of the kitchen through one of the open panels. There was no way he'd be going to Soledad. From what he'd read, it was a favorite for business meetings. Even with his beard, he couldn't be sure some banker or businessperson wouldn't recognize him. Besides, he didn't need to give Damien the chance to grill him.

"He's protective," Louisa said with a shrug, glancing back at him. "Boxer is too."

"They all are," Connor said. "Even Maria, and she's clearly still recovering from her past circumstances."

She made a sound of agreement. "Yes, but she's starting to flourish. Before she couldn't stand being touched, even by Jewel. Next up is our dining hall."

The large space was filled with rows of brightly colored picnic tables, the yellow walls decorated with Tuscan-looking sunflowers.

"You'll know we serve three meals to a max of eighty people a day. Not always the same people, of course. Some stay with us. Others come in from the streets. Damien and the other chefs in our network send over any day-old produce or ingredients, and of course, we have donors who send us food and other items from our Amazon wish list."

"I saw that. I never would have thought to do it, but it's an ingenious idea to give people a curated list."

When she beamed like that, she seemed taller, like she could fill the room all by herself. "I got the idea when I was buying a gift for a wedding. I was like, why can't we do this? Put our registry up at various places on the website. Amazon is great because people don't have to pay shipping on the items we've chosen. It's a win-win, especially for people who either don't have the time to volunteer or don't want to heft a box of canned goods."

They left the dining hall and turned down another bright yellow hallway. "Did someone donate all this yellow paint?" he asked.

"Yeah, but I ordered it yellow," she said with a laugh. "Damien and Boxer think I got a little carried away painting sunflowers everywhere, but they like to give me crap."

"You painted them?" he asked, stopping when she halted in front of a door.

"Yeah, and they're not too bad. I mean, I'm no van Gogh or anything. But they seem to make people happy. That's all that matters."

"Were the shelters you and your mother went to bright like this?"

She shook her head. "No, but the way we interact with the homeless has changed since I was a kid. People now have a better sense about how color and atmosphere affects mood and the like."

He'd only seen her on three different occasions, but every time, she'd worn a bright-colored top with jeans or dark pants. Now he wondered if it was another attempt to make her guests feel welcome and appreciated. He tried not to stare. She really was a beautiful woman, and the bold colors she chose suited her light brown skin and dark hair. He kept wanting to reach out and touch her, to reassure himself she was real. "And you're always reading up on something innovative to do, I expect."

"If you peek through the window in the door, you'll see one of my ideas in action," she said, "but be still. I don't want you to interrupt them."

He looked through the rectangular window to see a young girl of maybe six or seven sitting on a multi-colored rug reading a book out loud to the two guinea pigs he'd seen on the website. "Story time with Mr. Snuggles and Mrs. Cuddles. I couldn't believe it when I read about it. How did you ever come up with this idea?"

She gave him a small smile. "Before I moved in with my dad, I got really behind in reading. It took me a year of after-school tutoring to catch up. My tutor had me read to a teddy bear."

"Ingenious," Connor said, watching as the young girl traced the words in the book and continued to read to the animals.

"Only I felt a live animal might encourage trust in a way a teddy bear can't," Louisa said. "I've made up a wonderfully magical story about Mr. Snuggles and Mrs. Cuddles missing their own kids, who've grown up and moved away. Spending time with the guinea pigs builds their self-esteem. Homeless kids don't feel very special, let me tell you."

The glimmer in her eyes was its own kind of magic, and again he felt the impulse to touch her.

"And it worked better than I could have imagined. The guinea pigs are loving and affectionate, something most of the children are starved for."

"Incredible," he mused, hardly able to believe how still and yet engaged the guinea pigs seemed to be, sitting on the floor in front of the little girl. "Tell me about the child."

She sighed. "I can't go into details for privacy reasons, but what I can say is that she's like hundreds of kids I've seen walk in these doors. She's like I was."

He turned to her, and this time he had to touch her, but he only let himself put his hand on her arm. "And you triumphed."

Her golden eyes flashed to him as she leaned into his touch. "I was lucky."

"It wasn't just luck," he said, thinking about his current circumstances. He let himself caress her arm before pulling away. A quick glance into the room made him smile. "My God, that little girl just closed her book and is laughing. Now she's picking up the pig—"

"Mrs. Cuddles is her name. And she's not a pig."

"I stand corrected," he said, oddly moved as the little girl hugged the animal like she was her best friend. Michaela used to be like that when she was little, more comfortable with animals than people. He hadn't thought about that in forever. Part of him wished he'd paid more attention back then. "What happens now? Is the girl all alone in there except for the animals?"

"That room is connected to our daycare facility, but this door is locked. Staffers can check on her from the window in the other room. When she's ready to go back to the day-care program, she can. It's not a perfect system, but it's the best we have."

No, they dealt with a lot of situations no one would call remotely perfect, and yet they'd adapted. On the shelter's website, Louisa had talked about her reasons for creating the program. It was hard for mothers or single fathers to go job hunting with a child in tow. Most homeless kids didn't attend regular schooling, and some of them were too young to be left alone. "How many kids are you taking care of now?"

"About thirty children, anywhere from newborn babies to ten-year-olds."

Newborns? That made him a little sick. "And staff?"

"Eight, but we sometimes have more with volunteers," she explained. "Oh, here's Greta. She was on my list since you mentioned her when you talked about expanding the childcare program. You'll love her."

He nodded to the smiling gray-haired woman wearing a sweater dotted with laughing teddy bears. She had a palpable grandmotherly energy. "I just came from the kitchen. Carter is serving up some good treats like always. He said to come find you and meet your guest."

Louisa put her hand on his arm briefly, as if claiming him, and he liked it. He really liked it. "Connor, Greta. Greta, Connor. Connor is working with me on a new training program, and one of his ideas involves expanding our childcare program. Something for us all to discuss."

"I can't wait to hear more about it," Greta said. "Good to meet you, Connor. How long do you plan to be with us?"

"As long as it takes to help Louisa and the neighborhood."

She arched a delicate brow. "That long, eh? Welcome aboard. Our story time guest seems to finished. Would you like to meet her?"

Before he could answer, she was unlocking the door.

Connor stepped forward and watched as the little girl hugged Mrs. Cuddles to her and showed Greta the bright-colored book she'd been reading. Her eyes widened when she caught sight of him, and she hugged Greta around the legs.

"I think I scare her," he said, oddly hurt at the thought. Being the Big Bad Wolf hadn't bothered him with adults, but kids were different. Maybe he'd read too much into Jewel's comment. He was still scary.

Louisa put her hand on his back, her touch radiating warmth and comfort. "It's not you. She's wary of men, for good reason, something we try and heal as best we can. Kendra, I wanted you to meet another storyteller. This is Connor, and he's just written a new story for me that I can't wait to share with everybody. You'll be seeing him around a little, so I wanted to let you know he's my friend. Okay?"

The little girl ducked out from behind Greta's legs, her brown eyes shifting to everything but Connor before she finally looked him in the eye. "What's your story about?" she asked, her voice hesitant.

He'd been thirteen when Michaela was born, and so he knew to sink to a knee so he would be on her level. "It's about people who really want to follow their dreams. It shows them a road they can take to get there."

"When they're sleeping?" she asked, her arm still around Greta's leg as Louisa put away the two guinea pigs in the large cage in the center of the room.

He thought of how he might explain it to Corey's boys. "The dreams we have when we're sleeping are a little different than the ones we have when we're awake. I used to dream I could do anything I wanted." He almost laughed at himself. Now he understood what hubris that had been. All the money and power and intelligence in the world hadn't prevented the accident that had sent him down this spiral.

Kendra's small brows drew together. "Anything?"

"*Anything.*"

She was silent a moment and then she said, "I want my mom and me to have a home again. And enough food to eat every day. And a chocolate bar whenever I want it. That's a dream, right?"

Her words, so innocently spoken, wrenched something inside of him. Food and shelter shouldn't be a dream, but it was to this little girl. He wasn't sure how to respond, so he looked over to Louisa. "What say you, Ms. Evans?"

She sank to her knee as well. "Kendra, when I was your age, I wanted to have a home again too with my mom. As time went on, I got more dreams. I dreamed about growing up and getting a really good job and helping others. Now I have so many dreams I sometimes don't know what to do with them all." She glanced at him, her eyes glimmering. "And you know what? I dreamed about meeting someone who could help me do something important, and that dream came true."

His chest grew tight. Is that what he was doing? Yeah, and he'd better not mess it up. Before the training plan had been more cerebral to him, but meeting Kendra and the others had driven home how much it would affect—and hopefully help—real people.

Kendra nodded finally. "I guess I dream about going back to school and being with my friends. I'm afraid they'll forget me."

"Not a special girl like you," Connor said. "It was good to meet you, Kendra. I bet you're a really excellent reader."

She came forward to where Connor was still kneeling, and that simple action seemed to convey he'd won her trust. Again, his chest tightened.

"Thank you," she said, holding out her hand to him in what he recognized was a fist bump.

He gently touched her fist with his own, knowing he was going to remember this little girl for a long time.

"See you later, mister. Bye, Miss Louisa."

"Enjoy the rest of your tour, Connor, and holler if you

have any questions for me," Greta said, her hand on the little girl's shoulder. "Let's get back to the other kids, Kendra. You can tell them about your book."

Louisa was smiling as they left. "You did good with her." Crossing to the cage, she asked, "Want to hold one? I can't resist them."

He held up his hands. "Nice to meet them, but I'm not going to coo and fawn over them like that."

"Is that what I'm doing?" She laughed and put the gold-and-white guinea pig to her face like they were butterfly kissing.

"So you can be weird," he said, unable to resist teasing her. "I had a feeling the night we met."

"*I'm* weird? You were the one in nothing but shorts and a long-sleeved T-shirt in a snowstorm."

"I run hot, I tell you." Even hotter in her presence. "Why in the world did you choose guinea pigs instead of some therapy dog or cat?"

"There are lots of stray dogs and cats on the streets and not all of them are nice. Some are downright frightening. Guinea pigs are too small to make anyone feel threatened. They're social, so I bought two on the spot. Of course, we only bring out Mr. Snuggles and Mrs. Cuddles with kids and people we deem nonviolent."

"Do you have violent people in here often?" It chilled him to think about this little girl and Louisa being around someone like that.

"No, but sometimes it gets triggered by something you can't foresee, or someone might forget to take their meds or stop on purpose. I take safety very seriously. People have to feel safe coming and staying here. Especially kids. I remember feeling unsafe, and it's one of the worst feelings in the world, especially for a child. You know, the more I think about it, the more I love the idea of having a separate childcare program. We could put it off-site, and that would ensure the safety of the kids almost a hundred percent."

Had he ever felt unsafe, either as a kid or an adult? No. Never. His mind went to his parents then, to all they'd done to ensure he and his siblings had a sense of security. He wasn't sentimental, but if they were still talking, he'd text his mom to tell her thanks. But he couldn't. Not now. "Louisa..."

She stopped kissing the furry animal and looked over. "What?"

"What you're doing here is great. I just wanted you to know...I'm not easily impressed."

And he didn't want to let her down.

"So you keep saying." She put the guinea pig inside with a final coo. "I wonder who you've been surrounding yourself with to be so *unimpressed.*"

Some of the most powerful people in the world. But he'd decided to separate himself from the past, so he said, "Perhaps that's not the issue. Maybe there's just no one like you."

She had a spring in her step as she crossed to him and laid her hand on his chest. He captured it there and held it.

"I *am* an original," she said, "and I suspect you are too. I'm looking forward to when you finally decide to share your secrets with me."

He caught the flirtatious gleam in her golden eyes. "Think I will?"

"Some of the toughest people on the streets have told me I'm irresistible."

"I won't argue with that," he said, caressing the hand on his chest. "Were you thinking about me when you wrote that note on the board in the entryway?"

"You mean my daily love note? The one that said, 'When someone offers to help you against all odds, say thank you and let them.'"

He cringed. "Don't make this something it's not. I'm not a hero. I have my own self-interested reasons for helping you."

"I know, but you're still helping," she said, laughing. "I'm a cold, hard realist except when I'm not, and yes, you were on my mind. We also have some new volunteers who'll be arriving shortly."

She gave him a huge smile, something he was beginning to anticipate and savor. Then she stepped back and looked down at her watch. "Come on. You can meet them."

He only smiled. He knew exactly who was coming in.

He'd arranged it.

CHAPTER 6

CLARA STILL WASN'T SURE HOW SHE FELT ABOUT CONNOR'S plan.

So far all she'd done was dance to his tune, including exchanging the limo for a town car. Like Hargreaves hadn't navigated city streets before. Did the boy forget she'd lived in Manhattan for decades? Connor had emphasized the increased crime rate in the neighborhood like she was a silly old woman.

But despite her misgivings, she almost sighed as she walked into Sunflower Alley, taking in the sunshine walls painted with those tall gold and orange and red sunflowers. She gave their name to the young man sitting at the modest reception desk, and he welcomed them warmly and then jumped up to find this director they'd heard so much about. Her eyes fell on the hand-printed saying on the main wall, and she went all mushy, as Arthur would call it.

When someone offers to help you against all odds, say thank you and let them. #lovenote

Somehow she knew that sign was the start of their welcome party.

"I liked the sentiment until I read 'love note.'" Arthur harrumphed. "I'm not into that feel-good, fruity-tooty sentimentalism or that hashtag nonsense."

"Me either, sir, but I'm keeping an open mind," Hargreaves said, helping Clara out of her coat. "The shelter's website was very impressive." Clara had thought so too, and it hadn't escaped her attention that the proprietor, Louisa Evans, was a lovely woman.

"What are you going to do with Clara's fur, Hargreaves?" Arthur asked, putting his hands on his lean hips. "Hold it the whole time? Maybe the reception guy doubles as a coat check clerk. Bah! Clara, I told you to wear a different coat. We're at a shelter, for crying out loud, not a garden party."

"And I'm a potential benefactor thinking of donating a large sum of money," she informed him with a haughty raise of her eyebrows. "Also, I want to show people that anything is possible. In case you forgot, Arthur Hale, your friend and mentor and my grandfather came from nothing and had hard times in the Depression—"

"Only to strike oil out of hard work and luck," he finished for her. "Dammit, woman, I know the story. The Merriams were poor and homeless. Yes, I see. But *you* never were, and this coat and your perpetual strands of diamonds—"

"Enough! Arthur, it is a woman's prerogative to wear anything she wants, anywhere she wants. Especially at my age. You didn't hear me telling you to dress in a suit, did you?"

"I never even wore one when I was running my own newspaper," he barked. "Clara—"

"*Arthur.* Get your game face on, or go back to the sedan. We're here on an important mission."

He growled but squeezed her waist in an obvious apology. "I know it. I'm only feeling a little guilty now that we're here. This looks like a nice setup for a good cause."

Reminding herself they would be supporting a good cause even with the slight deception on Connor's part, she turned as Louisa Evans appeared. Wouldn't you know it, Clara's aggravating nephew was right beside her. Although he was taller by far, Louisa's powerful presence made it much less noticeable. Hmm...

Clara's matchmaking instincts had pinged when Connor had first talked about Louisa, even more so when she'd read about the compelling woman who'd started the shelter, but now she saw it for herself.

They were attracted to each other.

Which made the subterfuge Connor had insisted on even more ill-advised. Any matchmaker worth his or her salt would tell him not to play games with the woman he was drawn to. But she could tell from the way that he was regarding them—with the polite indifference of a stranger—that he expected her to go through with his cockamamie plan. Well, if he wanted her to pretend she didn't know him and vice versa, fine. As she'd proven before in helping his younger brother, J.T., she was a consummate actress. She only hoped Arthur could be equally convincing. Hargreaves didn't worry her. Nothing fazed the man.

Clara stepped forward, getting her inner Sarah Bernhardt on. "Louisa! I recognize you from all of the articles I've been reading about you. How wonderful to have you meet us the moment we arrived! This is my husband, the famed journalist, Arthur Hale."

"Not so much famed as old as dirt now," Arthur said, putting out his hand to the petite woman who rushed over to them with as much sweetness and energy as a triple crunch candy bar. "Wonderful to meet you, Ms. Evans."

She pumped his hand vigorously, Clara was pleased to see. So many people took one look at them and acted like a handshake would break them. Aging was for the birds.

"Please call me Louisa, Mr. Hale."

"Only if you call me Arthur. I'm a simple man."

Clara laughed gustily. "So he says. When he starts interviewing you, my dear, you'll soon learn otherwise."

"You mentioned that on the phone, Clara. We'd be honored to have a journalist of Arthur's caliber mention us in his article. Anything you need, you let us know."

"This is Clifton Hargreaves," Clara said, "my most trustworthy associate."

Arthur snorted. "*Associate*?"

"A pleasure to meet you, Clifton," Louisa said, shaking his hand.

"It's Hargreaves, miss," he said with a formal bow.

Clara linked her arm through Arthur's, hoping he'd get the message and behave. "If you have an opening for a chef in one of your upcoming competitions, we'd love to have Hargreaves compete."

"Hargreaves might be your chef, my dear, but he's not an actual chef," Arthur said, not getting her message.

This time she jabbed him in the side. "Arthur, my dear, you know many things, but not everything. Hargreaves has a degree in culinary arts from Le Cordon Bleu."

Even Connor's brows went up at that admission, and she gave him a kind smile with plenty of teeth.

"I hope you like Indian food, Louisa, because that's Hargreaves' specialty," Arthur said, nudging her back.

Oh, he was intolerable. "Hargreaves has a wide range, Louisa. Don't listen to him. He's grouchy after meeting with some pompous South Side city councilman this morning."

Louisa was biting her lip as if to contain her laughter. Well, at least she found them amusing. Better that than wanting to kick them out before they started step one in Connor's plan. "And your associate here, Louisa…"

The lovely woman put her arm around Connor in a gesture of surprising affection. For a moment, Connor's mask cracked. His eyelids opened just enough to convey his shock. His pleasure. Well, good. The Big Bad Wolf needed some shaking up, and based on the research Clara had done with Hargreaves, everyone seemed to think this tiny crusader for the homeless could make oil and water mix. Not a small feat.

"This is Connor," Louisa said, glancing up at him with a radiant smile, "and he's offered to help me plan my dream job training program."

Her entourage mumbled pleasantries and shook *her nephew's hand* like they'd just met on the street, and she had the urge to step on Connor's foot accidentally to let him know Louisa deserved better.

"You a native Chicagoan, Connor?" Arthur just had to ask.

Connor didn't break character as he replied with a straight face, "No...Arthur, was it? I'm just back for the time being."

"I was just giving Connor the nickel tour," Louisa said, gesturing to the hallway. "If you're okay with it, I thought we'd pick up where we left off, and then we can circle back to the kitchen and the dining room for the grand finale."

"Don't forget about the Story Room," Connor said, putting his hand to Louisa's back.

Arthur nudged Clara and gave her a sidelong wink like she didn't have eyes.

Some actor he'd turned out to be.

"You won't believe what she does for homeless children," he said, looking down at the woman with warmth and awe. She'd never seen him regard anyone like that before.

"I can't wait to see more for myself," Arthur said in a serious tone, and Clara thanked God for it. "No one should be homeless, but there's something downright barbaric about children living on the streets if you ask me."

"I couldn't agree more," Clara answered, following as Louisa started to lead them down the hall, introducing them to people as they came across them.

Some were staffers, like the man sitting at reception,

many of whom had once been homeless themselves. Others were homeless people coming in for lunch or stopping in to see their children in the shelter's daycare center, which captured her attention in a way nothing else had so far. The yellow walls painted with sunflowers gave the room a brighter atmosphere despite the wary eyes of some of the children. A couple of boys left their puzzles or books and trains and raced over to talk to them.

One of the little boys, who'd introduced himself as Howie, asked, "Are those diamonds real?"

Laughing, Clara sank to the ground—a task much easier now that she did yoga and Qigong daily with Hargreaves—and held them out for him to touch. "A lady wouldn't wear fakes."

His eyes were round as saucers as he gently reached for them, only to yank his hand back. "They're cold."

"That's why some people call them ice," Connor said, staring at her steadily, his mouth turned up.

"Do all ladies like the ice, Mr. Connor?" Howie asked, stuffing his hands in his back jean pockets.

"Some do, some don't," Connor said. "We know Clara here does, but I have a feeling Ms. Louisa doesn't."

Clara reined in her surprise. The Big Bad Wolf, good with children? Even though he was the oldest of seven children, she wouldn't have imagined it. Arthur nudged her as if to say he was surprised as well.

Louisa jerked her thumb at Connor. "He's pretty smart, Howie. Good thing he's on our side. All right, we've got to go. You guys have fun. I hear Carter is making spiced apple cider for you this afternoon to go with your snack. I might have to pop in if you'd have me."

"You know we would, Ms. Louisa!" Howie cried, ducking forward and hugging her legs. Turning back to Clara, he said, "It was nice to meet ya. Thanks for letting me see your ice, Ms. Clara."

"It was my pleasure, Mr. Howie," she responded, opening her arms to him.

He rushed to her, putting his small arms around her. Pure love, she thought, as her heart cracked a little at the thought of him being homeless. When they stepped outside, she turned to Louisa. "Can you tell me anything about Howie's situation?"

"Like I was telling Connor, unless we have permission to share someone's story, we keep things private. All I can say is that he has one determined mother, and we're doing our part to look after him while she works on getting things going in the right direction."

Well, that did it. Seeing this place, these people, made her even more eager to help. "I don't need to see any more. Louisa, I'm prepared to write you a check today. For a million dollars."

Connor had told her to only donate half a million, droning on about the absorptive capacity of nongovernmental organizations. Like she'd never given money to an NGO before.

Louisa grabbed her by the shoulder, her mouth open. "Did you say *a million dollars*?"

Arthur nudged her in the side, his craggy face transformed by a lopsided grin. "Yes, Louisa, she did."

Clara could all but hear Connor grinding his teeth as he attempted his own smile. Her nephew certainly didn't like to be sidelined or ignored. She shot him a look, but suddenly Louisa was jumping up and down like Jill Hale, Arthur's granddaughter, at a Bieber concert. Clara found herself bouncing in time with the woman.

"Oh, my God! Oh, my God! Oh, my God! Yes! Yes! Yes! Clara... You wonderful woman. No one has ever donated that much at once. This is going to help us get our training program off the ground faster. Oh, Clara, I just want to kiss you."

"Not on the mouth," Arthur said, laughing. "That's my prerogative."

Clara elbowed him. "You idiot. She was only jesting."

"No, I'm not." Louisa kissed her on the cheek and then squeezed her hard enough to make her cough. "Oh, I'm sorry. I'm going a little crazy now. But seriously! You just told me you're writing a check for a million dollars."

"Hargreaves will see to it."

"Oh, you're getting a kiss too, Hargreaves," Louisa said, grabbing him around the waist and leaning on her tiptoes to kiss his cheek.

Clara almost laughed at his appalled expression, but Louisa was already turning to Arthur, who had his arms open and waiting for her. "Make it good, Louisa. I'm an old man. I might die any day."

Louisa kissed him three times on the cheek and then fell back a few steps, laughing and crying. Connor caught her, anchoring her in place. He watched the scene as a by-stander, and Clara wanted to shake him to join in. He'd orchestrated this, hadn't he? Why wasn't he enjoying it?

"Do you have any idea how many people you just helped?" Louisa's laughter faded and tears trickled down her face. "How many lives you've saved? *Thank you*!"

Clara found herself wiping her own tears in response. "You are most welcome, my dear. From everything I've seen, no one deserves it more."

"Louisa, what in the Sam Hill are you shouting about?" a booming masculine voice asked.

Louisa rushed off, and then she was jumping onto the big black man coming toward them. "That woman just gave us a million dollars!"

"What?" The man's head swung in her direction. "No way! Oh, Louisa, honey!"

They embraced, both of them laughing and crying. Other staffers joined them in the hallway, asking what was going on, and Louisa proceeded to share the news, crying and hugging everyone who arrived on the scene. Soon it was a party, and Clara's heart swelled in response.

She'd been aimless for so long. Lonely and alone but for Hargreaves. Now she had a family. She had a beautiful connection with a village in Africa, home to the healing flower Michaela and her fiancé, Boyd, would bring to the world, and now she had this wonderful shelter too. Oh, to be eighty and to finally feel like she was doing something with her life.

She felt Arthur take her hand. "Well done, my dear."

Connor sidled up to them. "You were only supposed to give her a half a million," he hissed under his breath. "I won't give you an additional five hundred just because you got all gooey-eyed on the tour."

"Like I'd accept it, dear boy," she said, looking him straight in the eye. "This is my money, and *I'm* the one giving it to the shelter. You want to play your games, fine. I won't be a part of that. I believe in what Louisa is doing here, and I hope you're just as committed. From the way you look at her, I'd say you care. I know you're going through a tough time right now, and we're trying to be supportive, but there are more lives at stake than just yours. I hope you know that. Also, I really like Louisa, and given everything I've seen today between the two of you, you should think twice about continuing to deceive her."

With that, she yanked on Arthur's hand and propelled him forward to join the celebration. She was hugged and kissed and thanked, and people cried all over her in the best way possible—Arthur and even the inscrutable Hargreaves as well.

When she looked over to where Connor had been standing, he'd disappeared.

CHAPTER 7

CONNOR SHOWED UP AT EIGHT O'CLOCK BECAUSE HE AND Louisa had agreed on the time, but he fully expected her to back out. She would still be celebrating with her people, and he couldn't blame her.

It wasn't every day someone waltzed in and gave you a million dollars.

He wasn't in a good mood after Clara had up and turned the tables on him. He was supposed to be the one calling the shots. Not her. He'd calculated Louisa's shelter couldn't absorb more than half a million in its present form, but had Aunt Clara listened to the expert? No, and that pissed him off. It reminded him of how little control he had over anyone and anything. Connor Merriam wasn't in charge anymore, and the powerlessness of that made him feel like the sky was falling again.

Now Louisa would have a whole bunch of money to do numerous things with, and he wanted her to stay focused on the training program. That program would help get homeless people off the streets, which would ultimately make the neighborhood safer for Corey's family. It was where his plans most aligned with Louisa's.

He'd left the shelter, not wanting to be kissed or hugged—or affected. The joyful look Louisa had given him before hugging him as tears rained down her face had given him heartburn.

It felt like too much.

Already he was too affected. Little Kendra had made him fall to a knee to reassure her. Howie had charmed him. And Louisa...

She was dangerous to his emotions, way too open for his well-being. He had a job to do, and he was going to do it. This was supposed to be about making the neighborhood safer for Olivia and her boys. No more, no less. Only now he wanted that for Louisa and all the people she helped. The Kendras and Howies of the world shouldn't be homeless.

Whenever he was with Louisa, he felt the numbness he'd been trying so hard to achieve shifting under his skin, like car tires sliding dangerously on a snowy highway. Too much emotion, he'd be out of control again—he'd learned his lesson.

That was what Aunt Clara didn't understand. She wanted him to be open with Louisa, to tell her the truth, but if he let her in like that, he wouldn't be able to keep the distance he needed to stay sane.

"Connor!"

He turned at the sound of Louisa's voice. He'd been hovering near the front door, not wanting to seek her out in the dining hall. The more people he met, the less he'd be able to separate himself from what he was doing here.

"I didn't have time to change since everything has been so crazy." She threw her arms around him. "Oh, my God! This has been one of the best days of my life, and I'm so glad you were there with me to see it, although I wish you hadn't left so abruptly. I looked around for you when my feet found the ground again."

His heart wrenched in his chest as her golden eyes met his, her hands patting his chest as if she were still trying to express all the emotion bouncing inside her.

"I had somewhere to be." He hated stretching the truth. "Besides, you needed to celebrate with the people who'd made this happen. You and your staff have worked hard for this moment."

"We sure have, but having someone else honor that is a miracle, I tell you! Oh, Connor, I'm so happy. You might be going out tonight with the happiest woman on earth. I hope you can handle it."

He drew back. "You still want to go out? I wasn't sure."

"Yes, of course!" she said, her eyes practically glowing with joy. "First, I promised and I always honor my promises, and second, because I want to party. Gosh, I might even do shots tonight. Is that crazy? Or order a bottle of champagne. That's more celebratory, right?"

Her joy and openness made him feel like he was on black ice, and he feared he was going to take a hard fall at her feet. "If you want to celebrate with your colleagues or family and friends, I totally understand. As you said, it's a big day."

She slapped him on the shoulder. "Are you kidding? I figure today has to be one of the luckiest of my life. I'm rolling with it. Besides, my dad and Damien and a whole bunch of other friends came over the minute I sent a selfie of me holding a check for one million dollars." She spun in a circle. "I still feel like I'm dreaming."

So did he. The ground was unsteady under his feet again. "If you're sure…"

"I'm sure, but I didn't have a chance to change," she said, repeating herself again and tucking her arm in his. "Let me get my coat—I see you're still not wearing one, but I'm happy you have on pants and a sweater, at least. I need to pop into my apartment and change. After that, we can celebrate. It's about a fifteen-minute walk if we hurry."

Go by her place? That seemed way too personal. Did he want to know where and how she lived? Because he knew this wasn't a pretense for getting him into her apartment for sex. It was a step toward intimacy, connection. "You're walking? In this neighborhood?"

"Please. I've lived here my whole life. I know which streets to stay on. Besides, I'm trained in martial arts."

That didn't appease him, but he wasn't going to argue. The women in his family would have taken umbrage at his protectiveness. His heart hurt at the thought. He'd gone too far trying to protect them after Corey, and he'd only succeeded in driving them away.

"If you have any final things to wrap up, go ahead. I'm not in a hurry."

She patted his cheek playfully, a gesture he might have found sweet if his heart weren't tightening up in his chest, constricting normal blood flow. "I always have things to see to, but tonight I'm just going to grab my coat and your proposal. I didn't have any time to read it today in the awesome melee after Clara's donation, but I plan to look at it over my oatmeal in the morning."

He found himself fighting a smile. "You eat oatmeal for breakfast?"

"Every morning," she said, dancing backward down the hallway. "Sometimes I even add fruit. Oh, Connor, tonight's going to be so wonderful. Be right back."

She disappeared, and he found himself fighting the urge to flee. When he'd asked her for a date, he hadn't thought any further than his attraction to her—than his desire to touch and caress her, but this suddenly felt like more. He couldn't *let* it be more—he was damned if he'd take on someone else to love after what had happened with Corey and Michaela.

Except he couldn't bear to disappoint Louisa. She was so excited to celebrate with him. And he wanted to go with her...

He closed his eyes and reined himself in. He could compartmentalize. This was attraction and sex, not forever and happily ever after. Except he couldn't stop thinking of

the way her golden eyes had gleamed upon learning Clara
was donating a cool million. And he thought of the way
she'd sat beside him, a complete stranger, in the middle of
a snowstorm and refused to leave him. God! She was...way
too...affecting. He should—

"Okay, let's go," she said, barreling back into the foyer
like the force of nature she was. She blew kisses to what he
assumed were the sunflowers and then put her hand on
his chest. He noticed she was wearing the winter accesso-
ries he'd bought her, and his chest tightened again at the
sight—as if she were boldly claiming him, and vice versa.
The color suited her even more than he'd thought.

"You look beautiful in red. In everything."

Their eyes met, and he felt something click inside him.
There was no force on earth that would keep him away
from her tonight. If it damned him, then so be it.

She beamed as she ushered him out into the night.
"Tomorrow's love note is going to be epic. Man, I'll have to
stare into my oatmeal for inspiration."

He opened the door for her, falling further under her
spell. "Stare into your oatmeal? You are now certifiably
weird."

"I know! But I get some of my best ideas that way."

She spun in a circle again, the giddiness in her too
much to be contained in that small body, and he put his
hands out to make sure she didn't take a spill. There were
patches of snow and ice from the storm that hadn't melted.

"In this neighborhood, some people might think you're
high," he said, stepping to the outside of her so he was clos-
est to the street. "I mean, only I know you're ecstatic."

"Probably." She tucked her arm through his all date-
like. "But I'm known to the guys who sell drugs around
here. They won't think I'm high. Only happy. And I am...
Oh, gosh. You know, I thought I was lucky when you offered to help me design the training program, but I figured
it was going to take us a long time. And then Clara Merriam

Hale walked in today and gave me a million dollars."

It was weird to hear his last name come out of her mouth, and he felt a punch of guilt. He knew Clara was right. Louisa wouldn't like the subterfuge, but he needed it right now. It would maintain the distance between them, for one, and he also wanted—needed—to be a nobody right now, someone with no past.

"You going to let me blab all night?" she asked, stopping in the amber glow from Chicago's famous streetlights.

Her golden skin seemed even more luminous than usual, making his hands itch to caress the delicate line of her cheekbone. God, she was so beautiful. Inside and out. He was starting to think in clichés, but he couldn't seem to stop himself around her.

"Why would I stop you? You had big things happen today. I figure you can do or say anything you want to."

She took his hand and tugged him to the right, and he realized he knew the street they were on. This was where South Side met Hyde Park. He'd lived on this block with Corey when they'd moved off campus their junior year at the University of Chicago. He scanned the cross street, trying to gauge how far away his old place was. Then he stopped short.

There it was, the Greystone apartment building half a block up. Memories crashed into him. He and Corey hefting an oversized couch they'd bought at IKEA into their unit, only to realize it was too large. The *Star Wars*-themed party they'd held for Halloween one year. That one snowstorm where they'd watched a marathon of Jim Carrey and *Fast and the Furious* movies. Those were some of the best memories of his life. Back then, he'd felt as close to carefree as he'd ever been. He'd been foolish and naïve enough to think their friendship was unassailable. That he'd always have Corey in his life.

"What's wrong?" he heard Louisa ask.

He wanted to dismantle it brick by brick and howl at

the fates. Why did anyone pour so much emotion into relationships that would end? Every relationship ended in one way or another.

Breathing hard, his lungs started to burn with the cold.

"All right, whatever it is, you can tell me inside." She grabbed his arm and turned them down a sidewalk to a three-story brick house divided into apartments. Her grip didn't lessen as she dug into her purse for her keys and opened the glass door. He followed her up the red-carpeted stairs to the third floor and into the apartment on the right. She flicked on the lights and locked the door.

She lived across the street from his old building. Fate was laughing at him, all right.

Louisa turned to him and put her hand on her waist, studying him. "Tell me what happened back there."

Not a question, a direct order.

Right now he didn't have the energy for a clever equivocation. "I lived across the street a million years ago. No big deal. I just got caught off guard."

"You lived here a million years ago," she said. "No big deal?" The look in her eyes told him she knew it was a bunch of bullshit, but she didn't call him on it. "Okay, why don't you sit right here while I change?"

She all but pushed him into the chair and then disappeared. He took the time alone to grip his knees, forcing the images of Corey in the Greystone across the street from his mind. Except it was like whack-a-mole. He'd erase one image of Corey laughing at him, only to have another pop up.

God! He stood up and paced, running his hands through his hair. He'd thought he'd put this behind him, but he was coming apart.

"Connor."

His head swung in her direction. She was wearing

the same clothes, but his throat was too dry to ask her why. Then she was coming over to him and putting her arms around him. Hard.

He tried to nudge free, but she shook her head, something he felt rather than saw. "Don't you dare push me away right now."

"Louisa."

"I mean it, Connor." She tightened her grip. "Don't mess with me."

The steel in her tone soothed the acid coating his stomach. It felt good to have someone guide him through this moment, and he found himself tightening his arms around her and lowering his head to rest on top of hers.

She didn't pat his back or tell him whatever was going on with him would get better. No, she just held him in a fierce grip, infusing him with her strength. When he finally was able to take even breaths, he eased back. Her arms banded tighter.

"Not yet," she whispered, her tone softer now. "Just hold on to me a little while longer."

He thought about fighting her this time—when had he ever accepted comfort like this?—but then she nudged him with her body.

"Don't fight me. I'll win."

Oddly, he liked that threat. "Not to be weird, but sometimes you remind me of my mom."

"It's not weird, since that means she must be awesome," she said, her face pressed against his chest.

"She is," he said, his words a harsh rasp. God, he'd screwed up—with Mom and everybody. He'd hurt the people who cared about him. Pushed them away when they'd tried to help. Flown into rages. Forced them to fire him instead of explaining himself.

But how could he explain to them what he didn't understand himself? How could he let them back in when he was still such a mess?

Shit. When he'd left home, he'd thought no further than leaving Merriam Enterprises behind and fulfilling his promise to Corey. But what the hell was he supposed to do afterward? He had no plan. His uncertain future stretched before him, and it made him tremble. How could he have let it come to this?

"I'm ruining your celebration," he said, trying to step back. "I'm sorry. I should leave."

"You're not going anywhere," she said, her arms clenching even tighter. "And you're not ruining my celebration. Connor...I'm going with my gut here, but the place across the street... You lived there with the person you think you killed, right? That's why you're back here."

He jerked in her arms.

"I don't know your story yet, but that's a piece, right?" She made some space between them to look up at him, keeping her arms tight around him like she expected him to bolt. "You don't have to tell me anything. But I'm here for you. I don't have the same story as you, but I know how painful it feels to think you're the cause of someone's death. It's one of the worst feelings in the world."

"I don't want to talk about it," he said, trying to break free.

She let him. "That's okay. I respect it. Now, I'm going to change so we can go."

He stopped short. "You still want to go out with me after this display?"

Her face went all soft, like it had when she was looking at some of the homeless children. "You bet. In fact, this is my second miracle of the day."

He went speechless. A miracle? Falling apart in her arms? "You are officially now more than weird."

"So I'm a compassionate lunatic, but I'm good with it," she said with a wink. "Make yourself comfortable. I'll be a sec."

If she'd pushed harder—asked him to talk about his *feelings*—he might have backed out, but he didn't want to let her down. He'd let down so many people lately. Besides, what awaited him? A night of insomnia and regret in a dark apartment that wasn't home? Yeah, it was certainly more luxurious than that other place, but he didn't like to linger there.

He ignored the pull to cross to her front window and look at the place across the street. No, it would be better to lock it out like everything else. Compartmentalize. Focus on what was in front of him. He scanned her small living room, taking in the dark red walls. Of course her home would be colorful. The mantel called to him, decorated with brightly framed pictures of her with various people. He recognized Damien in one of them with a tall, older black man. There was something about his smile that made him think of Louisa.

"That's my dad," she said, appearing in the doorway, a vision in a full-length stretchy black dress with boots. "You've met Damien."

"Coach Evans," he mused, setting the picture down, trying not to stare. "I remember Boxer saying that. What does he coach and where?"

"Basketball, of course—the only sport worth playing—and at a high school in Washington Park."

Another troubled neighborhood close by. "Please tell me you're not a fan of Kobe Bryant or LeBron James."

"And you claim to have lived in Chicago..." She made a tsking sound. "No one was better than the one, the only, Michael Jordan."

He decided to yank her chain. "I'm not a Bulls fan. Not a basketball fan really."

She made a face. "You might have to leave after all. I'm not sure I can go out with someone who just said those things. You admitted them out loud to a native."

"The Bulls were overrated," he said, hiding a smile.

"What the Lakers did—"

"Are you crazy? The Bulls won six championships in seven years."

"The Lakers have won sixteen, and that's not even as many as the Celtics."

Suddenly she was rushing over to him, poking him in the chest. "You're playing me. Not a basketball fan, huh? You have given yourself away, my friend."

He put his arm around her waist, testing the waters. "You're too easily provoked on this topic. I'll have to re-member."

Her hand settled on his chest. "I won't bite the hook again. I have self-control."

He couldn't help but smile. "We'll see about that. You're beautiful when you're outraged."

"Cliché but I'll take it." She leaned back to look him straight in the eye. "And you're even more handsome when you tease me. I like seeing this side of you."

He'd shown her another side of himself too, but his embarrassing display hadn't fazed her. Part of him wondered if it was more dangerous that it hadn't—if he'd been foolish to think there could be anything simple between them. "You know," he found himself saying, "we're heading into some serious waters here. Do you think we should reconsider the personal side of our relationship?"

"I haven't changed my mind." She stepped back. "In fact, I'm more intrigued and on board than ever. If you've changed your mind, that's on you, but where's the man who asked me out earlier today?"

"A fair point. I don't want to back out, but I'm feeling way too much here."

She nodded. "Ditto." She paused, as if to let that sink in, then said, "So, last chance. What's it to be?"

He'd run away from way too many things lately. She wasn't running. If she could take it, then so could he.

They'd stray into dangerous territory together. "Forget my minor breakdown."

"Good," she said, coming back into his arms. "We might as well get the whole first kiss thing out of the way."

"You might be a hardcore basketball fan, but you're no romantic," he murmured, tucking her dark hair behind her ear.

She snorted. "And you are? Please."

"I might be—on some occasions." He was thinking this might be one of them. What would she do if he lifted her in his arms and took her into the bedroom? Laid her on the bed and undressed her ever so slowly?

She must have caught the gleam in his eye, because a slow smile spread across her face. "I might be a romantic too on some occasions, but at the moment I'm too hungry."

"So am I." God, she smelled delicious. Like spiced apple cider from Carter's kitchen.

She pinched his cheek like he was a truant boy. "Predictable. Come on. If you're not going to kiss me yet, let's go."

He helped her into the long black wool coat she pulled from the closet, a touch dressier like the rest of her outfit.

"You should have kissed me when you had the chance," Louisa said as she opened her front door. "Who knows? After we share a meal, I might have changed my mind."

She was so full of it, but he found himself laughing while she inserted her key into the lock. "I don't want to get our first kiss or any other kiss we have out of the way. You might remember *that* after we share a meal."

She took his hand. "I might take that into consideration," she said, her eyes sparkling. "Thanks for sharing."

His heart grew lighter in his chest as they walked down the stairs and left the main house. But the moment he saw that familiar Greystone, the weight was back on his chest, as crushing as a steamroller.

He kept his gaze ruthlessly forward as they walked by,

aware that Louisa was looking at him, measuring. He told himself the past was the past; it didn't—couldn't—matter anymore. He was here to make things right for Olivia and the boys. He needed to remember that whenever his focus slipped.

CHAPTER 8

"YOU KNOW, WE'RE HEADING INTO SOME SERIOUS WATERS here," he'd said before they'd left her apartment.

As if she hadn't realized she was in trouble that first night, when she'd found herself attracted to one of the hard cases. To someone who needed help and didn't want it. To someone whose heart was as wounded as hers had been. Sure, it scared her, but she wasn't one to back away. Since meeting him, it had been one stumble after another, a rough patch of sidewalk she couldn't resist walking down. But tonight, when he'd exhibited both his vulnerability and his sense of humor, she'd gone down hard. Whatever his real story might be, she wanted to be with him.

"This date is slowly imploding," he said, tucked in the corner booth of the restaurant he'd chosen, toying with a glass of prosecco he'd ordered for her celebration. "I still can't believe you wanted to order one of Chicago's best Neapolitan pizzas with shrimp, mussels, clams, and calamari. The Italians would deport you for that."

She whacked his arm with a menu, careful of her own glass of bubbles. "It's on the menu, silly. You were the one who had to go all uptown with prosciutto and stuff. Thank God we could agree on a simple sausage pizza." His lips twitched, and she whacked him again. "Is your mind in the gutter? Seriously, Connor, what's with guys and sausage humor?"

They were both trying to keep it light after their exchange in her apartment.

"If you have to ask..." He raised her hand to his mouth, kissing it lightly.

Oh my. "You trying to up your romantic quotient for the night?"

"More like for the year," he said, lowering their hands but keeping them entwined on top of the table. "I haven't been out much."

"That's okay," she said with a slight smile. "I'll be gentle with you. Ease you back in slowly."

Those sexy lips curved. "Like you get out much. You said you were married to your job. You also said most guys run when they hear you work with the homeless."

He didn't forget anything. "Fine, it's been a while for me too. Obviously you still know how to research restaurants and make a reservation. Sorry we were a little late."

"No biggie," he said, taking a breath for reasons she couldn't fathom. Had the person he'd lost told him about this place before he'd died? She fought the urge to ask him questions. Patience was a virtue, after all, and something told her he would require a lot of it.

"So let me catch you up on Chicago sports," she said, biting back the questions she'd rather ask. They filled the silence with light chatter until their pizza came. He served her a slice before she could reach for it, giving her a sexy smile as he did so. She knew he was entertained, and frankly that was good. So was the pizza, and when she took the first bite, she uttered a low moan.

He nudged her. "Be kind to the rest of us, Louisa. We're men. We only have so much willpower in the face of food-gasms."

"So have one yourself," she said with her mouth full, making him laugh.

He turned to his own piece, but those uncanny eyes of his continued to watch her. Even when he paused to drink either his water or prosecco, he watched her. The space between her thighs found it arousing, and she was doing her best not to show him how much he affected her.

Usually she didn't want to jump someone on a first date, but she did with him. Her other dating experiences had been so different. Usually, she felt the need to go out with a guy a number of times before she trusted him enough to let him into her bed, but there was something about Connor... She'd trusted him immediately, even though she hardly knew anything about him. The candor in his eyes couldn't be faked, and even though he hadn't told her his story, she felt she understood him. But was that a good enough reason to have sex with him tonight?

"Is it weird being on a date with someone you can't ask questions of?" he asked suddenly.

Since she had food in her mouth, she took her time to chew while she thought of the best response. Somehow it was another question of import to him. "We both agree we're weird."

"You're weirder," he said, putting his hand on her thigh. His touch sent a jolt of warmth directly to her core.

"I'm used to lots of people who can't or won't tell me things about themselves," she answered, fighting the urge to purr at his touch. "Some don't even remember their own stories."

"The mentally ill," he said, nodding. "Do you see a lot of them in the shelter?"

Business questions. Good. This was reliable ground for them. "Across the Windy City, it's about thirty percent, but in our neighborhood, we have less than that. Mostly because the gangs run them off. Even the mentally ill can be police witnesses."

"Charming." He picked up a piece of pizza and took a big bite.

"The street is self-regulating in some ways," she said. "I don't always agree with it, but I have to understand it to deal with it."

"You seem to deal more with families."

"We do, not only because they represent a major group for us but because we've made it our mission to be a shelter where families can come and be safe. It's a rarity. I knew when I started out that I didn't want to simply be a nightly motel for the homeless. I wanted to help those who wanted to turn their life around."

"Unlike your mother," he said, his gaze soft. "Is that something I can ask about?"

"I'm pretty open about it," she said, lifting her shoulder. "What do you want to know?"

He did that thing where he focused his entire energy and attention on her. Some would cringe at the intensity. It only pulled her in more. "What do you want to tell me that you haven't told anyone else?"

The feeling of lightness between them snuffed out as surely as if a power surge had fried all the bulbs in the room.

She fell back against the back of the booth. "Wow. That's a big ask. Do I get anything in return if I tell you?"

His eyes shuttered. "Are we negotiating again, Louisa?"

"I'm doing my best navigating our so-called 'serious waters' here. You might put your oar in and help me row the boat."

"Fair point," he said, letting go of her thigh. "I can't think if I touch you, and I need to consider this carefully."

"I'm beginning to think you're more intense than weird, Connor," she said, putting his hand back on her thigh. "It's not an interrogation. If I ask something, you don't have to answer."

"If I say I'll answer, I will."

More steely focus. Who in the world was he? "Fine, take your time. I'll finish up my pizza and my drink. If you're still thinking, I'll file my nails."

He made a rude sound. "I've kissed your hand tonight, so I know you don't file your nails. You don't paint them either."

She gave him her best fisheye. "So I'm not a girly girl."

"I have a sister like that," he said, smiling for a moment, and then his face fell. In fact, he turned downright gray.

"How about you tell me about your sister?" she asked.

He swallowed thickly. "Not yet. Umm... I never say umm. Ah, how about you ask me why I knew my way around this campus."

"I already knew you went here," she said, setting aside the last of her crust since she was nearly bursting.

"You did?"

"You lived in a Greystone apartment 'a million years ago,' and you're what, forty plus. It also explains that worn University of Chicago T-shirt you had on the night I met you."

"I'm only forty," he said, "and I love that shirt."

Maybe it was all the stress he'd been under, but he looked a little older. Not that she'd mention that. "Fine. You went here..."

"Graduated with honors," he said cautiously.

"You think I'm going to try to look you up on the graduation roster back in the day? That would be like combing a haystack for a needle. Besides, I'd rather hear about you from you." But it was tempting.

"I appreciate that," he said, pushing his plate aside.

"And..."

"You want to know more?" he asked.

Pulling teeth went faster than getting this man to open up. "I do. Tell me something I don't know."

"You first."

She rolled her eyes. "About my mom? Okay, how's this... The only person who knows this is my counselor. I'm trusting you won't repeat it."

He met her gaze. "You can trust that."

"The third time my mom and I ended up on the streets it was around the holidays. She didn't have anything for me for Christmas and felt horrible about it. I'd realized early on not to say I wanted anything. It only made both of us feel worse. Anyway, she had me wait at the end of an alley the night before Christmas Eve. I know she had sex with a stranger for money so she could buy me a doll at the drugstore. It was an ugly doll with scraggly dark hair—the last one on the shelf, probably because no one else wanted it. I hated that doll."

He just looked at her for a moment, his level stare unflinching, and then edged closer and touched her face. "Louisa Evans, you are fast becoming my hero."

Her heart clenched. People had called her that before, but of all the things she'd expected him to say, this wasn't it. "Why?"

He looked away and blew out a breath before meeting her eyes again. "Because you give me hope that anything is overcomeable. Is that a word?"

Her tightness vanished, replaced by warmth. "I like that word. Whatever happened to you *is* overcomeable, Connor. I truly believe that. I'm living proof of it."

"It's not the only reason I'm attracted to you. Let's be clear on that." He squeezed her thigh to make his point. "You seem to be finished with your pizza. Do you want dessert?"

"Can't," she said, patting her belly. "I'm stuffed."

"Shall we get the check then?" he asked. "Walk a bit?"

A walk sounded rather romantic, she thought. "You really have no compunction about walking in the cold, do you?"

"None whatsoever."

"I'd love a walk, and yes, let's get the check." She paused, picking one question from the slew in her head. "But can I ask you just one thing? Where were you before you came back to Chicago?" Small steps, she told herself.

"Nowhere this cold," he answered. "Outside San Francisco."

She didn't hide her surprise. "Seriously? I thought everyone from there only ate tofu cheese on their gluten-free pizza. And you don't talk like a valley girl."

"Stereotypes, Louisa? I expected better." But he was smiling as he signaled for the check.

"Oh, I've disappointed you. Another blow to our date. I'm still going to come back and get that pizza with the octopus on it sometime."

"It was calamari, and if you're so dead set on eating it, I'll try it with you next time."

She edged closer and put her head on his shoulder. "So there's going to be a next time?"

"If you want it, yes," he said, kissing the top of her head. "I was going to ask you what you were doing tomorrow night."

She knew she shouldn't be so pleased. Just a few hours ago, he'd tried to cancel their date. The man was an emotional ping-pong ball, and yet she was glad for it this time. "You don't believe we should take it slow?" she asked nonetheless, baiting him. "Take the conventional approach?"

He made a rude sound as the server slid the check on the table. "Neither one of us has a conventional bone in our body. Besides, I want to spend as much time as possible with you—while I'm here. Now that we've agreed we're both on board."

"Where are you going afterward?" she asked, reaching for her wallet in her purse.

"I don't know yet," he said, his jaw tightening a fraction.

Fighting the urge to ask more questions, she pulled the check closer and then opened her wallet for a couple of twenties.

"Do you seriously think I'd let you pay?" he asked, his voice harsh. "Put your money away before you piss me off."

"But you're…" She stopped short, seeing his jaw slam together.

"I am not homeless. I am not poor."

He'd mentioned this before, but knowing he'd gone to the University of Chicago, she'd concluded two things: he was either wealthy—or had been—or he'd gone on scholarship, meaning he was even smarter than she'd thought. Tuition was about seventy thousand a year alone, and given the academic excellence of most of the students, they didn't give many full aid packages.

"I wasn't trying to piss you off," she said, trying to break the mood. "I usually go Dutch on first dates."

"Most of the guys you've gone out with are morons then," he said, taking out his wallet and laying down crisp twenties.

"Yes," she said, filing away the fact that he was also a great tipper.

When they stood, she noticed another couple give them an assessing, almost disapproving glance. Who knew what they were thinking? Connor took her hand and lifted it to his mouth. She smiled when their eyes met, but he cast an angry look at the couple.

Outside, she tucked her arm in his. "Something upset you?"

"Yeah, I didn't like how those older people were looking at us. Do you think it's because I'm white and you're mixed?"

She shrugged. "I try to not let other people's thinking affect me. Why does it bother you?"

He cast a look back over his shoulder at the restaurant. "Because it shouldn't matter. That kind of thinking keeps progress from being made."

"Not just progress, but meaningful connections like ours. My dad told me when I was real little that everyone was a color like in my crayon box—all special, all wonderful to play with. Maybe no one taught them that. We don't know their story."

"Don't know their story?" He studied her and shook

his head. "Louisa, you amaze me. I've never met anyone so open and accepting of other people."

Which was maybe the best compliment she'd ever heard. "Thank you. Having empathy for other people is the only way to change things."

He brushed a lock of hair back from her face, staring at her with more than his usual intensity. "Come on," he said after a moment. "Let's walk."

He led her through the college campus, and they fell silent. He seemed to be lost in memories, and she felt her best course was to be present. To him and their surroundings.

When they reached her house, he paused on the steps and took her face in his hands. She held his gaze as he lowered his head. The first brush of his lips was like a match firing to life. The second, deeper connection was more like dynamite. She leaned closer, and his hand came around her waist, bringing her against him.

The sound that came from her throat was low and needy. Her need for him, which had pulsed stronger and stronger as the evening went on, was desperate and insistent. She opened her mouth, and they feasted on each other. His hands gripped the back of her coat, and she wrapped her arms around his waist, savoring the strong feel of his chest.

He was breathing hard when he released her. "Tomorrow night. Same time. Be sure you want me and this, because I don't want to walk away next time."

Before she could debate asking him inside, he was striding off down the sidewalk. Stopping, he flicked his hand at her, as if to urge her to go inside. That was what stopped her from waving for him to come back. He needed to respect they were both equal, in bed and out. She fumbled for her key and opened the door. But he didn't leave until she was inside and had thrown the deadbolt.

Leaning back against the door, she took calm, soothing breaths.

Tomorrow night, she decided, they would be coming home together.

CHAPTER 9

SO MUCH FOR SECRETS.

Arthur heard Clara gasp as they entered the main room of their suite after returning from dinner. And no wonder. The entire Merriam family was gathered inside. Clara's brother, Shawn, and his wife, Assumpta, sat on one of the couches across from their girls, Caitlyn and Michaela, who were sitting next to their fiancés, Beau and Boyd, while the boys—Flynn, J.T., Trevor, and Quinn—stood in a huddle. Arthur's niece, Caroline, who was married to J.T., was nestled in with their group. Somehow he doubted this was about Clara's million-dollar donation yesterday.

"A pleasure to see everyone in the Windy City," Hargreaves said, not missing a beat. "I'll prepare the appropriate beverages. Excuse me."

"Well, this is a surprise," Arthur said, clasping Clara's hand hard, knowing she was searching for what to say. She'd be worried too, of what the others would think.

Assumpta Merriam stood as her husband rose to his feet. "I'd like to say it's wonderful to be back in my old city, but we're here on a serious matter, as I'm sure you've guessed from Flynn's illegal entry into your suite."

"Sorry about that, Uncle Arthur and Aunt Clara," Flynn said with a grimace. "There were too many of us to wait in the hallway outside your room. And the lobby was so drafty."

"Drafty, eh?" Arthur chuckled, deciding a direct approach was the best. "What? Afraid we might run? At our age?"

Caitlyn shot forward past her fiancé. "I knew you were up to something when we FaceTimed the other night and you wouldn't tell me where you were. Another honeymoon, hah."

"At our age, I can see how you might not have believed it possible," Arthur said. "But your aunt has decided we're always on a honeymoon. Now, come here and give an old man a hug."

Clara worried her rings. "We were only trying to help. That's important for everyone to understand."

"And we do," Shawn said, crossing to his sister and putting his hands on her shoulders. "I have to admit I was shocked when Flynn showed me pictures of you two with Connor at Corey's gravesite. But I knew you must have had a good reason for keeping it from us."

"A damn good one," she said, hugging him hard.

Assumpta joined them and put her hand on Clara's back. "We've come too far these past few months to doubt you. But tell me truly, how's my boy?"

Arthur knew Assumpta had a steel backbone, so the way her voice cracked as she called Connor *my boy* almost broke his heart. "Hurt and angry as you might imagine. We're still trying to figure him out, but he gave us a ringside seat on the condition we wouldn't tell you we'd found him."

Clara nodded. "He threatened to disappear, and we believed him."

"You were wise to," Trevor said. "He was giving us fits until he visited Olivia."

"Of course, we already knew you were watching Olivia's house too." Flynn picked up a file on a side table and started laying out large black and white photos of them on stakeout. "Nice flask, Aunt Clara. I never knew stakeouts could be so posh."

"Posh, smosh." Arthur picked up a picture of them at the graveyard and harrumphed. "How come I didn't see you?"

Flynn threw his thumb in Trevor's direction. "Since he went off grid, Trev here hired some ex-SEALs he uses for the more complicated oil and gas jobs. They were staking out Olivia's house, the only place we knew Connor might visit."

"And the only lead," Trevor said.

"We saw him at the gravesite first," Arthur felt inclined to add. "But Connor was running too fast for us to catch him."

"Yes, he seems to be running a lot," Quinn said, walking over to the photos and picking through them until he held up one of Connor in workout clothes. He was sitting in a park while it snowed, a brown-bagged bottle in his hand.

"Oh, that dear boy," Clara said, putting her hand to her mouth.

"You were right to agree to his terms, Clara," Shawn said, his mouth tight. "He's clearly not himself, but we knew that. This, however... I never imagined seeing my son look like this."

Voices were quavering, and Arthur reached deep for his journalistic objectivity. He walked toward Quinn and took the photo. "Where was this taken?"

"A park not far from the cash-only motel Connor was staying in," Quinn said.

"Which is why I couldn't find him," Flynn said. "I never thought he'd stoop to residing in a place like that. Thank God he's not staying there anymore. He's at some furnished rental in South Side now." He picked up another picture of Connor exiting the motel room number twelve and then another with him passing a few rough characters on the way down the stairs.

"When was the one in the park taken?" Arthur asked. "The snowstorm a week ago?"

Quinn's mouth was a ferocious scowl. "Yes, the night he visited Olivia. Trevor's team followed him after he left the house. He ran to Corey's gravesite at Oak Woods Cemetery—clocking about seven minutes a mile—and back to this park after a stop at a local liquor store. I believe you know the woman who talked him into coming out of the storm." He produced another picture, and Arthur heard Clara gasp again.

"That's Louisa!" she said, bustling forward.

"Well, now we know how they met," Arthur said, taking the picture from Quinn's hand. "I believe that's Boxer on the right."

"Yes, Levan 'Boxer' Irving," Quinn said. "An interesting story for another time. However, we're all very interested in this woman. Especially since you, Aunt Clara, gave her a million dollars yesterday."

"Yes, I did," Clara said. "Your brother only wanted me to give Louisa and her wonderful shelter five hundred thousand—and from his own money, which I refused to take—but after seeing the incredible work she's doing with so many brilliant people, I had to give her more. Right, Arthur?"

"Exactly so, my dear." Arthur picked through the rest of the photos on the table. "I see we figure prominently in these. How did you get someone to take photos inside the shelter? Did one of your ex-SEALs pretend to be homeless?"

"They did what they're paid to do," Trevor said. "I don't ask how they get it done."

"Aunt Clara," Michaela said, letting go of Boyd's hand on the couch and coming over and hugging her aunt. "Can you and Uncle Arthur tell us what Connor's up to? A lot of theories have been bandied around, especially after Olivia told us she sent Connor away without seeing the boys. She didn't think he was in a healthy enough state to be around them."

Arthur winced. Connor would have taken that hard. Now he understood that brown-bagged bottle.

"Arthur, would it be wrong to break our word to Connor and tell them what we know?" Clara asked.

"I think the cat's out of the bag, dear, but how about we play the Deep Throat game?"

"I don't know what that is," Michaela said, looking around the room.

Trevor snorted. "She's a genius in science, but not contemporary American history. He's talking about Watergate, Mickey. Here. I've got this. Uncle—is Connor helping Louisa Evans and her shelter as part of his strategy for improving South Side so it's safer for Olivia and her boys?"

"Bingo, Trev wins the prize," Arthur said with a firm nod of his head.

"Deep Throat game aside, Uncle," Quinn said, crossing his arms, "does Connor really think he can use Aunt Clara's donation to change the conditions in Mom's old neighborhood that fast? He's never been a patient man."

"Maybe he's still not thinking rationally," Caitlyn said. "You know how he's been lately."

"Rationality has more than flown the coop." Quinn stood angrily, fists at his sides. "He was drinking *out of a bottle* in a snowstorm and living in a rat-trap motel."

Arthur understood why the boy was peeved. No two Merriams had worked more closely together than Connor and Quinn, and now Connor had gone off on his own, leaving his younger brother behind to pick up the pieces. Although it had needed to happen—that picture of Connor in the snow was proof enough of that—it was a heavy weight.

Arthur sighed. "I can't believe you all flew in."

"That's our Connor out there," Assumpta said, her

back rigid but her eyes teary. "We'd go to the depths of hell to get him back."

"Well, there'll be no need for that," Clara said, brushing her own tears aside. "Enough Deep Throat, Arthur. I'm telling them everything we know. Connor has developed a business plan for a training center Louisa has always wanted."

"And you gave her the capital, Aunt Clara," J.T. said, rubbing the back of his neck. "I get it."

"But won't training take a long time?" Caitlyn asked. "I mean, when we drove by Grandpa Noah and Grandma Anna's old house—oops, I mean Olivia's—we were all shocked to see how bad things had gotten in the neighborhood."

Quinn put his hand on Arthur's shoulder. "I expect Connor has more plans."

"Yes, he does." Arthur glanced over as Hargreaves arrived with two silver trays from God knows where lined with a variety of drinks ranging from red wine to martinis to whiskeys neat. Knowing Hargreaves, he'd accounted for everyone's favorite drink. Arthur handed Clara a martini and picked up a whiskey for himself. "Take one and drink heartily. I'm about to tell you what the Big Bad Wolf hopes to do."

He waited until everyone had a drink in hand before dropping his bombshell. "Your brother—and your son—plans to buy up every available South Side property—"

"And bring in new businesses or more stable tenants," Quinn said, shaking his head. "We wondered about the trip to Switzerland and Luxembourg, but thought it might only be about money. That's why we've been sitting back watching until your donation, Aunt Clara."

"So, we're talking dummy corporations?" Flynn whistled. "No wonder I haven't cracked that."

"Not dummies in the illegal sense," Quinn said. "Legitimate businesses under various names designed to hide the principal's identity. He wouldn't want to draw attention to himself. It's brilliant actually."

"And I'm researching and refining urban renewal solutions for Connor to add to the mix," Arthur added. "I'm also hoping to school him a little in Chicago politics along the way. Connor seems to think he'll be able to implement whatever plan he has in mind with no interference whatsoever from city politicians."

Assumpta snorted. "When I was growing up here, if you voted for the wrong candidate, no one came to pick up your garbage for six months."

"I'm sure it's different now, Mom," Michaela said. "Uncle Liam says Chicago has made some major changes in how things get done."

"I hope so," Assumpta said, glancing up at her husband. "So my boy plans to make South Side safe in one fell swoop for Olivia and the boys? My God, Shawn. I thought I was scared before."

"But why?" Caitlyn asked. "Mom, it sounds like just the perfect project to motivate him. Plus, he'll be doing real good."

"People have been talking about cleaning up my neighborhood since I was a kid, and nothing much has happened," Boyd said. "Gentrification is controversial—people feel strongly about it, pro or con. What happens if he doesn't succeed? Or if he does, and people hate him for it?" Leave it to Boyd to say what they were all thinking. Michaela returned to him, taking his hand again.

Arthur and Clara shared a look before Arthur answered. "That's why Clara and I agreed to his plan. He needs all the help he can get."

"It would be easier all around if Olivia would move," Trevor said. "Dammit. Mom, can you talk some sense into her? This kind of pressure can't be good for Connor."

"Honey, she explained it to me, and I understand." Assumpta faced her children. "That's my parents' house, and this is my old neighborhood. If I were in her shoes, I'd do the same thing. You don't let bullies move you out. You stay and move them out. Connor is doing the right thing for her and a whole bunch of other people living there, and by God, I hope he succeeds. He knows better than to take away the things that make South Side unique."

"Connor has the Midas touch," Caitlyn said. "He can make everything a million times more lucrative. If anyone can make real change, it's him."

Quinn all but growled, putting all eyes on him. "That was the old Connor, before Corey died."

"He's still Connor," Shawn said, his jaw tightening.

"Yes," Arthur felt compelled to say. "Michaela, honey, the first thing he did when he saw us was ask about you."

Her face bunched up, and she buried it in Boyd's shoulder.

After a few more sniffs around the room, Shawn said, "So, knowing Connor doesn't want us knowing where he is, what can we do behind the scenes to help?"

"Can we give more money to this shelter he likes or other groups like it?" Caitlyn asked.

Clara shook her head. "He'd find out you were onto him. I think you're going to have to let us work with Connor and trust we're going to succeed. Right, Arthur?"

He looked around the room, knowing no one was going to like his answer. "I don't see any other option. Until he does what he's set out to do, he won't be ready to see you. The boy's embarrassed. He needs to regain faith in himself. That's what this is about."

Trevor muttered a curse, and Flynn and J.T. echoed him. Quinn fisted his hands at his sides hard enough to make his knuckles white.

Shawn sighed, and Assumpta leaned her head on his shoulder for a minute before looking at her husband and nodding.

"So be it," Assumpta said. "We trust you to handle it."

"Trev, I want you to pull your ex-SEALs," Shawn added. "I'm happy as hell they found Connor for us, but we don't want to push it. He still might spot them."

"Never," Trevor said, "but I hear you. I'll pull them now that we know he's safe. Aunt, Uncle, you'll tell us what you can?"

"Yes, of course," Clara said. "I'm so sorry it's come to this. I know we all feel awful."

"But at least he's not alone," Shawn said. "I have faith in you and Arthur."

"And Hargreaves," Michaela added with a firm nod, brushing aside her earlier tears. "I don't know where he went after leaving our drinks, but we all know he's more than just a butler."

"Indeed he is," Clara said. "Speaking of drinks, why don't we have a few? It's good to see you—"

"And it's been a stressful few weeks," Shawn said, lifting his whiskey in the air. "To Connor, whom we hope will be back with us all soon."

Arthur teared up with almost everyone then. No family should be at odds, particularly not one so close. He knew his old friend Emmits wouldn't want things that way.

"To family," Assumpta said. "*Slainte.*"

Drinks lifted. Toasts returned. When Arthur raised his glass to drink, Quinn said under his breath next to him, "A moment, Uncle."

Arthur nodded to the door leading to the study—Clara had found them a suite as big as their house in Dare Valley, Colorado—then watched as Quinn knocked back his whiskey and slipped into the adjoining room. After a moment, Arthur followed him. Quinn stood in front of the spacious window boasting a breathtaking view of Lake Michigan dotted with amber lights at her edges.

"I don't have much time," his nephew said, coming forward and closing the door behind him. "Trevor, J.T., Flynn, and I agreed not to say anything about this to the others, so I'm trusting you to keep it between us."

"I can't keep things from Clara, boy," Arthur said with

a pointed look. "She's my wife and my gal, my best partner. If that changes things…"

He ran his hand through his hair. "No, I should have expected it. Fine, tell her, but please no one else. Not my parents or my sisters. They're worried enough."

His stomach grew queasy. "What is it?"

"I need you to tell me more about Louisa Evans. Because something happened last night that's not normal for Con, and given his mental state…" Quinn pulled out an envelope from the lining of his jacket and took out another photo.

Arthur took it, his eyes flying to his hairline at the subject. Connor was in a serious lip-lock with Louisa. Not that he was surprised. They'd fairly oozed attraction to each other on the tour through Sunflower Alley, like Gable and Lombard back in the day.

"Ahem," Arthur said, scratching the side of his face. "Clara and I thought there were some sparks."

Quinn took back the photo and pocketed it. "Do you approve?"

"Of Louisa? One hundred percent. She's incredible. Truly. In fact, given the way he looks at her, she might just be Connor's linchpin back to himself. I mean, Clara and I are doing our damnedest to help the boy, but we're still part of what drove Connor out of Merriam Enterprises in the first place."

"No, you weren't," Quinn said in a hard tone. "His choices and his decisions did that."

As the person who'd run the board meeting that had resulted in his brother's ousting, Arthur was glad Quinn felt that way. Probably had to in order to get up in the morning and run Merriam Enterprises as its new CEO. "I wasn't saying otherwise, Quinn. As for Louisa and Connor, this visual confirmation is very heartening. I've interviewed thousands of people, and I must say Ms. Evans is impressive as hell. Smart. Determined. And with one of the biggest hearts out there."

"She won't crush him?" Quinn asked, his eyes shuttered. "Because I'm not sure he could take that right now. I mean..."

Arthur watched as the boy stalked to the window and looked out. "What, son?"

"He looked suicidal in that park, Uncle Arthur."

Arthur sighed, unable to disagree. "That was before he met Louisa, correct? He has a renewed purpose with this neighborhood. We're going to help him. So is Louisa."

"He's falling for her," Quinn said, touching the window as if searching for something. "I've never seen him look at a girl like that. Not even the one he dated for three years after college. He doesn't let himself get close to many people. Not even me really. Maybe this wouldn't have happened if I'd tried harder to talk to him."

So the boy was carrying around his own share of guilt. "Water under the bridge now. We can only change our behavior moving forward, son, not what we did in the past. It's a hard truth, but one I've learned time and time again."

His deep sigh filled the space. "Forget I said that. Uncle, I asked you in here because the guys and I have a theory about why Aunt Clara gave the money and not Con."

"He doesn't want anyone to know who he is," Arthur confirmed.

"That's what started worrying me after I saw the pictures of him with Ms. Evans. If Connor is as interested in her as I think, what happens if and when Ms. Evans finds out?"

Arthur answered him honestly. "I don't have a clue."

Quinn turned around. "Not what I was hoping I'd hear from the Matchmaker Jedi."

CHAPTER 10

FOUR CLOSINGS AND ANOTHER DATE WITH THE MOST BEAU-
tiful woman he'd ever met. Had he broken his string of
bad luck? Connor sure hoped so.

His reconstruction plan for the neighborhood was
coming together even better than he'd thought. His ano-
nymity had helped. The fact that he wasn't operating under the Merriam name had allowed him to negotiate for
harder margins and more incentives. No one wanted these
properties, given the asbestos removal issues or the demo-
lition expenses, and he'd picked them up for a song. He
was hoping to have the lots fresh and ready for new commercial development in early spring. Since he'd be carrying the major development expenses, all he'd have to do
was talk some cash-flush stores into coming in, and he had
a dozen who'd give their eyeteeth to have a deal like this set
in front of them.

Something was finally going his way, and he felt lighter
about everything that had brought him to Chicago in the
first place.

When he arrived at Sunflower Alley shortly before
eight o'clock, he nodded to the volunteer at reception and
glanced at Louisa's daily love note: *Sometimes dreams do
come true, and sometimes people are your miracle.* He

felt a catch in his heart. She was talking about him again. Perhaps not exclusively, but the note felt like a glimpse at her feelings.

She'd thought of him as she'd written it, he felt sure of it. "Hey!"

He turned and saw her striding toward him. She seemed eager to see him, her footsteps almost bouncing, but she paused to exchange a quick goodbye with the volunteer packing up at the front desk. According to Louisa, the main prerequisite for their reception-desk volunteers was friendliness and enough tech-savvy to buzz her or Boxer in their offices. She'd jokingly told him he should try it, but he'd bandied back that he wasn't sure his friendly quotient met the bill. That had made her laugh. Funny, he was good at making her laugh, although no one had ever considered him one of the more humorous Merriams.

God, her smile was radiant, and that catch in his heart turned into a full-on tug. She was ready to leave, decked out in the red winter jacket he'd met her in, dark jeans, and black snow boots. "You look pretty relaxed. Happy, actually."

"Miracles have a way of doing that," she said, pressing her hand to her heart. "I was waiting for you, counting all my blessings. I was up to about thirty-seven when you cruised in. Hi! How was your day? I read your business plan over oatmeal and ended up rolling in late because it's *ridiculous*!"

"Told ya I don't do anything half-ass."

"Half-ass?" She bumped him with her tiny body like those basketball players she loved might do after a game, and he almost laughed out loud. "More like *the* business plan of the year. Connor! It's incredible. The vision...the steps to implement the training program. It's more than I could ever hope for. And with Clara's brilliant donation, it's actually possible."

He wished he could tell her he'd made sure she had both

a fantastic plan and the means to implement it. "Would have been disappointing if you'd had a kick-ass plan but no way of actualizing it. I'm glad things worked out."

She put her hand on his chest, her touch electrifying with her added energy. "Me too. I really want to kiss you, but I'm refraining in here since I'm at work. Fair warning. When we leave here, I'm going to plant a good one on you."

He found himself chuckling. "Someone had a good day. So did I. Come on. Let's get out of here. I want to kiss you too."

Boxer appeared then. "Heard your voice, Connor. Good to see you. Read the business plan. It's incredible, man. I owe you an apology."

The big man strode toward them with his hand out, and Connor extended his own. Their handshake was a new sizing up, but this time, Boxer punched him in the shoulder after they'd concluded their male ritual.

"You're all right, man," Boxer said, his gaze friendly.

Connor laughed. "The jury is still out on you."

"Funny," Boxer said, "but we're all dancing on clouds around here. Aren't we, Louisa?"

She spun in a circle. "Clouds. Asteroids. The moon. Yeah, we're pretty happy. When I turned my phone on this morning, I was flooded with calls congratulating Sunflower Alley. Of course, some of those calls were about groups wanting to partner with us. A million dollars attracts a lot of attention."

"I imagine it would," Connor said.

Another reason Aunt Clara should have listened to him about the donation amount, but there was no changing it now. He'd called Uncle Arthur earlier in the day to see what their plans were now that the donation had been made. Turned out his uncle was still steadfastly pursuing his story and researching urban development. He'd just come back from another interview this morning, one with someone in the mayor's office, and he'd arranged for a big meeting with the head of Chicago's Department of Planning and Development tomorrow. He'd promised to brief Connor after he assembled his notes.

Hargreaves, amusingly enough, would be the guest chef in Sunflower Alley's upcoming Friday night competition.

That was all fine with Connor. He was knee-deep in reading through the city's complicated zoning laws while buying properties right and left through the four real estate agents he was using. Four separate agents further insulated his property buyouts from unwanted attention.

Oddly, in deciding upon a restaurant for his date with Louisa, he'd come across a helpful find. Daley's Restaurant—a place his grandmother had brought them many times—had moved to a new location across the street from its previous one. Its new site was part of the kind of development Connor was hoping to usher into the neighborhood. Woodlawn Station had a slew of apartments and fifteen thousand feet of retail space, right beside the Green Line's 63rd Street stop. And Uncle Arthur had said bringing about urban renewal in South Side would be hard. It was already happening, and he planned to add his touch.

"Boxer, we're out of here," Louisa said, holding up her gloved hand for a high five. "Rock it out."

"Every day," the man said, tapping her hand. "Have fun. Where are you two eating tonight? I might have to see what leftovers we have in the kitchen. I'm still hungry."

"You always are," Louisa said. "Where are we going, Connor?"

"I thought Parisi's, but they close at nine, so my backup was Leon's BBQ. Unless you have a better idea."

"No, I love Leon's," Louisa said. "You really do know your South Side staples, don't you?"

"Maybe someday our business wonder here will tell us why that is," Boxer said, opening out his arms as he walked backward. But he was grinning at Connor as if to say he didn't hold his secrecy against him anymore. "Louisa and I are starting to throw around ideas about who you are. I'd put ten bucks on you being some indie Hollywood director trying to do a gritty movie about South Side. You taking that, Louisa?"

"A director?" Louisa asked, laughing. "I like it, but I don't think so. Maybe an undercover journalist like Mr. Hale? And no, Boxer, I won't put down a ten. You know I don't gamble."

They were joking, but Connor's stomach did a flip. How would they feel when they learned the truth? "Boxer, I write great screenplays when I'm not doing business plans."

"I'll bet you do, man," Boxer said, lifting his chin. "Have fun. Be safe out there."

Connor opened the door as Louisa waved goodbye. As they walked down the sidewalk together, side by side, she reached for his hand. He curled his hand around her small fingers, fighting a wave of guilt. When they reached the street, she came around and stood in front of him. The amber light backlit her as she stripped off her gloves. He gave her a puzzled look before she cupped his face.

"Bend over a little, will you? I'm short."

He leaned forward. "You're pint-sized adorable."

"And you're way too serious sometimes," she said, stroking his jaw. "I thought this might be a good time to kiss you. I have happy lust with you, and I love it."

Laughter spurted out of him. "Happy lust? That's a new term for me."

"Prepare to discover its meaning," she said, still making him chuckle.

"I don't usually chuckle right before I kiss someone," he said, putting his arms around her. "Maybe I've been struck with this thing called happy lust."

Her smiling lips covered his, leading him, stroking him. He let his eyes close, soaking in the pleasure of her cold hands on his face, of her mouth opening under his. Yeah, happiness and lust could coexist, something he'd never experienced until now.

"Excuse me?"

Connor lifted his head at the intrusion, scanning the street. A young white man in a gray hoodie stood a few yards away on the sidewalk and looked to be dancing in his shoes. Something felt off. Drugs? He moved in front of Louisa, but she grabbed his arm before taking a step forward herself.

"Can I help you?" Louisa asked.

"I heard you might have some food here," the young man said, his body way too fidgety for Connor's peace of mind. "A place to stay for the night."

He put his hand to Louisa's back, ready to protect her.

"Hi, I'm Louisa." She was completely focused on the young man but didn't move closer or offer her hand. "And yes, we might be able to find you a plate of food. It's after our regular walk-in hours, but I could have someone call another shelter and see if they could put you up tonight. What's your name?"

Connor wondered why she'd offered to call another shelter. He knew she sometimes took people in after hours—hadn't she offered a bed to him that first night? Did she suspect drugs too? The shelter had a zero-tolerance policy.

"Jax," the kid said, stuffing his hands in the front of his hoody. "Like Ajax without the A." He huffed a laugh. "My mom meant to name me after it because she got knocked up cleaning houses, but since she was high when I was born, she forgot to put the A on the birth certificate. Hence Jax."

Some part of Connor revolted at the story. If the kid's mother had been a user when he was born, his life couldn't have been easy. Maybe it was the people he'd met over the last couple of days, but Connor had found himself thinking about how lucky he'd been. His parents had named him after a value: strong-willed. What might his life have been like if he'd been born to Jax's mother? Would he be who and where he was today?

Strangely enough, they were questions he'd never asked himself before coming to Sunflower Alley.

"I like the name," Louisa said with a smile. "It sounds lucky."

"Not so far. But thanks for the help. It's been a few days since my last real meal."

Connor felt pulled between his need to protect Louisa and the sympathy he felt toward the kid. He'd never been hungry like that.

Louisa didn't take her eyes off Jax, but she turned her body slightly toward Connor. "I'll hook him up with Boxer and be right back. Jax, come inside with me where it's warm, and I'll introduce you to my man, Boxer."

The young man had a jolting gait as he came down the sidewalk. When he got closer, Connor saw the wildness in his eyes. He put himself between Louisa and Jax as they walked back to Sunflower Alley's front door. There was no way he was letting her be alone with someone this high.

She rang the outside call button, not using her keys—which he found interesting. All the while, she talked with Jax, asking about where he'd been staying. "Here and there," the kid responded. Moments later, Boxer appeared in the front. Louisa introduced them, smiled at Jax, and said goodnight.

Back on the sidewalk, she put her gloves back on and clapped them together once, almost like it was a demarcation point. "Let's go."

"Let me order an Uber," he said, knowing her mood had changed.

"Not just yet, if that's all right. I need to walk a little."

They walked two blocks in silence, her steps brisk yet somehow agitated. Connor finally took her gloved hand.

"You've crashed back down to earth. Want to talk about it?"

"Order the Uber," she said, clapping her hands again. "I've fretted enough."

"You fretting about that kid?" he asked as he pulled out his phone. "He was on drugs, wasn't he?"

She nodded crisply. "Yeah, he was using, which is why Boxer will feed him and call one of our sister shelters which specialize in substance abuse. Boxer and I had to decide early on how our shelter would be set up, and we both agreed that we didn't want to take in people with substance abuse issues. It compromises the safety of our clients, especially the children."

She didn't regret it, he could tell, yet he heard the frustration in her voice. "I think that's a wise decision. You can't help everyone, Louisa, and if they're using, they aren't always ready to make a change."

"Thank God, there are other shelters who can handle clients like him. I'm not sure if he'll go or not," she said, her mouth tight. "I don't like turning people away, but keeping our shelter's guests safe is paramount. Especially the children. My mom used to scream at shelter workers who wouldn't take us in after hours, but I didn't blame them. Usually, she was high as a kite or drunk."

God, what she'd been through. He had to touch her. As gently as he could, he traced her face. Her fiery eyes flashed to him, but she didn't push him away—she moved closer.

"When you tell me stories like that, it stirs me up. I get really angry at your mother. I feel horrible for that little girl. But the woman you are now blows my mind."

"We all go through stuff," Louisa said, shrugging. "You're going through stuff. So is that young kid, Jax."

"Boxer will do what he can. If there's one thing I know, it's that he's as committed to helping people as you are."

She put her head against his chest for a moment. "Thank you for saying that. Yes, he'll handle things the right way, but that kid might not get the help he needs. Sometimes I just wish the world were a different place."

He thought about Corey dying on that offshore oil rig with other Merriam employees because of a damn earthquake. He thought about the moment he'd heard Michaela was sick on the trip he'd sent her on. He thought about Olivia being a widow at forty with two boys to raise alone. "I wish the world were different sometimes too."

She nudged him with her body. "Thanks for listening to me rant, and thanks for backing me up with Jax. It wasn't necessary, but not every man would step in like you did. Hell, most of them would have canceled our date and never looked back."

"I'm not most men," he said, cuddling her close as the wind kicked up. "And you're sure as hell not most women. But do you still feel up to going out?"

Her hand brushed his beard, almost as if she was learning his face. "Yes. I learned a long time ago to rant, and then let it go. My first five years, I had trouble leaving work at work."

He laughed as their car pulled up. "Just the first five years? Seriously? Didn't you read my business plan over oatmeal?"

"Fine, I try and leave it at work. Of course, my dad says that shouldn't be too hard since I work most of the day and then crash when I get home. Like he's any better. His players and the kids he mentors call him all the time." She made a face as she got into the car. "Does how much I work freak you out?"

Connor climbed in next to her. "I probably had you beat at twenty hours a day."

She raised a delicate brow and pursed her lips together before saying, "Twenty, huh? No wonder you could create a business plan like you did in a week."

He reached for her hand. "Louisa, I hate to burst your bubble, but I had that done in two days. I kept texting you because I couldn't stop thinking about you."

Her astonished cry delighted him and, at Leon's BBQ and Grill, so did her enthusiasm for their rib tips and hot links coupled with coleslaw and macaroni salad. She truly had put the incident behind her and was back to herself.

"Man, I'm so glad Leon's came back to South Side," she said, forking up more meat. "Did you know it closed for a while?"

"I read that online, yes." Actually, he remembered Corey mentioning it one time in a face-to-face call on the rig. Olivia had told Corey about it, and he'd been outraged at losing the best BBQ in Chicago. But he didn't remember Corey mentioning the restaurant had returned. Had he known? Would it have made him happy?

Before Connor could dwell on it, Louisa held her fork up to his mouth. "I know you like sausage."

Usually he'd have been put off, having a date feed him, but with Louisa, it seemed sweet somehow. He took the bite and savored it. "You looking after me by feeding me?"

"Yep. Got a problem with that?"

"Actually, I was surprised to realize I don't," he said. "Next time we should order the shrimp. I read some good reviews about it. When I lived in the Bay Area, I used to have seafood all the time."

"Sounds like you miss it." Her voice was casual, but he knew she was curious about his old life.

"I do, I guess."

"Anything else you miss?" she asked.

Of course, there were a lot of things he missed. His family most of all. But he'd decided to keep his distance for a reason, hadn't he? "A clam chowder bread bowl."

"Still seafood."

He snorted. "Dutch-crunch bread. Sourdough bread."

She made a humming noise. "So you miss food... Tell me what you don't miss."

He didn't have to think about it. "The daily grind. The

pressure. Hell, I don't miss most of the people. Maybe I'm becoming antisocial."

"Or maybe you're just finding the new you," she said, leaning forward and kissing him softly on the mouth. "I like having a front-row seat."

His heart gave a hard kick in his chest. Her affection and enthusiasm were doing things to him, things he didn't have words for. For a man who was accustomed to writing everything from emails to inaugural speeches, it was uncomfortable not being able to define something this unusual.

"That sounds like one of your love notes."

"You've been inspiring a lot of them lately." She pushed her plate away. "I'm finished here. How about you?"

He'd been done for a while, content to watch her eat with her usual enthusiastic delight. "Also done. Ready to go or do you want something else?"

"I couldn't eat another bite, so yes, let's go."

He wondered what she'd decided about the rest of their evening. God, he wanted to be in her bed tonight.

She picked up her napkin and meticulously wiped her fingers, driving him a little crazy. "I'm assuming you'll get all prickly if I try and pay for my share or treat you?"

"If prickly is your sweet Midwestern way of saying pissed, then yes, I will." He caught their server's attention and dug into his pocket for his wallet.

"I've noticed you manage to draw people's attention to you rather artfully," she said, holding up her hand. "It's a combination of your intense energy and the masterful flick of your hand. I think I have it down."

When she demonstrated, he laughed. "If I looked like that, they'd kick me out for indecency."

She put her head on the hand she'd propped on the table, regarding him as if he were a subject worthy of perusal. "How did you become so commanding? Did you come out like that and order the doctor and nurses and your parents around the moment you were born? *Weigh me. Feed me. Diaper me. Name me something good.*"

Her impression of his voice was even worse than her attempt to copy his gesture to the server, but he didn't laugh. Her words reminded him what he'd been thinking earlier when they'd met Jax. "Actually, my mother named me Connor because it means strong-willed in Irish. So maybe I was a demanding baby."

She leaned closer. "Can I ask if you're close to your family?"

"Close isn't the word I'd use," he said cautiously. "I'm taking a time-out."

She hummed, the sound all but begging for more. "That must make the upcoming holidays hard."

His heart clutched. This Thanksgiving would be the first one he'd ever spent away from his family, and it was only a week and a half away. Flynn's thirtieth birthday was a week later. Right now, he'd best steel himself to not think about such things.

"Do you spend your holidays with your people at the shelter?" he asked, not wanting to dwell on thoughts of his family.

She gave him a look. "You're purposely changing the subject."

Connor paid the bill when the server brought it and ordered them a car. "Yes, and patience isn't your strong suit. I told you there are things I don't want to talk about."

"So impatience is one of my flaws," she said. "*Mysterious* is one of yours, I might add, but it won't deter me. I still like you."

He tapped her playfully on the nose because he couldn't help himself. "I like you too, Louisa."

Her eyes were shining like El Dorado's famed gold. "Since you admitted to not liking many people, I know that's an epic compliment. I think our car just pulled up. Come on and take me home."

He liked to think he knew what she meant, but he found himself wanting to make sure. "And what have you decided?" he asked, aware his voice had deepened.

She stood up and shrugged into her coat, an impish smile on her face. "In the hopes of being mysterious, I don't plan on telling you until we arrive at my domicile."

He rolled his eyes. "Domicile? Really, Louisa."

"Isn't that the kind of vocabulary mysterious people have? I can be mysterious."

That was when he knew for sure. When he stood, she trailed her hand playfully across his chest. "I want you more than anything," he said and meant it, "but I feel like I still need to ask. Doesn't it bother you not to know my full name?"

She put her hand in his, and that physical connection conveyed everything he saw in her golden eyes: her trust, her warmth, and her strength. "I wish I had more information about you, Connor. But that doesn't mean I don't know you. That's what I tell myself when I ask myself questions like that."

He cupped her cheek. "Yeah, somehow you *do* know me. You have since that night in the park. Okay, let's go."

He opened the door for her, and they hopped into the car waiting for them at the curb. When they arrived, he trained his eyes away from the Greystone building. He didn't want to be beset by old memories tonight—he wanted to make new ones with the beautiful woman next to him.

Louisa patted his thigh, thanked the driver, and then opened her door. "We're home."

Home? Off-balance, he fumbled with his seat belt. When he exited the car, she was standing under the amber lamplight with her hand out.

"Come upstairs with me."

She'd taken her gloves off, and somehow that felt significant, like they were striking a new pact that required skin-to-skin consent. His heart started to race as he reached for her hand and took it.

The force of that clasp was like a cannon hitting his very bones, and he remembered what he'd told her before.

This was another moment that would change things between them.

Chapter 11

Connor's face looked almost stricken in the lamplight as he took her hand.

Was he bothered by the emotion and intensity ratcheting up between them? She wasn't going to fight it, but he might need some help. She tugged him down the sidewalk to her front door.

He was coming home with her, would soon be inside her, and suddenly the joy of it rolled through her. She started laughing, and he looked at her funny, but his lips twitched as if her mood was affecting him. Good. All she wanted was to be alone with him, so after securing the front door, she raced up the stairs to her apartment, Connor right behind her. At the door, she had her keys out and her door unlocked in record time. The moment the door was closed, she turned and pressed him against it.

"I don't know if I can be all slow and gentle with you," she said, peeling off her coat and dropping it to the floor. "Now that you're here, all I can think about is having your hands on me and getting my hands on you."

His uncharacteristically wide smile made him look a decade younger. "We can do slow and gentle later. Louisa—not to be a killjoy, but we need to talk about precautions. I brought my last medical checkup for you to see. It was three months ago. I haven't had a partner since then."

"Oh," she said, her joy meter dipping at his practical tone. "I haven't been with anyone in a year. Long story. I'm fine too, but I don't have a test to show you. I should have figured you might want that. I was just going to suggest we use condoms, and we still should, but... God, why is this weird suddenly? If you wanted to see my last test results, you should have said so last night when you delivered your sexy sidewalk speech."

"Stop." He put his fingers to her mouth. "I don't need you to produce a test, or I would have asked, and yes, condoms are fine. I brought some."

"Me too," she said, smiling. "Lunchtime stop. Okay, shutting up. You did warn me that you didn't do romantic. Now, show me your test results. It will have your full name on it."

That brought out a laugh from him. "I already blacked out both the middle and last one."

She trailed her hands up his chest. God, she couldn't wait to see him naked. "Clever puss. Wait. It still might tell me something I don't know. Like, are you a universal blood donor? Does your blood pressure indicate chronic stress? And is your cholesterol high because you eat too much fried food?"

Shaking his head, he chuckled. "No. Yes. No. In that order. Louisa..."

"Yes, Connor."

"I very much want to make love to you too. I was only trying to protect you."

There it was again—his need to protect—she'd noticed it from the beginning, when the only argument that had budged him from that bench was her insistence she'd stay with him if he didn't come inside. But she didn't want protective Connor right now, so she decided to lighten the mood. "You know, I just got to thinking. Maybe this is weird for you because you know too much about me? I mean, where's the mystery when I've told you basically everything about my life? Maybe I need to do something to throw you for a loop. Like reveal that I really am a nun after all."

He laughed again. "Good one, but not an issue, thank God," he said, touching her bottom lip. "You know something that isn't one of your very few flaws?"

His tone turned sexy—at last!—so she matched him, saying, "And what would that be?"

"Your sense of humor," he said, stroking the seam of her lips. "The way you laugh. The way your eyes light up when you're excited. The way you look at me when you're happy."

She crossed her eyes to be funny. "How am I looking at you now?"

"We'll leave that alone, but right before you made that weird face, you were looking at me like you were happy. I find I like it. I...haven't made too many people happy. Not for a long while."

She pushed away the sadness that confession caused and linked her arms behind his neck. "Connor, I am happy when I'm with you. Now, take me. And I'll take you right back."

His colorful eyes flashed before he lowered his head and caught her mouth up in a fiery, passionate kiss filled with heat and tongue. That was all it took for the fire to engulf her. She moaned deep in her throat and started pulling off her clothes. His hands covered her breasts when her bra came off, and she let her head fall back as her insides tightened in response.

"Your clothes..." she managed, making him laugh.

He started tugging off his shirt and his pants, showing her the rest of that beautiful body, pausing only to grab a condom. Her hands found his fabulous ass, and he turned her to press her against the door. Soon they were skin-to-skin and totally out of control. Fitting her legs around him, he thrust in deep and hard.

"Oh, God!" She pushed back, locked in their rhythm. All she wanted was him. More of him. All of him. "Oh, yes." She emitted a loud keening noise as he hit the perfect spot.

Someone banged on the wall. Her mind flashed to her neighbors. "Maybe we should—"

"Forget them." He lifted her arms overhead and thrust into her faster. "Come for me."

She closed her eyes and fought the scream as she came in an avalanche of deep pulses. "God!" He growled deep as he thrust into her hard, making the door creak. "Yes!" Pressing his face into her neck, he cried out.

She slumped onto him, suspended in the air. "Don't... let your knees give out." She was out of breath and focused on holding on and sucking in oxygen.

"I won't drop you. Christ. Give me a sec." He was breathing just as hard, his skin slicked with sweat, and he still had her pressed full-length against the door. His hot body and the unmovable cold door made the perfect contrast. She realized it might be the only way to have sex.

As the buzzing and tingling in her body began to soften, she became aware of how his hands covered her, firm yet gentle. Perfect. "Can I ask you something?" she whispered.

He kissed her shoulder and then laid a trail of kisses down her neck and across to her mouth. His lips settled over hers, and the emotions she felt from him—and her—made her chest swell as if it were a sea sponge. Pulling on her bottom lip in the most delicious way, he finally released her mouth.

"Now you can ask me," he said, letting her hands go but still keeping her pressed between him and the door.

"Are you some superhuman sex god or have I just had sex with suboptimal lovers? Because that wasn't like any other sex I've ever had. Usually I'd worry about a compliment like this going to your head, but seriously, Connor. If you're some superhuman sex god, we need to create a training program *you* can teach. Every woman in the world needs to have sex like this."

His mouth was twitching. "Of all the things I expected you to say... Louisa, I am not superhuman, but I'll take sex god as my new moniker."

"You didn't answer me, sex god," she said, aware there was some emotional revelation layered under her light tone.

He studied her in the lamplight in her living room before saying, "No, that's not like any sex I've had either."

Kissing him full on the mouth, she linked her arms around his neck, enjoying the feel of him still inside her. Was he still hard? She shifted against him and smiled when his eyes flashed.

"Yes, I want you again," he said.

"So I'm a sex god too," she said, doing her best to dance in his arms. "Oh, shit. My neighbor heard me. I don't know whether I should be embarrassed or unabashed."

"Never been that loud before?" He grinned. "You're about to get loud again. Maybe we should find your bedroom after I get cleaned up in the bathroom. You have pillows in there, right? I can help you muffle it if you want."

"No pillows in the bathroom," she said, her lips twitching.

"Funny."

She kissed him, long and languid, and he kissed her back. God, when had the kissing been this wonderful? Right, never, just like sex with him. Then he cupped the back of her neck, and she felt her heart swell again. All she wanted to do was nestle into him. Yeah, she'd never been the sort to lie to herself, and she knew she'd tipped over the side of liking him into something more dangerous.

She'd fallen for Connor.

"Bedroom and now," she ordered.

"In a minute," he said, his mouth traveling to the soft side of her neck and collarbone. "You look beautiful in this light, and I happen to like having you pressed against the door."

"I was thinking before it might be the only way to have sex," she said, her eyes closing as he slid his mouth along the underside of her jaw, "but I'm ready for you to prove me wrong. Fair warning. When you let me up from being pressed against this door, I plan on kissing, licking, and touching every square inch of you like the sex god I am."

"I'm good with that plan," he said, stepping back from the door. "Let me make a quick stop in your bathroom, and then we're finding your bed. I might need the pillow for myself."

They both did, and her neighbor banged on the wall again at one point, but she didn't stop. People in apartments had as much right to great sex as anyone, and sure they should be respectful, but tonight wasn't going down like that. Not when Connor was...

She moaned again. He slid inside her again. On and on it went, until she was sure she'd memorized ever angle, every ridge, every shape of him. When her bedside clock proclaimed it was four fifteen in the morning, she realized that was why her eyes were drooping. She kissed his shoulder, pressing into the hand caressing her breast. He liked to play, and she'd discovered she did too. He'd lingered over her as much as she had him, and glorious didn't describe it enough.

"You falling asleep?" His voice was a deep, baritone rumble of pure masculine sex.

"Apparently even sex gods need sleep," she said, cuddling into him. "Stay. It's cold out, and I'd really like to have sex with you in my kitchen over my morning oatmeal."

He froze for only a second, but they'd been so in tune, she felt it. Pushing up, she studied him in the warm lamplight.

"You can also go, of course," she said, ignoring the hitch in her heart at the thought. "Do whatever would make you happy. Only promise me we're going to do this tomorrow night, because I don't think I can face the day knowing otherwise."

She said it lightly, but she was awake enough to realize it was true. This couldn't be a one-time thing.

Leaning forward slowly, he settled his mouth over hers. She almost sighed at the gentleness, the sweet warmth in the kiss.

"I'll stay, but only if you tell me the truth."

She blinked at his tone. "What?"

"Do you snore, Louisa?" he asked.

"When I'm this replete from sex, I have no idea. We're in a whole new universe here."

He laughed.

"Do you?" She nudged him.

"No. I wouldn't allow something as pedestrian as snoring."

"Of course you wouldn't," she said, cupping his jaw. "I like your beard. I've never been with anyone with facial hair, and I was happy to discover the benefits I'd heard about are true."

"Are they now?" he asked, sliding his hand up her thigh. "Want to discover any more benefits?"

She kissed him slowly, this time putting all of her emotions into it. When he didn't back away, she put her hand over his heart. He covered it, and she started to glow inside, not from pleasure but from pure happiness. Breaking the kiss, she smiled at him.

"This is one of the best nights ever," she said, making sure to keep it light. His problems hadn't gone away because she wanted to help him fix them. That would take time—and willingness on his part. "I just wanted you to know that. In a totally non-weird way."

"Back at you." He picked up her hand and kissed it. He

stared at it, obviously thinking. "Louisa, what would you say if I told you I was a billionaire?"

"Because all sex gods are billionaires?" She laughed and patted his cheek with her free hand. "Is that a Christian Grey reference?"

"God, no!"

His horrified response sent her into giggles. "I knew guys watched those movies or read the books. Now me... What would you say if I told you I really did have an inclination to become a nun, but this night with you changed all that?"

He didn't laugh, but she did. Snorted too, in fact.

She put his arm around her waist, aware his body wasn't as loose as it had been moments ago. "Come on. Let's sleep. I have a feeling I'm going to be a little late to work, but I can't be too late."

He kissed the back of her neck and embraced her. "Louisa, you are like no one else."

"Damn straight," she said, closing her eyes. "Now, be quiet. This sex god needs some z's." She nestled into him with a final thought.

With his sense of humor, maybe he was actually a comedian.

Chapter 12

WHEN CONNOR WOKE UP BESIDE LOUISA, ALL HE COULD think was how he'd tried to tell her.

Okay, maybe not his last name or how he'd gotten fired, but he'd tried to share *something*. And what had she done? Laughed, thinking he was joking. He supposed he should have expected it. What billionaire would willingly stay at a fleabag motel? A desperate one. Deep down, though, he knew it wouldn't matter to her. Shit, he was going to start sounding like one of her love notes. *She liked him for him and nothing else.*

Up until now, he'd only experienced that kind of connection with his family. He wasn't the easiest person to like or get along with. He knew that. Too driven. Too intense. Too...much. Sure, those were the hallmarks of a successful businessman, but it didn't create a warm-and-fuzzy social circle. The women he'd casually dated in recent years had been chosen for convenience since his job had been his full-time commitment. None had made much of an impression long term, and he hadn't meant for them to.

Until Louisa.

She redefined making an impression. In fact, she was leaving an indelible mark.

He couldn't go back to sleep. Seemed unable to. Louisa

mumbled and nudged him. She wasn't a quiet sleeper. No, she was probably charging through her dreams with gusto, just like she did in her waking hours. Her alarm would be sounding soon enough.

Pushing aside her dark hair, he couldn't help himself. He kissed her neck softly so as not to wake her, luxuriating in the softness of her golden skin. She mumbled again, and he smiled.

The moment seemed to freeze, and he took inventory of himself. He felt peace. And something more, something he hadn't felt in so long he had to search for the word. Hopeful. Then she clutched the arm he had around her, and he felt something else: warmth for another human being. He wasn't ready to call it love. Truth be told, he'd never been in love before, even in his only long-term relationship. But he felt a warmth unfold deep inside him whenever he was with her, and she seemed to feel the same way.

The bedside lamps were still on, and he took a moment to study her bedroom. Like the rest of her apartment, the room was small in size, barely able to fit the queen bed. Not surprisingly, she'd chosen a bright ocean blue for the walls. More pictures of her and her family were on the dresser alongside a glass vase filled with white seashells. Not from Lake Michigan clearly, since only mussel shells could be found there. He knew. His grandparents had taken them swimming many times when their family had visited the city.

His family.

What was he going to do about them?

He knew what he planned to do with South Side, but he didn't have a clue what to do about them. If it weren't for them, he'd gladly put his entire past in a trunk and cast it into the deepest water in the Atlantic Ocean, so to speak.

His days as a CEO were done. He knew that, had made his peace with it. Was relieved to find he didn't miss it or the feeling of constantly being bombarded by different people. In fact, maybe he'd be happier in a solitary profession. Buying real estate and coming up with solid investment offerings might be just his thing.

Despite his success so far, it would take him a long time to pump some life into South Side. He knew that. Arthur had been right about the political machine. The imprint of Chicago's bureaucracy and political system could be seen in every single zoning law and local development requirement he'd combed through over the past few days. The people in control didn't want to relinquish any of their power. But he wouldn't give up. If his strategy worked, maybe there were other cities and neighborhoods he could start helping, places where he could put his expertise to some good.

Oh man, he was falling for her. He waited a moment for his stomach to knot or his heart rate to climb to aerobic levels. None of that happened. He only felt warmth and peace. That was significant, wasn't it?

Nestling closer, he enjoyed the feel of her body conforming to his own. Awe built inside his gut. When had he ever had a night like last night? She seemed to be of the same mind. Didn't that mean something?

The screeching of an alarm jolted him—and her, if her elbow connecting with him was an indication.

"Stop that!" she shouted.

Something crashed, Louisa cursed, and then the grating sound ceased.

"Oh, God, it can't be seven already," she said, moaning. "I'm too tired to get up."

He was filled with energy. "What time do you need to be in?"

She wiggled, situating their bodies even closer. "Nine, but I thought at one point last night seven made sense since we can't keep our hands off each other. I thought sex, shower, oatmeal. Then work."

"I like the way your mind works. Practical."

"I try." She stroked the arm holding her. "Did you sleep?"

"Yeah, some. I don't sleep much as a rule." Although he'd been sleeping more since coming to Chicago. Until last night, he'd thought it had something to do with his punishing ninety-minute runs. Now he wondered if it had something to do with Louisa and his new goal of turning the neighborhood around—a cause he believed in, and not just because of Olivia and the kids.

"I'm glad you stayed," Louisa muttered, sleep still in her voice.

"So am I," he said, kissing her neck. "Go back to sleep for a while."

She went slack again, and he realized it was a good opportunity to do something for her. He slid out of bed and headed to the family room for his pants. The soft morning light was coming in through her front windows, and he fought the screaming desire to look out to where he'd once lived.

Instead, he walked into her small kitchen, smiling at the funny knickknacks on the stove: a Chicago Bulls spoon holder, a cow and pig set of salt and pepper shakers, and a rooster egg timer. A memory flashed of a couple of Corey's finds for the apartment—a hula girl spoon holder and a set of the ugliest dogs-playing-poker shot glasses. Louisa would have loved him.

Stop that, Connor, he told himself. *Make the damn oatmeal.*

After opening a couple of mostly bare cabinets, he located the oatmeal, trying to keep his mind in check. He'd have to tell her he concurred with her choice of oatmeal. Steel cut Irish oats were the only way to go in his opinion. Opening up the refrigerator, he found a half-dozen eggs and a bag of grated cheddar cheese. But no sausage or bacon. He fished out the blueberries and settled into the rhythm of making her oatmeal. He stirred and stirred it, trying to ignore the building across the street and memories of Corey.

Finally, he had to turn the oatmeal off since it was more than cooked. Walking into her family room, he decided to face the specter across the street. Maybe he could stomach it now. After last night, he felt calmer than he'd been since the accident.

He crossed to the front window and looked out. In their haste, she'd forgotten to draw the curtains, so he had a clear view of the Greystone.

So many fabulous memories existed for him in that rickety old apartment. The past tenant had marked their kids' heights on the doorframe, and Corey used to talk about little Alice and Peter and how he couldn't wait to have kids of his own someday so he could tally their height the same way. Back then, Connor had joked right back about naming his own kids something like Alexander and Victoria, leader-like names, not ones from fairy tales like *Alice in Wonderland* or *Peter Pan*, even if the latter had been his favorite childhood book.

Corey had given him a serious look and said something he'd never forget. "Connor, your problem is you don't believe in fairy tales anymore. Maybe you never did. But man, sometimes I wish you thought the world was a brighter place."

Everyone used to say Corey was the positive, easygoing one and Connor the practical, driven one. Together, they'd balanced each other out. Which was part of the reason Connor felt so lost without him. He'd lost his silver lining.

Grief tore through him, and he pressed his forehead to the cold window, wishing he could travel back in time to those days he and his cousin had spent across the street. *I fucking miss you, man. Dammit. I'm so sorry.*

His nose started to drip, and his chest grew so tight he could barely breathe. Jesus, he couldn't lose it. Not here. Not now.

He hadn't cried a single day since he'd gone home from the funeral, a ceremony as empty as Corey's casket. His cousin's body had been claimed by the sea, something that had made it even harder to sit there stoically while the priest rambled on about eternal peace and resting places while Olivia and her boys sobbed quietly beside him.

"Shit," he said, rubbing his nose as he stepped away from the window, releasing deep breaths.

Arms banded around him from behind.

"Don't touch me right now, Louisa." He needed time to pull himself together, but he could only do that if he was by himself.

"I'm not letting go, so deal with it," she said, tightening her grip on him.

He was glad she couldn't see him since his nose was dripping as he continued to suck in oxygen to calm himself down. He squeezed his eyes shut to keep the tears from falling, and they burned like whiskey in the back of his throat. If she'd said anything or tried to see his face, he would have stalked out. But she didn't. She held him hard, her face pressed against the center of his back, a quiet, compassionate warrior.

When he felt more in control, he put his hands on her arms holding him. "I'm okay."

She kissed his back, and the gesture blew through him, closing his throat again. Damn, she had a way of eliciting the most incredible reactions in him.

"You made me oatmeal," she said, her voice soft. "That's another first for me. Thank you."

She was thanking *him*? "It's only oatmeal. You were right. You don't have anything here. You should eat your blueberries up. They're in their final hours."

He felt her shift and walk around him. Girded himself to face her. She was in a long navy robe, her eyes steady, her face calm. He fisted his hands.

"You going to say anything?" he asked.

"Do you want me to?" she asked, her tone just as direct.

"No," he said, needing to release a deep breath that rose up. "How much time do you have? I can heat up your oatmeal while you shower."

She took his hand. "There's plenty of time for what I have in mind."

Leading him back to the bedroom, he watched as she shrugged out of her robe with one hand. He stripped his pants off and sat down on the bed, watching her. She hadn't run from him moments ago. He wasn't sure she ever would. Peace settled over him as she stood naked in the morning light coming in through the windows, looking at him.

Finally, he stood. It felt important that he should be the one to go to her. He touched her face. "You are so beautiful." The words didn't feel adequate to describe her or what she was coming to mean to him, so he kissed her softly and took her back to bed.

She rolled until she was on top of him. Straddling him, she leaned over his body until she was inches away from his mouth. "And I think you're pretty wonderful."

He felt wonderful, he realized, even after the punch of grief he'd felt moments before. "*Louisa*," he said, stroking her back, his earlier awe returning. "Last night changed everything."

"I know," she responded, those beautiful golden eyes promising the world.

He wanted the world he saw there, he realized, and then he was pulling her against him. His eyes closed, and she kissed him gently on the mouth, moving to his jawline and then his neck. In her every touch, he felt something his mind could only define as loving tenderness. He'd never experienced anything like it with anyone else.

Cradling her neck, he kissed her back, wanting to pour himself into her, to give back to her the very tenderness she was giving to him. He knew what she'd gone through to become the woman she was, this tiny pillar of beauty and strength, and part of him wished he could have been there for her back then—when she was hurting and lost and the past was licking at her heels.

She shifted on him, and he felt her gently roll a condom onto him. Then she was taking him inside her slowly, so very slowly he could feel her heartbeat with every inch. When he finally opened his eyes, hers were waiting for him.

An emotion he'd never imagined filled him—peace, warmth, and awe all mixed into one. Her open gaze seemed to peer through him, but then the merest touch of a smile appeared on her face. He felt his mouth move in response as happiness entered the powerful chain of emotions cresting through him. His heart seemed to take flight in his chest, and with that lightness, he began to thrust into her. Slowly. As slowly as they'd started, so too did they finish, their eyes holding the whole time.

Her breath caught when she came, and her body tightened around him, but still she held his gaze as if unwilling to miss a single moment of their joining. He held her hips as he came, forcing himself to stay with her, look at her, be with her. Then she smiled and stroked his face, kissing him softly on the mouth. He pressed her head to his chest, and they held each other that way for a while.

He became aware that their heartbeats were beating in time, and the significance of it brought a smile to his lips. Stroking her back, he kissed the top of her head. She was precious to him in a way no one ever had been.

He was in love with her.

It didn't matter that it had happened in a nanosecond or that he hadn't told her everything. It was an indisputable truth the universe had opened to him. Before he could decide if he was ready to share those words with her, she leaned up and kissed him on the mouth. Smiled. And then she was heading to the bathroom.

"Care to shower with me? It's not the most spacious,

but I can share so long as you play nice in the shower. No water-in-the-face tactics or sneaky touches with the wash-cloth. Oh, and my hot water heater isn't the greatest. Fif-teen minutes is about all the hot water I get. If you'd like, you can use my shower crayons. Sometimes I write myself notes, and sometimes I doodle."

This is what she wanted to say right now? Of course it was. "Shower crayons? I thought you might want to talk about what just happened."

She covered her breasts with her hands. He wasn't sure if it was because of the cold or modesty. "It was pretty pow-erful. Sometimes words can't do justice to an experience. I'm good with that right now."

He cleared his throat. "Okay. When you find the right words, I'd be open to sharing mine."

"I'll keep that in mind." Her mouth tipped up on the right. "I do have a thought I want to say, though."

When she paused, he sat up. "Tell me."

She picked up her robe and shrugged into it. "You know I like you. A lot. After last night, you couldn't help but notice it. But you made me oatmeal, and you trusted me with your hurts this morning, so I wanted to mention that you might consider calling my old counselor, Dr. Jo-siah Edmonton. He's in the book, so to speak, and special-izes on working with tough people like us."

He braced at the words, and she held up a hand, wor-rying her lip.

"He's not your regular counselor. He might be able to help you with your grief and anything else you want to talk to him about. I only wanted to share it because I know you're coming out of some tough things, and it might smooth the path to get some help."

His family had suggested it, and he'd pushed them away. Other people talked to shrinks. Doing that would mean he was really out of control. He hadn't been willing to admit that. And he sure as hell didn't want to tell a total stranger private details about his life. Still didn't. "It's not easy for me to consider it."

She nodded. "I didn't want to go at first either, but it was a big aspect of what worked for me, and since you seem to admire me for getting past my baggage, I wanted to mention it. Connor, I want you to be able to look across the street and not get so upset. Only remember good things."

God, he did too. Was it even possible?

"Now, I'm stepping into the shower," she said, giving him a bright smile. "I hope you'll join me."

He sat there, mulling over her words. If anyone else had suggested someone to him, he'd have dismissed it. But Louisa was different. She'd been where he was, and if that man had helped her get out, maybe he needed to consider it.

"These shower crayons are getting lonely," she called, "threatening an ugly strike if they aren't used quickly. Especially the red and green ones. They're the ones to watch. You need to get in here stat before I get caught in the crossfire."

Laughter erupted from him before he could think. She'd have known he was stewing out here. Maybe she was stewing in there, and this was her way of dealing with it.

He joined her in the shower, aware he had something else he needed to think about.

She deserved to know who he really was.

Chapter 13

"WHAT DO YOU MEAN WE LOST THE BID FOR THE PROPerty?"

Louisa's outraged question stopped Clara outside the woman's office at Sunflower Alley, where they'd come for the Friday night cooking competition. Hargreaves needed to prep, and she and Arthur had decided to come early with him so they could talk to the shelter's staff and clients, including the retired math teacher who'd greeted them at reception. The lovely woman had said she was finding renewed purpose in her supposed golden years, something Clara understood all too well.

"How could there have been a last-minute bidder? No one wanted that broken-down old school building."

Clara imagined she knew the identity of that bidder and cast a look at Arthur and Hargreaves beside her. "Oh, no."

"That doesn't sound good," Arthur commented, looking so cute in the long-sleeved black shirt she'd had made for him. "Team Hargreaves" paraded across it in white text.

"Sound like anyone we know, do you think?" she asked.

"I can't believe it!" she heard Boxer exclaim. "How is this even possible?"

"Shh, I'm trying to find out," Louisa shot back. "I thought this was a slam dunk."

"We should probably step away, Madam," Hargreaves said, gesturing to the hallway they'd come down.

"Eavesdropping is part of good journalism," Arthur said, craning his ear toward the doorway.

She took his arm. "No, Hargreaves is right, dear. Let her tell us if she wants to."

"You ready to have your butt kicked?" someone asked. "Because Carter's in the kitchen with his game face on hard."

"I beg your pardon," she said before Arthur could open his mouth.

When she turned around, she spied Damien Evans standing a few feet away with a tall, slender black man with whom he shared an incredible resemblance in the brow line and mouth. She'd met Louisa's brother briefly the day of her million-dollar donation and found him to be a cheeky but likeable fellow. "I see your usual charm isn't suffering in this weather, Damien."

"Never, and you look as lovely as ever, Clara," Damien said with a flirtatious wink. "Good to see everyone, although I wish I was the one putting the smackdown on tonight. Louisa wrenched my arm behind my back until I gave up my spot for Hargreaves."

"Forgive him," the other man said, stepping forward with his hand out, a big smile on his face. "His competitiveness sometimes gets the better of his sense. I'm Horace Evans, but everyone calls me Coach or Coach Evans. You must be Clara. I'm happy to meet the woman who made my girl's dream come true."

His hand engulfed hers, and she craned her neck to look up into his radiant face. "It's wonderful to meet you, Coach Evans, and an honor to help your daughter with her important work here. This is my husband, Arthur Hale."

"A pleasure to meet you, Mr. Hale. I understand you're writing an article on the homeless. It's wonderful to have a journalist of your caliber writing about this problem. It affects a lot of families and communities."

"Indeed it does," Arthur said. "Good to meet you too, Coach. Please excuse my costume. My wife insisted I wear this ghastly T-shirt. Of course, she was supposed to wear one too, but it didn't go with her outfit at the last minute."

She waved her hand. "Hargreaves agreed with my fashion choices for this evening. Excuse us, Coach Evans, for the domestic banter. Please meet Clifton Hargreaves, my longtime assistant."

"Sometimes she calls him her butler," Arthur said, "and other times her associate. I still haven't gotten it straight."

She elbowed him, making him harrumph, and Damien spouted delighted laughter.

"A pleasure to meet you, Coach Evans," Hargreaves said with a formal bow. "As for your son, I regret to inform you, sir, butlers do not get their 'butts' kicked, regardless of how much of a game face Mr. Carter has put on."

Damien whistled. "Tonight is going to be fun. I can feel it. Damn, why didn't I think to make T-shirts for my team?"

"Perhaps because you don't have the following you imagine, sir," Hargreaves said, his demeanor as calm, cool, and collected as ever.

"Butler trash talk!" Coach Evans gave Damien a friendly push. "Son, be glad you're not facing Mr. Hargreaves here. You'd have your hands full tonight."

"Speaking of followings..." Hargreaves said, gesturing to Louisa as she appeared in the doorway of her office. She was indeed wearing a Team Hargreaves T-shirt, dear girl, but Clara's attention was on the frown stamped on her face. She also looked a little pale, her normal radiance gone.

"Sis, you wore his colors and not Carter's?" Damien asked, his mouth gaping. "How could you do Carter like that?"

"Damien, zip it." Coach Evans strode over to his daughter. "Can't you see she's upset? What's the matter, honey?"

"Long story," Louisa mumbled. "Not now."

Boxer appeared, also in a Team Hargreaves T-shirt, bless him.

Damien snorted and said, "Et tu, Brute?" under his breath.

Shooting him a look, Boxer put his hand on the upset woman's shoulder. "Louisa, you might as well get it out. The building we've been eyeing for the training program was sold to another bidder."

"You're kidding!" Coach Evans said. "That piece of junk? It's been all but condemned."

"I know." Louisa rubbed the spot between her brows. "I never saw this coming."

Clara caught Arthur's steely blue look. What in the hell was Connor thinking? Had he bought that property on purpose?

"I didn't miss the cook-off, did I?" she heard Connor ask and looked over to see him coming down the hallway.

He was giving his best nonchalant smile, nodding to them like they weren't family, and Clara had half a mind to pop him.

Arthur seemed to sense her outrage because he stepped over and put his arm around her waist, squeezing her gently.

"No, you didn't," Louisa said, stepping forward with her arms out. "Just some crappy news."

Suddenly her arms were around him—a declaration if Clara had ever seen one, given that her father stood across from them. The way Connor's mouth slackened said he recognized it too, but he held her to him.

Clara tightened her lips together to keep her own surprise from showing. Arthur made a humming sound in his throat. Oh, he was probably delighted at the sight, being that he'd dubbed himself the Matchmaking Jedi. But Clara wasn't so certain this was a good idea given that Connor had just bought that property out from under her. Did the boy have no scruples whatsoever?

"What happened?" Connor asked, tilting Louisa's chin up.

That's when Clara saw it in the way their eyes locked and held.

They've fallen for each other.

"I don't believe we've met," Coach Evans said, stepping forward. "I'm Louisa's father. And you're—"

"Dad, you know this is Connor because I told you all about him," Louisa said in exasperation. "In fact, let's shake off this unhappy news with something positive. I talked to Dad, and we'd like to invite all of you to join us for Thanksgiving next week if you don't have plans."

"What?" Connor asked, his arms dropping to his sides. "You don't—"

"I'd like you to come, Connor, and Clara, you and your fabulous entourage are more than welcome. If you don't have another invitation…"

"We usually spend it with family," Arthur said, giving Connor a knowing look, "but we expected to be here in the Windy City a while longer, so we'd be happy to join you. Won't we, Clara?"

She blinked. This was her first Thanksgiving since she'd reconciled with the Merriam family, her first year happily married to the man she'd loved all her life, and she'd had big dreams about how it would come off. She thought they'd do Thursday with the Merriams in California and then come back for a huge feast with the Hale family on Sunday in Dare Valley.

But with the Connor situation, they hadn't nailed down their plans. No Merriam wanted to talk about having the holiday without Connor, and she'd been reluctant to upset them by mentioning it. She stifled her disappointment and turned to her husband. "Are you sure you don't want to pop back to Dare Valley or elsewhere, dear?"

"Maybe you two should talk about it and get back to us," Coach Evans said amiably. "How about you, Connor? We'd love to have you. It will be a full house. We invite a lot of my players who don't have anywhere to go, and Boxer here usually comes. My son cooks all day at the restaurant, and honestly, we don't miss him."

"Haha," Damien said. "You miss me hard."

Boxer made a rude noise. "Maybe your food. Coach moans and groans about my cranberry delight, but he always has a helping."

Coach Evans grabbed the man and jostled him, and they both laughed. "It's not so much a delight as it is good hospitality to eat your fixings."

"I'll get back to you on coming. I appreciate the invitation." Connor looked at Louisa, his hand grazing her arm. "Now, will you tell me what happened?"

She made a face. "Just a little setback. I'll tell you later. We need to get going with the cook-off."

"Tell me now," he said, putting his hands on her shoulders. "You're obviously upset."

Arthur nudged Clara as if she weren't already watching the scene.

"Fine," Louisa said, a frown reemerging. "The property we wanted for the training program you've so awesomely written up was sold to another party."

Clara watched as his entire face flinched. "What?" Connor said, obviously shocked.

Arthur squeezed her elbow as if to say, *he didn't know*. Well, that was a relief, she supposed. But if he'd put in the winning bid, would his ignorance matter to Louisa?

"No one has wanted to touch that property in two years due to the asbestos and plumbing issues," Louisa said. "We put in an offer the moment Clara's check cleared, but we lost to someone else. I still can't believe it. Connor, you don't think someone got word I wanted it and bought it in the hopes they could get more money out of me?"

"No, I'm certain that's not the case," he said, his brow knit. "Don't worry, Louisa. We'll find somewhere else. There are plenty of properties for sale near the industrial parks—"

"But those aren't in South Side," Louisa said, her golden eyes firing. "It has to be here."

"Why?" Connor asked, his tone firmer than usual. "The jobs aren't here."

But wasn't that the boy's plan? To generate jobs? Was he thinking he had to put the training program somewhere else in order to make the neighborhood safer for the bigger stores he was hoping to attract? Clara hated this infernal arrangement or she would have asked him outright.

Louisa put her hands on her waist, staring right back at him. "This program needs to be in South Side because the people are here, Connor. They can't be traveling to a training center so far away from their community."

"They'll come if they want to be trained," he shot back.

"Okay, kids," Boxer said with a strained chuckle. "Let's table this for now. Maybe losing the asbestos heap is a good thing. That property might have been a money pit."

"So why did someone else want it so bad?" Louisa asked. "Okay, I'm letting it go. I don't want to ruin tonight's cook-off. Like Connor said, we'll find somewhere else. In South Side."

"We'll need to talk about that," Connor said, frowning. "But as you said, let's focus on the cook-off. Don't I get a Team Hargreaves T-shirt?"

Clara had to bite her lip not to give Connor a caustic reply. Oh, they were going to have it out tomorrow. She didn't dare talk to him about this situation at the shelter where someone might overhear, but she wouldn't keep quiet any longer.

Especially if he and Louisa were in love with each

other. How in the world had that happened so fast? Louisa didn't even know who he was yet. Usually Clara liked to believe love conquered all, but Connor's secret agenda for the neighborhood seemed to be at odds with Louisa's hopes for the training program. She was suddenly afraid nothing good could come of this, and she felt squeezed to death between a rock and a hard place being both the shelter's benefactor and Connor's aunt.

"Another traitor to Carter?" Louisa's brother said dramatically. "How did he incur so much opposition?"

"Boxer and I only did it to mess with him," Louisa said, sharing a conspiratorial glance with the tall man in question. "We're taking them off before the show starts. Neutrality is everything."

"I'd be happy to give you my T-shirt, Connor," Arthur said, tugging at his own. "I look like an idiot."

"You look fine," Clara said, aware acid was lacing her tone. Oh, this situation was getting to her, all right. "Louisa, shall we see to the cook-off now? I'm sure Hargreaves would like to set up and get his game on, as Damien said. Again, I'm sorry for your disappointment today, dear. If there's anything I can do, *anything at all*, you let me know."

Because right now, she was wearing a Team Louisa shirt, not a Team Connor shirt.

CHAPTER 14

A SOUTH SIDE training program that wasn't in South Side?

What was Connor thinking? Louisa was trying to let her disappointment go, but Connor's comments had fired her up. So far, they'd been on the same page. They'd spent every free minute together for the past four days. They'd hit a few more South Side staples like Parisi's Drive-In, but he'd upped his romantic quotient, or so he'd said, by taking her to things he knew she'd like: the thirty-three-foot sledding hill outside Soldier Field and Simone's Bar for trivia night.

Once their evening out concluded, he'd come back to her place and they'd make love, sometimes playfully and sometimes so raw, she'd simply closed her eyes and held him afterward, not needing to say anything. A few times, she'd felt like he wanted to tell her something about his past, but they'd either been interrupted or he'd thought otherwise. She knew he'd tell her when he was ready.

She felt more in tune with him than she'd ever felt with another person, body, mind, and soul. Was it starting to slip away?

"*Focus, Louisa,*" Carter said, sharpening his knives with eerie calm. "Now that you've tossed the Team Hargreaves shirt—still can't believe you'd hit good ol' Carter below the belt like that—I need you to MC the hell out of tonight."

She shook herself. The aluminum panels leading to the dining room were still closed and would remain so until right before the cook-off began, but she could hear the murmurings from the other side. They had press out there and one hundred guests from their three-tiered system. Some had paid an entry fee to attend the charity event, the tickets for the public selling out in minutes, and a lottery was held for those who hadn't acted quickly enough or didn't want to pay the full amount. Of course, anyone who'd lived in their shelter as a longer-term resident could attend for free. Drop-in homeless clients in need of a meal could grab a sandwich pack from the back of the shelter.

Carter was right. She needed to get her game face on. Especially since Clara's donation had hit the press. She'd be introducing the couple to the public tonight, along with Hargreaves as the guest chef, of course, and she and Boxer had also decided she would be announcing the future training program. It made sense to do it on the same night she introduced their benefactors, besides which, Carter figured largely into their plans for the future. He would head up the expanded culinary program, and ultimately, they were going to open a restaurant staffed by their trainees. That was going to excite people since they went nuts over Carter's food. She was going to ask for more donations for the training program tonight, and she knew they'd get them.

Of course, she'd hoped to have the property bought so she could announce the center's future address, but dammit, they were going to find another property close to the shelter. Proximity made sense, not only logistically speaking—they could transport food from the kitchen program to feed their clients at this location—but also in terms of making it easier for her and Boxer to oversee things.

Her spirits dipped a moment. That location had been so perfect, and it had been the right size and price.

"You're still brooding," she heard her friend call out.

"Keep sharpening your knives, Carter," she told him as she clapped her hands together to refocus herself. "I think you're going to have your hands full with Hargreaves over there."

"Thank you, miss," Hargreaves said, sitting calmly in a chair beside the stainless-steel counter, his black apron blending into the rest of his black uniform. "I believe 'my game' is fully locked and loaded."

"Great, then I'm starting the show," Louisa said, leaving the kitchen and heading straight to the head table in the crowded, noisy dining hall.

People started to clap as she appeared, and a few cabbie-like whistles pierced her eardrums.

"Cook-off, cook-off, cook-off," someone started to chant. Others joined in, and then the foot stomping started, shaking the floor like it would have at a Queen concert during "We Will Rock You."

She welcomed the energy and picked up the microphone, scanning the crowd and nodding to familiar faces. Arthur and Clara were sitting next to her father, but she didn't see Connor. Had he disappeared? He hadn't been himself earlier. Had she upset him by mentioning the counselor?

She scanned the dining hall and spotted him lounging in the back against the exit, almost as if he worried about having a quick getaway. At least he'd stayed. Relief went through her. She'd had to persuade him to come, and when she'd suggested introducing him as the brains behind their new training plan, he'd balked, saying he wanted to keep a low profile. She hadn't pressed.

When she'd told her dad earlier today that she was dating someone she wanted to invite for Thanksgiving, he'd asked for his name. He hadn't been happy to learn she didn't have a last name to go with the first. But he trusted her, and in the end, he'd said he knew she would be smart and to go ahead and invite him. As she studied his hooded face, she wondered again about his story. It was becoming harder not to know it, not because she feared anything bad, but because it was a measure of trust.

All right, Louisa, enough of this. Start the damn show.

"Good eve-ning, Sun-flower Al-ley fa-ns!" she drew out like a professional wrestling announcer, getting into character. "Are you ready for the cook-off?"

Boxer blew the air horn he'd begged her to allow for the competitions, and she laughed, feeling lighter already.

"Our man, Chef Carter, is in the house," she said, "ready to face a dark horse competitor, Clifton Hargreaves. Our guest chef originally hails from London, and he works with the wonderful couple who have just given this shelter its largest donation to date, Clara Merriam Hale and Arthur Hale. Please stand up."

People rained enthusiastic applause. Clara waved regally, and Arthur waved as if batting away the attention, his cheeks reddening in embarrassment.

"You've read about them. You've wondered about them. Let me tell you more about them."

She started walking to the right in front of the crowd, making eye contact with people as she slinked across the space.

"She's a humanitarian finding her true purpose in life at last, she says, and he's the Pulitzer Prize-winning journalist who founded the legendary paper *The Western Independent*."

A spatter of applause sounded throughout the audience, and she recognized some of it coming from reporters in the front. Yeah, they'd heard of Arthur.

"They're living their best life in so-called retirement, according to Clara, and have one of the most incredible love stories I've ever heard. They first met decades ago, and after reuniting this year, they married this summer at nearly eighty."

More applause.

"They're helping a village in Kenya distribute an herbal healing flower to the world, and in their spare time, somehow they managed to find out about us at Sunflower Alley and offer their help. For which I am eternally grateful." She blew them a kiss.

They blew her one right back, and she dramatically caught it and touched her heart. "I hope you have a chance to meet them. Frankly, I want to be them when I grow up."

"Me too!" someone shouted from the audience, and laughter rippled through the crowd.

"Arthur, Clara, and Hargreaves, thanks for being here tonight and celebrating our work at Sunflower Alley. Their million-dollar donation is going to help so many people, and I'm pleased to announce it will fund a new job training program I've always wanted to provide to this community. It's going to rock South Side. Anyone want to hear how?"

"Yes!" someone shouted.

She danced across the front of the audience again, doing her thing. "You know Chef Carter, right? Well, he's going to head up an expanded culinary program. Right now, we've been training three people a year, but that's going to multiply like pancakes at a pancake breakfast. And do you know what else? Chef Carter wants to open a restaurant with the school so *all of you* can enjoy his cooking. How does that sound?"

People whistled and cheered, and someone started chanting, "Chef," and it gathered force. She joined in, smiling. "This training program is going to do so much more. We're talking about preparing people who need a leg up for other industries. We're talking about creating a more extensive daycare and after-school program open to any kid who needs help, because our children are our future. Isn't that right?"

Her eyes sought Connor's, and even from this distance, she could see that his mouth was tight. He wasn't clapping with everyone else. What in the hell was he thinking?

The crowd was cheering, and she punched the air to refocus herself. "Yeah, that's right. It's going to rock this neighborhood! I'll be sharing more details with all of you, and if you're feeling generous, we'd love to have your help. There are donation booths by the door as you exit, or you can find me or Boxer or Chef Carter anytime after the competition. Speaking of... It's time for the cook-off."

Boxer blew the air horn on cue, and applause thundered in her ears. When it died down, she pointed to the judges' table. "For tonight's *mano-a-mano* gourmet fight, we've assembled some of the toughest judges in the city. We have a man who likes to make grown men cry. Chicago food critic, Blane Salisbury."

The air horn sounded, and Blane stood, waving at the crowd. She introduced the rest of the panel in her wrestling persona: a Michelin-starred chef from a downtown fusion restaurant, the star player of the local basketball team, one of the shelter's long-term guests who was up for a national high school merit scholarship, a local morning news show celebrity, and finally, a rapper and producer from South Side.

After explaining the rules briefly to the crowd, she signaled for Spicy to flicker the lights. Everything went quiet, as if the Chicago Bulls were about ready to make their grand entrance onto the court at the United Center—indeed, they'd inspired the idea. Then the spotlight they'd set up shone on the doorway to the kitchen.

"The one and only Chef Carter Robinson."

Carter emerged as the air horn sounded, flexing his muscles and jumping up and down like an athlete warming up for a game in an apron emblazoned with the saying "Real Men Cook Butt." Only Carter had crossed out "Cook" and replaced it with "Kick." "He's our in-house chef, and if you don't know his story, it's going to bring tears to your eyes. He came to this shelter our first year and turned his life around in record time. Convinced my brother, Chef Damien Evans of the legendary Soledad, to let him intern in his kitchen then took his burgeoning skills to culinary school and graduated with honors. Instead of heading downtown to a fancy restaurant like my brother's—Damien's heart is still broken, right, Dad?"

Her dad nodded his head enthusiastically, causing the crowd to laugh. Dad knew how to ham things up.

"So Carter called me up and said he wanted to be the new chef at Sunflower Alley. I told him we didn't have a chef, and he replied, 'Louisa, you do now. Homeless people deserve to have their own chef, so get that kitchen ready. I'm bringing my knives, and I plan to train people for the food industry.'" She patted her chest. "I still tear up when I think about it."

She blew him a kiss, and he put his hand to his heart. "I love this man, but tonight, I think he's going to have his hands full with our other contestant. Now...the mysterious Clifton Hargreaves..."

Boxer blew the airhorn as Hargreaves appeared in all black, standing calmly as the audience went crazy. Clara had given an opener, something she and Hargreaves had agreed upon. It was short and sweet, and Louisa knew the crowd—and the reporters—were going to love it. "His mystery is legendary, and unconfirmed stories about him abound. Who is Clifton Hargreaves? Only a chef's certification from the august Le Cordon Bleu in Paris exists. Were all the other records about him destroyed?" She put her finger to her mouth as if wondering. "He's a Renaissance man. Plays the flamenco guitar, and I've heard tales that his curry and naan bread have changed people's lives."

"Not mine," she heard Arthur Hale call out loudly, making everyone laugh.

"Chef Carter, you'd better be ready because this mysterious man in black might have your number tonight."

The air horn sounded, and Louisa bounced in her shoes. "Let's start the cook-off. Chefs, please go to your stations."

The lights came up as the panels in the kitchen were pulled back, revealing the two chefs and their stations.

"Coach Carter, what are you making for us tonight?" she called out.

He held up a recipe card. "My grandmother gave me this cherished family recipe on her deathbed."

She made a disbelieving face to the crowd, and the laughter kicked up again.

"It's classic soul food, the kind everyone loves. Fried chicken the Colonel would fear. Perfectly peppery mustard greens. And mashed potatoes so buttery even the Irish in South Side would write home to their relatives about it."

The Irish-American joke wasn't lost on the South Side crowd, and people whistled. Louisa nodded, walking closer to the kitchen. "Sounds pretty good, Chef Carter. But I have a feeling Chef Hargreaves has something special up his sleeve. Chef Hargreaves, would you please tell us what you're preparing?"

He nodded. "A lost recipe from the American cooking icon, Julia Child, according to my source..."

Even Louisa's mouth dropped at that. Clara and Hargreaves hadn't mentioned his plan in their meeting about the cook-off. "Wow! *Julia Child's lost recipe*? You're kidding, Chef. Where did you get it?"

He smiled inscrutably. "I knew a man in British intelligence who said he served with Ms. Child in Ceylon when she was working for the OSS during WWII. Again, he *said* she made this recipe for him on a hot Ceylonese night during the war. I'll leave it to you whether you believe him or not. Since the British and U.S. governments have made Ms. Child's service records public as well as my friend's, I felt comfortable sharing this recipe tonight with everyone here."

Louisa didn't have to work to make her mouth gape

like a fish. "Spies? Ceylon? Lost recipes? Am I the only one thinking this is one of our most memorable cook-offs ever?"

The flashes from people's cameras in the audience were blinding.

"And they haven't even started cooking..." she called out.

Her announcer voice triggered another air horn blast, and she made a show of fanning herself. "So tell us, Mysterious Chef Hargreaves with connections to WWII spies. What are you making tonight?"

"A Ceylonese black curry with duck served with coriander rice and spiced greens as well as my naan bread," Chef Hargreaves said.

She made jazz hands to the crowd. "I'm salivating already. Who else is getting hungry?"

People cheered and whistled, and she did a little dance in front of the chefs before stepping aside. "Let's start the cook-off."

The air horn sounded, and Spicy hit the playlist he'd created for the event, a mix of classics like "Wild Thing" and "Jump Around." The chefs started chopping, putting pans on the stove, and tossing ingredients right and left. The sizzle of meat sounded alongside the roasting of Chef Hargreaves' spices. The dining hall became fragrant with garlic, lemongrass, cinnamon, clove, cardamom, and black pepper.

"Something's starting to smell pretty darn good to me," Louisa said, feeling on top of the world as she watched the gourmet spectacle. Damn, she loved this event.

"Chef Hargreaves is giving a clinic in roasting spices while Chef Carter is showing us the dip and dunk technique for fried chicken."

Whereas Carter cooked like a bull, rattling pans, chopping like a woodchuck might its wood, Hargreaves cooked like a Zen master, adding in dried peppers to his roasting spices, moving smoothly across his station as he put together the ingredients he'd prepped before the cook-off.

Louisa danced over to Chef Carter. "How are those mustard greens looking?"

"Like they're going to rock your world," he responded.

She laughed and leaned forward to sniff. "They're tickling my nose. Let's go over and see Chef Hargreaves. How is that curry coming together?"

"With perfect harmony, Miss Evans," he said with a slight bow.

God, she needed a Hargreaves in her life. "I'll let you get back to it, Chef."

She watched along with everyone else as the two chefs cooked up their dishes, one with his usual chaos and the other with impeccable calm. When their dishes were plated, she and Spicy ferried them over to the judges.

Over the first few cook-offs, they'd honed their system. The judges didn't announce the scores publicly—it had been done that way in the first few competitions, and the judges had been negative Nancies, not the vibe she wanted. Instead, they offered general comments and turned in their scores to be tallied by Louisa or one of the other members of her team.

Each judge tasted the first dish and commented. Everyone agreed Chef Carter's chicken was fried to perfection while the mustard greens were tangy and not overcooked. Of course, all the judges railed about the buttery simplicity of the mashed potatoes.

"Who doesn't like butter?" she asked. "Well, it sounds like our judges enjoyed Chef Carter's soul food. Let's see what they think of Chef Hargreaves' exotic duck curry and sides."

When Blane Salisbury closed his eyes after the first bite, she knew Chef Hargreaves might have clinched the win. The Chicago food critic was known for his toughness on all things gourmand. They'd had him judge a few times, and he'd never closed his eyes in apparent bliss. A few of the judges blinked rapidly, and she wondered if the dish had been too spicy for them. The tension in the room was palpable as everyone finished by trying Chef Hargreaves' offering of steamy naan bread.

"Well, my mouth is watering," Louisa said, "and if I were sitting down, I'd be on the edge of my seat. Judges, from what I can see, you have a hard decision ahead of you. Please take your time deciding who tonight's winner is going to be. And while you're doing it, I'm going to snag a piece of this naan here."

Everyone laughed as she smacked her lips after eating a bite, but to make it even, she pinched a piece of fried chicken too. "I'm glad I'm not judging."

Spicy took the score cards from the judges and then disappeared to tally the final scores. When he returned, he held their signature blue envelope. The hundred people in the dining hall went silent as she took the envelope.

"It's been a battle for the ages, and one I know I'm going to remember for a while. Thank you, Chef Carter and Chef Hargreaves for competing in Sunflower Alley's monthly cook-off. It's time to unveil who the judges chose as tonight's winner."

She tore open the envelope. Gave herself a moment to think of something clever to say. "I think I have *The Chicago Tribune*'s headline for tomorrow. Spies Beat Grandma. Sorry, Chef Carter. Chef Hargreaves wins!"

The air horn blew, and the lights flickered as people cheered and whistled. Eminem's "Lose Yourself" started to play, and Louisa gestured for Chef Hargreaves to come forward. "Chef, thank you for sharing your fabulous meal with us tonight. I know everybody is going to enjoy it when we serve dinner shortly. Is there anything else you'd like to tell us about how you got this recipe? I must admit you surprised me and everyone else in this room. I mean, who doesn't love Julia Child?"

"I'm afraid I've shared all I'm able to, Ms. Evans," he said with a reserved smile, "but I hope everyone enjoys this recipe from the land of spices. Thank you again for the honor of cooking in this competition against an incredible chef and person, Chef Carter." He bowed slightly toward Carter, who came over and shook his hand.

"I had a bad feeling when you brought out that Julia Child spy stuff," Carter said into the mic, "but if my grandma's recipe had to go down, at least it was to Julia Child."

"True that," Louisa said. "All right, everybody. Our staff and volunteers are going to work with the two chefs to prepare both of these dishes for dinner tonight. Mingle. Talk to someone new. Grab a drink. We'll serve dinner shortly."

Clara bustled up to the front of the room, Arthur just behind her. "Hargreaves!" she said joyfully. "I knew you could do it. What a show. Louisa, this is incredible."

She beamed. "It's one of the best things we've come up with. Brings the community together in a fun way and raises a lot of awareness and money for the shelter."

"I know!" Arthur exclaimed. "I couldn't believe the tickets sold out so quickly at sixty bucks a pop. Hargreaves, congratulations. You'll have to tell me the whole story about how you got that lost recipe."

"A man like me has to maintain some confidentiality with his sources," the butler said. "As a journalist, you understand."

Arthur nodded. "Indeed. I want to go on record though. This won't change my bitching about weekly Indian food."

"Oh, Arthur, why do you always have to be such a killjoy?" Clara elbowed him in the ribs, which he playfully clutched. "Come on, we're helping Hargreaves and the rest of his team finish up dinner."

"Madam, I have plenty of staff to help with the preparations," Hargreaves said. "You and Mr. Hale should mingle. I expect Miss Evans here would like to introduce you to some people and raise more money for the new training center."

Thank you, Hargreaves. "Yes, I would, and I think you'd like to meet them too."

"Then we'll do that, of course," Clara said. "Lead on, Louisa."

She made the rounds with the couple, and they were magic. The reporters hung on the every word of the famed Arthur Hale. A few of them even made donations, a first. Clara was terrific with the politicians, making them laugh easily while talking about how important it was for them to help the homeless. More donations found their way into the center's coffers. People's enthusiasm for the new training center and restaurant had Louisa over the moon.

"Clara, I need to hire you and Mr. Hale as my spokespeople," she said as her dad came forward.

"What a night, honey," her dad said, handing her a few more checks. "More donations for you. This might be my favorite competition ever. Too bad Damien had to head back to the restaurant to handle a surprise visit from a food critic. He'll gnash his teeth when he hears about that lost recipe. Goodness, is it true, Clara?"

"Ask Hargreaves," she said, linking her arm through Arthur's in a sweet show of affection.

"I have some people I'd like Clara and Arthur to meet," her dad said. "Mind if I borrow them for a while?"

"Sure thing," she said, knowing they were in great hands. "I have someone I need to find."

She left them, searching for Connor again. People in the crowd continued to stop her, congratulate her on the new center, and give her money. It was life-affirming, their excitement and support, and it fanned her excitement even higher. When she finally made it to the back of the dining hall, she saw Connor crouched down in front of the exit doors in the most shocking spectacle.

He was holding a sobbing little boy in his arms, looking like his heart had been torn out of his chest, much like the man she'd first met drinking out of the bottle in the snowstorm. Somehow she knew that boy was the son of his friend who'd died, the one he'd roomed with in college. And she knew he needed help.

Story or no story, she was going to give it to him.

CHAPTER 15

ALTHOUGH CONNOR HAD WORRIED SOMEONE FROM THE press might recognize him at the cook-off, or perhaps someone familiar with the business world, the last thing Connor had expected was to hear someone call out "Uncle Connor."

When he'd turned at the sound of his name, he'd found himself looking at Corey's youngest son. Joseph's face had immediately crumpled, and then he'd launched himself at Connor and started sobbing. Connor had dropped to his knees and gathered the little boy to him, his heart an agony of pain in his chest. Joseph was clutching him for dear life, crying his heart out, and Connor had to squeeze his eyes together to fight his own powerful grief.

My God, he'd ruined this little boy's life. Olivia had been right to tell him to keep away. Was she here? He'd worried she might read about Clara *Merriam* Hale's donation to Sunflower Alley in the paper and sense he was up to something. He held Joseph tightly, doing his best to comfort him, as he scanned the crowd from their position in the back.

Which was when he met Louisa's eyes. She was standing at the end of the chairs in the back, her face soft with compassion.

Shit.

But Joseph was all that mattered at the moment. He picked the boy up and carried him out of the back exit, hoping to give them more time alone, away from questions.

Joseph pushed back, crying raggedly. "I...I...need...to find...my friend."

"Okay, buddy," Connor said, smoothing his sweaty hair. "We'll find him. Give it a second."

"You...You..." The boy was crying so hard he couldn't talk, and his whole body was shaking. Connor made himself force his own pain away, clawing for numbness. For compartmentalization.

He wrapped Joseph up again, and the boy pressed his face into his neck, keening, "My daddy..."

And with those words, Connor felt hot tears pop into his own eyes. He listened to Joseph cry and mumble against his neck, words like "Mom" and "Max" and "Daddy" and "accident."

Accident? What crap. Accidents didn't cause this kind of hurt—a little boy bawling his eyes out because Connor had reminded him that his heart was broken. That he'd lost his daddy, his hero. Of course someone was to blame, and that someone was *him.*

God, how could he ever make it up to this little boy and his brother and his mom?

He'd grasped on to this plan to make their neighborhood safer, thinking it would redeem him somehow, but he'd been fooling himself. There was no fixing this.

Joseph's crying leveled out to a few sniffs, and he wiped his nose on his sweater's sleeve. When he raised his head, the sight crushed Connor. Those blue Weatherby eyes were staring back at him from beneath dark brows...it was like looking at a little Corey.

"Why are you here in this place?" Joseph asked. "Why haven't you come to see us?"

All the spit in his mouth dried up at the accusation in

his voice. How was he supposed to tell Joseph his mother didn't think he'd be a good influence on the boys? Hell, how was he supposed to say she blamed him for Corey's death? That he blamed himself?

"I've kept Connor so busy for a few days he hasn't seen anyone," a familiar voice said.

He looked up, and his heart clutched. Louisa had Mr. Snuggles in her hands, and Connor instantly knew why she was here. She was coming to save him, armed with her unflappable compassion and a white and gold guinea pig.

He loved her. He wanted so much to tell her in that moment that he had to bite his lip. For a few nights now, he'd wanted to tell her everything, but he hadn't managed to get the words out, not wanting to disrupt the incredible rhythm they'd fallen into. He'd been enjoying himself, feeling free and easy for the first time in months, maybe years, and he hadn't wanted to risk messing with it quite yet. Even if part of him thought it cowardly.

"Hi, I'm Louisa, and this is my good friend, Mr. Snuggles," she said, crossing to them and sinking to one knee.

The boy put his little hand out formally, and they shook. "I'm Joe, but some people like Uncle Connor still call me Joseph."

"Nice to meet you, Joe."

The boy still had his arm around Connor, but he touched the guinea pig, who was grunting. "It's okay to pet him?"

"Yes, he told me he wanted to meet you," she said, smiling. "He likes making new friends."

Connor met and held Louisa's gaze as Joseph petted the guinea pig and talked to it. The light in her golden eyes captivated him, and her soft beauty stole over him, as powerful as an unstoppable ocean wave. His heart tightened in his chest. No matter how he felt about her, she deserved more. Hell, he hadn't even told her his whole story yet. Once she knew, she might feel differently about him.

"You're the lady who hosted the contest tonight," Joseph said, his mouth lifting on the right when Mr. Snuggles grunted again. "You're funny. You must watch wrestling. You sound like the men on TV."

"Why, thank you, I try," she said, extending the guinea pig. "Would you like to hold Mr. Snuggles?"

"I shouldn't," Joseph said, frowning now. "I need to find Tommy. He's my friend. He begged me to come with him. His parents are always taking him to things like the museum and concerts and soup kitchens. They say it does something to the mind. I don't remember what."

"Expands it maybe?" Louisa asked, her lips twitching.

"This is the best show Tommy's begged me to come to," Joseph said. "I hope the food's good. If it's not, his parents will probably take us to the vegan place they like in Avalon Park. It's disgusting. Tommy and me try not to throw up."

"I tried a little bit of the food tonight. I thought it was delicious. I don't do disgusting food either. Do I, Mr. Snuggles?" She kissed the guinea pig. "How about I help you find your friend, Joe, while Connor watches out for Mr. Snuggles. He's a little scared of crowds."

For a moment, Connor thought she was talking about his reticence with crowds, but it struck him that she meant the guinea pig. Maybe both of them felt that way.

"You aren't eating dinner here?" Joseph asked. "Oh, please, Uncle Connor, stay. I've missed you so much."

"I've missed you too." He made himself smile and touched the boy's nose. "Another night, man."

Please God, don't ask me when. I can't say, and it will break your heart even more.

The boy went silent and then asked, "Do you miss Dad too?"

That did it. Tears took up camp in his eyes again, threatening to fall. "Every minute of the day."

"Me too," Joseph said, knuckling away more tears.

"Max keeps telling me not to cry in front of Mom, but sometimes I can't help it."

"Connor's the same way," Louisa said, putting her hand on Joseph's shoulder.

"He is?" The boy's face lit up. "But he's the Big Bad Wolf. Everyone calls him that."

"Not anymore, sport," Connor said. "I've put away my hood."

"Little Red Riding Hood had the hood, Uncle Connor," Joseph said, sniffing and wiping his tears with his sleeve.

"Hey!" Louisa exclaimed. "I have an idea. If you could meet one of our judges tonight, who would it be?"

"That's easy! Derrick Franks. He's a beast on the court."

"I'll introduce you." Louisa stood. "Come on, Joe. Say goodbye to your Uncle Connor and Mr. Snuggles, and don't worry. You'll see them both again sometime."

He couldn't fault her for saying it, but he wished she hadn't made a promise.

Joseph wrapped his arms around Connor and held him tight. Connor squeezed his eyes shut. *I'm sorry. Christ, I'm so sorry.*

"Wait by the door a sec, Joe," Louisa said, tousling his hair gently. "I have to whisper something to Mr. Snuggles here."

"Okay," the boy said, kissing Connor before he stood on his own two feet. "I don't like the beard, Uncle Connor. You should shave it. Max says girls don't like beards."

He swallowed thickly at the mention of his other godson. God, he missed him. "And how would Max know?"

"He's always saying weird things like that now that he likes Amber," Joseph said, rolling his eyes. "She's in junior high."

Louisa chuckled. "An older woman, I'm guessing?"

"Yeah, and it's messing with his brain," Joseph said,

kicking at the floor, shoelaces dancing. "You'll come visit us, right?"

Here it was. He nodded, not able to say any more. "Love ya, man."

The boy smiled valiantly. "Love you too." He looked at him once more and then walked to the door, a small, brave soldier.

As Corey's son walked through the door, giving him a final smile as he did so, Louisa reached out to Connor. She touched his chest. "I'm assuming you're going to go now. If you'd like, come by my place after you take a run. Here, hold Mr. Snuggles and take him back to his cage for me. The door's unlocked right now."

He took the wiggling guinea pig and settled him against his chest. She fished into her pocket and pulled out her keys.

"Louisa..."

"The gold one is for the front door, and the silver for my apartment. Don't worry about the hour. Come any-time."

She stuck them in his pants pocket and stepped back from him, her golden eyes locked on his face.

"Don't make me hunt you down. I love you, you know."

His throat seized up. So she'd said it, and in the mo-ment she imagined he most needed to hear it from anoth-er person. It was just like her.

"I shouldn't say it back after this," he said, holding out one of his hands helplessly. "You don't know what you've gotten yourself into."

She leveled him a glance that promised a good butt-kicking for how he was acting. "Don't treat me like I'm stupid, Connor."

"I love you too," he whispered harshly. The words were wrenched from his chest. "But you might wish oth-erwise once you know everything."

She smiled, her eyes a little watery. "I'll be the judge of that. Time for us to talk. Tonight. Don't you dare make me find you, Connor."

As she walked through the door, going over to Joseph and taking his hand so sweetly, Connor realized the die was cast.

He couldn't walk away from her.

CHAPTER 16

THE LIGHTS WERE ON IN LOUISA'S APARTMENT WHEN SHE returned home.

Relief coursed through her as she closed the door and locked it. He hadn't left her. All night, she'd pushed away the fear that he might disappear. That her declaration of love, and his to her, would send him running.

He rose from the chair he'd pulled in front of her front window. His hair was still wet from a shower, she guessed, given he was wearing brown pants and a navy sweater instead of his running clothes. His face looked stricken, and he shrugged. "I'm here."

"I'm glad," she said, tossing her purse aside, shrugging out of her coat, and crossing to wrap her arms around him. "I got away as soon as I could, but I was ready to gear up for a manhunt if you didn't come. You saved me and a few other people a long, cold night."

His arms came around her. "Who else?"

"I'd planned to ask Boxer, Carter, Spicy, my dad, Damien, and anyone they wanted to bring along. They all have their own posses."

"They would have helped you look for me?" he asked, astonishment lacing his tone.

"Of course," she said, pressing back and cupping his

jaw. "You may not believe this, but you matter to me, and because of that, you matter to a lot of people. Boxer's starting to like you, and the others will if you let them get to know you."

He pushed her head back against his chest, running his hand down her straight, dark hair. "Your so-called posse sounds a lot like my family."

"Are you going to tell me?" she asked, her heart tight in her chest.

"Yeah, but it won't be easy," he replied. "I've thought about telling you a couple times, but I faltered. Maybe staying like this is best. I don't want you to see my face."

Shame. Its dark specter had a way of wrecking lives. But she knew its calling card. If he could only tell her like this, she'd be grateful for it. Afterward, she'd do her best to burn his shame away with the love in her heart. "I'm just happy that you're holding me."

"Good." He coughed, as if clearing his throat. "I don't know where to start. It's unusual. I always knew where to start until recently."

"Start with the first thing that comes to mind," she suggested, falling back not only on her own counseling but on her training with people in need.

"Corey's boy sobbing in my arms," he said, tightening his hold around her. "That's all I've been thinking about. Louisa, I ruined that little boy's life. I came here thinking I could help Corey's family, but what I did can never be undone."

"Corey was your employee and friend who died in that natural disaster you told me about," she said, urging him on.

"He wasn't just an employee or a friend." He coughed again. "He was my first cousin and my best friend since we were born. God!"

She tightened her hands on the arms he had around her as the pain in his voice echoed in the room. "Tell me about the accident, Connor."

"I ran the company that had him and a few hundred others working on an oil rig off the coast of Indonesia. An earthquake hit. He and seven other people lost their lives that day. I can name every single one of them and their families, their ages, their hometowns."

Why did people feel so responsible for the deaths of other people? She'd felt guilty about her mom well into her twenties. They'd talk about guilt later, but right now, he needed to talk about events, not feelings. "Then what happened?"

Had he been fired? Had he been blamed? Or had he simply taken the blame for himself? She was betting on the latter.

"I decided to stop all future offshore oil projects, a policy I pursued without anyone else's consent," he said. "First blip, so to speak. I would have sold every offshore rig we had, but I knew I couldn't get away with it."

Right, because oil was big money, and what company wanted to give up money? "Then what happened?"

"Ireland happened," he said, putting his face in her hair. "Since we weren't doing offshore projects anymore, I told my brother to buy some land onshore. Only he didn't agree with my decision. To make matters worse, he fell in love with the land's owner. When I pushed, Trevor pushed back. It got ugly. There were things about this woman I didn't know, and one of my actions ended up hurting her. My family thought I was acting unlike myself because of Corey's death. I couldn't hear that. I fought back. But they stood against me, and I finally backed down."

His entire body was rigid enough with tension, so she refrained from asking any of the questions she had about his family. From what he was saying, it sounded like some of them worked in the business together. "Then what?"

He fisted his hands around her. "I sent my youngest sister on an assignment to Kenya. She almost died. When I found out, I kinda lost it. I was desperate to find her, and I hired the people who seemed best suited to do that. I knew I was crossing some lines, but it made sense to me at the time. Again, my family stood against me."

She found herself getting angry with his family. Sure, she didn't know their side of things, but she loved him, and that meant she had his back. "Keep going."

"They wanted me to explain myself and my actions." His grip tightened again. "I was too angry and upset to see straight. I told them to eff off. They thought I needed counseling. It had been mentioned before. I went crazy. Long story short. When I didn't explain myself, they called a vote to question some of my actions as a leader. I goaded them into it. If they were against me, I couldn't run anything. I didn't want to."

"So they fired you," she concluded, rubbing his back.

"Yeah," he said heavily. "So I packed up a bag, got some cash, and came this way. I'd promised Corey I'd take care of his family. Keeping that promise was the only thing I had left. Then I got here, and his wife wouldn't let me. She even... Oh, God, this is the hardest thing to say out loud. She..."

Louisa gripped him tightly to help him find the courage to speak.

"She told me she didn't want me around Joseph and Max," he said harshly. "Not given my recent behavior. They were having a hard enough time dealing with their grief. Christ. I failed Corey, and now I've failed them. I knew it when Joseph sobbed in my arms tonight. I've ruined that boy's life. And his brother's. Forever."

"Okay, stop," she said, turning around and taking his face in her hands. "Now I'm talking, and you're going to listen."

He tried to move his head out of her hands. "*Louisa.*"

"No, Connor, you need to hear this," she said firmly, "and I'm going to say it because I love you."

His face fell. "You shouldn't, you know."

"Stop that too," she said, rising on her tiptoes so he had no choice but to meet her eyes. "From where I stood tonight, that little boy had nothing but love for you."

"He doesn't know I'm to blame," Connor said, his face crumpling. "Even his mom thinks that—"

"And she's crazy with grief too. You *aren't* to blame," she said, putting more resolve into her voice. "Babe, listen to me."

His mouth was bunched up as he looked at her. "You've never called me that before, and you shouldn't."

"Stop telling me what I should and shouldn't do. That ship has sailed. I love you, and you love me. We deal with what's now. Now hear me out. Did Corey want to work on that oil rig?"

He blew out an aggressive breath. "I know what you're going to say. I've heard it before. I've even tried to tell myself. *You're not to blame.* But dammit, Louisa, it's just not how I feel in here." He pounded his chest. "In here...it's my fault. We should have had earthquake sensors on that rig or been in contact with nearby seismologists. Dammit, it's an area known for earthquakes. How did I miss that?"

She knew the way the logic worked. *If I'd just done this, this would or wouldn't have happened.* "Connor, how many people worked in this area with you?"

He rubbed the bridge of his nose. "Thousands. But it doesn't matter, Louisa. I was the leader—the buck stopped with me. My dad always said everything fell at the CEO's feet. I failed Corey and all of those men. Left their wives widowed and their children fatherless."

"So you have a God complex," she said, and he met her gaze, shock rippling over his face. "Think you can outwit and outthink nature? You can't. Are you going to let this ruin your life? Ruin your chance to make a difference?"

He shook his head. "I like that you didn't sugarcoat it and pat my face and tell me I'm a good man and everything is going to be all right."

She knew to tread carefully. "Connor, you are a good man, and like I said the other day, you need counseling. Whether you get it is up to you. No one knows better than me how hard it is to accept that something isn't our fault. For years, my guilt story went like this. Are you ready? Because it's as ugly as it gets."

He nodded, focusing on her.

"I thought my mother wouldn't have become a drug addict after she got back from the war if I'd been a better daughter. She wouldn't have taken to the streets with me if I'd been a good girl. And she wouldn't have frozen to death on those same streets if I'd loved her enough. Because by the time my dad got full custody of me, I didn't love her very much anymore. At times, I hated her. For a long time, I thought knowing that was what had finally killed her. Knowing that her own daughter hated her."

"Oh, Louisa," he said, caressing her cheek.

"No, not *oh Louisa*." She put her hand on his chest. "You don't get to tell me I wasn't to blame for her death and then push me aside when I tell you the exact same thing about your cousin. Because the details might be different, but it's the same horrible story. Something happened out of your control, and someone died because of it. You're no more at fault than I was, Connor."

"You were a child, dammit," he said, his brows slamming together. "I was the president of the whole fucking company. I was responsible for everyone. It *is* different."

"That's what you think," she said, "but honey, it isn't different. You can't be responsible truly for anyone but yourself."

"*Honey*?" He stalked away from her toward the window and looked out at the building where he'd lived with Corey. "I don't deserve those sweet epithets. I killed my best friend. I made his little boy cry. Louisa, I'm a monster."

She couldn't stop the tears from filling her eyes. "That's

impossible," she whispered harshly, clenching her fists at her sides. "Do you know why? Because I love you, dammit, and I can't love someone who's a monster. I wouldn't."

He lowered his head. "You're killing me here."

She strode over to him and banded her arms around him before he could resist. "Good, because you need to hear this. I love you, and trust me, I've known monsters. You aren't a monster. Connor, I'm just going to say it. The only person who can stop you from seeing yourself as a monster is you. But trust me when I say that Joseph doesn't love a monster. He loves his Uncle Connor, and even more so, he needs him."

He turned around and pressed his face into her neck. She held on, sensing the tension in him cracking under the pressure of the truth and her love.

"You can't seek counseling only because of someone else. It never lasts unless you're the one who wants to get better. But that boy is a damn good reason to want to get better, and I expect his brother is too. Then there's me."

He pressed back, and she felt like another miracle was happening. He had tears in his eyes. "You're the best part in all this. A light in my darkness."

She couldn't let her own tears fall. She had to be strong here. It was her only chance of reaching him. "If you and I have any chance of making this work, you'll need to face the darkness like I did. The thing is... I know you. No one is braver and stronger and more stubborn, and trust me, you're going to need all of that to make it through. But you have me."

Tears trailed down his face, and he knuckled them away. They were some of the most beautiful tears she'd ever seen.

"And I expect there are a few people in your corner you don't know about yet," she said, pushing aside his hands when he went to brush those tears away in shame. "You take the first step and give it your all, and we'll be there

with flowers and cake and all the love and encouragement
you need to keep going on the days when you feel like you
can't go on."

"Flowers, huh?" He sniffed and rubbed his nose.
"What about my family? Louisa, I don't know what to say
to them. How to make this up to them. I'm the one who
pulled away, but dammit, I miss them. Despite everything. *Every last one of them.*"

She finally had to brush aside her tears. "If they wanted you to get help, that's a good step. There are others
you can take. When you're ready, we can go visit them together."

He traced the line of her tears. "You're crying for me.
That's enough to bring me to my knees."

"I love you," she said, touching his chest. "It comes
with the territory, I guess. Connor, I've been trying not to
be attached to what you decide. Only know this…I want
to support you. I know it's a little different, but if my dad
hadn't been with me when I had to face all the junk going
on inside me, I don't know if I would have gotten through
it."

"Yeah, you would have." His eyes held her own, the
love in them palpable. "You're too strong and stubborn to
do otherwise."

"So are you," she said, tracing his jawline. "And when
you need reminding of how incredible you are, I'll tell
you. My dad used to say, 'I won't give up on you if you
don't give up on yourself.'"

"A tall order," he said with a deep sigh. "I think I'm
going to like your dad."

She wanted to jump in the air at that admission. Future talk was the most promising kind. It meant Connor
intended to stay and see things through. "He's going to
like you."

He laughed harshly. "So long as I don't hurt his little
girl."

She poked him in the chest. "Then don't."

"Right," he said, nodding. "I'm sorry things got intense there. I thought I'd run out all of my emotions before I got here."

"How long did you run?" she asked, taking his arm and leading him to the couch.

"Two hours give or take," he said, laying his head back and studying the ceiling.

She could feel the exhaustion he'd been fighting settle over him. "Where did you run to?" She pulled the crocheted blanket onto them.

He lifted his head and cuddled her closer. "Where I always run. Where Corey is buried. In Oak Woods. And then along the lake."

She leaned her head against his chest, listening to the beat of his heart. "I'd like to put flowers on his grave if that's okay with you."

He kissed the top of her head. "I'd like that, and I expect he would too. I...talk to him. Is that weird?"

Leaning back, she caressed his beard. "No, not to me. As part of my counseling, I wrote letters to my mother. Told her things I wish I could have said. Things I needed to say."

"Corey would have liked you a lot," Connor said, raising her hand and kissing it. "I realized that tonight. He'd have been happy I'd found you. Joseph liked you. It struck me later how significant that was. You were good with him."

"He's a good kid," she said, her heart going out to that little boy. "Plus, I had Mr. Snuggles. Everyone likes Mr. Snuggles."

He snorted, the sound music to her ears. Some clichés had gained that status by being true, and one of the ones she liked most was *laughter is the best medicine*. "Mr. Snuggles. Thanks for coming to my rescue. I didn't say it earlier, but I knew the moment I saw you with your pig."

"That's guinea pig to you, buckaroo," she said, climbing onto his lap. "Now, how about we shift the energy? I believe I told you I love you tonight. How do you feel about that?"

He blew out a breath. "I kinda suspected, but you shocked the hell out of me by saying it then. Only I wasn't surprised. It was just like you."

"I like to keep people on their toes, but you didn't answer my question."

His eyes looked off before coming back to her. "Humbled. Awed. A little scared."

"Did happiness play into it at all?" she asked, her own chest tight suddenly. "Because I was worried you might skip out on me. It wasn't the easiest thing to say, especially in that moment. I've never felt this way about anyone."

"Neither have I." He traced her cheekbone. "I've known a lot of incredible women, Louisa, but you might be the most courageous and incredible of them all."

She melted like wax on the inside and linked her arms around his neck. "And you, Connor, are one of the most incredible men I've ever met. I hope to love you as long as you'll let me. Tonight I'm hoping that's an awfully long time. Just so you know."

She smiled to lighten the mood, but his face darkened. "You going to ask me what my last name is?"

"I was hoping you might tell me, but I can wait if you're not ready."

His heart started to pound so loudly. "It's Merriam. Connor Merriam."

"I like it," she said, and then her mouth parted. "Wait! Isn't Clara's maiden name Merriam?"

He winced. "Another long story. They didn't like keeping it from you."

She felt a punch of anger. So, her epic good luck had been less luck and more planning. *His* planning. "And you did?"

"No," he said, holding her gaze, "but it was necessary. I didn't want anyone to know who I was."

"Explain." She nudged him for good measure. "Make it good."

He told her, and she finally rubbed her forehead, trying to make sense of it all.

"So you decided to help me with the training program, anonymously, because your cousin's family lives in this neighborhood and you want to do something for them. Okay... Unconventional and over-the-top, some would say, but somehow so you."

"Are you upset?" he asked, stroking her spine.

"I'm still taking it in," she said, shaking her head slowly. "There's been a lot tonight. Oh, God. I suddenly remembered. You made that joke about being a billionaire."

"You were cute, laughing at me." His mouth turned up at the corners. "I wanted to tell you something about myself without saying everything."

Oh shit. "You really are a billionaire."

"Yes."

"Huh," she said, breathing out a bunch of pent-up air at the thought. "Honestly, I like knowing you have enough money for food, clothing, and shelter. Question. Why were you staying at Ferguson's?"

"I didn't want my family to find me. Cash only. Plus, they'd never think to look for me at a place like that."

"God, they sound like the mob." She made a fist. "I'll fight any of them if they hurt you again. I swear."

"Spoken like a girl from South Side." He brought her fist to his heart. "My grandma was born and raised here. So was my mom. Corey's family lives in my grandparents' old house."

He'd said she reminded him of his mom. Now she knew why. "We South Side girls are as tough as they come."

"Don't I know it," he said, threading his hands in her hair. "Apparently I needed a tough girl."

"I'd say," she said, sliding closer on his lap until there wasn't an inch between them. "But I can be gentle too."

"Wait," he said, leveraging his head back. "I need to tell you something else, and it really might upset you. In all fairness, I didn't know your plans."

His mouth tightened, and her belly flip-flopped with nerves. "Spit it out."

"I'm the guy who outbid you on the property you wanted for the training center," he said. "I also didn't expect another bidder. It's a crap heap."

She put her hands on his shoulders for grounding. "So why would you want to buy it? I don't understand."

He sighed. "Part of me doesn't want to tell you. You were so upset at me when I suggested having the training program in another part of town."

A hard ball lodged under her ribs. Helping the shelter wasn't his only plan—she should have known a man like him would think bigger. "What are you doing, Connor?"

"I'm buying up property in South Side with the intention of creating urban renewal. Bringing in key stores and more shopping and housing complexes like the one on the Green Line, for example."

Her chest was tightening with every revelation. "You want to flip South Side."

"What I want," he said, pausing for emphasis, "is for this neighborhood to be safe for my cousin's family and for you and everyone else here. What I want is for the needles to be off the street and the gangs to move on."

She'd heard outsiders talk about helping South Side before. But they usually wanted to change it, fashion it into some homogenous downtown suburbia. "I want the neighborhood to be safe too. And I sure as hell don't want needles or gangs on the street. I'm on a lot of community boards, and it's important to balance the progress you're talking about with maintaining the best aspects of South Side. There's a culture here too."

"I realize that," he said, his gaze steady, "and I respect it. My mom is still proud of where she's from. But the other crap going on... It's nothing to be proud of. You're doing something about it. I want to do the same."

"Because you promised your cousin you'd look out for his family," she said slowly, trying to stay open-minded. "All I'm saying is that we have to address key community issues. Connor, people need affordable housing. If they can't afford to live in South Side anymore, you'll be pushing them out of their neighborhood. You might end up making more people homeless."

"So we need to bring in more prosperity too, which is part of my plan," he said. "Training for higher-paying jobs is a good start, but I'm not in favor of free rides, Louisa."

He hadn't answered her concerns about housing, but she could continue to remind him of its importance as they moved forward. Introducing him to other community leaders and hard-working people affected by increased rents would be a tangible way to show him what she was talking about without trying to talk *at* him. That only closed people down to other ideas.

"Long term, I agree, but sometimes people need a hand up while they're getting there. That's what Sunflower Alley does. That's what I want this training program to do. In South Side."

"Hear me out. I wanted to put it in the industrial park because the land is less expensive long term. Also, investors want neighborhoods to look a certain way before they come in."

She saw where he was headed with this. "They don't want a homeless shelter or a training program for the homeless down the street from the corner Starbucks. Of course, I'd like to think I can work myself out of a job someday, but I'm not that naïve. Connor, you need to remember how much people love this neighborhood and how your plans are going to affect matters, especially for vulnerable populations."

"I know we see things differently," he said cautiously, "and I like to bulldoze my way through a problem."

"You're kidding, right?" She made herself smile. "So do I. Continue."

"I'd like to hear your side of things. In a show of conciliation, I'm prepared to give you the land you want for the training program. I don't want to lose you over this."

This time her heart felt like it was going to beat out of her chest. Maybe they could make this work. That he was willing to give her the land… "I'm grateful for the conciliating. I plan to pay you for it. No free rides."

His mouth tipped up. "It's no wonder I love you. Be patient with me though. I'm still working my way through how to make this all work, my plans and other people's. Remember how I told you I don't miss working with people all day long?"

His vulnerability had her reaching out and tracing his beard. "Yeah. You really struck me as a people person the night we met." She was starting to believe he was more comfortable in smaller groups, like most introverts she knew.

His snort made her smile. "I'm finding I do like buying up property and making plans for it. Thinking about the right investment groups to approach. Being hands-on. That kind of thing. It's exciting."

Clearly he hadn't felt that way in some time. She still needed to tread carefully here. He was making big changes and trusting her after a horrible string of events, but he still carried a lot of pain and guilt with him. It would be easy to crush him, and that was the last thing she wanted to do. They could continue to talk about the right balance between investment and revitalization. "I'm happy to help you on stuff like this, and I'm looking forward to talking about it more. That's what partners are for, and I happen to know the neighborhood like the back of my hand and all of the hot-button issues that matter to the people here. Lucky you."

"Yeah," he said, tracing her lips. "Lucky me. Meeting you is the best thing that has ever happened to me. I'm convinced of that. I just never want to let you down."

"So don't. I don't want to let you down either, you know." The love shining in his eyes called to her soul. "I'm pretty lucky too, Connor. I have a feeling meeting you was one of the best things to ever happen to me as well. Let me show you how much we have to be grateful for."

And so she did, kissing her way across his skin in benediction. They stripped out of their clothes, and he lifted her into his arms and carried her into the bedroom. Following her down onto the bed, he touched her softly, slowly, and with so much care, she sighed in bliss.

Tonight was different. This was lovemaking, the kind that fused two people together for more than one night, the kind that held the power to fuse them for a lifetime. She knew it as he traced the line of her bones. Did he? When he sighed into her mouth and pressed his face between her breasts, she heard the answer. Yes, he most certainly did.

She nudged him onto his back, fitted him with a condom, and slowly eased down on him. His knees came up to cradle her back in support as she started to rock. He gripped her hips, rising to meet her downward thrust. Her head fell back as the rhythm overtook them, the slow, deep slide taking her to a new level of urgency. She came over him and heard him cry out in response. Her mate, she thought, perfectly matched for her. Their bodies had known before their hearts did.

She settled against him, a new warmth and sweetness settling in her skin. There was nowhere else she wanted to be but right here. Right now.

He kissed her head and put his arm around her. They remained silent for a long while until he said, "I'll call the counselor in the morning."

She went to sleep with a smile on her face.

CHAPTER 17

ARTHUR DIDN'T LIKE BEING BETWEEN A ROCK AND A HARD place.

He sure as hell didn't like Clara fretting. His beloved wife had been mumbling under her breath all morning, twisting her diamond bracelets as she paced the cavernous suite. They'd invited Connor for a meeting, at Clara's insistence, and he was due to arrive any minute. It could end up being a showdown. With Connor, it was hard to tell.

Joseph Weatherby had told his mother he'd seen his Uncle Connor at Sunflower Alley last night. The poor little boy didn't understand why his Uncle Connor was in town and hadn't come to see him. Olivia was freaking out, so much so that Shawn and Assumpta were flying in from California to talk her down.

No wonder Connor had disappeared from the cook-off. They'd gone to look for him after they'd finally done the rounds with Louisa and Coach Evans, only to come up empty. They'd asked Louisa if she'd seen him, and the girl had denied it without indicating any concern. He suspected she was an excellent actress.

"You don't think Connor's flown the coop, do you?" Clara asked, staring out their high-rise windows with the view of the lake.

"Dear, he told you he was coming when you texted him," Arthur said from his perch on the sofa.

He shared a look with Hargreaves, who brought in a tea tray. "Maybe it was a ruse. He asked for a different time than I wanted."

"Clara, it's Saturday morning," Arthur said. "Not everyone wants to meet at eight in the morning."

"Connor is used to it," Clara said, stomping her foot. "Oh, I'm so frustrated. I feel like everything is coming apart. Olivia put two and two together about me helping the shelter, and she thinks Connor is up to something. Shawn and Assumpta need to calm her down."

Arthur knew better than to try and pour his own tea—probably a green one given Clara's health kick of late—so he let Hargreaves execute his butler duties. "You'd think you'd want to relax after beating the pants off a celebrity chef last night, Hargreaves."

"Winning a cooking competition is independent of my duties, sir," the man said as if he hadn't been applauded and cheered like crazy last night.

"You're unflappable, Hargreaves."

"Thank you, sir," he said, bowing formally. "I'll see to the sandwiches for Master Connor's visit."

He reached for his teacup and scalded his mouth. "Arrr... It's hot."

"It is tea, sir," Hargreaves said. "Would you like an ice cube?"

Arthur almost picked up his *Chicago Tribune* and threw it at him. "You made the paper. Did you know that?"

"A wonderful picture of me with Miss Evans, I thought," Hargreaves said. "I'll leave you to your tea."

"Come sit, my dear, and have some of this tea," Arthur said, patting the seat next to him. "If I have to drink it, I'm not doing so alone."

A knock sounded on the door.

"Finally," Clara said, crossing to the sofa but not sitting down.

Why in the hell did Hargreaves always have to be the one to open the door when someone else was closer?

"He's right on time, dear."

Hargreaves moved into the room like he imagined butlers of old had done: without haste, fuss, or noise. Most days Arthur marveled at his poise. Today, his stomach was too sour for him to do anything more than stretch to take Clara's clenched fist. She fitted her hand into his and gave him a brave smile.

"It's going to be fine," he assured her.

"Master Connor," Hargreaves announced, "and Miss Evans."

Arthur stood up at the mention of a lady. Some courtesies were ingrained. The couple walked in, hand in hand, and the force of them had him rocking back on his heels. The Matchmaker Jedi knew a unit when he saw it. Whatever had happened had happened with cement, not glue. They were fused together, and damn if they didn't look good together. Hope shot through his chest, and he tightened his grip on his wife's hand.

Perhaps this meeting would go down better than he'd thought.

"It's good to see the two of you," he said, waving them over. "A surprise, but in the best way. Come, sit down. Clara ordered green tea, but from the look of you two, maybe we should break out the champagne."

"Perhaps in a little while," Louisa said, crossing to the couch and greeting them both with a kiss on the cheek. "Hargreaves, I know you might think it's improper, but I'm kissing you too. Especially now that I know how you're connected to Connor here."

"I wouldn't dare stop you from being improper, Miss Evans," Hargreaves said in a droll tone, but he actually leaned into the woman as if her show of affection pleased him. Shocking.

"So the cat's out of the bag all the way, eh?" He felt a smile break out across his face, and Clara's hand tightened around his. This was what they'd hoped for.

Connor nodded, his eyes meeting Louisa's. "It's like you say, Uncle Arthur. Some women are worth everything."

"And the truth is one of our greatest treasures," Louisa said, sitting down on the love seat across from where Arthur and Clara sat. "I'd love some tea. Connor?"

"Sure," he said, coming over and joining her. "Thank you, Hargreaves. I didn't congratulate you on your victory last night."

"I believe the supposed lost recipe gave me the edge, sir," Hargreaves said, pouring two more cups of tea. "If you'll excuse me, I'll bring in the sandwiches."

"We already ate at a greasy spoon, Hargreaves, so no need," Louisa said, patting her belly. "Well, I can feel the tension in this room. Whew! Perhaps I should start off by saying how incredibly happy I am to know Connor is related to you wonderful people. And how much I love your nephew here."

Clara's mouth flapped open like a prize trout while Arthur wanted to jump to his feet and lift his hands to heaven. "Love, eh? Well, I can't say I'm not thrilled. We've been awfully worried about this one. I assume you know everything if you're here, Louisa."

"I do," she said, sipping her tea. "Oh, this is good. Jasmine? Yes, I know what happened with Corey and his old job, and the fact that Connor is a billionaire. You should know he's agreed to sell me the property he bought yesterday. He didn't know it was the place I was eyeing for the training program."

Arthur studied Connor. "Well, love has a way of surprising everyone, doesn't it?"

"Yes," Louisa said with a laugh. "It's been a fast, wild

ride so far, and I can't wait to see what happens next."

"She didn't kick me out when I told her everything," Connor said, gazing at Louisa as if the sun rose and set on her. "Only listened with that giant heart of hers." Connor lifted her hand to his mouth and kissed it.

The poignancy of the gesture made Arthur's own heart warm. He squeezed his bride's hand. Although he'd never admit to it aloud, especially not to Clara, matchmaking and love were starting to be up there with writing articles for newspapers. He loved that life could still be so surprising.

Clara was teary-eyed. "I just knew there was a spark between you two. I was hopeful despite other…issues. Louisa, you're everything anyone could hope for."

"You're not bad either, Connor," Arthur said with a smirk.

Connor shook his head. "Of course, I know falling for a great woman doesn't undo any of the problems I've caused. I know I have issues to face and apologies to make. I'm working on it."

Louisa handed him a cup of tea. "Tell him one of your first steps."

He folded his hands after setting his tea aside. "I called a counselor Louisa recommended this morning and made an appointment. After seeing Corey's son last night at the competition—"

"We heard, dear," Clara said, fingering her bracelets. "It's one of the reasons we wanted to speak to you."

"Let me guess. Olivia freaked out and called my mom." Connor ran a hand through his hair. "Crap, I knew it was a possibility, but I couldn't tell Joseph to keep seeing me a secret."

"Of course you couldn't, Connor," Clara said, her face somber. "He's only a boy and doesn't understand what's going on. I spoke to your parents this morning, and they're coming back this way to talk to her."

Connor leaned forward, all his energy focused on Clara.

Arthur wanted to roll his eyes at his wife's slip-up, but kept his mouth shut.

"What do you mean 'back this way?'" he asked, his tone hard.

"Before you pounce," Arthur interjected, feeling the Big Bad Wolf's hackles rising, "you should know your brother Trevor is a master at finding people. He had former SEALs staking out Olivia's house. They knew you were in town the moment you showed up. Turns out SEALs don't halt their stakeouts for snowstorms, unlike hardened journalists." He was still put out about that.

"Oh, give it a rest, Arthur. I wasn't going to let you or me sit in a parked car in a snowstorm," Clara said, clucking her tongue. "Connor, I know we had an agreement, but what were we supposed to do? Your entire family was waiting in our suite when we came home the night after I made the donation, all of them worried sick about you."

Connor stood up, his body coiled with obvious tension. "*Everyone*? You mean they've known this whole time, and you didn't say anything?"

Arthur stood as well, facing the boy. "What was there to say? They promised not to interfere, which is what you wanted, right? We kept helping you like we'd agreed. Son, they were worried about you. We all were. But it seems like you've found a new purpose here in South Side. Meeting Louisa and wanting to help her has been the best thing for you. And when your parents arrive, that's what we plan on telling them."

"Excuse me, I need a moment," Connor said, crossing to the balcony and opening the door.

Even from this distance, Arthur could see the man gripping the cold metal bars of the balcony.

Louisa glanced at him too, as if she wanted to go to him but knew he needed a moment alone. Turning to Arthur, she said, "He's torn up about his family, and he doesn't know how to make things right."

Arthur nodded. "It's been difficult for everyone, but they love him and only want to help."

"He has to want to help himself," Louisa said. "Trust me, I know this by heart. When are his parents coming?"

"They were hoping to leave today, so I expect late tonight," Clara said.

"If they find a flight." Louisa looked back over to where Connor was standing.

"No, they're...not flying commercial," Clara said, clearing her throat.

Louisa gave an ironic laugh. "Right. They probably have their own plane."

"Several, in fact," Arthur said with a laugh, sitting down again. "But that's not important now. Is Connor more afraid to face his parents or of what Olivia might say to her boys about him?"

Louisa put her hand to her mouth before saying, "I don't know. If I were in his place, both, I'd imagine. Okay, he's had enough alone time. I'm going to him. Clara, where would Hargreaves have put my coat? Just because that man runs hot doesn't mean I'm going out there like this."

Hargreaves appeared with Louisa's coat moments after Clara called his name. That man had a knack for anticipating everyone's needs, no doubt about it.

"Wish me luck," she said, charging out the door like a determined bull.

Arthur looked at his wife. "My dear, I believe we all just hit the jackpot with that one. What she's done with him is nothing short of miraculous. This matchmaker is starting to think love might be the answer to every problem."

"I only hope it continues, Arthur." Clara worried her diamonds. "I don't want her to get hurt. His volatility might be better, and I'm glad he's getting help, but it can't be gone."

No, it likely wasn't, but Arthur had a feeling Louisa could take care of herself.

CHAPTER 18

HIS PARENTS WERE COMING.

Was he ready to face them? As he gripped the balcony's rails, his insides roiled. Olivia must have been crazy upset for them to up and fly to Chicago.

Learning his entire family had known where he was all this time had pain lashing across his temples. He couldn't believe *no one* had contacted him. Gotten in his face. Punched him. They'd left him alone.

Like he'd wanted. Did that mean they'd stopped caring? No, they'd all come to Chicago to talk to Arthur and Clara. Maybe they didn't know what to say to him either.

"All right," he heard his favorite tough girl say, stepping up beside him at the balcony. "You're clearly upset. Want to tell me why?"

He punched the frosty air. "Isn't it obvious?"

She rested her elbows on the rails, and he was relieved to see she was all suited up in her winter gear. Otherwise, he'd have gone inside so she wouldn't freeze.

"I try not to read minds when people are upset," she said, her head turned in his direction.

"You read minds all the time," he said, feeling contrary. "You're one of the most emotionally intelligent people I've ever met."

"Thank you," she said with a pat on his back. "But back to you. Connor, why are you so upset?"

"You do realize that whatever Joseph said to Olivia last night upset her so much my parents felt it necessary to make a special trip to handle her."

"It wasn't your fault you and Joseph ran into each other," she said in her normal fair-minded way. "In fact, why not look at this from a different angle? What if the two of you running into each other was the best thing that could have happened for both of you?"

She would say that. "Louisa, it sounds like he went home crying. How is that good?"

"Let's talk about you first. Seeing that boy helped break you down to the point where you decided to get some help. Personally, I think that's pretty incredible."

He growled. "Joseph wasn't the only reason. Our talk last night factored in. I love you, and I don't want to lose you."

She hugged him briefly and kissed him on the cheek. "Logical but romantic."

"I'm not at my best right now," he shot back. "My parents are coming…"

"So you're not dancing on clouds right now," she said. "You don't have to be anything but what you are."

"What I am is upset."

Resuming her posture against the railing, she said, "I know. You still haven't answered why."

"Because I'm forty years old, and I feel like I've gotten in trouble. Again." He swore under his breath. "I hate that I upset the very people I'm trying to help, even more so because my parents have to come smooth things over. It makes me feel like a kid again. A delinquent."

She took his face in her hands then. "The question we need to get to—*you* need to get to—is why you feel so responsible for other people's lives and emotions."

"Maybe it's the first child bullshit." He swore again.

"My parents were always asking me to look out for the younger kids. I hate sounding like a cliché."

"You're no cliché," she said, "and you do swear impressively. You could give some competition to Carter on a bad day, let me tell you. But I think it's more than being the oldest. I think..."

"I thought you didn't read minds," he said, his mouth twisting up at the corners.

"This is more analysis, which you like. As I was saying..."

He touched her nose playfully. "You're so damn good for me, Louisa."

She smiled, her face radiant. She hadn't put on much makeup. They'd showered together, and he'd watched her get ready in the small bathroom. He'd known before that she didn't doll up her face, but now he had the inside knowledge. All she used was bronzer and mascara with some lip gloss.

"You're also more beautiful than Rihanna," he said, tracing her cheek.

"Aww... If I tweeted that, I expect I'd have millions disagree, but we digress. Back to you. I think you have a god complex, probably because everyone expected you to take over the big family company. You think it's on your shoulders to take care of everyone, to make everyone happy. Connor, you're one of the most honorable men I've ever met."

He put up his hand, his insides twisting for a different reason now. "No, I'm not. I can be as ruthless as they come."

"Maybe you've been ruthless, but on the inside, I expect you were doing it for a damn good reason."

"Didn't make it right."

She shook her head. "Didn't make it wrong either. Damn, you're so stubborn. You can't make a friend of everyone in business, but we're digressing. Let's cut to the chase. Are you planning on seeing your parents today?"

His diaphragm seized up. "I've never thought of myself as a coward, but right now, I just want to put on my running gear and speed off. That pisses me off too."

"Do you want to kick the rail?" she asked, testing it for him. "Seems pretty sturdy. So you're upset. Under that, you're hurt. Because here's the kicker. You think Olivia freaked out because she's worried you'd hurt Joseph."

Shit. His eyes burned. "I would *never*."

She rubbed his back. "What you have is a perception problem."

That caught his attention like the first tug of a ninety-pound black grouper when he'd gone deep sea fishing in Florida with his brothers. "Tell me more."

"You've exhibited unusual behavior since Corey died, correct?" she asked, her direct golden gaze drilling into him.

He nodded. "The reasons don't matter. They think I'm...acting rash. Volatile. They aren't wrong, Louisa."

"You're processing your grief," she said. "Doesn't make some of the actions right, but have you explained yourself to your family? Listened to their side? Maybe your parents coming here is just what you need."

"After the way I ran off, I was afraid I'd lost them," he whispered harshly. "And that I couldn't get them back."

"Babe, listen to me. Look through those windows."

He followed the line of her fingers. Clara had started pacing, and Arthur was scratching a pen onto a newspaper sitting on the couch.

"That's your family, and they're here." She put her hands on his chest. "Your parents are coming—for the second time. Connor, I've seen a lot of families go through troubles, and last night, hearing some of your pain, I threatened to punch them for hurting you. But today, I'm reserving this fist of mine. Meet with them. Tell them you're sorry. Tell them you're going to see a counselor. Share what's in here." She beat his chest softly, where his heart lay.

Share what was inside him? No one wanted to hear that. *He* didn't want to hear that.

"Babe..."

"I like that name," he said, taking her hand. "I'm stewing about all of this sharing. It's not what I'm used to. People used to look to me for decisive, unemotional responses. It's hard to act differently."

"If it stays inside, it festers. I know. And trust me, if your family still loves you, you have every chance of making things right. You know when I knew we'd lost my mom for good?"

He almost didn't want to hear it. Sometimes hearing what she'd gone through broke his heart anew. But if she could be courageous enough to tell him, he could listen. "When?"

She took a deep breath. "Not too long after she bought me that horrible doll, she got even deeper into drugs. This time it was heroin. She said the old drugs weren't making her feel good anymore. It's a common issue with drug users. Anyway, she got hooked on heroin, and things started to go south real quick. One night when I was waiting for her outside this heroin shack in an underpass, some guy approached me..."

His gut wrenched. Until now, he hadn't thought of the danger she'd have been in. Why hadn't he?

"He was a predator. I'd seen enough of them to know." Her mouth tightened. "They all have the same feral look in their eyes. I ran inside to find her. There were about ten people in this place, all lying on these dirty, sick-smelling cots. I went to my mom and shook her. Told her I wanted to stay with her. She looked past me and said it was too hard to take care of me and that I should go away and leave her alone. When I told her I loved her—something I did to bring her back—she closed her eyes and said it wasn't enough. *It didn't matter anymore.*"

He pulled her into his arms and held her tightly.

"I'm okay. Really. It took me a long time to share that story with anyone, and when I finally got it out, I couldn't stop crying. Then I got angry. And then I cried again. It was one of the worst moments of my life. I remember looking at her thin, slack face. Her hair was dirty and tangled, and she had dirt smudged on her skin. She was so thin. She didn't look anything like the strong, brave mom whom I remembered. The one who went off to war to serve her country. She looked hollowed out. Almost dead. And I realized, even though I was a kid, that inside she was."

Kissing the top of her head, he found it hard to speak. "Nothing like that is *ever* going to happen to you again. I swear."

She tightened her arms around him. "I know that, and I didn't tell you that story to make you feel bad for me. It's to show you there's hope with your family. They haven't given up on you, and from what I can tell, they won't."

"I'm glad you told me, Louisa," he said, taking her hands. "Dammit, I love you. And your love will always be enough."

Pressing her head into his chest, she burrowed into him. "Your love will always be enough for me too."

In that moment, the whole world opened up for him. As he looked across the lake, he wondered if this was how his Grandpa Noah had felt coming back from the war to a woman he'd fallen in love with through letters. Letters across an open sea, his grandparents had called them.

His grandpa had always been open about the difficulties of life on the front, and how coming home had posed its own set of challenges. Chicago had been new to him, and although Grandma Anna's brother, who'd died in action, had been his best friend and brother-in-arms, he'd never met her in person. His return home had been fraught with anxiety and hope. Grandpa had often said letting go of what he'd done during the war had taken more courage than what his duty had called him to do.

Surely Connor had that much courage inside him. "I'm going to see my parents. Ah... Would you like to meet them? If it goes well?" Because that was a possibility, right?

"You don't usually hesitate," she said, looking up at him. "Do you want me to?"

"Yes. You're important to me." His diaphragm eased its grip of his ribs. "Of course, I wish it were under different circumstances."

"Nothing is ever as perfect as we think." She laid her head on his chest again. "You're making some pretty big progress."

"Does that mean I don't have to talk to your counselor?" He was mostly kidding.

She snorted. "Like I said, it's your choice, but I still think it would be a smart move. Besides, he's good at helping people figure out what they want to do next beyond overcoming some emotional issues. You might find value in that."

"I might indeed," he said, "since I have all this time on my hands. If I don't have enough to do with it, I'll go crazy."

"I have a feeling you're going to be fine," she said, stepping back. "Ready to go inside? Your aunt and uncle appear to be fretting."

"We have been out here awhile."

"And you without a coat," she said, touching his hand. "Come inside with me. We'll warm you up. Then you and your aunt and uncle can brief me on your parents."

"You're staying?" he asked. "I might want to talk to them alone first, and if that goes well..."

She waved him off. "Don't lead with the negative. That was one of my love notes last month. Expect the best, Connor, and you might be surprised."

"You don't know how bad it's been, Louisa." He gave her a pointed look. "When I say I've screwed up, I mean it. I've made a mess of everything."

"So apologize. You feel remorse. Trust me, there's

nothing worse than someone apologizing and not meaning it. That really pisses me off."

He fought a smile. "You're adorable when you're pissed, I suspect."

"You're not, by the way. As ferocious-looking as they come. Maybe dial that back a bit when you talk to your parents. Hear them out. You might not like everything you hear, and some of it might hurt like hell, but that's part of reconciliation. You can do it, babe. I have faith in you."

"Are you *always* this positive?" he asked, excited on some level to learn everything there was to know about her.

She held her hands up to the sky. "I am mostly. My dad helped me with that. You should hear his halftime speeches. Epic. After what I went through, I figure it's all easy street now. I try to stay grateful. Look for the good in life and people. I saw it in you, didn't I?"

"Yeah, you sure did," he whispered, suddenly emotional. "You saw it when I couldn't."

She squeezed him tightly for a moment, and he savored the contact. She talked about miracles all the time, but he knew the truth. She was the miracle.

"Last point," she said, making space to gaze up at him with those beautiful golden eyes of hers. "I figure we can choose how we want to feel, and I've decided I want to feel good and stay positive. I hope you join me, babe, because I'd hate to do it without you."

He watched her sail inside, and he took a moment to mull over what she'd said. She was right. He'd forged a company with his vision and attitude. It was time to use the same focus for his life. Because he wasn't about to lose the best thing that had ever happened to him or this second chance, and it wasn't fair to ask her to carry all the water.

She deserved the best he could be, and he wanted to give it to her.

Now all he had to do was face his parents.

CHAPTER 19

LOUISA SHRUGGED OUT OF HER COAT ONCE INSIDE, KNOW-ing she'd done everything she could to inspire Connor to take the next steps.

He had to do it for himself, but since she understood him, she'd been able to reach him. She'd have to tell her dad about her whole "perception problem" line. He might be able to use that with one of his players.

"You look pretty pleased with yourself," Arthur commented, tossing aside his newspaper. "I hate to burst your bubble, but your purse has been vibrating. Clara and I were torn about fetching you since it seemed you and Connor were having a deep conversation."

"From your smile, it looks like the conversation went well," Clara said, coming over and putting her hands on Louisa's shoulders. "I can't tell you how grateful we are for you, my dear."

"I'm grateful too." Her purse started buzzing again, and she crossed to it. "Excuse me a sec. I only have a few phone numbers programmed to go through when I have my phone on Do Not Disturb, so it's important."

When she picked her phone up, she noted six missed calls and then a bunch of texts from Boxer. Pulling them up, she read them quickly.

There's a woman here insisting she speak to you.

I've tried to tell her you aren't working today, but she's pushy.

Not homeless. She won't tell me her name or why she wants to speak with you.

I can't get her to go nicely, and I don't think calling the police and having them make her leave is the way. She isn't crazy. Just very upset about something. Don't think Mrs. Cuddles will help even.

If you aren't answering the phone, I know it means you're doing something else. Wink. Holler when you can. I have her installed in my office for the moment.

She shook her head. The wink was about her having sex. If only he knew what she was really up to right now. She wondered who the woman was. Running a homeless shelter, it could be anyone. God, this is the last thing she wanted to deal with, but if Boxer couldn't make her leave, she'd have to go.

"I need to talk to Boxer," she said, turning around as Connor finally came back inside. "Is there somewhere I can go for a minute to make the call?"

"If you'll follow me, Miss Evans," Hargreaves said from the doorway, "I'll show you to a private spot."

"What's wrong?" Connor asked, his body instantly alert.

"A shelter thing," she said, waving her hand. "I might need to pop over there and come back. Give me a sec to call."

She followed Hargreaves to a lovely study with dark wood built-ins. Goodness, this was one hell of a suite. After Hargreaves shut the door, she dialed Boxer.

"Hey! Sorry I wasn't picking up. It wasn't for the reason you thought. I'll explain later. About this woman... Will she talk to me on the phone? I'm downtown right now, and with traffic, it would take me about forty minutes to get back to the shelter. Plus, I'd have to come back here."

"Yeah, sorry about this. I've tried to get her to talk to me, but she's remained adamant. Let me see if she'll talk to you. Hang on."

She gazed out at the beautiful view. The last twenty-four hours had been life-changing, but then again, the transformation had started the night she'd met Connor. If there was one thing she knew about life it was that it was important to roll with things. Here she was in this incredible suite of a couple she'd come to care about even before she'd discovered they were the family of the man she'd fallen in love with at record speed. Later, she'd be meeting his parents.

Please let their talk go well. Help them remember why they love each other.

That was going to have to be her new love note: *Remember why you love each other.* It was the most important thing.

"She understands the inconvenience and apologizes, but says she needs to speak with you in person," Boxer said. "I asked about making an appointment for this week, but she said you'd want to hear this today. That the shelter's well-being might depend on it. She didn't tell me that earlier, and I'd like to dismiss it, but she seems to believe what she's saying."

"The shelter's well-being, huh? All right, I'll head out shortly. This had better be worth it."

"You're telling me," Boxer said. "I've had to watch her like a hawk, and she's put me behind today."

"Sorry about that. I'll see you soon."

"Thanks, Louisa," Boxer said. "I hated to bother you."

"I know it. Don't give it another thought. Bye."

She hung up and went back to the main room. Connor was standing beside the couch, talking with Arthur.

"Everything okay?" he asked, coming over to her.

"I need to deal with something at the shelter," she said. "It shouldn't take too long. I'll swing back here when I'm finished."

"You sure? I can go with you."

"No, stay here. You need to be settled for your talk with your parents. This will only distract you. Besides, you'll only have to wait at the shelter for me, and Carter might finally make good on his threats and put you to work in the kitchen."

"I doubt it," he said, "since I'm all thumbs in there. Okay, let me call you a car."

He had his phone out before she could say anything about taking the "L" train back. Traffic wouldn't be great, but at least she wouldn't have to sit through all the stops on the train. "Thanks."

"It will be downstairs in five," Connor said, pocketing his phone. "I'll walk you down."

She decided to let him and hugged Arthur and Clara before she left. Hargreaves too, although it seemed to alarm him. Connor took her hand in the elevator, and that was when she felt it. They'd become a unit. It felt like the most natural thing in the world for him to reach for her hand and hold it. In the lobby, she headed for the doors. He pulled her back.

"You'll get cold waiting on the street. I'll tell you when the car's out front."

More consideration—this was the kind of gentlemanly gesture that didn't chafe. When the car arrived, she made to dash for the door.

"He's here for you," Connor said. "No need to rush. You sure you don't need me to come?"

She shook her head. "No, I'll be fine."

"Text me when you're ready to come back, and I'll call

another car," he said, arranging the scarf he'd given her higher on her neck to keep out the cold. "I mean it, Louisa."

"Yes, sir. See you." She leaned up and kissed him on the cheek.

He cupped her face. "Uh-huh." The kiss he laid on her mouth was one of the sweetest and gentlest she'd ever experienced.

When he released her, she sighed. "I really like that."

Smiling, he opened the door before the bellman could. "So do I. Be safe, okay?"

He was worried, she realized. "Always."

She headed to the car and chatted with the driver briefly before pulling out her phone to text her dad.

Gave a halftime speech to Connor you'd have been proud of. Shared with him some of the things you taught me. Just wanted you to know how grateful I am that you're my dad and how much I love you. You're the best.

Goodness, she was feeling emotional, but perhaps that was par for the course. She was in love, a new and powerful feeling. This relationship with Connor was reshaping the course of her life. She could feel it. Her dad texted her back.

Big words on a cold day. Warms my heart to hear them. Can't wait to hear more. And I'm grateful for you too. Love you to pieces.

She sent a heart emoji and set her phone aside. Putting her hand on her heart, she fell into the moment. Everything was exactly where it needed to be, and she trusted in that. Once she'd found her faith in life, it had never let her down.

At the shelter, she said goodbye to the driver. She spotted the kid from the other night up the block with two local gang members she recognized. What had his name been?

Jax? She called out a greeting to him. He hadn't seemed like the gang type. Maybe he was looking for drugs?

They all turned and looked at her, the two gang members staring her down. She stared right back.

"You doing okay, Jax?" she called out when he lifted a hand quickly, a half wave he seemed ashamed to have initiated when the guys next to him turned their feral gazes onto him.

"Yeah. Later." That was all the reply she received before the trio started walking in the opposite direction.

Good, she thought. They should know she didn't like any gang members or drug dealers this close to the shelter. She and her staff had put the word out, and their boundaries were usually respected. After she met with this mysterious woman, she'd talk to Boxer about the trio.

When she walked in, she fixed her gaze on her newest love note. *Miracles happen every day when you look for them. Pay attention.*

She greeted the staff member at reception and headed down the hall, shrugging out of her coat as she walked to Boxer's office. In the doorway, she noted the short brown hair of the woman sitting in front of her friend's desk. Dressed in a black sweater and jeans, she was tapping her foot.

"I'm Louisa Evans," she said, smiling at Boxer when he looked up. "I understand you want to speak with me."

The woman rose and turned around. "I'm Olivia Weatherby. I see from your face that you know who I am."

Well, this was unexpected. "Yes, why don't we go into my office and talk?"

"Thank you, Mr. Boxer," Olivia said. "I know I was a little pushy."

Boxer put his hand over his mouth like he was holding back a response. "You sure you're good, Louisa?"

"Yes, Olivia and I will be fine. I'm in the next office, if you'll follow me."

The woman's boots echoed on the tile floor as they entered her office. Louisa hung her coat up on the hook behind her door after closing it behind them. "Please sit down, Mrs. Weatherby."

The woman did, clutching her knees. "I'm sorry for being so insistent about speaking with you, but after what Joseph told me about last night, I didn't feel I had a choice."

Louisa gauged the woman's bloodshot eyes and pale face, deciding it was best to tread lightly. "What exactly did Joseph tell you?"

"That his Uncle Connor is working with you at this shelter." The woman rocked in her chair. "I didn't believe it at first, but Joseph was so upset about it, I couldn't dismiss it. I mean, he was supposed to be sleeping at his friend's house, but he wouldn't stop crying about his uncle and why he hadn't come to visit. The boy's parents brought him home."

Louisa's heart hurt for the little boy, but she let the woman speak.

"His brother got upset too, hearing about Connor, and after I finally got them calmed down and off to bed, I looked up your shelter. Of course, I'd heard about your cooking competitions. When I saw that Clara Merriam Hale had given you a million dollars, I just knew Connor was behind it. I'd hoped he'd left town as I told him I didn't want him around the boys."

Louisa told herself to remember what this woman had been through. "Mrs. Weatherby, I'm deeply sorry for your pain, but I'm still not clear on why you wanted to see me. This is a family matter."

The woman's eyes narrowed. "If you're working with Connor like Joseph said, I'm here to tell you not to. He's made a recent string of volatile reactions and can't be trusted right now. We're all dealing with Corey's death. I lost my husband. But Connor's actions are irrational and out of bounds, and everyone in the family knows it, or he wouldn't have been fired."

Louisa had to bite her tongue to keep from defending Connor. That wouldn't help. Olivia clearly was dealing with her own pain and needed to rant. When she finished, Louisa would do her best to respond in a calm, patient manner. But man, this woman was pushing her buttons, telling her what to do.

"I want you to tell him to leave town," Olivia said, her tone hard. "I don't know why he's helping you, but it's not out of the goodness of his heart."

Not out of the goodness of his heart? Louisa fisted her hands under the desk. After everything Connor had done for and with Corey's family, this woman had every reason to believe he had a good heart. She'd agreed to let him be the godfather to her sons, for Pete's sake. Sure, he'd done some regrettable things out of grief, but he wasn't a bad man.

"Mrs. Weatherby, it's not for me to give Connor any messages for you. Perhaps you might consider leaving him a note. I can pass it along to him when he comes in." Of course, she feared what the note might say, but she couldn't control events. Long ago, she'd given up trying. All she could do was tell Connor he was a good man if he read otherwise in Olivia's note.

The woman pulled at her sweater, gripping the edges with her hands in clear distress. "I told him when he visited me that I don't want him around the boys. Clearly he didn't listen. If he thinks working with you at some homeless shelter like Saint Connor is going to soften me up, he's wrong. Joseph hasn't been this upset since his father's funeral, and I won't have it. Do you hear me?"

Boxer opened the door and stuck his head in, clearly worried about the shouting, but Louisa motioned him off.

"The boys don't understand why Connor is a bad influence right now, and I don't have the heart to tell them.

I forbade them to visit this shelter when they asked if we could come here to see Connor."

Forbade them? Louisa weighed what more to say. She didn't want to get in the middle of this. Connor had finally decided to speak with his parents, a monumental step, and they were coming to town to speak with Olivia. She didn't want to hurt anyone's chance at a reconciliation. "Again, I'm sorry for what you're going through, but I'm afraid I can't help you. This is a family matter."

Olivia stood up, her muscles stiff with anger. "I've read about you in the papers, and everyone says you're a nice woman and good for the community. From where I'm standing, they're wrong. Otherwise, you'd know he was a danger and help me."

That was the last straw. "Mrs. Weatherby, I won't defend my actions to you, but I also won't let you assassinate my character in my own place of business. Now, I've done my best to listen to you and be kind. I would ask you to extend the same courtesy."

"You don't understand," Olivia said, holding her hands out. "My husband is *dead* because he loved Connor and wanted to help him. He preferred to stay on an oil rig nine months out of the year for Connor than to be home with his own family."

So there were cracks in the marriage before his death? Louisa was sorry to hear it, but her anger at Connor was starting to make sense. She'd been angry before her husband had died. That he'd died on the job had likely only made it worse.

"I'm doing my best to raise my boys without my husband, but Connor isn't making that any easier, hanging around here. I would have thought he'd know that after seeing Joseph last night. My son was inconsolable. If you aren't willing to help another woman in need, who came to you out of concern for the shelter's welfare and your own reputation, then fine."

Louisa took a deep breath before answering. "Mrs. Weatherby, your concern for the shelter and my reputation is unfounded. While I'm aware of Connor's recent predicaments, I'm here to tell you that he is a good man and one I trust. I appreciate you disagree with that. That's your prerogative. But I will continue to work with him. That's *my* prerogative. I wish you and your boys all the best in healing from an unimaginable loss, but Connor is trying to heal from that loss too, and your approach won't be helpful for any of you. I'm a certified counselor, so you can trust me on that."

"You're blind," Olivia said, walking to the door and opening it. "He needs to be stopped from himself. I guess I'll have to do it alone. Don't say I didn't warn you."

She stomped out, her boots echoing in the hallway before fading away. Too bad Louisa couldn't make their meeting fade away. By God, no wonder Connor had been sitting out in the snowstorm after his meeting with Olivia that night. She took a deep breath. Okay, she wasn't impartial when it came to Connor, but she knew people—always had—and she wasn't wrong about Connor.

"You want to tell me who the hell that woman was and why she was shouting at you?" Boxer asked from the doorway. "Carter and Spicy came charging out of the kitchen when they heard her. I had to talk them down from going in there."

"It's a long story, and a personal one," she said, rubbing her temples. "Let's put it this way: if I'd thought there was even the smallest chance she'd listen, I would have suggested she seek grief counseling. Man, that wasn't what I expected when I got up this morning."

Boxer came over and rubbed her shoulders. "Been a while since you've been yelled at like that. Guess I should have called the police instead of ruining your Saturday."

"No, I...learned some important things," she said, thinking about Connor and his family. "Not sure what I'm going to do with them yet, but I'll give myself a little time before I decide."

"What brought you downtown?" Boxer asked.

"I'm meeting Connor's parents tonight." She cracked her neck. "I'll need to be in top shape."

"You're meeting Connor's parents? Louisa, girl, that's pretty fast."

She shrugged. "When have I ever done anything slow? I love him, Boxer. Like maybe the forever kind."

He whistled. "Does he expect them to have any issues about you being mixed?"

"No, I don't believe so. From what he tells me, their values about people being people are like ours."

Nodding, he said, "Love shouldn't be sullied with that kind of crap. This may have happened fast, but you've got a good head on your shoulders. I know you're going into this with your eyes wide open."

"I finally know his last name and his story," she said, pushing out of the chair.

"Figured you'd get it out of him. Is his story anything like you expected?"

She chuckled, her heart lightening up. "Not a bit. But you didn't get it right with the director thing." Not that any of her guesses had hit the mark either. She never would have pegged him for a billionaire.

"Isn't that how life is?" Boxer said. "We try to control it. Folly. Every time. So, anything you can tell me?"

"He's Clara's nephew," she said, laughing as Boxer's mouth went slack.

"You're kidding. But she's—"

"Rich as Midas? So is he. Only he's in a serious career transition. Long story. One he can share with you if he's willing. Now, I need to eat and get ready for tonight."

After meeting Olivia, she planned to be ready to go nine rounds with his parents if it came to it.

CHAPTER 20

L OUISA HAD A KNACK FOR GETTING TO THE ROOT OF A STO-ry, and that gift was never more on display than when she returned to the suite to tell everyone about her encounter with Olivia.

"What do you mean, she came to the shelter to see you?" Connor asked. And he'd thought he was upset about his parents' visit. This felt so much worse. "Damn it, I didn't want you to get sucked into my crap."

"I handled it," she said, handing her coat to Hargreaves. "I had some time in the car to figure out what to tell you. Here goes. You're not the only one who's exhibiting uncharacteristic behavior due to grief. It's time to stop feeling guilty and accept that grief sometimes messes people up for a while, you notwithstanding."

Since he trusted Louisa's instincts about people, he knew she must be right about Olivia acting differently. When he'd visited her it had been so brief, and he'd been too caught up in his own feelings to really assess how she was doing. He'd assumed poorly, but clearly there was more to it.

Uncle Arthur poured her a cup of tea and extended it before Hargreaves could. "Well put, my dear."

Aunt Clara fiddled with her bracelets. "I imagine Olivia

will be calling my brother and his wife to express her un-happiness that you didn't go along with her wishes."

Connor's stomach, already a popcorn machine of ten-sion, tightened. "If she badmouths you, Louisa, I..." He reined his emotions back in.

"Don't worry," she said, "I can handle myself with your parents if it comes to it. We'll see when they arrive."

For the next two hours, Uncle Arthur and Louisa en-tertained them by telling colorful stories about their re-spective professions. Of course, Connor knew they were doing their best to keep the mood upbeat. He appreciated their moral support and did his best to listen, but his ear was cocked toward the door.

When a knock finally landed, setting Connor's heart to racing, he watched as Hargreaves opened the door for his parents. No one had said they'd be joined by more of the family, but Michaela and Boyd filed in behind them.

He flinched, seeing the baby sister he'd failed so bad-ly.

The next thing he knew Michaela was running across the suite and throwing her arms around him. He clutched her to him and realized she was crying. What was he sup-posed to say?

"Oh, Connor, I'm glad you're here. I was so scared we'd never see you again."

Her love blew through him, and he pressed his face into her familiar curly brown hair. A memory surfaced of him doing the same when she was little. She'd fallen and skinned her knee, trying to catch a wounded bird, and he'd let her play with his briefcase until she smiled. The words tumbled out of him. "Mickey, I'm so sorry. For how I acted. For everything. I know it's not enough—"

"Shut up," she said, pushing back, scrubbing at her tears. "Don't you ever say that you're not enough. Con, we love you. I love you. And yes, it was awful, but not nearly as awful as you shutting us out and disappearing.

I thought it was my fault—that what happened with me might have been the last straw—so I'm sorry too."

He brushed back the damp hair at her temple, aware his own nose was running. He swiped at it. "You didn't do anything. I flipped out when I heard you were sick and we couldn't find you, but I know that's no excuse. I could have handled it better, but hell... I..."

His heart needed an anchor, and he turned his head to Louisa. She was standing next to Clara, tears in her eyes. She smiled at him, simply smiled, and he found the courage to do what she'd suggested—share his heart.

"Losing Corey was the worst day of my life, but when I thought I might lose you too—after I sent you on that trip myself—Mickey, something inside of me snapped. I would have torn the world apart to find you. With Corey, I couldn't even do that. He was gone by the time I found out, and I...couldn't accept that. Again, I'm sorry. I'm so sorry."

She hugged him again, crying against his chest. Something cracked inside of him, as if he were made of ice and he was thawing from the warmth of her love. Tears began to run down his face, and he pressed his face into her hair, ashamed of them but unable to stop the flow. If this was healing, it fucking hurt.

Then he felt another pair of arms come around him, and the welcome familiarity of them made him release a sigh.

"Mom," he whispered, shifting so he could put one arm around her.

She was crying softly too, patting his back like she'd done when he was a child, upset about a toy not working or, later, getting an A minus. "Oh, honey. We've missed you so much."

Stronger arms banded around him, ones so like his own. "Dad."

"Yeah, son." His father's voice was hoarse with tears. "Welcome home."

More tears streaked down his cheeks, but he didn't want to let go of anyone to brush them away. His chest was hurting, his head was pounding, and his nose was running like a faucet, but it didn't matter.

Somehow they'd found a way back to one another.

"Oh, God, I'm getting snot all over your sweater, Con," Mickey said, easing back. "Sorry."

"A handkerchief, Miss Michaela?" Hargreaves asked, stepping forward with an assortment of finely pressed linen. That man never missed a beat. "Anyone else?"

Connor took one and wiped his face. "Well, that was intense. Sorry I cried. Not my normal."

"Me either," Michaela said after blowing her nose. "Caitlyn's the crier in the family."

"Nothing wrong with that," Dad said, wiping his eyes. "We all had a lot of emotion about this."

He met his father's eyes. Searched for judgment. This was the man he'd idolized, the man who'd trusted him to take over their family company. The man he felt he'd failed. Inspired by Louisa, who was standing a short distance away, he decided to say as much. "Dad, I let you down with the company."

"Hey!" His dad gripped his shoulder. "No, we're not going there. You were hurting, and we didn't do enough to help you. That's on us. Now, you apologized. I'd like to do the same. I'm sorry we didn't fight you harder. I've been beating myself up since this all happened. Son, I think the reason you've felt so responsible for everyone started with me."

It felt like a bucketful of cold water had hit him in the face. "Sir?"

His dad tightened his mouth. "When we were on the yacht when you were eight, Quinn fell in and almost drowned. Do you remember?"

Heat blasted in his chest, opening up a door to old memories. "He and I were playing with paper airplanes, and Quinn's flew too close to the edge. He made a grab for it and fell between the bars." He could hear the splash and then his brother's cries. He'd stood rooted in place, shocked and unsure of what to do.

"I jumped in and fished him out," his dad was saying over the roar in his ears, "but I yelled at you for not watching him. For not jumping in and saving him."

He felt tears fill his eyes again. He remembered his dad shaking him, his angry shouts raining over him as Quinn stood next to them crying, dripping wet. "You were upset," the adult in him said.

"I blamed you." His dad's mouth twisted. "I was supposed to have been watching you boys, but I was working on budgets. I told you not to tell your mother. That wasn't good parenting. Maybe if we'd told her, she would have talked some sense into me."

"Shawn," Assumpta said, stroking his back. "Honey, we discussed this. There's an epidemic of beating oneself up in this family. Just apologize to Connor."

His dad put his hands on both of his shoulders. Connor had thought he was done crying, but all the emotion barreling through him, plus the tears in his father's eyes, was enough to send another tear down his cheek. He'd been so upset about what had happened with Quinn he'd cried himself to sleep that night. And anytime they'd been near water on family trips, he'd always watched his siblings like a hawk, not wanting anyone to get hurt.

"I'm sorry," his dad said, gripping him.

"It's okay, Dad." He was aware of some peace opening up in his chest as his dad hugged him hard. He hadn't thought about that incident in years, but given how painful it had been, surely it meant something. He'd have to ask Louisa about that later.

"No more second-guessing," his mom said, joining in their hug. "You're ours, Con, and we love you. That's all that matters."

When they let go of each other, he let himself look at Louisa. She had a handkerchief in her hand, and her eyes were trained on him. She nodded at him to continue. He wiped his nose again when it dripped. "I still embarrassed the family. Hurt the company. There are board members—"

"Connor, I love you so much," his mom said, putting her hand on top of his dad's on his shoulder, "so you hear me when I say that we're handling it. Let it go, honey."

He wasn't sure the others would feel that way. Would Quinn? He'd had to clean up Connor's mess. But Louisa was right—he couldn't control the way other people reacted to him. He could only apologize to his brother and everyone else and hope they'd embrace him like Mickey and his parents had.

"What else do we need to get off our chests here?" Connor asked. "Boyd? I'm sorry for how I acted with you in Kenya. There was no excuse for it."

"Well, I probably should apologize for punching you," Boyd said, coming forward and holding his hand out. "Tempers were high. I'd like to bury the hatchet if you will."

He took his hand. "I appreciate that. At some point, I hope Uncle Arthur and Aunt Clara can take my apology to the Maasai tribe as well."

"We'd be happy to, my boy," his aunt said, waving her own handkerchief at him.

"There's probably more to discuss," Connor said, "and I should tell you all I've decided to see a counselor. I also imagine Olivia has shared her opinions about the woman who runs the Sunflower Alley homeless shelter."

"She did, indeed," her mother said.

"That's not how I wanted you to first hear about Louisa," he said, holding his hand out to her and trying to give her an encouraging smile as she came toward him and took it. "Everyone, this is the most incredible woman I've ever met. She also happens to be the woman I love. So if we need to clear anything up about what Olivia said, I'd rather do it now. None of it would be accurate given how angry Olivia is with me."

Louisa held up her hand and said, "Hi, everyone."

Michaela raced across the room and grabbed Louisa by the shoulders. "Connor loves you? That's awesome! I mean, he doesn't even like most people."

Louisa laughed. "I'm aware of that, but I figure he might just need to find a new tribe."

"Yes," Michaela said. "Oh, I love you already."

"Me too." Connor's mother went over to Louisa and extended her hand. "I'm Assumpta, and this is my husband, Shawn. It's wonderful to meet you, Louisa."

"You too, Mrs. Merriam," she said, to which his mom immediately suggested—or rather insisted—she use their first names.

His dad held her hand warmly before releasing it. "Welcome to the family, Louisa."

Although Connor hadn't seriously thought his parents would hold Olivia's assessment against her, part of him had feared it, and his heart flooded with crazy emotions as he watched them embrace her.

"Thank you, Shawn." Louisa turned to Connor. "I'd say that's a pretty good second half. Wouldn't you, Connor?"

He knew she was referring to her game-time speech on the balcony. "To use one of your words, I'd call it downright miraculous."

"See, my positive influence is taking root." She buffed her nails against her shirt. "My work is nearly done."

He was laughing when Michaela said, "Con talking about miracles? Oh, my God. I'm in shock. Wait till I tell Caitlyn. Mom, you're going to have to tell Olivia she's not thinking straight. I mean I know she's upset, and I feel for her..."

"About Olivia," Louisa said, "I agree she's in a lot of pain and could use some counseling herself. Given her reaction today, I'd prefer it if she didn't know about my relationship with Connor just now. But I'll leave that up to you. I don't want to get in the middle of anything."

"Neither did we, frankly," Assumpta said with a sigh. "Sometimes I wish my brother hadn't left South Side for Arizona. He could have handled this. Sorry, Louisa, Corey was his son, so he's the boys' grandfather."

"It'll work out somehow, Assumpta," Shawn said. "All along, I've thought it would do the boys good to see you, Connor. I mean, I understand some of Olivia's reticence, but the notion that you'd do anything to hurt those boys is ridiculous."

His throat clogged up. "Thanks, Dad."

"Raising kids is tough," his mom said, "and no one can tell you how to do it."

"I agree," Uncle Arthur said, "but there's common sense too. Those boys love Connor, and he adores them. He's one of their connections to their father. Why keep him away? We get over our grief together. Not by putting up walls. And now I'll shut up."

"No, you're right," Assumpta said, pushing her gray hair back behind her ears. "I'll see what we can do about that. Louisa, I am sorry Olivia put you in a difficult position, but after meeting you, I know you can handle yourself. You're a South Side girl, after all."

"Damn straight," Louisa said. "I understand you are too, Mrs. Merriam."

"Assumpta, please, and it's like I tell my family, 'You can take the girl—'"

"Out of South Side, but you can't take South Side out of the girl," they all finished.

Michaela whistled. "Man, two South Side chicks in the family. Dad, do you think we're going to be able to handle it?"

He put his arm around Michaela. "I think we'll be luckier for it."

"Everyone else is going to flip when they hear about this," Michaela said.

Connor's stomach turned over at her words. "I haven't figured out what to do to reach out to everyone else. Frankly, I didn't expect to see you today, Mickey."

"Boyd and I decided to come so we could see you, of course, but we also wanted to talk to Aunt Clara and Uncle Arthur about their next trip to Kenya. And get their take on the best neighborhoods in Dare Valley."

He was so out of the loop. "What? You're moving to Dare Valley? When did this happen?"

She held up her left hand. "Since Boyd and I got engaged."

Happiness radiated from her, and since he appreciated anything that would make his little sister this joyful, he nodded to Boyd. "Congratulations, you two."

Kissing his cheek, she beamed. "Thank you, Connor. Despite what happened, we owe you for bringing us back together."

He hadn't considered that. "I only wish I'd been more... Never mind. Tell me about your move."

"The new company is going to be in Dare Valley," she continued, "so it seems only smart for us to be on-site. J.T. and Caroline are over the moon."

"So are we, Michaela," Aunt Clara said with a warm smile. "We'll be able to see each other anytime we want. Even for coffee at Don't Soy with Me."

"Over-priced frou-frou coffee," Uncle Arthur grumbled.

"That's your granddaughter's place," Michaela said.

"She knows it," Uncle Arthur said. "Of course, I also like to give her a hard time."

"Wait!" Connor held up his hand. "What new company?"

Michaela shared a look with their dad, whose expression turned serious as he folded his hands in front of him.

Somehow Connor knew to brace himself. This news was going to hurt.

"For a number of reasons we can go into later if you want, Con, Merriam Enterprises is selling off the pharmaceutical division to Evan Michaels' new company. Mickey and Boyd here will be leading up the plant science division—"

"Like we've wanted all along," Michaela said, coming over to him and taking his hand.

"What am I missing here?" he asked, sensing the tension in the room.

"It hasn't been announced yet, but the feeling was that our pharmaceutical division was a little vulnerable after what happened in Kenya. Your brother fired the head of the division—"

"I get the picture," Connor said, rubbing his brow. "That's a huge profit loss for Merriam. If I hadn't screwed up—"

"Boyd and I might not be working together and moving to Dare Valley," Michaela finished, pulling away his hands. "This is exactly the opportunity we've always hoped for. Connor, I know you feel bad. That's why Quinn was waiting to release the press announcement about the sale to Evan's company."

"You were holding up a billion-dollar business deal because you were worried how I'd react?" He swore. "Jesus, now I really feel like crap. I've been wondering how Quinn's taken all of this. Now I know."

"Hey!" His mom stepped closer. "Whatever you're thinking. Stop it. Your brother might be dealing with some things, but he's still your brother. He's been as worried about you as the rest of us. Don't sell him short. Okay?"

"If it were me, I'd be so pissed to be the one left holding that bag," Connor said. He'd have to offer his face to his brother for a solid punch.

"Before you start falling back into the rabbit hole of

shame," Louisa said, poking him in the chest to garner his attention, "how about we refocus on the positive? Aren't you relieved your family still loves you?"

His mouth twitched. "Yes, babe. I sure am."

"Oh, my God, she's like a wolf whisperer," he heard Michaela whisper to Boyd.

Arthur barked out a laugh. "That's a good one."

Louisa clasped her hands together. "Now about that celebration. I know this great place for steak. Babe, why don't you invite your family out to dinner?"

He rubbed her arm when what he really wanted to do was kiss her. "Why didn't I think of that? Where are you thinking?"

"Soledad," she said, linking her arm through his. "My brother won't deny us last-minute reservations."

He turned to his family, and it was wonderful to see them standing there. His parents were holding hands, beaming at him. He found it easy to smile at them in turn. Yeah, it was downright miraculous. "Would anyone like to go to dinner with us?"

"We'd love that," his mom said.

"Anyone mind if I invite a few people for brunch tomorrow too?" Michaela asked. "I figure the rest of the family can be here in the morning if they take a private plane. Maybe even Trevor."

Everyone? They all looked at Connor, waiting for him to respond. His insides did a wildly uncomfortable dance, but another part of him felt the pull to move on this. If he could make things good with the rest of his family before the holidays, he needed to do it, no matter how hard.

"Call them," he said, jolting as Louisa poked him in the side.

"Good job, you. Now, I need to call my bro."

Louisa sailed over to her phone, and his mother sidled up to him. "I always thought a girl from South Side would suit you."

He laughed and shook his head. "You have no idea how much."

She'd helped him find his wings again.

CHAPTER 21

RECONCILIATION WAS GOOD FOR THE SOUL, CLARA KNEW from experience.

But she hadn't realized how good karaoke was for the soul until today.

"How did I never know how much fun this is?" she asked Flynn, who was sitting next to her on the large benches the entire Merriam party had co-opted for their karaoke Sunday brunch.

Flynn, J.T., and Caitlyn had embraced Connor with their usual ease upon their arrival at the suite in the morning. Trevor had flown all night and rolled in right before brunch and proceeded to pretty much man-hug Connor off the ground and threaten to send his ex-SEALs after him with machetes if he ever disappeared again. Then he'd looked Connor in the eye and said, "I felt guilty as hell about Corey too since it was on my watch, but it wasn't our fault. Corey wouldn't want you to beat yourself up like this."

To which Louisa had said, "Man, I love this guy. He's your brother?"

Connor's mouth had lifted on the right, and he'd said, "They say I'm the serious brother."

"Word," Caitlyn and Flynn had said at the same time—and proceeded to exchange a high five.

Leave it to dear Louisa to suggest a karaoke brunch to set everyone at ease. The girl had a knack for helping people, no question about it.

Clara was flying high as she watched the Merriam kids banter with big grins on their faces. She'd worried those days were over. When she and Arthur had come to Chicago, they'd thought this would be their hardest assignment to date. And yet, they'd barely helped on the matchmaking front. Instead, they'd poured their efforts into helping Connor achieve his goals. She'd given Sunflower Alley a million dollars for a new training program, Arthur was working on his article, and Hargreaves had helped raise money for the cause at the cooking competition.

"Arthur," she said, leaning into him. He'd been complaining nonstop about the noise, but she suspected it was because his crotchety comments made the others laugh.

"What?" He cupped his ear. "I can't hear you. There's a cat wailing on stage."

That "cat" being some tone-deaf millennial singing Mariah Carey's "Daydream." It was a rather horrid rendition, she had to agree. She grabbed his sweater and pulled him so she could speak into his ear. "I think I've discovered a universal law of matchmaking on this assignment."

"That sounds deep," he said, his blue eyes twinkling. "Let me guess. That earlier rendition of 'Rocket Man' inspired you."

"You think you're so funny," she said, making a face at him. "What I was trying to say was this. When you help people meet their goals, it's easier for them to fall in love. And sharing a goal brings people together."

"I assume you mean Connor and Louisa," Arthur said with a nod at the happy couple settled amidst the Merriam kids. "Sounds like common sense to me more than a universal law of matchmaking."

She leaned away from him, not caring if he heard her. "Sometimes you are such a curmudgeon."

"I love you too," he replied with a flirtatious pinch at her waist, proving what she'd suspected all along. He damn well heard everything.

"Of course, we're not completely flying in cloudless skies yet," Arthur said, cozying up to her ear. "Quinn is making a stand by being the last sibling to show up."

Clara thought Quinn's late arrival was poppycock. Everyone was trying to smooth it over, but Connor had said Quinn was sweating him out—and that he didn't blame him.

And that wasn't the only pickle in their fruit salad. Shawn and Assumpta had made a quick visit to Olivia this morning while the siblings talked and caught up in the suite. They hadn't said much when they'd returned from her house. Only that Olivia's stance hadn't changed.

Connor hadn't shown surprise, but it had to hurt, didn't it? Clara had joined Louisa in trying to keep up everyone's spirits. Arthur needed to do more if you asked her.

Clara glanced at the bright stage as two young people stepped off after singing a heartfelt rendition of Taylor Swift's "Shake it Off." Personally, she felt they could all benefit from shaking off their troubles. "Arthur! You and I are going to sing. Come with me."

He held out a forkful of French toast. "Woman, not on your life. Singing on a full stomach is bad for you. Go sing with Flynn. He has a nice voice. Better yet, ask Hargreaves."

She hated it when he wouldn't cooperate. "Fine, finish your brunch."

Arthur must have heard the pique in her tone, because he patted her hand and winked at her. "Too bad Beau had a concert last night. If he sang, he'd have everyone on their feet cheering. Louisa!" he called out. "You're good at crowd engagement. Take Connor away from his worrying about Quinn and go sing something."

"I'm fine," Connor said, although his mouth tightened into a thin line.

Louisa set her mimosa aside. "Arthur, I hate to burst your bubble. My wrestling announcer voice is top shelf, but my singing voice is pretty depressing. I'm more into listening than going on stage."

"Connor has a great voice," Michaela volunteered. "Come on, Con. Take your woman up there and sing something. Uncle Arthur's right. You're fretting over Quinn being late."

"Mickey, I don't fret." His crossed arms suggested otherwise. "I understand why he's pissed, and I know he's busy. That job never ends."

"I'm glad you've moved on," Louisa said, pressed up against him. "Oh, was that the wrong thing to say?"

Flynn was fighting laughter, and Trevor put his hand over his mouth to cover up his smile.

"Not in this family," Caitlyn said, smiling. "We're pretty expressive."

"Except for this one, but he's learning," Louisa said, standing up. "I mean he's finally figured out he's an introvert, so working on his own might be the best thing for him."

"Louisa."

"Don't 'Louisa' me. You told me that the other night. Come on. I'll muster the courage to sing in front of everybody if you will."

He groaned, but he stood up. "I know that look. Okay, but you have to pick the song. I won't be bothered with that."

"Goody," she said, taking his hand and leading him to the front.

"Why didn't I know he was so unhappy being the president?" Shawn put his hands on the table as if testing it for solidness. "I always thought he wanted to do it."

"Shawn," Assumpta said, turning in her seat, "this isn't the time."

"I know the job is hard," he continued. "Hell, I had it

for twenty-plus years when my dad retired. I never asked him…"

"That's enough, Shawn," his wife said again with all the children looking on. "Let's enjoy being together."

Clara sent her brother what she hoped was an encouraging look. Their father had worked all hours of the day, so she had some understanding of the pressures of running Merriam Enterprises. It certainly wasn't a job for everyone. Connor might have been a good CEO up until the end, but she suspected the lifestyle hadn't suited him. He seemed happier now than he'd been before. She knew it could happen at any age. She'd finally found her spark, her purpose, at nearly eighty. As far as she was concerned, Connor was lucky to have found it at forty.

"Daddy," Caitlyn said, patting his hand, "this is a great time for all of us to tell each other how we really feel about things. I mean, I wanted to start my new perfume line because I wasn't completely satisfied with my work at Merriam. Trevor's delegated more of his workload so he doesn't have to work or travel like he used to."

"Connor's right," Trevor said. "It was crushing at times. J.T., you know."

"Yeah," J.T. said, leaning back and putting his arm around his wife. "I put in twenty-hour days sometimes. Hard to have a life and family. Really glad I changed things up. I work a lot of hours at the art museum, but it's with my beautiful bride here, so I'm happy."

"Working with your partner in life is a pretty great way to go," Michaela said, leaning her head on her fiancé's shoulder. "Boyd and I couldn't agree more."

"Well, I would *never* have wanted to work with your father outside of having a family and raising you kids," Assumpta said, making Arthur bark out a laugh in the midst of stuffing his face with more French toast.

"Arthur and I love working together as matchmakers,"

Clara said, tapping her fingers on the table to garner his attention. "Don't we, dear?"

"If I agree, I'll get a kiss later," he had the audacity to say, "but if I'm contrary, God knows what she might do."

"Have Hargreaves put extra starch in your shirts," Clara said.

"Hargreaves would never do such a thing," Arthur said, giving her another cheeky wink. "Too ethical."

He was right. Darn it. She was losing this argument, so she turned her gaze back to the stage. "It looks like Connor and Louisa are about ready."

"I can't wait to hear what Louisa picked," Flynn said, pocketing his phone. "I'm kinda in love with her."

"Me too," Michaela said, taking a gusty sip of her mimosa. "Total girl crush. I mean, she's incredible."

"He hit the jackpot," Trevor said, a smile cresting over his face. "I couldn't be happier—or more relieved. She's just what he needed and at the perfect time."

"South Side girls rule," Assumpta said with a little smirk.

The kids groaned, and Caitlyn said, "Mom, you always say that."

"Because it's true," Assumpta said, pointing at her daughter for emphasis. "Look, they're up. I can't believe it. If someone had told me Connor could loosen up this much, I never would have believed it."

Clara would have, and another song lyric came to mind: "That's the power of love." It had a wonderful way of transforming a person. Look at her with this sometimes curmudgeonly, mostly wonderful old guy. She leaned over and kissed Arthur on the cheek despite the fact that he had some maple syrup there.

"What was that for?" he asked, but his hand crept around her waist in response.

"You know," was all she answered.

He patted her backside, signaling he surely did, the sweet man.

***

Since Connor had ceded the music selection to her, Louisa traced a finger down the list of karaoke songs, looking for something inspirational. Although Connor was trying to act like Quinn's absence was no big deal, she sensed it mattered quite a bit. And she had a fist with Quinn's name on it if he didn't shape up quick.

"Aha. We have a winner."

"I can't wait," Connor said, his body getting stiffer by the minute, and not in the way she usually enjoyed.

"You're going to be fine," she said, already tapping her feet. "Fair warning. What my voice lacks, I make up for in showmanship." Okay, she'd played down her love of karaoke, fearing Connor wouldn't go on stage with her.

"Why do I feel like this is about to be embarrassing?" he asked. "You weren't telling the truth earlier, were you?"

She ignored that. "This will be good for you. Babe, I picked this one with you in mind. Remember these lyrics as we wait for Quinn to arrive, okay?"

"Oh, God, what did you do?" He tried to see the screen, but she threw herself in front of it.

"Not yet! I need to introduce us."

There were two microphones up front, and she tapped Connor's before handing it to him and then ran through a mic check for her own. "Hello, everybody! I'm Louisa and this is my main man, Connor. Are you guys enjoying this incredible karaoke brunch today?"

"You were so lying," she heard Connor mutter.

"Let's give some love to the owner, Wally Clay, and his incredible staff. Wally, I love you, man. It's so good to see how far you've come."

"Let me guess," Connor whispered in her ear as Wally gave her a jaunty salute. "Another graduate of Sunflower Alley? You didn't mention that."

"I can't keep track of everything I say," she whispered back. "Ready, babe?"

The iconic piano intro started for Journey's "Don't Stop Believin'," and she pumped her fist in the air at the crowd. "Sing it with us if you know it!"

"You're kidding," Connor murmured, rolling his eyes.

Clapping her hand to her thigh, she put the mic to her mouth and starting to sing the classic tune. Thank God, Connor joined in or she would have punched him. He did have a great voice, one she hoped to hear a lot from now on. Channeling her inner rockstar—the one she usually only let out in the shower—she did her best impression of playing her air guitar while the other patrons sang back the words with feeling, especially the group in the far corner who looked to be having a birthday party of some kind.

She looked over to the Merriam table and was pleased to see Flynn, Caitlyn, Michaela, and Clara on their feet. All of them were singing their hearts out, and Trevor let out a piercing cabbie whistle, yelling, "Go Connor! Strut it!"

Turning to him, she put her hand on his chest and sang the song to him, sending him a message as she did so. *Don't stop believing, babe. Not in your family or this brother who's late. Or us.* She patted his beard, and he surprised her by pulling her close and dipping her at the waist. It was cheeky, and man, did she like it.

Facing the crowd again, she clapped her hands overhead when the song went back to the melody section. People got on their feet, and then they were really rocking. She mimed more strokes on her air guitar, and Connor laughed and brought out his own, pretending to pick the strings.

Man. He'd come so far it brought tears to her eyes.

She scanned the group and noticed a haggard man in a dark suit approaching the Merriams. Shawn stood up first and put a hand on his shoulder, and then Assumpta was hugging him warmly. That would be Quinn, then. Well, he'd better not mess up this reconciliation, or she'd air guitar his nuts back to California.

Since Connor didn't need the distraction, she stepped

in front of him, air guitaring her heart out in time with him. He was smiling now, and he laughed as she started to stomp her feet in time with the beat. This was the kind of moment she loved. Letting go completely in front of total strangers for a good cause. It jazzed her up.

She fell to one knee, tipped her head back, and sang like it was the last song she'd ever sing. Connor's voice was growing in strength and power, and she jumped back up, wanting to sing the end to him. She was such a mush ball sometimes.

"'Don't stop believing,'" she sang with him, and his eyes fastened on hers.

That flash of light in them had her heartstrings doing their own air guitar routine in her chest. He was so different than that night they'd met, covered in snow, all alone in a park. Now she knew the why. She'd met all the characters, heard about his past. How the story would end was still a little unclear, but one thing was certain. She loved him, and she'd help slay any dragons in his path.

They finished the song together, holding the notes in a harmony only lovers could achieve. She traced his cheek and then faced the audience, punching the air. "Yeah! All right!"

The patrons started clapping, and she clapped right back at them.

"You're incredible," Connor said, setting their mics aside and putting his arm around her waist. "Damn, I love you."

Then she felt the tension lock his muscles, and she knew he'd seen his brother. As the applause died down, they walked off the stage.

"You remember what I said," she told him, fidgeting with the button on his shirt just so she could touch him.

He cupped her face and kissed her slowly, almost sighing with her as the sweetness of it rolled over them both.

"I remember," Connor said, putting his arm to her back and leading her back to the Merriams.

Quinn turned his body, giving Connor the alpha male chin nod thing. He returned it.

"Let's go," Connor said, and then Quinn was following him out of the restaurant. It looked, for all the world, as if they'd planned it, only Louisa knew they hadn't.

"Where are they going?" Caitlyn asked, clenching her teeth.

Louisa tracked their progress to the front door. "I believe they're taking it outside."

"Men." Michaela threw up her arms.

"Hey!" Flynn said, touching his chest. "That kind of stereotyping hurts right here."

"You know what she means," Caitlyn said, throwing a napkin at him. "Do you think they're going to punch each other?"

"Then have a whiskey?" Trevor asked. "Probably. That's what Connor and I have always done."

"When?" Mickey asked.

"Never you mind," Trevor said, waving his hand. "Hey, Louisa! You got any contacts on the police force in case it gets a little rough and rowdy out there?"

"If they get carted off to jail," Assumpta said, standing up, "*no one* is bailing them out. Do you hear me?"

All of her remaining children nodded, and Louisa had to laugh. "Sometimes a night in jail does a person a hell of a lot of good. You should ask my dad. He doesn't bail any of his players or students out if they get into trouble. Looks on it as a life lesson."

"Exactly," Assumpta said, her arms folded across her chest. "They have to settle things their way, and if there are consequences, they take them."

Yeah, Connor's mom was so from the old neighborhood. Louisa fist-bumped her, making Arthur laugh.

"And women say men are vicious," he said, standing

up. "Personally, I miss the good old days when I could punch a man in the face without worrying he'd break me into bits. Age sucks."

"Arthur Hale," Clara said as everyone started to laugh, "when in the world did you ever punch someone in the face?"

"I thought about hitting your dead jerk of a husband when I heard him talk out of turn about you on your own wedding day," he replied, grabbing a piece of bacon.

"Me too, Arthur," Shawn said, his mouth a downright snarl now. "Too bad we didn't follow through."

"I never knew!" Clara leaned down and kissed him and then took the rest of his bacon. "Thank you for the thought."

So Arthur Hale could be a badass, Louisa thought, and so could Connor's father. And Connor's mom was a badass without question. Clearly the apple didn't fall too far from the tree. She glanced over her shoulder, but there was no sign of them yet.

"It's probably too early for whiskey," she said with a shrug. "Another round of mimosas while we wait?"

"Yes," everyone replied.

She was really starting to like these Merriams.

CHAPTER 22

CONNOR DIDN'T THINK ANYONE WOULD FOLLOW THEM OUT, Louisa included, but he wasn't going to bank on it. Plus, if Quinn needed to yell at him—and maybe he needed to yell back, who knew?—it would be best if they did it away from the restaurant and the downtown Sunday throng.

He faced his brother on the sidewalk. "There's a park on the lake we could walk to."

"Fine," Quinn responded, tucking his suit collar up to protect him against the wind.

"You want to go back in for your coat?"

His brother's level stare would have been answer enough, but he said, "I can stand it if you can."

He kept his mouth shut, feeling the anger rolling off his brother like steam issuing from hot asphalt. When they finally made it to the park, he called it out there. "You have every reason and then some to want to kick my ass. I have no way to make up for what I did, but I'm sorry. Sorrier than you know. I understand the kind of position I put you in."

"You made me fire my older brother," Quinn shot back, unbuttoning his suit jacket and taking on a fighting stance. "You wouldn't talk to anyone. Hell, you didn't even talk to *me.*"

"I know I didn't give you a choice. I don't want you to feel any guilt over that."

His brother's eyes filled with fire. "You don't? Well, good for you, Con. Unfortunately, you don't get to tell me how to feel. You have no idea how hard you've made things."

He wanted to hang his head, but Quinn deserved more from him. He had made things difficult—he knew it.

"You have no idea how many people have asked me how it feels to fire my own brother after he went off the deep end. And I know they're all looking at me and wondering if I'm going to crack up if there's another godawful tragedy. Dammit! I know you're sorry, and I'm sorry too. Fuck."

His mouth went dry. What was he supposed to say? Then he remembered Louisa's halftime speech. *Share your heart*. Dammit, it was so much harder with Quinn for some reason, but he had to find the courage to be open with him.

"Corey's death messed me up bad," Connor said in a low voice. "I'd like to think I would have been that upset over any employee dying, and it bothers me that I can't be sure. I don't know what kind of president you'll be except a damn good one, but I'm afraid there's no way of knowing how you'll react in this kind of situation until you're in it. And I really hope you don't find yourself in that position anytime soon."

His brother tugged on his tie, his throat moving.

"Maybe there was something wrong with me on the inside that caused me to 'go off the deep end,' to use your words. Dad seems to think it all started the day you almost drowned. I don't know. All I know is that losing Corey like that haunted me. I played the footage right before the earthquake over and over at night when I couldn't sleep. And I wasn't sleeping at all in those last months. No one knows that. Not even Louisa." He didn't have to ask if Quinn knew who she was. Of course he did.

"Why didn't you talk to me?" Quinn punched the air. "Dammit, I'm your brother. I was your freaking vice president. I could have stepped in for a while if you needed some time off. It didn't have to go down this way, Con. It shouldn't have."

"No, but it did, and I'm living with that." He slipped his hands in his pockets. "I'm sorry you have to live it with it too. I know I changed your life. That you've had to move back to California. I can't change it back. What else do you want me to say?"

"I want you to swear to me that you won't shut us out again." His hands formed fists. "Do you have any idea how much Caitlyn's cried or... Never mind. Maybe I should have pushed harder. I thought giving you the space you wanted was the best approach. Neither one of us likes to talk about our feelings." He spat the word out like it was spoiled meat.

"No, we don't," Connor said, "but I have someone who's helped me understand that's exactly what I need to do if I want to turn my life around. I'm going to see a counselor and figure this shit out. Do you want to know why? Because I don't want to let you down again. Any of you."

"Forget letting me down for the minute." Quinn stormed over to him. "Dammit, take care of you."

They were so alike, he and Quinn, down to the Saville Row suit his brother wore. God, he hoped Quinn wanted to play that role. "That's what Louisa says."

"She's right, and I can't wait to meet her, but seriously, Connor... Do you want to know what the worst part of this was for me?"

He really didn't, and his entire body tensed at the mere question. But he owed it to Quinn to listen. "What?"

"You didn't leave your office the night before the board meeting. Not once. I had to check with employees to make sure you were okay. Know why? Trevor and I got scared you might have hanged yourself."

The words were a harsh slap against his face. "I wouldn't have done that."

Quinn stalked off a few paces, prowling. "When I saw the pictures Trev's boys had taken of you in the park drinking out of a freaking bottle in the middle of a snowstorm, I thought it was still on the table. You could have died."

Except what should have been one of the worst moments of his life had ended up being the best, because that was the night he'd met his love, his angel. What had her love note said that night? *If you're reading this, something wonderful is about to happen.* Yeah, it sure as hell had.

He rubbed the space between his brows before looking up. "Honestly, I'm not sure how things would have gone if I hadn't met Louisa that night. After Olivia told me she wouldn't let me see the boys, I was beside myself. I came here thinking the only thing I had left was the promise I'd made Corey to look after his family. After leaving there, I felt like a monster."

His brother cursed. "You shouldn't have faced any of this alone. You didn't have to."

"I'm not alone anymore," Connor said, his chest tightening thinking about all of the support he had now. "I know it might take some time for you to forgive me. But dammit, Quinn. I love you. You're my brother. I'm sorry I fucked things up for you. I hope we can move past that at some point."

His brother looked away toward the lake, and Connor held himself still, awaiting his response.

"I love you too, man," Quinn said quietly. "Mom texted me earlier to say that's the only thing that matters, and for once I agree. Also, it's not your fault Corey died, and I'm sorry as hell you lost your best friend. If that had happened to me, I probably would have lost my shit for a while too. And if or when something like that does bring me down, I'm counting on you to kick my ass or sing a Journey song to get me back on track."

Tears burning his eyes, he managed a snort. "Thanks for that. You heard the song, huh?"

"Your woman is a *badass*," Quinn said, his mouth lifting at the corners. "I wondered who would be able to handle your crotchety old moods."

"I'm less crotchety since I'm not working with so many people these days." Perhaps it was time for him to extend an olive branch. "Maybe you should have taken over for Dad in the first place. Maybe I wasn't made for the president's shoes just because I'm the oldest. I'm sorry no one, myself included, thought about it."

Quinn waved him off. "Forget it. Kept me from getting gray hairs earlier. Hell, this week alone, I've popped four new ones. Flynn is trying to convince me to do that Just for Men hair dye thing."

"Don't do it, man," Connor said with a shudder. "If you start dyeing your hair, next thing you know you'll be waxing your back hair."

"You're the one with the back hair, moron," Quinn shot back, smiling with the quip. "Does it bother Louisa much? Women hate that crap, right?"

Since he didn't have any in the first place, he didn't feel bad about making up a pretend answer. "No, she loves me despite it." Which was true. She loved him despite everything.

"I should probably meet her then," Quinn said, refixing his tie to its usual perfect knot. "I want us to be good, Con. I can't promise I won't get pissed every once in a while, but I want you to know it's not targeted at you. Running Merriam is a bitch right now."

He didn't feel it was right to apologize again, so he only nodded.

"Also, I don't know why Dad brought up me falling off the boat and almost drowning," Quinn said, scratching his head. "He's going through some weird cycle of regret about our childhood ever since Caitlyn thanked him for giving her some soap when she was a teenager."

"What?" Connor asked, confused.

"Not the point. Anyway, I know Dad yelled at you that day and blamed you for not watching me. Or jumping in after me. That was crap. It was my fault, but it didn't seem to matter just then. I remember dripping water on the deck as Dad yelled at you and then me. All I wanted was for someone to bring me a towel and wrap me up in it."

He'd forgotten about his dad yelling at Quinn once he'd finished with him. "You just fell in. It was no one's fault."

Quinn cursed. "What I'm trying to say is, I still don't get close to water, so we all have our own neuroses."

And so the olive branch was taken. His brother extended his hand, and Connor took it, his chest tight. Then he pulled Quinn in for a brief man-hug, which had them both clearing their throats and coughing with emotion.

"You think they expect us to come back with black eyes?" Quinn asked, elbowing him in the side.

Connor chuckled. "Probably. If you need to get it out of your system, you get a free pass. I won't hit back. This time."

"Nah, I can't hit someone who won't hit back," Quinn said.

Connor gestured to his brother's suit. "You freezing yet?"

"Hell, yeah. Of course, you're like a freaking volcano, so the cold doesn't penetrate your thick hide. Can we finally head back in? My feet feel like ice."

They'd somehow found the common ground of brothers again, and in that moment, he knew they were going to be all right. "If Mom doesn't have a cure, Louisa will. They're from South Side. Just ask them. You'd think they'd gone to the same college or something with all their neighborhood talk."

"You telling me they're going to be intolerable around family events? Talking about being tough from the old neighborhood?"

There it was again. Even Quinn was assuming Louisa was one of them now. He figured they were right on the money. Pretty soon, he'd have to decide when he wanted to ask her officially how she felt about that. But first he'd start counseling, get a little closer to coming to terms with the past and putting it in its place.

"Probably, but when she pulls out her wrestling announcer voice or her karaoke rockstar act, no one is going to care."

"No, they're probably not." Quinn tipped his head toward the path leading out of the park back to downtown. "Do you think she'd sing one with me?"

Since Connor knew he was joking, he returned the favor. "I'm sure she'd love to do 'A Whole New World' with you once I tell her you dressed as Aladdin for Halloween one year."

Quinn nudged him with a shoulder. "Does she know you dressed up as Peter Pan yet?"

He nudged him back. "Mom dressed me in that, and if you tell Louisa, I'll kill you." Actually he'd chosen the costume. The guy could fly and hung out with a cool fairy and fought a pirate. What wasn't to like?

"Oh, I'm so scared," Quinn said, picking up his pace when the wind started gusting.

Connor flashed back to that Halloween so many years ago. Corey had begged to visit so they could trick-or-treat together. He'd dressed up like Captain Hook, Pan's evil nemesis, and he'd spent all night threatening to fight Connor for his candy. They'd made a pirate ship out of dining room chairs and sails from some old sheets in the linen closet and ended up falling asleep in their costumes, their hands in their candy sacks. It had been the best Halloween of his young life.

Grief welled up again as the mental images faded, but its claws weren't as sharp this time. He noted it. Realized it was because he was feeling grateful for that time with Corey. He'd have to tell Louisa later. She'd say it was progress.

Yeah, it probably was, and he was grateful for it as he slung his arm around his brother's shoulders like guys do, and they walked back to their family.

Together.

CHAPTER 23

LOUISA STUDIED THE OFFICIAL PRESS ANNOUNCEMENT for the new training program on Monday morning.

Now that Connor was selling Sunflower Alley the property they wanted, she thought it was time to share more news about their plans beyond what she'd announced at the cooking competition. She was pleased with her draft, but she wondered if Arthur would take a look at it. It wasn't every day a person could get feedback on their writing from a Pulitzer Prize-winning journalist, and he'd offered to help in any way he could. Picking up the phone, she called Clara, her point of contact.

"Good morning, dear," Clara immediately answered. "Recovered from the wild night?"

Just the thought of their party, which had raged late into the night, brought a smile to her face. "Are you? I didn't know your hotel allowed karaoke in its rooms. I'm still shocked we didn't get in trouble. We were so loud."

"Flynn assured me when he rented the machine—God knows where—that he'd handle any problems. That boy is slick as rain, let me tell you."

He was pretty adorable. "The most easygoing of all the brothers, I think."

"Your duet of 'Islands in the Stream' with him was one of my favorite parts of the night."

"Flynn knows how to ham it up," she said, laughing. By then, Connor had been almost completely relaxed. However he and Quinn had handled things had worked for them. Yesterday had inspired a new love note for her board: *It's never too late to forgive someone and laugh again.* "Is Arthur around? I wanted to ask him something."

"He's reading the paper. We begged off after an early breakfast with everyone. Missed you, dear."

Oh, she loved these people. "I needed to get to the shelter. Besides, I thought it might be nice for Connor to have some time alone with his family before everyone headed off."

"Have you decided what you'll do for Thanksgiving?" Clara asked. "This is the first Thanksgiving I've looked forward to in decades. I told Arthur that I want to spend time with everyone: his granddaughters, my family, and yours too. I so enjoyed meeting your father at the cooking competition. Of course, it will be a tad difficult to do everything given the location of the Merriam Thanksgiving."

She needed to call her dad about their plans. "That's a lot of turkey, Clara, but I understand wanting to do them all. I'm grateful the Merriams invited me, of course, but I'm still mulling it over."

Connor's family was planning to spend the holiday in Ireland with Trevor and his wife, Becca, as their hosts. They'd asked her to join, and she was tempted—how could she not be?—but Connor had insisted there was no pressure either way. He knew she'd never been away from her own family save for those horrible holidays she'd spent on the streets with her mother. But he'd made the decision to join them—he felt it was an important step for his recovery, especially since some of his early actions had hurt Becca.

"Arthur tells me that three invites means we must be doing something right," Clara said with a laugh. "All I know is that it was wonderful to see the family come together after what happened with Connor. Rifts are horrible to live with."

Yes, she'd heard all about Clara and Shawn's rift from Caitlyn, who'd seemed as chatty as Flynn was easygoing. "Forgiveness doesn't have a shelf date. Thank God."

"You couldn't be more right," Clara said, suddenly muttering at someone. "Arthur is growling at me to hand him the phone, and since his ears are red, I'd better... See you later, dear."

"You too."

"I thought she'd never let me talk. Hello, Louisa. Still have your voice this morning? I've never seen anyone sing with such gusto, although Flynn came close. Too bad Beau couldn't join us. That boy would have made us weep. He has a gift."

"I can't wait to meet him," she said, aware of how much her life was changing as she said it. Although she'd heard of Beau Masters, of course, every woman in the country had, she'd never expected she'd find herself dating his soon-to-be brother-in-law. "I was wondering if you'd give me some feedback on my first official statement to the press announcing the training program. I want it to really shine. Everyone keeps asking me what Sunflower Alley is going to do with a million dollars. I figure it will cut down on all the calls I have from people suggesting they could help me spend it."

She'd been surprised by the outpouring of interest, even more so by the downright avarice of some parties. The worst offender had been a port-a-potty company who'd called and suggested they could add some additional bathrooms-to-go for people on the streets unable to stay in the shelter. She'd vetoed that one pretty fast.

"Money brings out the flies just like honey," Arthur

said matter-of-factly. "Sure, I'd be happy to take my red pen to it. Can you email it to me? This hotel must have a business center where I can print it. Wait. Clara is volunteering Hargreaves for that duty. Wonderful, that man is finally useful to me."

She had to bite her lip to keep from laughing. Arthur might bark about Hargreaves, but he clearly liked and respected the man. So did she. She'd even seen him tapping his foot from the doorway as Flynn, Caitlyn, Boyd, and Michaela had sung "Bohemian Rhapsody." Hilarious.

"I'm sending it now," she said, hitting the button on her laptop. "I'm not sure when I can dash over for your comments."

"Clara says Hargreaves will bring it. I love having my own personal courier. Clara, we should have used him like this months ago."

"I'll look for him then," she said, her shoulders shaking. "Carter will try and enlist him to cook for dinner, wanting a rematch, but tell Hargreaves it's all in good fun."

"If he's planning on serving me Indian food tonight, you can have him, my dear. All right. I'll let you get back to work. By the way, my article is coming along. It's turning into a great feature. Now go do what you do best. And don't get all keyed up when you see my changes. I'm not a Pulitzer-winning journalist for nothing."

"I'm pretty tough."

"Yes, you sure as heck are," he said with a laugh. "Talk to you later."

She said goodbye and checked her texts, hoping for one from Connor. Aha! He'd read her mind. *Missing you. Sounds crazy since I just saw you a few hours ago. Hope you're having a good day so far. Caitlyn cried when she left, and it got to me. I'm so glad everyone flew in. Thanks for helping me with everything. I couldn't have done it without you. Love you.*

She smiled to herself as she responded. *Love you too,*

and you carried most of the water. Having a good morning so far. Planning on having a great afternoon. Have fun with your parents. Everyone else left, right? I'll see you when I finish up here. Earlier than usual, I hope. Night in? My place? Your place? We could order pizza.

She still hadn't seen his place, although he'd told her it was a soulless furnished apartment in South Side. She didn't care. Now that she knew who he really was, she wanted to know everything about him.

Should she go to Ireland with him for Thanksgiving? Oh, she didn't know. That sounded like a big deal. Maybe it was too much too soon, a thought that immediately made her laugh at herself—when had that ever bothered them? For some reason, hurtling along at this pace felt right.

"Daydreaming?"

She looked up to see her brother standing in the doorway. "You're awake before noon on your day off? Have zombies taken over the city?"

"Didn't see any on my way here," Damien said, shrugging out of his leather jacket and tossing it on the back of the chair before sitting down. "I was worried about you."

She tilted her head to the side and gave him a look. "I was hoping you wouldn't do this."

He put his feet on her desk, but she decided not to say anything. "I have to. I'm your brother. Plus, on some level you wanted me to get involved, you know, given you took *billionaire* Connor Merriam's family to my place for steak on Saturday night when you could have gone to any old chophouse. And don't tell me it was because you knew I'd make room for you because you're family. You wanted me involved."

"I'm surprised you're not thrilled to find out Connor's successful and not some sort of con man," Louisa said with a snort.

"I read up on him yesterday, Louisa. He's had some big emotional things lately. Business articles don't speculate like the tabloids, but he got fired for conduct unbecoming. That's pretty serious stuff, even for a white guy."

"Dad would cut you a look for that kind of talk."

He cut her a look himself. "Dad doesn't know what I know. Yet."

She leaned back in her chair. "I know the full story, and yes, it was serious. It's being handled. He's going to see my counselor after Thanksgiving. He's made up with his family. He's on the right track, and that's something I plan on telling Dad, FYI."

Damien grabbed her coffee cup, sniffed it, and made a face before setting it back down. "I need to get you a fool-proof coffee maker. Okay, I had to say it. His family does seem nice. I mean, Clara Merriam Hale gave Sunflower Alley a million bucks, didn't she? My staff also said they treated them well and tipped generously—something not everyone with money does."

She'd found the same when she'd worked as a hostess in high school. "You checked up on the family too? Of course you did. Damien, I'm fine. In fact, I'm more than fine. I'm happy. I love him."

He nodded slowly. "I know you do, and I know that's big. I'm keeping an open mind since he's helping with the training program. Dad told me Connor gave you the property you had your eye on."

"I'm paying him for that property," she clarified, hoping it was still true. It wasn't like she'd cut him a check yet since the property hadn't closed.

"Okay... Here's what's bugging me. What guarantee do you have that he's going to hang around, sis? How can you be sure this guy isn't going to head back to California and take some other high-powered job?"

"Damien, I'm hoping it's going to work out," she said honestly because he was her brother, "but I'm also trying not to be attached to it. No one knows better than I do how fast something can change, but I won't stand back and play it safe. I'm going to love Connor one hundred percent until something happens and pray every day that it doesn't."

"Crap." He swung his feet down and leaned forward to fist-bump her. "You're braver than I am, and you had way more junk to mess you up."

"You'll open your heart when it's the right person," she said, a soft smile playing on her face as she thought of how lucky that woman would be. "I'd like to think you aren't so much an emotional coward as a discerning soul."

A laugh burst out of him. "Tell that to Dad. He still worries that I haven't stepped all the way into my 'man shoes.'"

"He only wants you to be all you can be," she said, treading over familiar ground. "I think you're doing pretty great. He just has a harder time seeing being a chef in a fancy restaurant as contributing to society. You know him. He believes helping people is our sole reason for being here."

His sigh was dramatic, and she laughed.

"You and I both know you make a difference in your own way. You're always willing to give Carter's people the benefit of the doubt. A quarter of the people in your staff used to live here. Hell, who gave Carter a second chance?"

He lifted his shoulder, but she could feel the chip on it. He'd had it since he'd told their dad he wanted to go to culinary school and not college. What a row that had been.

"You're the best, Louisa. You know? I came by to make sure you know what you're getting into, and you turn this into an 'Inspire Damien Moment.'"

She stood up and came around to poke him in the chest. "You know you can come to me whenever you're feeling sorry for yourself for being such a hugely successful ol' chef. I'll have Carter kick your ass."

"Where is the big ox?" he asked, cracking his knuckles. "Maybe I need to disrupt his kitchen today. Tell him I'm more qualified to run the new culinary training program."

She pulled on his hair playfully. "Please don't. I beg you. It's only Monday."

"Of course, the one I'd really like a shot at is Mr. Hargreaves." His wide smile was downright cocky. "*A lost recipe of Julia Child's.* Even I'm not sure I could have overcome that."

"You couldn't have, but then again, Hargreaves is more mysterious than you. Now, I'm pushing you out. We would love your help with the culinary training program as a guest chef."

"Done!"

She hadn't thought any differently. "If you'd like to feel like you're helping people today, I have some children who would love to be read to by someone good at story voices. You could hold Mr. Snuggles and Mrs. Cuddles and do your magic trick."

"Who could pass up story time with some little kids?" He kissed her cheek loudly, knowing she hated it. "Last word. If that guy does anything to hurt you, I'm coming at him with my sharpest knife, regardless of what you say. I'll wait until he's signed the property over to you, of course."

Connor wouldn't renege on that, no matter what happened between them. "So noted." She pushed him toward the door. "Make sure you pop in and say goodbye before you leave. Also, you might prepare yourself to have dinner with me, Connor, and Dad."

"Fine. But I'm not cooking."

She rolled her eyes. "We'll go out. Keep it social. You can give us your thoughts on the culinary training program. I'll also give you a list of approved questions if you want."

"I can handle my own questions," he said, tossing his jacket over his shoulder. "Or maybe I'll just rely on Dad. He likes to make sure everyone is fulfilling their life purpose. Imagine what he might ask Connor. Oh, this dinner is sounding better and better. Tonight?"

"No, moron. Now, out. It's not one of my days off."

He blew her a kiss. "Check you later, sis."

He did check with her later, and so did Boxer when he came in. Hargreaves arrived with Arthur's changes in the early afternoon. She didn't faint seeing his edits, but she did grimace.

"Mr. Hale prides himself on providing excellent input," Hargreaves said, his calm presence ever a balm to the soul.

"As should we all," she said, steeling herself. "I'm embracing the excellence. How incredible is it to have this kind of support, right?"

"Excellent perspective, Miss Evans," Hargreaves said with a slight bow. "It's one of the things I most admire about you. Now, I believe I will visit Chef Carter and see if I can be of any service in the kitchen. Madam gave me the rest of the day off."

"It's nice of you to help, Hargreaves," she said, wanting to hug him. "I know you could have gone to a museum or something."

"There's a particular kind of art here, Miss Evans. The human kind has always made a bigger impression on me. If I were a Chicago resident, you could count on me as a permanent volunteer. I'll let you get to your changes."

With that, he simply left, and she melted. "He's a total peach. Art of the human kind? I need to make that into a love note."

She was jotting down various permutations of Hargreaves' sentiment when Boxer appeared in the doorway. His face was grim, and she instantly went on alert.

"You have some visitors asking to see you, requesting shelter. Our volunteer snagged me as I was coming back in from a meeting. They're pretty upset. I thought you might want to talk to them in the Story Room."

"Okay. What am I missing?"

"They're Connor's nephews or something," he said, clucking his tongue. "Babies with the saddest faces I've seen in some time. They wouldn't come down the hall with me. Told me they'd wait by the entrance for you."

"Oh, no." She stood up and followed Boxer out of her office, waving at their volunteer at reception.

When she saw them, her heart simply broke in two. Joseph was holding the hand of a slightly older boy who had the same dark hair and eyes. They were bundled up in blue winter coats, and their backpacks, both of them stuffed to the brim, were visible over their little, drooping shoulders.

"Hi, Ms. Louisa. Do you remember me? I'm Joseph."

She rushed forward and got down on her knees in front of them. The other boy was staring at her, his chin an angry thrust of attitude. "Of course I do. Is this your brother? I can't remember his name."

"It's Max." The little boy nudged his brother.

"Hi," he said, his tone hesitant.

"Hey, Max. I love that name. One of my favorites. Joseph, did you tell your brother about our guinea pigs? I was just going to feed them. Would you both like to help me?"

She wasn't going to ask why they were there. She already knew.

"Sure," the boy said, shifting his heavy backpack up on his shoulder. "Is Uncle Connor here?"

Bingo. "No, not right now." She shot Boxer a look, and he nodded, taking off. He understood she'd want to deal with this by herself. "Were you hoping to see him?"

"Yeah," Joseph said, nodding fiercely. "Since our mom won't let us see him, we're coming to live here. That way we can see him anytime. Max looked on your website, and it says you take in families in need. We've brought our pajamas and toothbrushes. A change of clothes. Everything. We promise we won't be a bother. We just want to see Uncle Connor."

Chest tight, she gestured for them to follow her to the Story Room. When they arrived, she was pleased to see it was free and let them inside. She waved to Greta, whom she could see through the window to the daycare room. What in the hell was she supposed to do here? "We usually only take in families who don't have a home."

"We don't have a home anymore," Joseph said, woeful beyond his years. "We've run away."

The first whisper of fear rolled through her. No parent should ever have to feel the terror of not knowing where their children were or if they were safe. She would need to contact their mother soon. But she couldn't betray these boys by doing that just yet. Not given what she knew about the situation. It wouldn't help anyone if they left the shelter only to run away somewhere else, where no one could find them. "Come, let's talk about that."

"There's nothing to talk about," Max finally said. "We've run away, and we aren't going back. If you try and talk us out of it, we'll run away from here and wait for him outside."

There was enough anger in his voice that she believed him. She helped Joseph off with his coat and backpack and put them on the shelf. Max eyed her with mistrust, but he shrugged out of his outer gear and carried his stuff over to set it carefully next to his brother's things.

"Would you like to meet Mr. Snuggles and Mrs. Cuddles?" she asked, crossing to the cages to give herself time to think about how best to handle this. Should she call Connor and have him bring over Shawn and Assumpta?

"Are you thinking about telling on us?" Max asked as she picked up the first guinea pig. "I meant it. We'll only go somewhere else. We're not going back home."

"Our mom hates us, and she hates our Uncle Connor too," Joseph said, a sad little soldier in a red sweater and brown cords. "She's been awful since our daddy died."

She held out Mr. Snuggles to Joseph, who took him gently. "Nestle him against your chest, and he'll do the rest. Max, do you want to hold Mrs. Cuddles?"

The boy shook his head, so she picked up the guinea

pig herself. Max sat down with them in a small circle on the carpet, his eyes screaming anger, a look she recognized well. She'd worn it a time or two.

"You know, I ran away when I was about your age," she decided to tell them. "Quite a few times, in fact. I was angry at my mom too."

"What did she do?" Joseph asked.

"She was mean to me too," Louisa said, falling back on every scrap of training she'd had with kids. "She fought in this horrible war far, far away, and when she came back, she still looked like my mom, but she didn't feel like her anymore. It was like something had hurt her so much that she'd changed. I imagine losing your dad hurt your mom real bad."

"It hurt us too," Max said, his voice louder this time. "We don't get to yell at her or order her to let us see Uncle Connor."

Tread softly, Evans. "What did she tell you about your uncle?"

"She told us we couldn't see him and that was that," Max said, clenching his little fists. "But we overheard her talking to Aunt Assumpta and Uncle Shawn. We know she's mad at him for Daddy dying. But it's not his fault. He died because of that stupid earthquake. She's crazy."

She had a moment of awe for the wisdom of children. They saw things so clearly. Adults could learn from them. "You're right. Your Uncle Connor didn't have anything to do with it."

"Exactly," Joseph said, rubbing the guinea pig under the ears. "We tried to talk to Mommy after Aunt Assumpta and Uncle Shawn left, but she yelled and yelled at us. That's when we decided to run away. If we stay here, we can see Uncle Connor anytime we want."

"He might even let us live with him," Max said. "I couldn't find out where he was staying, or I would have gone there."

"Uncle Connor said we could always count on him," Joseph told her, nodding very seriously. "And Daddy always said it too."

Oh, God. "You must miss your daddy very badly, huh?"

Joseph nodded, the first hint of tears filling his eyes. Max hunched over, hiding his face from view.

"It's not fair he's dead," Max whispered harshly.

"No, it's not," she said, opening one of her arms to Joseph, who took the invitation and scooted closer so she could put her arm around him.

"It's not fair Mom won't let us see Uncle Connor either," Max said, still looking down. "We know he got fired. I read about it on the internet. But we don't care."

"We love him anyway," Joseph said with the earnestness of a little boy. "Mommy's just being mean."

Louisa wanted to sigh. The complications just kept coming. Connor was the person she needed to call. This situation wasn't one she could or should handle on her own. He could involve his parents if he thought it best. Given Olivia's anger toward him, she was going to recommend it. The woman would only blame Connor for the boys coming to the shelter.

"I'm going to call your uncle right now, but can I get you a snack while we wait for him? We have some nice treats here."

"You promise you're not calling our mom?" Max asked.

Man, the mistrust. "I promise. Only your uncle."

"Okay, we'll have a snack then." Max held out his hands hesitantly. "I can take your guinea pig so you can call him if you'd like."

She smiled and deposited Mrs. Cuddles in his little lap. "Thank you, Max. I'll be right back. You guys stay in here, okay?"

Moving swiftly out of the Story Room to her office, she passed Boxer in the hall.

"Poor little tykes," Boxer said, shaking his head.

"Yeah," she said, blowing out a breath. "When did things get so messed up?"

"Adam and Eve?" He gave a harsh laugh and patted her on the back. It was an old joke between them.

Picking up her phone, she called Connor. He answered right away.

"Hey! You about finished or just missing me like crazy?"

"Missing you, but not finished." Not even close, she thought. "There's no easy way to say this. Joseph and Max are here. They came looking for you. They've run away. Can you come here? I don't know whether you want to involve your parents, but I suspect it would be a good idea to have them in the wings. I'm afraid of how Olivia will view this for you."

"Jesus. Those poor kids. Yeah, I'll talk to my parents. We'll need a united front, and even then, I'm not sure she won't banish me forever. Louisa, I'm sorry you got dragged into this."

"It's okay," she assured him. "I had a bad feeling when Olivia said she'd forbidden them to come to the shelter to find you."

"We'll be there as fast as we can," he said rapidly. "Thanks for taking care of them for me."

"I'll take care of them as if they were mine. See you soon."

"Yeah. Love you."

Always a silver lining. "Love you back."

She dashed to the kitchen to discover Hargreaves chopping carrots next to Spicy. "Hey! I hate to ask but could someone rustle up a snack? I have two runaway boys in the Story Room."

Maria put down her knife and wiped her hands on her apron. "I'll bring you something."

"Thanks. Gotta get back."

When she arrived back in the room, she noted how

the boys had edged closer together. Oh, her heart hurt for them. "Your uncle is on his way and so are your snacks."

"Thank you for not getting mad at us and throwing us out," Max said, and she noted his eyes looked less distrustful.

"I told you she was nice to me," Joseph said, his mouth tilting up on the side. "I told Max you had to be okay since Uncle Connor liked you."

She sat down in a cross-legged pose, smiling. "He's helping me with some things around here."

"Like a new job?" Joseph scrunched his nose. "He was busy all the time with his old one and couldn't visit us much. I hope you don't make him work that hard. Daddy was always telling him he worked too much."

"So did our dad, dummy," Max said without heat. "What's he helping you with?"

Their snacks came in while she was telling them about her plans. She asked them about what they liked to study. Max said he liked to build things like his dad had and that he wanted to be an engineer when he grew up. His eyes filled with unshed tears when he said that, and so did Louisa's. Oh, the hero worship of parents. Before her mom had left for the war, she'd talked about being a soldier herself. She wondered if Max would end up changing his mind like she had—if he would someday realize he just needed to be himself, not his father.

When Connor rolled through the door, the boys handed the guinea pigs off to her and ran to him. He was on his knees with his arms open as they knocked into him. Joseph was already crying, but Louisa knew Max wouldn't let his tears fall. He'd already become a tough guy. The poor little kid.

"We're staying here so we can see you," Joseph said, his arms clenching Connor. "Mom is so mean."

"Hey, now," Connor said, his eyes meeting hers briefly. "She's only trying to look out for you."

"No, she's not," Max said, pushing back and standing his ground. "Dad said *you'd* always look out for us. And you promised it too."

"I did," Connor said, "and you can always count on me. Right now, though, your mom wants me to stay away. We need to respect that."

"It's not fair!" Max yelled, his hands clenched at his sides.

Connor's sigh was audible. "I know it's not, but she's your mom."

"I don't care," Max shot back. "No one cares about us anymore. Mom won't let us see you. Now you're telling us a pile of crap."

"Max, that's not true," Connor said, still holding Joseph. "Please, come here."

She tightened her arms around her waist as she watched him open up his other arm to the boy. *Please go to him. You need each other so much.*

But Max was too angry for that. He sat down in front of Connor, his whole body locked in anger. "You'd better not lie to me. I'm not a little kid anymore."

Her throat clogged with tears at that, and she watched Connor raise his eyes to meet hers. The pain in them was tangible, but he took a deep breath and looked back at Max. "I know you're not. And I won't try and talk to you like one. You're right. Your dad dying wasn't fair. What's happening now isn't fair. I got so mad about everything when your dad died. I didn't act like I was supposed to."

"Did you cry?" Joseph asked.

"Yeah," he said with a sigh. "But there's nothing wrong with crying. Do you know any boys who get into fights at school?"

"Kelly Brown gets into fights all the time," Joseph said with an emphatic nod.

"Well, if I were in school, I'd be like Kelly. That's why your mom wants me to stay away right now."

The courage it must have taken him to admit that slayed her.

"But you wouldn't get into fights with *us*, Uncle Connor," Joseph said, pointing to himself and his brother.

"No, but your mom thinks I'm a bad influence right now, and since she's your mom, that's up to her."

"But she's wrong!" Max shouted. "You couldn't be a bad influence. Ever. You were our dad's best friend."

"And he was mine," Connor said softly. "The best friend I'll ever have probably."

Times like this, Louisa wished she'd known Corey Weatherby.

"We want to stay with you," Joseph said, clutching him and starting to cry again. "Please don't make us go back, Uncle Connor. She's only going to be madder at us."

"My mom and dad came to take you home," Connor said, chucking Joseph under the chin. "They'll talk to your mom."

"It didn't help before," Max shouted again, shooting up off the ground. "It's not going to change anything. She won't listen. She'll just ground us forever. This sucks." He raced off to the corner of the room, hiding his face again.

Louisa didn't think it would change anything either, and she hurt for all three of them. They wanted to be together so badly. She felt the pull inside her to do something, like talk to their mom again. But that would probably only make it worse. They hadn't exactly hit it off.

Connor continued to pat Joseph's back as the boy cried in his arms. God, the poor little guy. But Connor had him in hand, even if his face did get more haggard with every sniff and soft wail.

She walked over to Max and knelt down beside him. Knowing he didn't want comfort, she went for truth. "I know this sucks. Like your uncle said, none of it is fair. I wish we could make it all go away, but we can't. I won't lie to you. You might not see your uncle for a while, so why don't you go over and hug him instead of standing in the corner all by yourself?"

He turned his body slightly so he could glare at her. "Would you talk to our mom? I read on the website where it says you've won lots of awards for helping people. Can you help us? I know we're not homeless or anything..."

Oh, crap. Now she was going to have to tell him. "Your mom already came and talked to me after she heard your uncle was working here with me. It didn't go well."

He lowered his head, his shoulders slumping in utter defeat. "She hates everything right now. She said Dad dying was the worst thing that could have happened, but she was wrong. The way she's acting is the worst. I mean, we were used to Dad being gone most of the time. I miss him, and I wish he could come back, but Mom was the one we saw every day. She used to be fun and nice."

"Losing someone sometimes changes people for a while," she said, meeting his eyes.

"Do they ever get back to being how they used to be?"

She couldn't lie to him. "Some do. Some don't. It's the person's choice, really. They have to decide if they want to keep being happy. My dad always says he doesn't think anyone who truly loved us would ever want us to stop being happy just because they're not around anymore."

Max nodded slowly. "That makes sense to me. Your dad sounds nice."

"He's pretty great, but he had some rough times too. Choosing to be happy got him through them. So did doing good for others. He says those two things get him up in the morning."

"So what you're saying is that my dad wouldn't want me or my brother to stop being happy—not even if my mom is being stupid right now."

He was a smart boy and ahead of his years in many ways. She expected he'd been like this always. "Sounds like a good approach to me. I can tell you it's what finally turned things around for me. For a long time, I was really mad at my mom—even after she died. Every day I got up, I wanted to punch something. But after a while I realized I was only hurting myself."

"My mom is hurting me and Max and Uncle Connor besides herself." He kicked the floor. "I hate that. I can't wait until I'm eighteen. Then I can do anything I want. See anybody I want."

No truer words had ever been spoken. "You're right, but in the meantime, you still have the power to choose certain things. Like whether you want to be happy. You can do that no matter how your mom feels. Or even your brother."

"Yeah, he cries a lot, but I figure it's okay. He's little and he misses Dad."

And this boy didn't consider himself little anymore. She wondered if he ever had. "I'd say you're pretty grown up for your age. That's a compliment."

"Thanks." He lowered his chin and shrugged. "And thank you for not treating me like a dumb little kid. I like you. You're not like other grown-ups."

She smiled. "Thank you. I'd like to think I'm special. You are too, by the way."

"I wish we could come here to visit you too," he said, glancing at her for a moment before looking away. "I can tell Uncle Connor likes you a lot, and he doesn't like a lot of people. That's what Dad told me. Since he's really particular about who he spends time with, and he always wanted to hang out with Dad, Dad used to laugh and say he had to be the best person in the world."

That made her smile. "Since your Uncle Connor loves you so much, you have to be pretty awesome too. He doesn't like you just because of your dad, you know."

He jerked his little shoulder. "I know. Okay, we'll go with Aunt Assumpta and Uncle Shawn when they show up. But I'm not going to say I like it."

She bit her lip to stop from smiling again. "Lying about how you feel is the worst thing any of us can do. It's like taking rat poison."

"Ugh." Max made a gagging sound. "I hate rat poison."

Laughing, she held out her hand to him. He took it. "Come on. Let's hang out until your aunt and uncle get here. Want to hold the guinea pigs again?"

"Sure. I bet my brother will too."

They took out Mr. Snuggles and Mrs. Cuddles and walked over to where Connor was still holding Joseph.

"Hey," Max said, patting his little brother on the back. "You okay?"

Joseph sniffed loudly but he edged back, knuckling away tears. Connor wiped his nose as well.

"We're going to hang out with Uncle Connor until his parents get here. Then we're going to go home and not tell Mom we came here."

"Max—"

"No, Uncle Connor, it'll only make everything worse if Mom finds out. Aunt Assumpta and Uncle Shawn can drop us off. We can hide our backpacks in the garage and get them later. She'll go crazy if she finds out we ran away."

"I'm not sure lying about where you went is the right move here," Connor said slowly.

"It's my choice, and I'm making it."

Louisa winced. "That's not quite what I meant, Max."

"You said we make choices about how we want it to be. We don't want Mom to get any madder than she already is. Right, Joe?"

The little boy nodded.

"We're going to do our best to be happy and that means hanging out with our friends after school and on weekends. Every chance we get. The more time we spend away from home, the better."

"Your mother loves you," Connor said, his shoulders slumping in sadness. "She's just mad about your dad."

"No, she's not," Max said, his eyes full of fire again. "She's mad about everything! I don't want to be around her right now, and that's *my choice*. I get to make some choices. That's what Miss Louisa said."

She couldn't fault him for feeling that way. Of course, being away from the kids might not be good for Olivia's recovery. "When she starts to be herself again, you can reassess. Right, Max?"

"Right. Joseph, you good with this? We're not going to get ourselves in trouble or Uncle Connor."

"Don't worry about me," Joseph said, crossing his heart. "You're the one I'm worried about. You've been mad too."

"Don't be worried," Max told him. "We have a plan. Thanks, Miss Louisa."

She wished she could recommend family counseling to all of them, but she didn't think Olivia would accept it. "You'll have to see if your aunt and uncle will agree. They might not like lying to your mom."

"Then we'll take a cab or something home," Max said firmly. "This is how it's gonna go."

A knock sounded on the door, and she glanced over toward it. Hargreaves was standing in the hallway. "Would you hold Mrs. Cuddles for me, Joseph?"

The little boy took the guinea pig, and she rose to open the door for Hargreaves.

He nodded to her but stayed put in the hall. "Boxer mentioned the two Weatherby boys were here," he said in an undertone, "and I wanted to extend my services should they need to be driven home."

Perhaps Max's guardian angel had heard them talking and arranged the ride? Louisa stepped into the hallway. "Connor's parents are coming from downtown, but with traffic, it could take a while. We were just discussing getting them home. Hang on."

She crooked her finger at Connor, who kissed Joseph

on the top of his head and then headed over. "I didn't know you were here, Hargreaves."

Casting a glance at the boys to make sure they were okay, she was happy to see them playing with the guinea pigs.

"I wanted to spend my time off with Sunflower Alley's staff and residents, Mr. Merriam," he said, always formal. "I heard about the Weatherby boys and was telling Miss Evans I would be happy to give them a ride home if it's helpful."

They shared a look. "Is it wrong to go along with the wishes of a ten-year-old?" Connor asked.

She let out a long sigh. "Will it help anyone if their mother escalates the situation? It's a fine line, but these boys need to know they have some control here. They only ran away because they felt like they didn't. Now they do, and they're going home, and I feel like they're in a better frame of mind. I don't feel like they're going to try to run away again. If I did, I'd never suggest agreeing to this."

"Agreed," Connor said. "I don't like it, but they shouldn't get punished for something like this. It kills me to think about them running away. This is my fault."

"No, it's not, and that's not productive." She put her hand on his arm. "My gut says we do it Max's way. If we don't, I feel like he's only going to get madder and strike out again."

"I hate this." Connor cursed. "Sorry, Hargreaves."

"No need to apologize, sir," he said, his face inscrutably calm. "This is a delicate situation."

Connor thought for a moment and then heaved a sigh. "Fine. We go with your gut, Louisa. You deal with angry kids all the time and used to be one. If it comes out, I'll take the fall. Say I went along with their story so they wouldn't get into trouble."

She squeezed his arm. "More adults should listen to kids. They're a lot smarter than we give them credit for.

Okay, Hargreaves. I can ride with the boys and see them as close to their front door as possible. Better me than you, Connor." Plus, she was good at keeping out of sight from the old days on the streets. Olivia would never know she'd been there.

"All right, I'll text my parents and tell them to turn around." He dug out his phone. "Last I checked, she didn't know they were gone."

"I'll pull the car up in front of the shelter and have it warmed for the boys," Hargreaves said with a bow before taking off.

"Is this crazy?" Connor asked, his worried eyes locked on her. "Am I being irresponsible here?"

"It's a crappy situation," she said, gesturing to the window where they could see the boys talking. "I don't want to encourage lying, but I also don't think it would be productive for your parents to tell Olivia. You'll remember I had the opportunity to meet her. She's not very receptive right now, and from what your parents said the other day, she didn't listen to them either. The boys are right. She's mad as hell right now and not acting like herself."

"I'll go tell them what we've decided then." He glanced through the window again. The boys were sitting cross-legged on the carpet, watching as the guinea pigs nosed a small rubber ball forward on the carpet back and forth, one of their favorite tricks. "Damn, this might be the last time I ever see them."

She put her arm around him, hearing the sorrow in his voice. "You can't think about that right now. Just go in and tell them what you need to say. Then I'll take them home."

He opened the door, his shoulders braced as if he were heading in for battle. "We found you another ride. Louisa is going to go with you, and before you argue with me, it's better that I don't go, in case your mother sees me."

"He's right," Max told Joseph. "If Mom sees him, she'll go nutso."

"Fine," Joseph said, stroking Mr. Snuggles' fur. "At least Louisa is going."

Connor knelt down in front of the boys. "It might be a while before we see each other again, but I want you to know a few things. I love you. No matter what. Okay?"

Joseph teared up immediately, and Max's chin went out as he said, "We love you too, Uncle Connor."

"Good, now hear me out. Until your mom changes her feelings about me, you need to steer clear of the shelter and all talk of me. Got it?"

"Got it," Max said, his eyes narrowing. "Doesn't mean we have to like it."

"I don't either. But I'll be watching out for you from afar as much as I can. I wish it were different, but we're going to do the best we can and hope this is only going to be for a short time. Now come here."

Louisa took the guinea pigs, and the two boys rushed their uncle, hugging him tightly.

"Don't worry about us," Max told him when he stepped away. "We're going to be okay. And when we get older, we'll find you. If Mom hasn't changed her mind by then."

"How old will that be?" Joseph asked, wiping his eyes.

"Eighteen. We'll be adults, which means we'll be able to do whatever we want."

"But that's a long time," his brother said. "Too long."

"It will go by in a blink," Louisa told them. "Somehow time starts to speed up the older you get. Let's see to your coats. Did you know you have an actual butler taking you home? Actually, Joseph already knows about him. He's the man who won the cooking competition the other night."

"That was pretty cool," Joseph said. "Usually I don't like Asian food, but his was good. Is he really going to take us home? Also, what's a butler?"

Louisa laughed, putting the guinea pigs back in their cages and grabbing the kids' coats. "I'll explain in the car. Or you can ask Hargreaves directly." She'd love to hear more about him from his own mouth. The man truly was a mystery.

She handed Max his coat. He was too grown up for her to think of helping him. Connor helped Joseph, and she could see him lingering over the final ministrations. He was savoring these final moments.

"Your dad loved you guys so much, and he was so proud of you." Connor zipped Joseph's coat up finally and cupped his face. "And he was right. You can count on me. Even if it takes a few years for everything to be sorted out. Got it?"

"You going to be okay, Uncle Connor?" Joseph asked. "I mean, you said you were like Kelly Brown who gets into fights all the time."

She all but melted at the simple sweetness of the question.

Connor's mouth tipped up. "I'll be okay, Joseph. I'm mending my ways. Aren't I, Louisa?"

"You certainly are," she said with a smile. "Okay, let's go to the front and see if Hargreaves has his car waiting for us. I figure there's no reason for us to freeze. It's crazy cold outside. Connor, why don't you grab their backpacks while I get my coat? You can meet me there."

She wanted to give them some final time alone too. As she was leaving, Joseph ran into Connor's arms again, sniffing. "I don't want to go."

"We have to, Joe," Max said. "Come on. I've got your back."

Yeah, that young boy did, and she knew he always would. Joseph and Max were lucky to have each other. She'd often wondered if things might have been different if she'd grown up with a sibling during those tumultuous times, but then she was glad it had only been her on the streets with her mom. She wouldn't have wanted Damien or anyone else to go through that.

Connor and the boys weren't at the front when she arrived, but she saw a black Escalade double-parked on the street, exhaust coming out of the back. She'd tell Harg-reaves they were right behind her. She pushed the door open and stepped outside, heading down the sidewalk.

A male figure appeared at the end of the street, and she recognized it as Jax. She glanced around, noting he was alone this time, but after seeing the company he kept, she felt even warier about him. She braced herself. If he want-ed help finding a place to sleep, she'd direct him to another shelter, but she wasn't offering a meal. She wouldn't invite him back inside until he made some different choices.

"Hey, Louisa," he said, holding up his hand briefly. "You going out?"

He was fidgety again, so she suspected he was high. "Yeah, I have some precious cargo I'm transporting. Jax, we're full up tonight, so if you need a place to sleep, you might check out Ashland. Boxer called them for you last time. Remember?"

He took a few uncoordinated steps toward her, and she edged back, her body going on alert. Something didn't feel right.

Don't do anything stupid, Jax.

"A couple guys on the street said some rich lady gave you a million dollars."

Her solar plexus tightened, and she noted the odd line under his jacket. He was carrying. Not good. "She gave it to the *shelter* to fund some great programs we have in mind. You'll have to check them out. One's a training program to help people find great jobs so they can get off the street. Now, I need to dash since I have people waiting."

Stepping off the sidewalk and onto the snowpack, she tried to circle around him toward the car.

He blocked her, using his body to make her step back. She did so, only because she didn't want to escalate the sit-uation. She never used her martial arts training unless it was a last resort. "You need to let me pass, Jax."

He waved his hands in a way she suspected was meant

to be intimidating. "I need some of that money, Louisa. I owe some people."

For drugs likely. She'd been afraid of that, seeing him with those gang members. Jax didn't look like a recruit. It didn't mean he wasn't dangerous, though. He'd come here with a gun. She needed to get him away from the shelter, and then she'd call the police. But protecting the people inside was of the utmost importance.

"I don't have the money, Jax," she said, holding his frantic gaze. "It's in the shelter's *bank account.* Now, come on. You're going to leave, and I'm going to get into my car. We're going to forget about this. This isn't who you want to be." She rarely lied, but it was the right move right now.

He made a hasty grab for her purse, but she took another step back to evade him. Could she move him onto the street away from the front of the shelter?

"You got your purse right here," he said, pointing at her, his eyes gleaming. "We're going to the ATM up the block. I want some of that money, bitch."

Not good. She needed to deescalate this fast. "Jax, the daily limit for an ATM is five hundred dollars. Do you really want to go to jail for that small of a score? You strike me as a smarter guy than that. Come on, let's forget this. I'm asking you to leave."

He shifted into what she recognized as a more threatening stance, opening his jacket enough for her to see the butt of the gun. She was walking a fine line—she'd have a better chance of disarming him if she got closer, but he was more likely to pull it if she moved.

"This is your last warning." She set her weight in her martial arts stance. "Jax, this isn't going to go down good for you."

He flung his hands out, walking toward her. "I don't care! I can't go back empty-handed. We'll have to go into a bank or something. I'm not settling for five. You listen to me, bitch. I need more money, or they'll hurt me again."

Ready for him, she felt someone open the door behind her. She knew it was Connor. With the boys. Her heart rate kicked up. *Oh, God.*

"Stay inside!" she yelled.

"Bitch!" Jax lurched forward, getting in her face. "You shouldn't have done that. *Why* did you do that? He's going to call the cops."

"Then you'd better leave," she told him in a hard tone. "Now, Jax."

"Excuse me, miss," Hargreaves called out calmly. Keeping her eyes also on Jax, she glanced over quickly to see the older man walking toward them.

What was he doing?

"I'm your Uber driver," he continued casually, "and you either need to get in the car or I'm leaving."

The lie told her that Hargreaves had some ruse in mind, but he was elderly and breakable, and she didn't want him to get hurt. "I don't need a car anymore," she called out briskly. "Please go ahead and leave."

She heard the door open again. Connor.

"Let her go." Connor's voice boomed across the cold expanse of the front walkway.

"Stop right there," Jax shouted. "You too, old man. I've got a gun. I just want some money."

She had two bystanders to worry about. Time was running out. If she didn't handle this situation soon, it was going to blow out of control. "Here, take my purse." She shoved it at Jax. "If you use my ATM and credit cards, you might get a couple thousand. Leave now. Run before the cops get here."

Jax clutched the purse to him and pulled out his gun, training it first on Hargreaves and then Connor. "You two got any money?"

"Take mine." Connor threw his money clip. "Now put the gun away and leave. Louisa, get over here."

Who was he kidding? He wasn't trained for this. "Connor, dammit, go inside. I've got this."

"Lady, I have the gun, so I'm the one who makes the rules. Shut up." Jax waved the gun in Connor's direction and her stomach clenched.

She only made it a couple of steps toward Jax when Hargreaves pushed her out of the way. If her weight hadn't been set, she would have fallen to the ground.

"Take my money," Hargreaves said, moving quickly toward Jax as he reached inside his coat, presumably for his wallet. "I run a driver service. Here, let me get it for you."

Jax's gaze followed Hargreaves' hand. What was Hargreaves doing? She had to cut him off or he'd get hurt. She started to move forward again.

But before she could move an inch, Hargreaves' other hand was on Jax's wrist, redirecting the gun away from them to the ground. Jax cried out a split second before the gun fired, the sound reverberating in her eardrums and making her jerk in surprise.

"Louisa!" Connor cried.

Hargreaves squeezed the kid's hand, and the gun clattered to the ground. The boy cried out, holding his wrist. "You broke my hand!"

"You okay, Hargreaves?" she asked, rushing forward.

"Yes, miss."

She picked up the gun and secured it as Connor ran to her. His entire body was hot, and his heart was pounding. He wanted to kill Jax—she could feel it vibrating within him. "Stop. I'm fine. Now go inside."

She pushed him toward the door, but he wouldn't budge. "I'm not leaving you."

"It will be easier for me if you go inside," she said. "The boys will have heard the gunshot. They'll be scared."

"I'll stay with her, sir," Hargreaves said, his eyes trained on Jax.

Connor's mouth bunched, and he said, "Dammit!" as if acknowledging she was right. He gave her a final look before heading back inside.

Boxer stuck his head out, his brow creased with worry. "Louisa, you good, girl? Cops are on their way."

"Yeah, keep everyone inside," she said, noting a few of their people pressed up against the glass.

She turned back to Jax. "You stay put! What the hell were you thinking? You could have killed someone."

"I didn't want to hurt anyone," he cried, cradling his hand. "I'm sorry. I couldn't take them hurting me anymore. I just wanted some money."

His knees gave out, and he started sobbing, horrible gut-wrenching sounds coming from his throat. She wanted to yell at him.

Needing to get a grip on her anger, she turned to Hargreaves, who was wiping his brow line as he watched the scene. A trace of sweat? Who was this man?

"Where did you learn that, Hargreaves? Because it sure as hell wasn't in cooking school." She stood there, trying to ignore the anguish coming from Jax.

"The man who knew Julia Child in Ceylon taught me karate," the older man answered, patting her briefly on the back as if in comfort.

"The spy?" She shook her head. "What a wild night. After today, you should tell me his name."

He handed her a handkerchief. "It was my father, miss. Also, you have blood on the side of your mouth where you bit it."

Wiping it off, she stuffed the handkerchief in her pocket alongside the gun. Jax was still crying, huge sobs being torn from his chest. Yeah, he knew he'd messed up bad. No stone-cold criminal ever cried when they were caught. His hand flopped at an awkward angle, and she pulled the gun out and handed it to Hargreaves.

"Put this someplace safe until the cops arrive, will you?"

He took the gun from her after meeting her gaze for a long moment. Yeah, they'd escaped disaster tonight. "You know I was trained in martial arts, Hargreaves. I could have handled myself."

"I was not aware of that, miss, until it was too late to walk away."

Yeah, that's what she'd thought. Crossing to Jax, she knelt in front of him. "Jax, what were you thinking?"

He looked up, his eyes huge and puffy in his lean face, his body jerking with sobs. "I'm...ah...sorry, Louisa. Really...sorry."

Oddly enough, she believed him.

His eyes gleamed with tears as he forced his sobs back. "They said...they'd...beat me up again...if I didn't pay."

They might have killed him even, and she suspected he knew it. "Did they give you the gun?"

He nodded. "I'm so...sorry. I didn't want anyone to get hurt, but they said..."

She could imagine what they'd said. This neighborhood had seen violence from them time and time again. God, sometimes the world sucked. "I know, Jax."

"I couldn't take it anymore, Louisa. I just couldn't."

She remembered feeling like that after another cold day on the streets, her hands red and bleeding from the wind. She'd felt like she just couldn't take it anymore. Compassion started to fill her, and she let her anger ebb away. It wasn't going to help anyone.

"Nobody cares about me," Jax whispered, hunching forward. "Maybe I should have let them kill me."

He started crying again, and she put her hand on his arm. He winced. His body was so thin he was almost skeletal, and she suspected he had fresh bruises under his worn clothes from the gang members' warning. "Don't say that. I care about you, Jax."

His sobbing began anew. Her time on the street flashed through her mind, as well as the stories of hundreds of people who'd told her what had happened to them. In that moment, he became yet another wounded human being to her—and she the person who could comfort him.

Scooting closer to him, she did the only thing she knew to heal hurts. She put her arms around him as he cried his heart out.

When the sirens came closer, she hugged him tight and then pushed back. "The police are coming to take you away, Jax, but I'll come see you if you want. Be sure to tell them who put you up to this, okay? It will go easier for you." Her dad had some guys who worked in the prison ministry who could check on him as well.

He wiped his nose. "You're *way* too nice. You know?"

She chuckled, the sound almost wry even to her own ears. "So I'm told."

"But yeah...I'd like it if you come to see me." He held his hands up as the cops swarmed out of their cars. "Again, I'm really, really sorry."

Standing up, she started walking toward the cop she knew as some of the other officers cuffed Jax and read him his rights. They'd want a statement from her and from Hargreaves too.

The faster she could finish the interview, the faster she could talk to Connor, because she knew she had more fast-talking to do tonight.

CHAPTER 24

S HE'D ALMOST DIED BECAUSE OF HIM.

When Boxer had told him the reason Jax had held her up at gunpoint, he'd wanted to rip the kid's head off. But pain had ridden in on the coattails of all that fist-squeezing rage.

He'd done this.

That kid would never have gone after Louisa if Connor hadn't put Clara up to donating such a large sum to the shelter.

Through the waves of guilt and pain and rage, he felt confusion too. How could Louisa have held the kid like that after he'd turned a gun on her? The guy had almost killed her. He just couldn't understand her. Right now, it was beyond him.

Louisa was out front talking to the cops, and he was in the kitchen with the boys, standing by while Carter and Maria fussed over them. Although he was grateful for their help, he needed to get Max and Joseph as far away from this place as he could. God, they could have been killed too. What if Joseph hadn't needed to use the bathroom at the last minute?

He was going to be sick.

No, he couldn't. The boys needed him. He fought the gorge in his throat.

Hargreaves walked into the kitchen, the appearance of calm, as if he hadn't disarmed a gunman earlier. Connor stepped forward to speak to him.

"Miss Evans has more questions to answer with the police about Jax's alleged associates. She suggested I might take the boys back since I've given my statement. The police are moving my vehicle to the shelter's back entrance. We thought it best not to take the boys through the front."

"Good idea. I was just thinking about getting them the hell out of here. You okay, Hargreaves?"

"Of course, sir." He was pulling on his black gloves. "A butler is prepared for every eventuality."

"Even violence?" His aunt hadn't exactly led a dangerous life up until recently.

"Your aunt is a wealthy woman, as you know," he said in that same casual way of his. "When we lived in Manhattan, I made sure to guard against robbery and the like. She is known for her art and jewels."

He'd never thought of it that way. Most of his suits were worth thousands, and the watch on his wrist was a Patek Philippe Calatrava, all chosen for their understated style and perfection. He'd never worried about being attacked because of it. Maybe it was a sort of blindness only guys possessed. Otherwise, no guy in his right mind would buy his girl a big engagement ring. "How did I not see that before, Hargreaves?"

"Perhaps you have a brighter world view than I do, sir."

He studied the white-haired man. "Are you joking with me, Hargreaves?"

"At a time like this?" The man smiled thinly. "I wouldn't presume. Sir, you might say goodbye to Miss Evans before we depart. She's tough as steel, but any person would be affected by today's events."

Yeah, that was Louisa. She was made out of the toughest substance on earth, and he seemed to be made of glass right now. "Are you affected, Hargreaves?"

His mouth quirked into a facsimile of a smile. "A butler is trained not to be affected, sir, but I might have had a moment or two. I'll see to the boys and make sure the car is warm."

After making sure the boys were okay to leave, Connor left the shelter and walked to where Louisa was standing. Red and blue lights were still flashing from police cars parked in the street. A crowd had gathered along the string of yellow police tape. Jax was in one of those cop cars. He hoped the kid would rot in hell.

Boxer was speaking to a cop taking notes in a small black book. Louisa was gesturing to another officer with her hands. When she spotted him, she excused herself. He braced himself, not knowing what to say, and she didn't move to hug him. Instead, she stopped short in front of him.

"You're blaming yourself," she said in a voice only he could hear. "I can see it in your face. This could have happened for any number of reasons."

He fisted his hands at his sides. "Don't do this right now."

She worried her mouth for a moment. "Take the boys home. I don't see how you can just drop them off. It will be all over the news. They might need counseling. I have crisis counselors from other shelters arriving for our clients and staff shortly if you want to wait a bit."

Counseling. Christ. As if the boys didn't have enough to deal with. "It's late, and I'll need to talk to Olivia about that. Maybe it's better this way. Corey would want me to try talking to her again."

"He might at that." She rocked on her heels. "So, where are you going after you drop them off? Up for a late pizza? I'm not hungry now, but I imagine the adrenaline will wear off. Dad and Damien would probably like to wrap me up in a blanket tonight and feed me tea or coffee, but I'm not up for that."

She was babbling.

"I'm not sure what I'm doing," he said. "My parents... They might have seen the news. I need to text them. I don't think they're leaving tonight."

"You going to see them after you talk to Olivia? Good idea. Be good for you to be around people you care about after this." Again, she rocked back, but this time she lost her balance.

He laid his hand on her arm, and her eyes flashed to his. Hargreaves was right. Under that tough exterior, she was hurting. Some of his rage dispersed. "Come here."

She shook her head, but he pulled her into him. She was trembling, he realized, the tremors too small to be seen by the naked eye. "I'm okay. Just shaky."

It never should have happened. "When I finish with Olivia, I'll swing by the apartment. Have Boxer or your family take you home, okay?"

He kissed her hair and made himself let her go even though he didn't want to leave her. A few steps away, a thought struck him. She was already walking back to Boxer and the cops.

"Louisa?"

She stopped and turned around. "Missing me already?"

The arrow struck his heart. Yeah, he was, and it hurt like hell. "Will there be any gang retaliation over what happened here?"

Her face went blank. She took a few steps toward him, but not all the way. "We don't think so, but the cops are picking up the two gang members I saw Jax with the other day. He already named them. My dad, Carter, and Boxer will be talking to people in the community. We're going into Green mode here at the shelter. Have some new security items to consider with a donation of this size."

All he could do was incline his head. He'd brought this to her door.

"*Connor.*" She swallowed thickly. "This is a good problem to have. We'll handle it."

A good problem to have? Who was she kidding? "I need to get the boys home."

"Tell them goodbye for me. I'm sorry they had to be here for this. They're good kids. I wish I could have met their dad."

He wished that too. He lifted his hand and went back inside.

Hargreaves had the boys in the back of the Escalade with hot chocolates in their little hands. The scent seemed almost too innocent for what had taken place at the shelter, which was likely the reason Hargreaves had arranged for the treat. Hot chocolate was the antidote when the big bad world came knocking.

God, people used to call him the Big Bad Wolf. Tonight, he was scared shitless.

"Is everything all right, Uncle Connor?" Joseph asked, his little gloved hand wrapped around the coffee cup.

"Is Louisa safe?" Max asked, his face lined with worry.

They'd heard the shot outside, and the boys would probably find out anyway—these days all you had to do was access a news site online—so he went with the truth. Losing the trust of these boys would kill him. "Someone wanted some money from her, but she and Hargreaves here handled it."

"Could she have died like Daddy?" Joseph asked.

The gorge in his throat was back. This time he had to lie. When he'd heard that shot go off...

"No, Joseph. Now, let's talk about what happens when we get you guys home. I'm going to talk to your mother alone. Can you go upstairs? We can say goodbye here in the car."

It wasn't ideal, and the boys didn't like it, but in the end, they were troopers. After Hargreaves parked the car, they both gave him long and sniffly hugs. He took their hands and walked them up to the door. When Olivia opened it, her eyes immediately narrowed, and he felt a blast of rage from her.

"You were supposed to be at friends' houses. Dammit, I should have known you'd pull something like this, Connor."

Max pointed his finger at her. "Mom, we're going upstairs so Uncle Connor can talk to you about what happened, but we're okay. Don't be mad at him. We only ran away because we wanted to see him."

"*You did what*?" Olivia gasped.

"We're not stupid. We had a plan and everything. Come on, Joe. Bye, Uncle Connor."

Joseph teared up and hugged Connor's leg. "Bye," he said in a small voice. "I love you."

"I love you too," Connor whispered, pain rocketing through his heart. He ruffled Joseph's hair and kissed the top of it, wondering if this was the last time he'd see them.

The boys linked hands and walked up the staircase.

Connor stepped inside to stop the cold from pouring into the house. "I can't imagine how angry or upset you are, but can you give me a minute of your time please?"

"A minute? Do you have any idea how irresponsible this is? You went against my wishes in seeing them."

He put his hands on his hips, aware the boys would be listening at the top of the stairs. "I didn't arrange this. The boys found me because they missed me, Olivia. They don't understand why you won't let us see each other. I tried to explain that I'd made some bad choices before coming here, like Kelly Brown at school."

"Who's that?" she asked, her tone as brittle as her face.

"Never mind. Just listen. They found me because they didn't know why they shouldn't. They miss me, and whether that's right or wrong, it's true. Blame me for what happened tonight. Not them. There was an incident at the homeless shelter that'll probably be on the news. I want you to know they were inside and safe the whole time, and I feel worse than you could ever know about them being there."

She grabbed the edges of her black sweater. "I told you when you came here something would happen to them if they followed you. Just like Corey."

His jaw locked. "Okay, you were right. Just don't blame them, Liv. They're only kids, and they've been through enough. Dammit, I'm a grown man, and I can barely take it."

He hadn't called her by that nickname since her first years of being married to Corey. They'd all been so young and carefree then.

"Don't tell me what they've been through." Her face crumpled. "I'm here every day. Connor—"

"Listen, I'm going to honor your wishes. I'll stay away. I won't even email them if you don't want that. But I hope you'll change your mind someday because I love those boys."

He looked to the top of the stairs, and he saw Joseph crying softly, Max sitting next to him with anger in his eyes.

"I set up college funds in each of their names," he continued, "and a modest trust fund for meals and incidentals. I'll send you the papers after I leave. Beyond that, if you ever need anything, please know I'm here for you and the boys. Corey wanted me to take care of you, and I hope you'll let me. That's all I wanted to say."

He turned to leave, but the sound of a door slamming upstairs stopped him in his tracks, reverberating so loudly that the family photo on the side table fell over. He looked up to see Joseph still crying. Max was gone.

"They really ran away?" Olivia asked, tears appearing in her eyes.

"Yeah," he said, tucking his hand into his pocket. "They're hurting, Liv. We all are. Someone recently told me hurting people act out sometimes. Tonight, it was the boys' turn."

Except Olivia had been hurt by the boys' actions too. Maybe they were all locked in a vicious cycle where the only thing that was going around was hurt.

"I miss Corey too, Liv," he said, lowering his walls and not fighting the tears that wanted to fall. "I love those boys. Take good care of them for me."

"I was so jealous of you," she whispered, biting her lip. "Sometimes I thought Corey loved you more than he did me."

Shit. "Don't think that. Don't ever think that. We were best friends since we were born, Liv, and cousins to boot. He didn't love you less or me more. He loved both of us. He was on that oil rig because he wanted to take care of his family and give you and the boys a good life. You know that."

She scrubbed her face before saying, "I know he wanted to provide for our family, but he was also on that rig because of you. Because he wanted to work with you in the one way he knew how. He knew he wasn't a corporate desk jockey. He liked to be in the field. He used to tell me how much he loved wearing the Merriam logo on his clothes— even when he was home—because it reminded him that he was part of something bigger, something you were expanding."

He hadn't known that. He used to tease Corey for always asking for Merriam swag. That was all gone now, and another wave of grief engulfed him. "Again, I'm sorry I failed him, and you guys. I should go."

His hand clenched the door handle, but the sound of soft crying stopped him from turning the knob. Should he leave her to her grief? Then he thought of Louisa. She wouldn't leave. No, she'd take Olivia into her arms and comfort her. She'd done that with him, and it had helped, hadn't it?

Turning, he cautiously took a step toward her, his arm out. Would she push him away? Yell at him to get out?

Bracing himself for that possibility, he pulled her to him and tucked her close.

She gripped his coat like a mountain climber who'd lost her grip on the rockface, tunneling her face into his chest. Her body started shaking, and he banded his arms around her like Louisa had done for him, anchoring her, letting her know he wasn't going to turn tail and run in the face of her hurt.

"Oh, Corey," she cried out, and then she was pouring out her tears.

"I've got you, Liv," he whispered, tears filling his own eyes.

Joseph caught his attention, crying softly at the head of the stairs with a teddy bear clutched to his chest, and he held out a hand to the little boy. He ran down the stairs, his arms wrapping around Connor's leg. Putting his hand on the boy as best he could, he held them both, his eyes trained to the second floor.

Come out, Max. Please come out.

He waited and waited, but the boy didn't emerge. Hearing Liv's and Joseph's sobs tore at his heart, and he found his own tears falling with theirs. He thought of Corey and all they'd lost, and he wondered if this pain would ever go away.

Then Max appeared, his hands gripping the banister as if he wanted to tear the rungs from their anchors. Connor understood. He'd felt the same way for months, but he was sick of feeling angry, and he didn't want that for Max.

"Come here, son," he called out softly.

Olivia shifted in his arms, looking over at Max as he tromped down the stairs, anger in every step. She stepped away from Connor and faced her son.

"I'm so sorry, Max," she said, crying softly. "I promise to do better from now on. Just don't run away again. Okay?"

His face crumpled, his jaw locking as if he were fighting

it all the way. Then he lunged forward and wrapped his arms around his mother. "*I miss Daddy.*"

The boy's wail decimated what was left of his walls. Connor picked up Joseph and walked over, bundling up Liv and Max. They sank onto the floor, all of them crying now, missing someone who would never return.

And yet, Connor could feel the power of the moment. This, too, was the kind of moment that changed everything.

CHAPTER 25

THE WAIT FOR CONNOR WAS INTERMINABLE.

Louisa leaned forward on the couch and checked her phone on the coffee table again. Just after eleven. Still no messages from Connor. Had he up and left after what had happened tonight? Her heart seized up with pain at the thought of him leaving over this. She knew he blamed himself, and she wasn't sure how to convince him otherwise.

Truth was, the incident had shaken her too. Maybe it should have dawned on her, but she'd never considered anyone trying to rob them for donations. After the police had left, she and Boxer had gone to her office to return calls from the press and other concerned parties.

"It's a weird situation, Louisa," he'd told her. "People hear a million dollars, and they go crazy. Of course, gang-bangers and drug users don't read our annual reports. Otherwise they'd know our donations run into the six figures every year. If they did, maybe this would have happened before. But now it has, and we'll make some changes."

But would it be enough? She'd made call after call, re-assuring people it would be, but it hurt to know they'd fall-en so short of the mark.

Security had been one of their biggest thrusts at the

shelter, both for the staff and for the people they served. That sacred trust had been broken tonight. They'd had some people leave the shelter, especially ones with kids, saying they didn't feel safe. Even Kendra's mom, who'd said she had to watch out for her baby girl.

That had about killed Louisa.

It was the first time they'd ever lost clients because of safety concerns. And part of her feared it wasn't the only thing they'd lose. Would volunteers stop coming? Would people no longer be interested in attending their monthly cooking competitions?

Parents wouldn't bring their children to a shelter that had been on the news for an armed robbery over a charitable donation.

She took a sip of the tea she'd made to soothe her dry throat, trying to keep calm. Someone could have been killed tonight. They'd all been lucky.

But what about tomorrow? And the day after that? Was the upcoming Thanksgiving holiday to be mired down with more danger?

The cops assured her they would be driving by more to mitigate any additional trouble. She was always grateful for their support, but their heightened presence might only serve to remind everyone that there had been—and might still be—trouble.

Tonight she didn't have much in the way of answers, and her usual strength seemed elusive. She could feel that scared little girl from her past reemerging, the one who hadn't felt strong enough to handle what was next.

She still needed to write tomorrow's love note. What the hell was she going to write? *Stick with us. We'll protect you.*

Who would be inspired by that? She'd run like hell if she read that.

A key sounded in her lock, and she jumped up, the blue throw she'd covered herself with falling to the floor. When

Connor appeared in the doorway, she almost ran into his arms, not only out of relief but the need for sanctuary. But years of hard training had her gauging his face, his body language.

Something had changed. The tension was gone from his body, but he looked older. She wouldn't have been surprised to see white hairs had sprouted at his temples, as if the fear and rage had leached his very vitality.

"Hey," she said, almost wincing when she heard how weak and unsure her voice sounded. "I'm glad you came."

He locked the door with the precision of a military officer checking off roll call. "Sorry it's so late. Olivia and I put the boys to bed and then started talking, and I didn't feel like I could take out my phone. I worried it would break the mood."

Her throat thickened as she thought about what could have happened if those boys had stepped outside with Connor. "You've been with her the whole time? That's good, right?"

He shrugged out of his coat, groaning as he rolled his neck. "It's what people who're in war call a fragile peace. She's agreed to let me see the boys at the house when she's around, with the promise of more once she feels comfortable. Also, after hearing what happened tonight, she would like the boys to talk to a counselor. I suggested it might be good for them to talk to someone about Corey too, and she agreed. Could you give me a couple recommendations?"

"Of course," Louisa said, swallowing thickly. "That's some good news at least. I'll text you some names. The boys are okay?"

He lifted a shoulder. "They had a breakthrough with their mom, so yeah, I think they're going to be all right."

She decided to call out the elephant in the room. "What about you?"

He rubbed the space between his brow. "I'm all over the place actually."

"Me too," she said, trying to smile.

When he looked up, the tension in his face was palpable. "Do you have any idea what it did to me to see you being held at gunpoint? I could go on about the donation I put Clara up to making, but honest to God, right now I'm so tired I don't have it in me. I just want to hold you. Is that okay?"

That sounded encouraging. She padded forward, the hardwood floor cold under her bare feet. "I could use some good holding. It's been a day."

"An understatement if I've ever heard one," he said, pulling her to his body and wrapping his arms around her. "How are you?"

She pressed her face against his chest and clenched her eyes shut, reaching for her strength. Her hands fell short of their mark. In its absence, she reached for some quip to ease the moment, but again, her fingertips only touched the edges before falling into nothingness. "Honest to God? Pretty scared. That's not easy for me to admit—to you or anyone. I've been telling everyone we will rise again."

A soft kiss landed on her hair, and she squeezed her eyes shut again. "I won't tell anyone, don't worry."

"I know you won't," she said, wanting to clutch him to her and never let go, but knowing they both had to stand tall in this moment and see just how much they could support each other. "What happened tonight isn't over."

"I read some news reports online as Hargreaves took me back here. Can you believe he waited all night for me? When I left the house, there he was, reading a mystery in the Escalade with the car running. Like it hadn't been hours."

She was aware he hadn't given his impression of the news reports or what she'd said. "Hargreaves is amazing. I was trying to gauge the best way to disarm Jax with you two present, but I'm glad he stepped in like he did. When I first saw him coming forward and then you..."

"I couldn't leave you out there." His arms tightened. "*Louisa.*"

The torture in his voice tore at her heart. "I know it was bad tonight, but I'm trained in martial arts. I don't advertise it, but I'm a brown belt in Krav Maga, and I take refresher classes four times a year to keep up. Dad thought it would help me feel more empowered after what I'd faced on the streets, and he was right. Of course, I've never really had to use it much."

He was silent for a long moment, so long her stomach had the opportunity to do a front and back flip. "But you have had to use it before, haven't you?"

It seemed important to look him straight in the eye. "Only a couple of times. Gunpoint is new, though. This is rare, Connor."

His eyes shuttered. "And all I can think is that once is plenty. What about after that shot went off? Did you even wonder if that kid might try to wring your neck as you hugged him?"

She searched for the right words, knowing how important it was that he understand. "I knew the danger was over, or I wouldn't have approached him. It's actually one of the few moments today that felt okay. I know that sounds weird, but I felt like both of us had a breakthrough in that moment. Jax realized someone actually cared about him, and I figured out my anger and fear is never greater than my compassion for another human being. Even in a moment like that. Honestly, I wish my mother were alive because I might have been able to love her more tonight than I ever did toward the end."

He stepped away from her, turning his body so she couldn't see his face. "He could have killed you, Louisa. Part of me understands because I know you, and I want to admire you for it, but the other part... You scared me to death. When I think about why Jax attacked you in the first place...and the fact that the danger might continue because I'm a billionaire..."

"That's horseshit," she immediately said. "Don't go there, Connor."

He held out his hand in an entreaty. "No, hear me out. Tonight, Hargreaves helped me see that money makes people a target. Did you know that's why he learned martial arts? He wanted to be prepared to protect my aunt from burglars or muggers. Maybe it's a guy thing, but when I walk out on the streets, I don't think about getting mugged. I don't worry about someone breaking into my house if I buy a new painting."

Crap, she hated that she understood him here. "The men I know are the same way unless something has happened to them or someone they love, but let me emphasize again how rare this kind of thing is. We're adding new precautions."

"Rare or not, it still happened. And could again."

How was she supposed to fight this new brand of fear? "But you have a security system at your old home, right? Connor—"

"Hang on. Yes, back home I have a security system, but so do most of the people I know. I've never thought about how our wealth makes us a target, especially in a neighborhood like this where there are people like Jax who will hurt people to get it."

She pinched the bridge of her nose, hoping to focus her thoughts. "That's a simplistic view of the world and a pretty shitty view of this neighborhood, which I love. Let me point out a few things here. You all but admitted to living in an ivory tower moments ago, and tragedy still found its way to your door when Corey died. Connor, you can't continue to live your life in fear. Things happen. No matter how much we try and protect ourselves from them."

He cursed under his breath. "You're not hearing me.

This isn't about *me*. It's about you. Louisa, it would destroy me if you were hurt or killed because of me and my money. I can't do that to you again. Ever."

So she was going to lose him after all. The pain in her chest intensified as she hit the wall of cold reality. "I've wondered what I would say to you about all of this. What I could say to you. I've been trying to encourage you to move past your fears, but right now, it seems we're knee-deep in both of ours. I'm fighting mine. Will you do the same? You're wrong to think you put me and the shelter in danger—"

"I don't think it," he spat out, his eyes glaring. "I know it."

His certitude was as hard as diamonds, and she knew there was no way she was cutting through it. "You also think I'm a little batty for hugging a man who'd just tried to rob and maybe kill me," she continued, putting her arms around herself. "I don't know how to explain it except I saw him crying and talking about being hurt, and suddenly he was just a hurting human being. Connor, I don't know his whole story or all that he's gone through, but trust me, he must have suffered a world of hurt to do what he did tonight."

"You're being way too Pollyanna here," he said, his tone hard.

The accusation stung, especially from him. "Maybe, but I know when someone does something out of malice or greed or anger or even because they like it." She took a breath. "I've known people like that my whole life. Jax isn't one of them. It doesn't justify what he did, but in that moment, I felt compassion for him. Anger and fear weren't the main emotions coursing through me, and I'm grateful for that. It means I've won a battle over emotions I don't want running my life. Connor, it's a battle I want you to win too."

He walked over to her mantel and fingered a few of the photos there, a couple with her family and one with her and her wonderful staff at Sunflower Alley. "I thought of you when I took Olivia into my arms. She was crying as I went to leave. At first, I figured she'd want me to go, but then I thought about what you said...about how we're all hurting, and I figured maybe I could..."

Her heart wrenched in her chest, hearing that. Maybe everything wasn't lost. "What?"

"I could comfort her in her hurt. Like you did with me."

His voice was tight, and she cleared her throat as emotion poured in. "And what happened?"

"She cried in my arms, and then Joseph ran down the stairs clutching his teddy bear and joined us. Max had shut himself into his room, but I found myself hoping, *wishing* he'd appear, and he did. He came tromping down, and Liv held out her arms and said she was sorry and that she'd try and do better, and then he was crying out for his dad. God!" He pressed his fist to his mouth.

She fought her own tears. "It does sounds like a breakthrough for all of you. I'm so glad. That's the kind of positive momentum you cling to as you keep going, Connor."

He lowered his hand. "Breakthroughs aren't going to keep you safe, Louisa."

His decision was in his voice, and she clutched her arms around her body, waiting for him to finish.

"I know you love what you do. It's part of you. Something I'd never want you to give up—despite how scared I was tonight."

Tears started filling her eyes.

"But if word gets out that you're dating a billionaire, you're going to have even more trouble. Users like Jax and his gangbanger friends could ambush you outside of Sunflower Alley. Try to rob you, maybe even kidnap you. I won't do that to you."

Her heart fell into empty space, and in that moment, she knew there was nothing more to reach for. "I was afraid of how you might react after what happened, so here we are. Part of me wants to argue with you, to try convincing you that counseling will help you get through this and connect with how you really feel, but I'm just not up for it right now. I can't keep reminding you that you can't control everything. You need to realize that for yourself."

His brows slammed together. "It's about keeping you safe. Nothing else can matter. Not how I feel or even how you feel."

She didn't know how he could say their feelings didn't matter. To her, they were everything. "So you say. I'll agree to disagree. I wish our time together had been longer because I really love you."

Tears filled his eyes. "I really love you too. That's why I'm doing this."

She knew he believed that so she nodded, and finally her fingers touched the bedrock of her strength. "I've always known sometimes love isn't forever, which is why we have to enjoy every day. Connor, I'm glad I met you, and I'm hoping you'll decide to take life as it comes. I'll be rooting for you because you truly are wonderful and have so much to give."

He studied the floor, his pain evident. "You have to trust me on this, Louisa. It's safer this way."

For whom? She wiped at the wetness on her face and crossed to him. "Again, we'll have to agree to disagree. You'll have to choose to go the rest of the way. You have your family back. Let them help you, okay?"

He met her eyes, and his face fell. "I've hurt you, and I never wanted that."

She had to stay strong, so she took his jaw in her hands because he was hurting too. "And you gave me great joy for a while. That's pretty wonderful if you ask me."

He turned his head and kissed the center of her palm. "I thought you'd fight me more on this."

"I can't fight this, Connor." She let her hands drop by her sides, digging her nails into her palms. "No one should ever have to fight someone to continue to love them or stand by their side. I figure that's why marriage vows are so important between people. You both know what you're signing up for. That's not what we're meant for, it seems."

His hand traced her cheek. "For a few moments, I dared to wonder otherwise. I thought this might be that kind of love."

She felt a tear fall but didn't swipe at it. "So did I."

Kissing him lightly on the mouth, she made herself step back when he turned into her and started to deepen the kiss. The pull to make love with him one last time was strong, but what would it serve? He was only going to leave later, and it would hurt even worse if she let herself pretend otherwise.

He tucked his hands into his pockets and stepped back, putting distance between them. Funny that they could find the strength to walk away from each other and not to stand together. Maybe sometime later she could find the irony amusing.

"You're one of the best people I've ever met," he whispered, his eyes on her face. "Right up there with Corey."

She had to bite her lip not to cry. "Thank you. I know what a compliment that is. And you're still one of the most incredible men I've ever met."

He shook his head. "On that, we can agree to disagree. You'll never know how much your help has meant to me. Without you, I don't think I could have ever found the courage to reconcile with my family."

"You did that. Remember that when you don't think you can move mountains." She needed to remember that too right now.

His mouth quirked up. "I'll send you the deed for the school building when I have it."

"You'll have to tell me where to send the check."

He waved a hand. "No."

Pain lanced her heart. "Connor…"

"Louisa, I believe in you. At least let me do this for you."

She could insist, but she knew it would only hurt both of them more. Instead, she nodded. "All right, but you've already done plenty."

His sigh gusted out. "Let me do this for you. I want to. So much. Just please don't use my name for your sake."

Her lip trembled. "Of course. Thank you. I'll text you the counselor names shortly."

"I appreciate it," he said, staring at her intently. "I'll miss your halftime speeches. Louisa, if you ever need anything..."

No, not this. She shook her head. She couldn't be one of his responsibilities. "Don't worry about me, Connor. I'm going to be fine."

Unlocking the door, he pulled out her keys and handed them to her. "I know you will. You'll be safe. Goodbye, Louisa."

She couldn't force the words out, and as the door shut, she saw his coat resting on a side chair. Yanking open the door, she dared to hope he might have left it there on purpose, as a way of coming back to her.

"Hey! You forgot your coat."

His head appeared on the second floor. "I don't need it, remember? The cold doesn't bother me."

One final smile, a forced one, and he disappeared from view again. She walked back into the apartment and closed the door, forcing herself to stop listening for his final footfalls. His coat was still in her hands, and she burrowed her face into it, inhaling deeply. His scent, so distinct and masculine, filled her nose, and because of it, tears filled her eyes.

He was right. The cold never had bothered him.

But it bothered her. She put his coat on and crossed to the window, sensing...something.

He was standing across the street, in front of the apartment building where he'd lived with Corey. She watched him continue to remain there, and she wondered if he was making peace or only piling more regrets onto his shoulders.

Then he strode off, and she stumbled back from the window.

No, the cold didn't bother him much, but there were different kinds of cold. There was the debilitating cold of isolation and loneliness, and as she finally let herself start to cry, she feared it would be his constant companion because of what he'd chosen today.

CHAPTER 26

CONNOR DIDN'T LOOK MUCH LIKE THE BIG BAD WOLF HE'D once been called.

In fact, Arthur thought he looked like a man who was holding on by his fingernails. He was sitting at a table in a corner of the Wild Irish Rose's dining room, along with his brothers, Quinn and Trevor, and their parents—the only other early risers in their group. Arthur and Clara sat at an adjacent table, close enough to be companionable but far enough away that they could talk privately. The rest of the Merriam family were in bed in another part of the inn. The Wild Irish Rose was beautiful, as always, and the weather was fairly pleasant for Ireland at this time of year, but so far, the family's Thanksgiving trip had been a somber occasion.

"I thought we'd seen Connor hit rock bottom in Kenya," Arthur leaned in and told Clara.

"Anger doesn't make one hit rock bottom, Arthur," his lovely wife said in a low voice, frowning as she set a buttery scone aside. "Heartbreak does, and he has it in spades."

They'd left for Ireland the day after the violent event at Sunflower Alley, after Connor had told them he and Louisa ended their relationship. No prodding from *anyone* had produced the full story from him, although everyone in the family thought they had a line on what had led to the breakup—Connor's guilt and fear about putting another person he loved in danger.

Balderdash, Arthur thought, and he wasn't the only one.

"I'm still surprised Louisa didn't fight with him more. The boy collects guilt like it's his hobby," Clara said in that same low voice, picking up her mimosa and taking a sip. "Wasn't I the one who gave her a million dollars? He wanted me to give five hundred thousand. Maybe I should have listened. This might not have happened."

He took the champagne glass from her hand and set it aside. "In the vernacular of our host, has jet lag addled your head? Clara, that's the most darn fool notion I've ever heard. You tried to help the shelter and what she's doing there. Stop talking like that. You sound like Connor."

"I couldn't agree with Master Hale more, Madam." Hargreaves set his knife and fork down from eating the full Irish Clara had insisted he partake of with them given the holiday. "That young man would likely have attempted the same thing regardless of the donation. He was desperate for money to stop those gang members from beating him up again or killing him. This kind of thinking is foolhardy and counterproductive."

Clara's brows rose. "Well, thank you, Hargreaves. For once, you have a strong opinion about something."

"On this? Absolutely, Madam." He picked up his fork and speared a rasher. "On other topics, I keep my thoughts to myself as per my training."

"Thank you for breaking butler protocol, Hargreaves." Arthur gave a sound harrumph to make his point.

Clara fiddled with her diamond bracelet. "I was so sure he and Louisa were perfect for each other."

Arthur had felt the same way. "Are we washed up as matchmakers then?"

She popped him in the shoulder. "Never say that, dear.

I'm just finding my groove. I want to honor their decision, but I don't believe they're so convinced this is for the best either. I mean, when I think about how incredible they looked doing karaoke. They were magic together."

If karaoke was the measure of a good relationship, the world was going to hell in a handbasket. "So what do we do about this?" he asked, his mouth twitching as he watched Trevor tap the window. Buttercup, the resident lovesick alpaca, had appeared and pressed her lips to the glass.

"Your girlfriend is here, Trev," he heard Quinn tease. "Does your wife know?"

"Becca probably told Buttercup to say hi when she went out to her dyeing room," Trevor said, waving at the alpaca. "I tried to tell her that we don't work on Thanksgiving, but she informed me that she's still Irish, thank you very much, and she has things to do today."

"It was nice of her to let us take over the entire inn," Assumpta said, fiddling with her strawberry-covered scone.

"When you rent out all the rooms, how could she say no?" Trevor said. "Just kidding. Hey, Con. Why don't you come see the extra rabbits Flynn bought as part of his investment in Becca's yarn-making enterprise? They'll cheer anyone up."

"Maybe later," Connor said, the corners of his mouth lifting briefly before falling flat. "I'm going to take a walk. See you guys later."

"We'll save you some scones, honey," Assumpta called. She waited until he was out of sight, and hearing, before turning to everyone. "All right, what are we going to do about this? I thought being here with everyone would cheer him up, but clearly it's not helping."

"I was just asking Clara the same thing," Arthur said, scooting his chair out so he could better see everyone at the table. "He's miserable."

"I say we leave him alone," Quinn said. "He's getting back on his feet with his family. If he and Louisa decided to end their relationship, that's up to them."

Trevor cleared his throat. "We've just got him back and talking to us. If we butt into his personal business, it might drive him away again. I know he's upset, but we can't force this."

"Did Louisa say anything when you talked to her, Clara?" Assumpta asked. "I'm trying to be thankful Connor is here with us and that he and Olivia somehow managed to come to terms with each other for the boys' sake, but he's hurting, and I don't like it."

"Louisa said the same thing Connor did," Clara said. "Which is to say she didn't tell me anything." Of course, Assumpta knew that—they'd had this conversation more than once—but they were all hopeful there was some missing piece they could slide into place to fix things.

"The girl's got her hands full at the moment," Arthur said, tapping his fingers on the table. "It's a slow news week with the holiday, and somehow the incident is being cast as more appalling given it happened during 'this season of gratitude,' according to a few overly sentimental reporters. They demean the profession with that kind of hyperbolic reporting."

He got riled up every time he thought about it, but it comforted him some when Clara patted his arm.

"So far she's on top of things," he continued. "But some of those reporters aren't helping matters, interviewing unsavory characters from the neighborhood who wouldn't have a good thing to say about anything, least of all a homeless shelter. When I get back to Chicago, I'm going to wrap up my article. It can't come out quick enough."

He had a rough draft started, but the piece was missing something. Dicey issues with a lot of prejudice behind them needed something special, something extra, in order to open people's minds up and help them understand new points of view. He had to dig deeper.

"I'm so grateful no one was hurt," Assumpta said, putting her hand on her husband's arm. "When I think about what could have happened..."

"But everyone was safe," Shawn said. "Again, I need to thank you, Hargreaves. If it hadn't been for your quick thinking and help—"

"Please, sir," Hargreaves said, standing. "No thanks are necessary. I was grateful I could be of service. Miss Evans is an exceptional woman, and I do hope this cloud of misunderstanding will pass. Her work at Sunflower Alley is admirable. Now, if you'll excuse me, I'm going to leave you to your breakfast."

As he left, Trevor shook his head. "We should know by now not to thank him. It only makes him uncomfortable."

"I'm sorry I drove him off," Assumpta said, "but it needed to be said again. Back to Connor. Does anyone have any ideas? I was up with the girls brainstorming after everyone else went to bed. But I'll be honest, all of our ideas involved getting Connor and Louisa back together."

"I still think we should respect their choice," Quinn said, wiping his mouth and tossing his napkin on the table. "None of us know what went on inside their relationship. Isn't it a bit presumptuous of us to think we know better?"

No one said anything in response, and Arthur sighed deeply. "Quinn could be right, but my gut tells me this isn't over."

Clara patted her belly. "Mine too. Let's give ourselves a little more time. Something has to come up."

Thinking could only get a person so far. What they needed was a miracle.

Then again, Ireland was a land known for such things.

CHAPTER 27

THE VIEW FROM THE IRISH CLIFFS, WITH ITS BRILLIANT AZURE sky and the midnight blue lapping waves of the sea, would have taken anyone's breath away.

Anyone except for Connor Merriam.

All he could see was his own hubris. Before the accident, Connor had signed off on plans for an offshore oil field miles out to sea from Becca's land. Afterward, he'd torn those plans up, not wanting to construct another potential gravesite. Not even if it went against every corporate rule he'd been taught.

He'd first fought his family about the land he was standing on, thinking to buy it so they could protect their employees from the dangers in that sea. In forcing the issue, he'd almost lost his family. Today he was back with them, and on a holiday he'd never missed with his family—one he'd feared he'd spend alone weeks earlier, one he'd wanted to spend with the woman he loved.

Louisa.

God, he missed her.

Was she doing all right? He'd watched her press conference and read every post she'd written about the shelter. She was trying to turn around the narrative, but she had a perception problem. A big one. His hands itched to help, but he was part of the problem.

"Are you all right there, Connor?" he heard someone call out in a lilting Irish accent. His sister-in-law, Becca.

He turned away from the view, surprised to see her standing a few yards away with her Irish setter, Boru. "You made it out this far? I didn't realize you'd made that kind of progress with your condition. Sorry, that sounded rude. I've been a bit out of the loop."

Becca had a tight grip on the dog's leash, likely as an anchor, but her smile was friendly, even after the trouble he'd given her in the beginning over wanting this land. "I've been working with my new doctor almost four months now, and it's helped get me out this far on my own with Boru here by my side. I can't make it all the way to the cliffs without your brother yet, something that irritates me to no end. But I try to be grateful for the progress and remember every step I take outside my inn is a victory."

"You sound like Louisa," he said, smiling for a moment before his heart caved in again. "Never mind. I'm glad you're making such incredible progress. I can't imagine what it must be like to overcome something like that."

Can't you? The knowledge that those words had come from him—from a place deep inside—made him break into a cold sweat.

"There's a saying in Ireland about us all having our crosses to bear," she said, her hair flowing in the breeze. "I personally wish we could just burn those crosses and get on with it. Your brother reminds me that that's why I have him. When I'm too tired to keep carrying mine, he picks up the weight of it so I won't have to stay in one place."

Again, he thought of Louisa.

A smile touched Becca's face. "Oh, I'm sounding Irish now. Forgive me. I just wanted to check on you."

"Worried I might jump?" He winced, remembering what Quinn had said. "Sorry, that wasn't funny. Again, I'm not fit for human company right now. Maybe I shouldn't have come. Please. Forget I said any of this."

She set her shoulders in response and took one halting step forward and then another until she reached him. There was sweat on her temples, he noticed.

"What are you doing?" he asked, wondering if he should call his brother.

"I was coming out to you," she said, biting her lip. "But I'll admit I'm not in my usual easy way of things when I have to go outside my comfort zone."

"Then why did you?" he asked, his hands falling slackly to his sides.

Boru must have sensed her tension because he pressed his head against her leg, and she caressed his ears. "You sounded like you needed a friend, and as someone who has felt that way, I thought maybe I saw you out here because I was meant to. Now you'll say I'm really Irish, talking like that. But the truth is, you helped me get this far out to the cliffs. You know, you put me in mind of the famous Irish King Brian Boru, who my beloved dog is named for, what with the way you were facing the sea as if it were the enemy itself..."

He looked out at all that dark water. "I was thinking about what lies out there and what happened with my cousin."

"I expect you were," she said, stroking Boru's head. "Do you know what I see when I look out there? Usually from the upstairs windows, of course."

"No, what?"

"I see the miracle God put in the ground that brought your brother to me," she said, her eyes closing as the wind rushed over her. "Before him, I never imagined having the strength or purpose to venture this far out of my tower again." She gestured to the two towers built at the edge of the inn. The one on the right was where she and Trevor lived.

"Louisa said I lived in an ivory tower."

"Did she now?" Her head tilted to the side. "And why would she say that?"

Maybe it was because Becca's tone was warm, or maybe he just desperately needed to unburden himself, but he found himself saying, "She told me I'd put myself there to protect myself and yet tragedy found me anyway."

"Who would have thought you and I had so much in common?" She flashed him a wry grin. "I've tried to do that with my own place after tragedy found my parents and me when I was a child."

He knew they'd been murdered before her eyes on an assignment with Doctors Without Borders in Angola. The trauma had caused her agoraphobia.

"You know, I did everything I could to make this the most wonderful place on earth. And yet, I still felt like I was trapped and isolated from the outside world. Still do some days."

He found himself warming to her honesty and directness. "And yet you gritted your teeth and came out to join me. You mentioned strength and purpose helped you move forward. How did you find that?"

She patted her chest. "You have to find it in here first, but Trevor gives me a little of his strength when I need it. But mostly, it's love that moves me forward, and knowing he's there to hold my hand or have my back when I need him."

Louisa had done that for him, and the loss of her unyielding support had left a hole in him. "What if your very presence puts the person you love in danger?"

"Ah, we're to the crux of it then," she said, meeting his gaze head-on. "I've heard the talk of what happened with your lady friend. Will you tell me your side?"

He cleared his throat. He hadn't bothered explaining himself to the others, knowing they'd only tell him he was being an idiot, but somehow he knew Becca would listen to him and not judge him so harshly. "If I hadn't asked Clara to give her that money, Louisa never would have been held at gunpoint."

"And if you could stop earthquakes or prevent them, your sweet cousin wouldn't have died," she said softly. "I used to think that if I'd burst out of the closet my parents had stuck me in to protect me from the rebels, they wouldn't have killed my family. It's hard to live with that kind of guilt, Connor, especially when it's not true. But you and I know it doesn't matter. We're caught in the tangled web of our own stories."

He nodded, his chest filled with those tangled knots she spoke of. "People tell me all the time it's not true, but it *feels* true."

Then his mind flashed to that memory from childhood. His dad was yelling at him, shaking him, while Quinn stood dripping wet on the deck of the boat. Now, he understood that his father had been scared that day, that he'd been reacting from a place of fear and guilt, but he hadn't known that at the time. He'd really thought he was to blame for the accident. Could that be the root of some of his issues?

"I want to believe them, but in here, it feels different." He pounded his chest. "I just don't want anyone else to get hurt because of me."

She touched his forearm, and the compassion in her blue eyes had his throat clogging with emotion. "Ah, boyo, of course you don't want that. I can tell you what everyone else has told you, that you're not to blame, but it'll do no good until you believe it."

"That's what Louisa said, but you didn't see that druggie holding a gun on her. I dreamed about it again last tonight. I put her in danger when all I wanted to do was love her."

He turned away.

"You'll likely have those dreams for some time," she

told him. "I won't lie about that. I still dream about my parents being killed."

"How do you stand it?" He swung around. "How do you stand gritting your teeth every day and trying to take another step outside your tower?"

Tears filled her eyes, and he stepped forward and put his hand on her shoulder.

"I'm sorry. I didn't mean to—"

"No, I like that you don't dance around it," she said, waving a hand and wiping at her tears. "Your brother doesn't either. I like that about you Merriams. It's no wonder you're part Irish. You want to know how I stand it? Some days, I bake three batches of scones. Other days, I go out to my dye room. And then there are days when I simply cuddle up with your brother and push everything else aside. Guilt, regrets, fears—they'll nag you until you're too weary to raise your head. But your brother's smile or a newly dyed skein of yarn or this beautiful dog of mine—those things get me out of bed in the morning. They give me the strength to overcome anything. The question for you is this: is the love you have for your Louisa that kind of motivation?"

"Yes, dammit. But I have to be realistic. I'm a billionaire. Once people find out about us, she'll be in even more danger. I mean, the money I told Clara to give her almost got her killed, and that's only an iota of what I want to shower on her."

She cocked her head. "I suppose the only solution to your problem would be for you to give away all your money, but that's a crazy notion if I've ever heard one."

He took her by the shoulders. "Why?"

"Because someone in the village over was robbed for twenty pounds the other night outside the Horse and Hound Pub," she said with a pointed look. "The amount of money doesn't seem to matter much to criminals. They'll rob pretty much anyone."

So Louisa had said, he remembered. "So what's the solution? Will counseling help me get over this?"

Becca's head turned, as if she sensed something in the air, and he looked over to see Trevor waving at them. Well, more likely at Becca, who waved back with a wide smile on her face before shooing him away.

Once Trevor disappeared back into the inn, Becca met Connor's gaze again. "Maybe. It's surely helped me. What you must ask yourself is if she's worth gritting your teeth over. I can tell you that your brother surely is and then some. I wouldn't part with him in my life for anything. In fact, I've come to believe that maybe it's love and our connection to others that helps us feel the safest. You might think that's crazy given what happened."

He stared at her as her words sunk in, and his mind flashed to the image of Louisa hugging Jax. The moment that had so startled and disarmed him had been revelatory for her—it had made her realize she could overcome her own feelings of anger and fear and choose love. "No, I think that's brilliant. And yes, she's worth all of that and more."

"So why are you here in Ireland?" She gestured to the sea. "Call your plane and go back to her. Right this minute. Tell her she's worth all of that and more to you."

He could feel the energy building, coursing through his very bones. "She might not want to take another chance on me."

She smacked him in the shoulder. "Then think of something to prove yourself to her! Come on, you're a smart man. All of you Merriams are."

Yes, he was, but he had a perception problem, like Louisa would say. He'd started to perceive himself as something he didn't want to be. It was time to change the story of himself. If he didn't, he couldn't write a new one with Louisa.

"Becca," he said, taking her hand and raising it to his lips in a gesture that was unusual for the man he'd been but very much a part of the man he wished to become. "You're wonderful. I can see why Trevor did everything in his power to stand beside you, even when it meant standing up to me. I'm glad he did it, and when I go inside, I plan to tell him."

"We're all just happy to have you back with the family, Connor Merriam. You've been missed. Now, off with you. Your girl is waiting."

He extended his hand. "I can go back to the inn with you."

She closed her eyes and raised her face to the sun. "No, I made it out this far. I plan to savor it as long as I can. Feel free to send out your brother after you share all your brotherly admiration with him. He's going to be a puddle by the time he gets to me, but I'll be ready for him."

"Thank you, Becca," Connor said, looking out at the sea one last time. "You know...I used to be good at feeling things out when it came to business, and until recently, I wasn't often wrong. But sometimes a gut feeling is more than just that, and Becca, I think you're going to be traveling to the village or anywhere else in the world you want to go pretty darn soon."

Her eyes were sparkling when she looked at him. "Thank *you*, Connor."

It might be cliché, but even the various shades of Irish greens around him suddenly seemed brighter. "Maybe you're right about that miracle in the ground out there in the sea." It had brought him to this moment, after all, one he'd never forget.

"I'll make sure to tell the selkies and the fairies you're grateful," she said, opening her eyes briefly before closing them again, "so when you bring your lady back to our beautiful land, they'll make sure there's extra magic waiting for you both."

He liked the sound of that. As he strode off, he called over his shoulder, "Tell them to send some of that Irish luck my way too."

"Oh, off with you," was all he heard in response, which had his mouth lifting.

When he entered the inn, he wasn't surprised to see his brother was waiting at the window just inside the door. "How did she get all the way to the cliffs by herself?"

He walked right up to Trevor and wrapped him in a bear hug. "She overcame her own fears because she was 'connecting' to someone else. Man, I sound like an idiot, but I'm seeing everything in a new light. I need to call the pilot. I'm headed back to Chicago, bro. Oh, and Becca is great. Wonderful. You're one lucky son of a bitch, and I can see why you picked a fight with me to support her."

Trevor put his hand to Connor's brow. "You got a fever, man?"

"No, I've had a breakthrough. God, I hope it's enough. It has to be enough. Where are Flynn and Uncle Arthur?"

"Probably with the rabbits. Flynn and Aunt Clara love those little guys. Con, you sure you're okay? What did you mean about calling the pilot? It's Thanksgiving, remember?"

"I know, but this can't wait. Good thing this flight crew is Canadian." He didn't want to bulldoze over anyone's holiday, his family included. The moment they finished Thanksgiving dinner, he was out the door.

"That's why they were on call for the holiday. Okay, I'm still behind. Why are you taking off again?"

"Trev, I have to return to Chicago and win Louisa back."

"You're going to need a ring, right?" Trev asked, grinning. "I could call the jeweler I used for Becca's engagement ring. He could probably be here in a couple of hours."

He wanted to spend the rest of his life with Louisa. But he needed to convince her that he could be counted on—that he knew what he was signing up for with her. "Yes, I need the best ring in the world for my girl, but no diamonds. She doesn't like them."

"You'll have plenty of help in the ring department. Trust me."

The knowledge that his family would be there for him warmed his chest. "But first I need Uncle Arthur and Flynn's help."

"With what?" Trevor asked.

The way to win her back was clear to him now. "Louisa's perception problem."

CHAPTER 28

THE SUNDAY AFTER THANKSGIVING DIDN'T FEEL MUCH LIKE a day of rest to Louisa.

Although she was at her dad's house for an impromptu brunch, her brain wouldn't stop spinning, thinking about her ongoing task list, Connor, and even the items she needed to pick up from the grocery store. She was out of laundry detergent, and the unusual number of times she'd thought about that was a clear indication she wasn't herself.

Then again, it had been a hell of a ride since the incident at Sunflower Alley. She'd talked to hundreds of people, everyone from board members, donors, volunteers, and the families and other people they served, to politicians, city leaders, and the press. Her voice was shot.

Volunteers had canceled right and left, so she'd ended up spending Thanksgiving at the shelter with the rest of the staff, serving their community. They'd all been running on fumes trying to glue everything back together, and there was no end in sight.

Her mind should have been too busy for thoughts of Connor, but they were always there in the background.

"Louisa, how do you want your eggs?" Damien called, jolting her out of her funk. He stood in front of the kitchen island, spatula in hand. "If Carter here is going to make me his short-order bitch, the least I can do is serve up individual orders. Go sit down, man. You're supposed to be taking a break. I've got this."

They were all running on fumes, so she'd convinced Carter and Boxer to come to brunch while the rest of their trusted staff took care of things for a few hours.

"You wish you were my short-order bitch, Damien," Carter said, waggling his brows. "And I can still flip some bacon. Cripes, don't treat me like I'm old. Besides, you need supervision. Your restaurant is so not known for breakfast. You don't have enough heart to pull off soul food."

"We don't serve breakfast, you idiot," Damien shot back with a grin. "You don't win a Michelin star serving eggs and bacon. And I have plenty of heart. All the ladies say so."

She couldn't help but snort at that one.

"Bacon is good for you," Carter said, flipping an entire pan of delicious-smelling smoked bacon. "That one ingredient alone should win you a star."

She wasn't too hungry, but she could still feel the pull to throw down some bacon. It was like dark chocolate kisses or hot buttered popcorn for her in terms of comfort food.

"They're going to rag on each other all morning," her dad said, pouring her some whole milk. "Drink, Louisa. You sound like a bullfrog."

"She needs hot water with lemon and honey, Coach," Boxer said, sitting across from them at the kitchen table tucked in the corner against the wall.

"You going to rag on me too, huh?" her dad said, taking her hand and fitting the glass in it.

"I don't need all of you guys fussing over me." Her words came out in a harsh whisper, and she had to fight not to clutch her throat. Crap, her glands hurt, and on top of everything, she was getting sick. She couldn't get sick. Of course, she hadn't slept more than a few hours since that night, kept awake by her memories of the incident and thoughts of Connor. Damn, she missed him, but she would have to find a way to heal and move on. There was no other way. "I'm fine. Mostly."

They all paused what they were doing and gave her "the look."

"Your heart is crushed," Carter said, "and you've been working like a madwoman."

"We all have," she said, getting misty-eyed just thinking about how much they'd done. "You've talked to as many people as I have, and Carter, I know you contacted a few people you'd rather not associate with in the gang responsible for the robbery."

"I've been assured the leader is making sure everyone knows we're off-limits again," Carter said, his mouth twisting. "Those two gangbangers acted against his wishes, and even though they're in jail, he'll send them a message, I imagine."

She didn't like to think about that, and she tried to tell herself they'd put themselves in that situation. "Jail should be enough," she said, drinking her milk with a grimace. "Perpetuating violence isn't the way."

"People like that only respect strength, and those guys disrespected their leader by going against his wishes," Boxer said, cracking his neck from the tension they'd been under. "We need the word on the street to be that no one is going to try and steal any more money from us."

"I hate this part," she said, rubbing her temples. "I wish we lived in a world where we didn't have to deal with this kind of crap."

"My daughter," her dad said, putting his arm around her, "the idealist."

"I'm just like you," she said, taking another drink to soothe her sore throat.

"That's what makes me so proud," her dad said.

"We're all proud of you," Damien said, brandishing the spatula. "Now, how do you want your eggs?"

Oh, these men. How she loved them. "Scrambled. With cheddar cheese and some of that bacon mixed in."

"Me too," her dad said, pouring her more milk in an obvious move of fussing over her.

"Me three," Boxer said, reaching for more coffee. "Now that the gang situation is under control, we still have some work to do with the greater community. Most of our volunteers have canceled for the week. People have also canceled their tickets for next month's cooking competition."

Her mood tanked again. Were they ever going to get beyond this? "Speaking of problems, I should check my phone. Dad, where did you hide it?"

"I took your phone because you need a break," her dad said, his dark eyes studying her face. "If there's an emergency, they'll call Boxer."

"Maria, Jewel, and Spicy have the kitchen under control, and Greta has all the families and kids in hand," Boxer said, patting her hand. "Girl, you need to chill. We're going to weather this."

She was usually the cheerleader of their group, but right now she didn't have the energy. Leave it to Boxer to take up the torch. "I'm trying." She slid her coffee cup toward him. "I need another cup."

"You've had two already," her dad said, putting her milk close to her again. "I know you're running on fumes, but no more caffeine."

"I'll make you a cappuccino later, Louisa," Damien said, cracking eggs into a bowl.

"He's never paid me much mind," her dad said, rolling his eyes. "But if he had, he probably wouldn't have become the kick-ass chef I'm so proud of."

Her brother dropped an egg on the floor.

"Man, watch it," Carter said. "I hate cleaning up eggs."

"You're proud of me?" Damien asked, his usual bravado gone. The eggs had lost his attention for the moment.

"Of course I am," her dad said, shaking his head. "Don't

I tell all my boys sometimes you gotta fight to be who you want to be? I'm just sorry you had to fight me. But I learned a good lesson. I don't do that anymore."

Louisa smiled easily for the first time in days. She'd needed this. "No, you just push milk on your daughter when she doesn't want it. Damien, didn't I tell you?"

"What?" Her dad shifted his chair around. "He didn't know I was proud of him? Well, damn, son." Then he was standing up and crossing to Damien, giving him a massive bear hug.

"Thanks, Dad," Damien said when they broke apart. "Now I can sleep in peace. I mean, maybe that's been the cause for my insomnia lately."

He was back to his usual teasing, but she knew how important this moment had been for him. Maybe later when he got home he'd pour himself a whiskey and enjoy it. Men were so silly sometimes.

That made her think about Connor. How was he doing? What was he doing? Had he gone to Ireland with his family? Was he okay? She reminded herself these were not the kinds of questions she needed rolling around in her brain, but they were like a tin can in the wind, hard to catch and pin down.

"Serve up the eggs," her dad said, "and let's get down to eating some of this soul food. Carter, I have some pancake mix in the pantry."

"Don't make me cry, Coach," he said, miming wiping some tears from his eyes. "I'll whip up a batch from scratch."

"Feed Louisa first," her dad said, plucking up a strip of bacon from the plate and taking a bite of it. "She's hungry."

"Apparently so is someone else," Carter said, already opening the refrigerator.

They plied her with eggs, but honestly she ate more bacon, because why the heck not? Carter was flipping the pancakes, and Damien was cutting up some apples and mangoes when the doorbell sounded.

"Excuse me a sec." Her dad left the kitchen. "Louisa, come here. You've gotta see this."

She rose and walked to the entryway. "Coming."

When she reached the front, she stopped short. Connor was standing just inside, holding a newspaper in his hands. No coat, of course, even though it was in the teens outside. His navy suit, white shirt, and maroon silk tie were a little jarring to her. She'd never seen him dressed so formally, but he looked good. Really good, in fact, with a sparkle in his two-color eyes, and it wasn't only because he'd shaved off his beard. Yeah, that looked good too. Her heart clutched at the sight of him. It shouldn't feel this good to see him. They'd agreed to part ways, and despite how much they loved each other, she still knew that was the right decision.

"What are you doing here?" she asked, her voice raspy.

"I invited him," her dad said, crossing and kissing her cheek. "He managed to convince Boxer, Carter, your brother, and me to let him make an appearance and talk to you. Since you know we're no pushovers, we think you'll want to hear him out."

Her dad walked off, and she found herself gaping after him. "You talked to all of them? When?"

"Yesterday," he said, closing the door behind him. "It took some doing since everyone was so busy, but I was determined. I knew I needed to talk to you today."

She wanted to play it cool, but it was beyond her. "I'm tired and my voice is shot, so say what you came here to say and make it brief."

He nodded. "I'm sorry I hurt you, and I'm sorry I caved in to my own fears on the day when you needed me the most. I swear to you on Corey's grave that I will never, ever let you down again."

Oh my God. He wanted her back? She crossed her

arms. "I'm not sure that's something you can promise, Connor." Sadness coursed through her at the thought.

"Aren't I one of the most incredible men in the world?" he asked, forcing a smile.

She wanted to bite, but the hurt was too fresh, the talk they'd had too strong in her mind. "Connor, before you go any further—"

"I know we have some trust to rebuild," he said, stepping toward her. "That's why I brought you today's paper. You'll want to open it to the Op-Ed. And after that, we need to turn on the TV. There's something you should see—" He checked his watch. "In about three minutes."

When he handed her the paper, she took it, flipping to the back. The headline caught her attention: "The Antidote for South Side's Problems: Louisa Evans."

"What? But the press has been beating me up…" She checked the writer of the piece and clutched the paper a bit too hard, tearing the edges, when she saw Arthur Hale's name.

"Keep reading," Connor said, checking his watch again. "I'll find your father and put on the TV. Come find us when you're finished."

She watched him walk out, but she fastened her gaze back to the article and started reading.

In nearly six decades of reporting, I've written more articles about issues than I have about people. Perhaps it's because people come and go, but the issues remain. My recent time in South Side has borne that out. The community is still experiencing what many call chronic issues: lack of economic opportunities, cycles of violence, racial divides, homelessness, unemployment, and limited educational resources. In this neighborhood, the effects of public policies bent on dividing races and creating isolated communities in one of the world's most prosperous cities is ever apparent. South Side is known for its grit and working-class culture. Steel was forged here in factories long since closed. The breakfast cereal boxed at the General Mills plant put bread on people's tables. Those economies are long gone now.

So what is the answer to this storied community's problem? It's not more social programs or funding alone. Those have been done and done again. No, it's a woman working in the trenches who is running programs with a different fuel. That person is Louisa Evans. You might have heard about her in the news recently. She runs a homeless shelter called Sunflower Alley, a safe haven for families and others who live on the street. But her programs weren't in the holiday news cycle. What happened to her was.

She was the victim of the very violence she is trying to prevent. I personally know this because my wife, Clara Merriam, gave her the million-dollar donation her assailant claimed to be after.

Normally I might indulge in a rant regarding how apocalyptic it is that we live in a world where helping other people puts us at risk, where a donation intended for service would attract a dark kind of violence. I won't devolve into that kind of digression today.

Louisa's story is too inspiring for a sideshow. As you've likely heard, the gunman was disarmed, by her and someone else close to me, Clifton Hargreaves, who was volunteering his time in the kitchen on his day off. But that's not why Louisa Evans is the antidote for South Side's problems. It's what she did next.

The news cycle will be showing a recently released tape of her hugging the young man after he broke down and apologized for attacking her.

Cynics might want to dismiss such an embrace as reckless, crazy, naïve even. But watch the tape.

People, this is honest-to-goodness compassion, and we need more of it if we are to rebuild communities and bring people back together so they aren't bowling alone all the time. The young man in custody has a story we so often hear on the news: born to a drug-addicted mother and a father he never knew, he was kicked out of the house after failing out of school and getting involved with drugs. There is never an excuse for criminal activity. The rules are clear, and we have them for good reasons. They are not, however, the antidote to violence, not when you look at crime rates or recidivism.

Louisa Evans is the antidote to the problems in South Side because she is willing to see the people causing those problems as human beings. She is willing to listen to why they are participating in violence and economic exploitation. She is willing to speak to a part of the community that most of us want to turn a blind eye to, wall off, or send packing. Her shelter has gained attention because she's committed to helping families and other individuals find a leg up after setbacks that put them on the street.

But it's her willingness to embrace what most of us would find repulsive and scary that makes her special. Look out, South Side. With Louisa Evans in your camp, there might be an urban spring around the corner.

She clutched the newspaper to her chest, shock falling over her like cold water. Arthur had written *that*?

"Louisa, come here," Connor called out.

His tone broke apart some of the shock. He was back to being commanding. It must be the suit.

She went into the living room. He was standing in front of the TV, holding the remote. A local station was playing a commercial.

"Just remember," he said, inhaling deeply as if nervous, "Boxer approved all this."

"I did at that," her friend called. "You can kill me later if you need to."

The credits for one of Chicago's morning shows rolled, and then the host appeared.

"This morning we're bringing you more information about the assault on the director of a South Side homeless shelter right before the holiday. New footage from the shelter's security cameras reveals that Louisa Evans not only disarmed the gunman with a man identified as Clifton Hargreaves, but moments later, she hugged the very man who'd held her at gunpoint. Think you heard me wrong? Watch the tape."

The front of the shelter appeared on camera, and sure enough, there she was, being held at gunpoint. She watched the scene unfold almost as if outside of her body. It was weird to hear her own voice and see herself in the scene. Then Jax was on the ground crying and she was walking over to him and hugging him.

"Billionaire businessman Connor Merriam witnessed the event, and he's with us this morning. Good morning, Connor."

He appeared in the split screen, wearing the same suit he had on now.

Louisa gaped at him. "What did you do?"

Gesturing with the remote, he said, "Watch the interview."

"Good morning, Leslie," he said with a polite smile. "Thanks for having me on this morning."

"Of course," the host responded. "You were at the shelter that evening and witnessed this incredible scene. Why were you there?"

"Ms. Evans and I have been working together on the shelter's new training program for the homeless."

"Your aunt, Clara Merriam Hale, was responsible for the million-dollar donation involved."

"She was," Connor replied. "After seeing how Louisa handled the situation, I've also decided to give Sunflower Alley a donation that I hope will help her expand programs to help the South Side community. My mother was born and raised there, and me and my family have deep roots in this community."

"We'll talk about that in a minute," Leslie continued. "Would you be willing to share with us the size of your donation? I believe it's going to get our listeners excited."

"Yesterday, I gave Sunflower Alley a check for twenty million dollars, along with some additional properties I've recently acquired, one of which is for a state-of-the-art training program."

Louisa's mouth dropped open. "*Twenty*?"

The Connor on the screen smiled at the host. "Louisa doesn't do anything small, and neither do I. She's one of the most incredible people I've ever met in all my years in business. She has a lot of people she'd like to help, everything from making sure they have a safe place to stay to providing targeted training so they can break the cycle of unemployment and disfranchisement."

"That's a lot of money for one homeless shelter, Connor. In fact, we've done our homework, and it's one of the largest donations ever to a nongovernmental organization of this size."

"With her ambition, drive, and heart, she has the ability to make her organization as expansive and influential as Big Brothers, Big Sisters or the Red Cross. Trust me, Louisa is more than up for it."

The screen went black. "The rest of the interview is pretty chatty. You can watch it later if you'd like. Boxer has the check and a list of the properties I'm donating. I figured we could talk later about bringing in some key economic drivers to help create jobs and stability. Of course, we'll want to ensure there's affordable housing and the like. That is, if you won't object to me hanging around and helping."

Hanging around? Louisa shook her head as she croaked, "Why are you doing this? Before you were scared your money put me in danger. What changed? Was the guilt too great? Dammit, I told you I didn't want to be one of your responsibilities."

He set the remote down. "First, you're not a responsibility. You're a joy, and I love you very much. You had a perception problem, and I had an idea to help you turn things around so everything you created would continue—so your program could blossom and grow. Louisa, that tape needed to be seen. People need to know there are people like you out there. Uncle Arthur agreed, which is why he wrote that Op-Ed."

"You didn't have to do any of that," she said. "I was handling it. Not that I don't appreciate it. But Connor, you can't just give the shelter twenty million dollars."

"Yes, I can." His mouth tipped up. "I was hoping you'd understand the significance, but you're pale, and you really have lost your voice, haven't you? It must have been a rough couple of days."

"It has been," she rasped out.

"The donation was purposely high because I wanted you to know I won't give in to fear anymore. My sister-in-law helped me understand what I was too stubborn to grasp on my own. I want to stand by your side even on days when fear has me in its grip because I love you so much."

Her heart rolled over in her chest.

He took a step forward. "When the fear comes back, I'm going to grind my teeth or stare it down. I won't let it come between me and what I want anymore. There's a lot I want right now, but nothing else comes close to how much I want you. You're my everything, babe."

She remembered how she'd started calling him that, an endearment signifying how easy and right they were together. "Oh, Connor…"

Moving until he was right in front of her, he held her gaze. "I know it might take some time for you to trust me again. I am committed to counseling. Not just because I love you, but because I want to feel good about myself and life again. I started to feel that way because of what we were creating together. Not only personally but professionally. You helped me find the courage to reconcile with my family and Olivia, and to envision a new life for myself, one with you. I know I have a lot to learn, but I'm committed to standing beside you as you share with the world the incredibleness that is Louisa Evans. I plan to figure out how to share what I have inside me too."

Every word rang with certainty and purpose, and his gaze didn't stray from hers. In her gut, she knew he'd turned a corner. She had to give them another chance. She loved him too much.

He reached into his pocket and pulled out a small black box, and she started shaking her head.

"Hear me out, please," he said, sinking to one knee and opening the box to showcase a beautiful emerald ring.

"Oh, my God," she whispered.

"I'll talk about the stone in a minute, but first I'd like to tell you about the engraving inside the band. I thought the sunflowers would tell you what I wanted to say. In here."

He touched his chest, and her breath caught as he struggled with his emotions.

"Take your time," she said softly.

He cleared his throat. "I know what sunflowers mean to you. That they're both strong and beautiful. That they stand up in any condition. I wanted... No, I needed you to know my love for you would be like that."

She felt tears fill her eyes. "And the stone?"

"You said you didn't like diamonds, but I thought you might like an emerald. Caitlyn knows all about the meaning of stones, and she assures me this is the stone of the heart. It embodies courage and infinite patience. Flynn said to tell you that you'll need a lot of the latter to deal with me, but I swear to you that I will make it worth it every day of our life. Louisa, I love you. Will you marry me?"

Heart thudding in her chest, she was amazed to find her mouth twitching. "Infinite patience, huh? Oh, Connor... You make this seem one-sided. I might require some of your infinite patience too. I work a lot, and sometimes I don't have good boundaries about clients."

"Leave it to you to make me feel better," he said, standing up and reaching out and gently tracing her cheek. "Take all the time you need to give me an answer. I'll wait years, if that's what it takes. I just wanted you to know I heard you when you said vows are about two people knowing what they're signing up for. I know what I'm signing up for, and I can't wait to do it if you agree to marry me. I mean it. I can't promise you we'll never fight, or that you'll never get mad at me, but I give you my word that I'll never let you or me down again like I did the other night."

Louisa put her hand over her mouth, emotion flooding through her. "I know you won't. Gritted teeth and all."

"I'm glad you believe me," he said, his eyes scanning her face. "I was worried. But you need some rest, babe. Maybe some chicken soup."

He was fussing over her? She liked it. "How is it you look so chipper?"

"It's the fresh shave I got this morning at one of South Side's legendary barber shops. I looked pretty haggard before."

She fingered his lapels. "And the suit helps. I like you clean-shaven. Oh, and I'll marry you."

He blinked. "You don't want to tell me later? You'll really marry me?"

"Yes, because I trust your word." She slid her arms around his waist. "And I trust my gut. It's telling me to wrap my arms around you and never let go."

He framed her face. "Thank God. I was afraid I'd blown it—even after I managed to convince four of your biggest advocates that I was serious about loving you and supporting you."

And they weren't pushovers. "Later, you'll have to tell me how that went."

"You'll need a whiskey. Hell, I'll need a whiskey. I was sweating bullets."

She leaned up and kissed him, and he sank into her. His arms came around her, and her mouth moved under his. The love in that kiss was something she knew she'd always remember.

"How do you feel about a second wedding in Ireland after we get married here around your community?" he asked when they broke apart. "I have someone special I want you to meet. I'll tell you more about that later too. Also, my family came back to Chicago with me, hoping you'd say yes and prepared to offer moral support if you didn't. But Flynn is an eternal optimist and has rented another karaoke machine. We would like to invite your family to join us for a little celebration. I thought about calling Liv and seeing if she would bring the boys."

He'd come so far since that desolate night in the park where they'd first met. In fact, he seemed downright triumphant. She certainly felt that way too. "That sounds wonderful. All of it."

"Did you say yes, Louisa?" her brother yelled from the kitchen.

She laughed out loud. "Yes, I did."

A cork popped then, the sound of a champagne bottle being opened. "Good, because I think I'm going to like having Connor in the family. He didn't flinch yesterday when I said I was going to punch him. In fact, he said he deserved it."

Shaking her head, she gave Connor a look.

"It's a guy thing. But if Boxer had wanted to hit me, I might have declined. He might have broken my jaw."

She touched his nape, feeling a swell of gratitude for those she loved. "You're mine now."

"I have been since that first night." He looked down,

his throat moving with emotion. "Promise me you won't ever stop challenging me. The other night...I know why you didn't...but it scared me."

It had scared her too—all of it. "I promise. We only have good things ahead, babe."

He smiled. "Will I get my own personal love notes every day?"

That was a great idea, she thought. With a caveat. "I figure we both pony up a love note. Even and odd days. Keep it equal. Like partners do."

"Deal. Want to hear my first one?"

Tears sprung into her eyes. Yeah, he'd definitely turned a corner. "Tell me."

"Love truly is the greatest force on earth," he said, his eyes shining with it. "Your love is, and I hope you trust mine is too."

She kissed him softly again.

"There's nothing I trust more," she said as her own love note for tomorrow sprung into her mind.

Loving someone makes the heart sing like nothing else, so what are you waiting for? Go out and love someone...

CHAPTER 29

THERE WAS NOTHING BETTER THAN SEEING THE MERRIAM family celebrating together after everything that had happened. Arthur lifted his glass in a silent toast to his old friend and mentor who'd started it all. *Emmits. I miss you, but your family continues to be everything you hoped and more.*

Flynn's birthday was another party in what had been a string of them since Connor and Louisa's impromptu engagement party in Chicago. Tonight they were in a fancy hotel ballroom in the Big Apple. Even so, part of him looked forward to doing some down-home partying with his Hales in Dare Valley. He and Clara had been traveling nonstop, and although he was grateful Caroline had been able to make it, he missed the rest of his family of blood.

"I've never envisioned becoming such a jet-setter in my golden years," he told Clara, who was dancing in place next to him, watching the gala below.

"Looks good on both of us," she said, humming with a glass of champagne in her hand.

Only Flynn would think to have a three-tiered birthday party—one for each decade, he said—kicking off with the intimate family-only dinner they'd just enjoyed at one of Manhattan's best restaurants. They were now in Stage

Two, an elaborate gala for friends and family of all ages in a gilt-edged ballroom downtown decked out with a full orchestra playing everything from Frank Sinatra to Elton John. Over-the-top in his opinion, especially since it required him to wear a monkey suit. He still couldn't believe he'd let Clara talk him into wearing one, but when in Rome...

After this, the young people were going clubbing at a VIP lounge to top things off. He and Clara sure as hell wouldn't be attending that eardrum-breaking event.

Lifting his champagne flute, he nudged his wife. "I'd like to propose a toast."

She turned, ever beautiful in a midnight blue chiffon gown, her hair gathered up in some fancy twisty thing Caitlyn had done to it.

Clara beamed, and he fell in love all over again. "We've had a million toasts tonight," she said, "but I have a feeling this is going to be about our matchmaking."

"Yes, although frankly, I think you and I have to relinquish our trophy to Becca on this one."

She swayed as Billy Joel's "Piano Man" began to play. "Given how fitting it is that she's the one who helped him, I won't complain. After the way things started between the two of them...well, let's just say Ireland's magic was never more on display. Of course, I wish she could be here."

Tapping their flutes together, he said, "She will be soon, I expect. Trevor told me Connor's belief in her gave her another boost of confidence. Likely because he's been such a tough customer."

Clara took a sip. "The Big Bad Wolf seems to have disappeared. My God, he's practically beaming with Louisa on his arm. Of course, who can blame him? She's wonderful."

He spotted the newly engaged couple dancing in the ballroom. They were cheek to cheek, moving as in tune as if they'd been married thirty years. "He's found himself again, perhaps even better than before. They'll keep each other happy and balanced. They're going to do a lot of good in Chicago together."

"Yes, they are, and I'm excited to have contributed a little on that front. You also did a wonderful job with that Op-Ed, Arthur Hale, and I don't mind telling you I'm proud as hell of you. Don't let it go to your head."

His lips twitched. "The only thing likely to go to my head at this age, dear, is if you were to tell me I'm the most incredible lover you've ever imagined."

Her snort made him grin. "I might toast to that later if you're a good boy tonight."

Yet another reason to find a way to slip out early. "I'll be sure to mind my p's and q's. So let's talk about who's next? Flynn here?"

He found Boy Wonder in the crowd, laughing in a group of young people, surrounded by at least three beanstalk models who looked to have been air blown at some fancy salon. How much goop did one have to use to achieve that look? He didn't want to know.

"Or Quinn?" Clara responded, sipping her champagne. "He's thirty-eight."

"Bah. Age doesn't have anything to do with matters of the heart. Look at us. We're old as dirt and got hitched at eighty."

"Arthur Hale, I'm seventy-nine until February, and I plan to keep saying so until my driver's license proves me wrong."

"Don't know why you bother having a license when you have Hargreaves drive you everywhere. Where is he, by the way?"

She grinned. "I told him to take the night off. I'm hoping he got in touch with one of his lady friends."

Arthur almost spewed his champagne. "Hargreaves has lady friends?"

She crooked her finger to a nearby server and swapped out her empty glass for a fresh one. He tossed his back, because why the hell not, and grabbed another too.

"He's a man, isn't he, and a very interesting one at that." She made a sound filled with warmth. "Of course, I'm partial. He's been my friend for almost sixty years. I don't know what I would have done without him."

Arthur was glad she'd had him too, even if the man did serve him Indian food and starch his shirts. "Well, good for him. Everyone could use a night with a lady. Now, back to who's up next for us. Quinn seems too preoccupied with his new job as the CEO at Merriam. Every time I've spotted him, he's talking to some ancient businessman. Not a model like Flynn."

"Which makes you wonder... Is Flynn ready to give up every model in every port?" She laughed at herself.

"It wasn't that funny, Clara," he said, but gave her a wink to tell her he was teasing.

"You're right," she said. "Flynn's more open to life. Meets more people. Quinn is too mired down in work. Plus, Boy Wonder has been looking for his next best thing. He's been moaning about everything Louisa has done in comparison, even though I told him she's a few years older. Still, he feels like a slacker."

He barked out a laugh. "In comparison, he is."

She popped him in the shoulder. "They're different people. Flynn will find his purpose, and perhaps true love with it. They seem to run together. I mean, look at our other Merriam couples."

He found Caitlyn and Beau and Michaela and Boyd dancing in the crowded ballroom. J.T. and Caroline were cuddled close in the corner talking to the head of some museum here in New York. Clara had made the introductions earlier. "You might be right. Care to engage in a bet on the matter?"

"Does it involve grand passion and sex?" she asked, her blue eyes coquettishly lowering a fraction.

He loved the way her mind worked—never more so than when it came to enjoying sex at their age, when everyone seemed to think they should be dead from the waist down. "When we slip out of here, I'll whisper some suggestions into your ear in the back of the limo."

"I can't wait," she said, touching his arm before turning back to the ballroom. "My bet is on Flynn then, and you should know, Arthur Hale, I'm very competitive. I'll do anything required in order to win."

Their bet would be win-win for both of them, but he wasn't going to point that out right now. Not when she smelled so nice and looked so beautiful in the soft light from the chandeliers. "Then I'll take Quinn because he's all that's left, and I'm a gentleman."

She snorted again, and he found himself grinning. "Not too much of a gentleman though, I hope."

He cupped her cheek. "Never. Would you care to dance before we slip out of here and talk bets, Mrs. Hale?"

"I'd love to, Mr. Hale."

When she took his hand with an impish sparkle in her blue eyes, he'd never been happier.

When they joined the rest of the Merriams on the dance floor, she pressed her cheek to his, and they started to dance like they'd been doing it all their lives.

***

IT WAS OFFICIAL.

He was thirty years old.

This was the second morning of his new decade, the day when the party was over, when it was time to get down to business. Flynn rolled over onto his back and shoved the plush white duvet off his chest, surveying his penthouse bedroom in his Manhattan apartment. Everything was neutral in palette—just like in his life.

Something had to give.

His twenties had been filled with loads of life adventures, everything from finishing college to taking his place at Merriam Enterprises to traveling to the world's most beautiful cities and romancing some of the world's most stunning women.

Except it all had started to feel stale in the past year, and he'd been hoping to find some new inspiration by the time his birthday came around.

Instead, he was waking up this morning late after another great night of partying, fairly happy, but not fulfilled. He was grateful Connor was back in the family, at least, especially since his brother seemed happier and more open than he had been in years. And no wonder. Louisa's work was awe-inspiring, and talking to her had made him question what he was doing with his life. Because thirty was supposed to be grown up—wasn't it?—and he still needed to figure out what the hell he wanted to do with his life.

Something would turn up. He checked the clock. It was almost ten. Quinn was crashing with him, and they hadn't gotten back to his place until around four. His parents had made arrangements for a final family brunch before everyone headed home, and they needed to be at the restaurant by eleven.

He headed to the shower, picking up the basket of new body products Valentina had given him for his birthday when she'd popped by his flat yesterday. He and Valentina had hit it off when they'd met in Milan at a fashion show but never like *that*. Still, they liked to hang out every now and again, when they found themselves in the same city. Despite being an internationally famous model, she was funny and down-to-earth with no drama. She'd told him it was the only brand she used—and since she was reputed to have the most beautiful skin and hair, notwithstanding her incredible body, he believed her.

He hadn't heard of Bilberry & Co. before, but he'd given them all a good sniff, and the scents had intrigued him as much as the names. The shampoo and conditioner were called Black Forest Luxury, the body wash was called Alpine Mist, and the Old Bay Rum shaving soap made him think of pirates.

But he winced at the lotion. If his brothers knew he was using lotion, they'd take away his man card. But privately he thought the Towering Cedar smelled pretty good—and it made his hands feel good too.

Snagging all of the products into his arms, he headed into the shower. The shampoo made his scalp tingle in the most incredible way, like it was clearing his head of a bunch of junk. The conditioner was so silky soft, he was almost embarrassed to admit his shower was turning into a sensual experience. The body wash lathered up thickly on his body, and yeah, through the steam in the shower, he could almost feel the alpine mist.

But it was the shaving soap that almost did him in.

The rum blended with the herbaceous citrus of lime in a way that had his eyes closing, and it made his cheeks as soft as a baby's bottom—something he would never admit out loud.

He wondered if he was going crazy, groaning over body products. His family teased him about liking the finer things in life, and after talking with Louisa, he'd started to think he was shallower than he'd like. Quinn would tell him if he'd lost it. He was Big Bad Wolf Number Two, after all, although maybe he was top wolf now that Connor had decided to give that character up.

Wrapping a towel around his waist, he headed to the spare bedroom where Quinn was staying. He knocked and heard a grunt of an answer. When he opened the door, his brother was sitting in a white robe in front of his laptop at the desk in the corner of the room, ignoring the incredible view of Central Park below him. Philistine.

"Like I expected," he said, coming inside. "You're working."

"All I do is work," Quinn said, rubbing his eyes. "You just wake up? Damn, must be nice to have no real responsibilities."

They both knew he worked at Merriam and kicked ass. "You're cranky and I can work whenever I want to." Normally he wouldn't have felt the tip of that arrow, but he did today. "I woke up in a bit of an existential crisis, and then I tried these products Valentina gave me for my birthday. I need you to tell me they're not as incredible as I think they are."

"I'm working," Quinn muttered, already turning back to the screen.

Flynn walked into the en-suite bathroom and turned on the shower and arranged the products neatly on the marble ledge. "Come on, princess," he called. "You have to take a shower sometime."

"I'm not at your beck and call," Quinn shot back.

Typical. Maybe he needed a little brotherly roughhousing to kick off his thirties. He came up behind his brother and locked him in a vise, pulling him off his chair.

"What the hell, man?"

Quinn started to struggle, and they toppled to the floor, wrestling.

"Get in the shower."

"Go to hell."

He snagged his brother's robe off, revealing his color-coordinated pajamas—of course—and he got an elbow in the chest in response.

"Don't make me kill the birthday boy."

He only laughed. This was the most fun he'd had in years with Quinn. Then his towel fell, and they both stopped struggling.

"Now it's weird," Flynn said, grabbing it in front of his jewels. "Please just get in the damn shower and tell me I'm not crazy thinking these products are pure gold. Merriam business neurons are firing."

Quinn shrugged into his robe after shoving him back one final time. "Only because it's your birthday and Mom and Caitlyn might cry if I have to kill you."

He followed his brother. "You mean Michaela won't?"

"No," Quinn said and slammed the bathroom door in his face. "I'm locking this door since you've taken a weird pill this morning."

He was smiling as he sank to the ground in front of the door. Quinn must still be feeling some birthday good-will for him if he was actually trying the products. Too bad J.T. wasn't here. He was the only other brother who appreciated a good body product like Flynn did.

When the door opened a little while later, he fell onto his back into the bathroom.

Quinn looked down at him, his hair wet from the shower, his face clean-shaven. "You're not crazy. This shit is the bomb. Some of the scents remind me of London. Damn, it made me homesick. California isn't the same."

Flynn hadn't thought to ask how his brother was tak-ing his recent move from London to the Merriam head-quarters outside San Francisco. "You okay with the new job?"

"I haven't decided." His brother held up the shaving cream bottle. "Bilberry & Co. Is it a British company?"

Flynn hopped off the floor and headed to his brother's computer. "Let's find out."

He typed in the name and clicked on the website. Stylish. Professional. Elegant. Just like the packaging. He clicked on the About page and did a double take at the smiling blond-haired, blue-eyed woman in the picture. She was standing with her arms crossed in front of three little blond, curly-headed girls playing in the background in a magical cottage garden. The older two looked like twins. God, they all were adorable.

"Annie Loudermilk," Quinn read as he peered at the screen beside him. "Are those her daughters?"

Flynn quickly read her bio. "Yeah. So cute. Now, let's see where they are…"

She marketed herself as a small business owner and the single mama of three beautiful, independent little women. They lived on their family farm, from which Annie sourced some of her organic products like goat's milk for her artisan soap collection. There was a charm to her voice that struck him emotionally, and as a tech person, he knew how important it was to convey that kind of feeling over the internet.

"Nemo, Ohio," Quinn said. "Okay, so not England. It sounds like a small town."

Like either one of them had ever been to Ohio. "I'll pull up a map later," Flynn said, navigating the site. "She has an Etsy store in addition to selling from her personal website."

"Over eight thousand reviews on Etsy," Quinn said when he pulled it up. "Not bad. We should get in touch with her and see if she can handle our holiday gift baskets."

"Good idea, but I'm buying some for family members first," Flynn said. "Let me text Valentina and get Annie's phone number. She only has a contact form on her site. I'd rather call her anyway. How many baskets do you need?"

"According to my assistant, who emailed me about this at six this morning, about five thousand. Can you believe Connor used to make decisions like this? No wonder he went crazy. A CEO shouldn't be looking at Oprah's favorite things before he's had coffee, if ever. I wanted to poke my eye out. This makes it easy for me."

"You need to delegate, man," Flynn said, leaving the bedroom. "Or you'll explode too."

"Yeah, but it's a full-time job to figure out how to restructure things," Quinn said. "I'm beginning to think our dad was superhuman."

"Word," he said, picking up his phone to text Valentina a playful message.

Morning. You were right. I need more Bilberry & Co. in my life. Can you send me the owner's number? I need to make a big order.

Her reply was immediate.

Great! So happy you love the products. Didn't I tell you? Annie is terrific. So smart and talented. Sending the contact info now. Happy birthday again!

"Tell me you and Valentina have banged," Quinn said baldly. "She's beautiful."

He was already calling the number she'd sent. "Never clicked like that."

"Tragic," Quinn said, shaking his head. "Maybe you are losing it."

"Bilberry & Company." The voice sounded like it belonged to a young girl, maybe one of the daughters.

"Hi, I'm Flynn, a friend of Valentina's. Can I talk to Annie?"

"You're a friend of Valentina's? Hmm... What is your occupation?"

Her little voice was so at odds with her serious tone, he couldn't help but smile. "I'm in business."

"Hmm," she said again. "Send me your picture. I need to see what you look like."

Mysterious... "Okay, I'll text you a selfie right now."

Quinn gave him a puzzled look as he snapped the picture, making sure it was a headshot. He only had a towel on. He sent it and heard the text ring on her end.

"I've got it. Oh, you look nice."

This was so weird. "Were you trying to see if I was good-looking?"

"No, silly, nice. Mom says Valentina is always hanging around with bad men because of her job. I can always tell if I see a picture. I'm her helper. Sometimes I help Mom too."

"So, sweetheart, how about you tell me what your name is and how old you are."

"We're not supposed to talk to strangers, but since you're a nice man, I'll tell you. My name is Amelia, and I'm four. How old are you?"

His interrogator was four? "You must be a prodigy. I'm thirty."

"You look younger," she said. "Since you're Valentina's nice friend, I'll call my mom. I only answered since we take customer service seriously in this family. She's in her lab creating a new lotion, and she's swearing a lot under her breath although I'm not supposed to hear. Excuse me."

Customer service? "You need to hire the daughter, Quinn. You should hear her."

"Just get me those baskets," his brother said, rubbing his eyes.

A few moments later, he heard, "Hello, this is Annie at Bilberry & Company."

"Hi, Annie. This is Flynn Merriam. Like your daughter probably told you, I'm a friend of Valentina's, and she gave me your number. I just tried your products and they're incredible. I wanted to order five thousand gift baskets for the holidays. We can—"

"Five thousand baskets?" She started laughing, an engaging, infectious sound. "Amelia, we got punked. Nice try, Steven."

The phone went dead.

"Hello?" Flynn held his phone out, frowning at it. "I think she hung up on me." He dialed back, but his call went to voicemail immediately. Like she'd declined it.

"What?" Quinn asked.

"She said I was punking her about the order," Flynn said. "You should have heard her laugh. Maybe someone's played a joke on her before or maybe it was too much for her. I mean, how much could she sell online?"

Quinn's eyes narrowed. "We should buy her company.

If the rest of her products are like the ones Valentina gave you, we'd be getting a bargain. I'll send someone tomorrow."

Flynn's insides clenched. Who knew who Quinn would send? Would he be an acquisitions shark and take advantage of that nice lady and her adorable little girls? "No, I'll go. She's a friend of Valentina's."

"Go soon," Quinn said, clapping him on the back before turning around and heading back to his room. "I need those baskets."

He rolled his eyes. His brother was made for the CEO job if that officious tone was any indication. Flynn pulled up the website on his phone again and clicked over until he saw that photo of Annie and her daughters. He studied the smallest little girl, suspecting she was Amelia. There was something about them...

Looked like he was going to start off the new decade by heading to Nemo to acquire bath products.

Not exactly the existential answer he was looking for regarding his life purpose, but after seeing Annie's setup and talking with the little girl on the phone, he knew he was going to enjoy the trip.

Dear Reader,

This book made me feel better about the world, and I hope you loved it as much as I did writing it. If you missed the story about how a real billionaire inspired this story (yes, you heard me right) along with a few others, make sure you pop over to the Acknowledgements section and read all about it. Like Arthur Hale would say, I got the scoop on some pretty remarkable life stories. Of course, the joy is weaving in inspiring examples like theirs into our beautiful friends in this book because I truly believe values like love and kindness and empathy multiply the more people it touches.

Hargreaves continues to be "the man," as my editor said. I can't wait to see what he and Clara and Arthur get up to in Flynn and Annie's book, A FOREVER OF ORANGE BLOSSOMS, the next book in our fabulous Merriam series. I've been in my proverbial lab making lotions and shampoos and the like as research for this book as well as a non-fiction compendium. It's going to be fabulous sharing this story and the outcome of so much research. The four year old, Amelia, is already chatting happily in my head, and she's adorable. I already know she might become our Baby Matchmaking Whisperer.

Thanks again for all of your beautiful support to me and these beautiful books we all love.

Lots of love,

Ava

ABOUT THE AUTHOR

 International Bestselling Author Ava Miles joined the ranks of beloved storytellers with her powerful messages of healing, mystery, and magic. Millions of readers have discovered her fiction and nonfiction books, praised by *USA TODAY* and *Publisher's Weekly.*

Women's World Magazine has selected a few of her novels for their book clubs while Southwest Airlines featured the #1 National Bestseller NORA ROBERTS LAND (the name used with Ms. Roberts' blessing) in its in-flight entertainment. Ava's books have been chosen as Best Books of the Year and Top Editor's Picks and are translated into multiple languages.

Made in the USA
Coppell, TX
24 January 2020